Published by Bookouture

Previously published as *Now You See Me*

An imprint of StoryFire Ltd.
23 Sussex Road, Ickenham, UB10 8PN
United Kingdom
www.bookouture.com

ISBN: 978-1-78681-226-1
ISBN: 978-1-78681-463-0
eBook ISBN: 978-1-78681-225-4

FORGET
ME
NOT

Detective Jess Bishop Se

FORG
ME
NOT

KIERNEY SC

bookouture

For Gina Calanni, the Jess to my Lindsay.
And for Alistair, the best decision I've ever made.

God, he loved a good hunt. Obviously, the kill was better. But a kill was over too quickly. No matter what he did to prolong it there was a finite amount a person could take before they gave up. That's always what happened in the end. People just gave up. It was such a shame because there was always so much more he wanted to do, but eventually they stopped fighting for the next breath.

There was an art to it, getting as much use out of someone without wasting a kill. If he got greedy or miscalculated, he would miss the moment and they would just drift into the slumber of death. That was a wasted kill. Nothing worse. There was hardly any point if he didn't get to see the terror fade into a glossy-eyed acceptance. The point where the eyes went vacant, that was the best.

But like an orgasm, that part only lasts a few seconds, if you're lucky, so you have to enjoy the buildup. That's what the hunt was: the buildup to the climax of a kill.

He glanced at the time on his phone. Almost. She was due here at seven thirty-seven. That was as good a time as any for the game to begin. Shame she wasn't going to enjoy playing, though to be honest it would ruin his enjoyment if she did.

The hardest part was right at the start, the moment right before the prey fell into the snare. If there was one thing he had learned from the hunt: people have an incredible capacity for self-preservation. He both loved and hated that fact. There was no guarantee that every hunt would end with a prize but that made the win all the sweeter.

Sadly, he was his own biggest stumbling block. But he was getting better. Women were experts at reading people, all the subtle micro expressions that gave away character and motivation. If they were scared, even a little, he lost. Luckily, he had now almost mastered the facsimile of genuine emotion.

He pulled down the visor above the driver's seat and examined his reflection in the mirror. He grinned. It was too wide, which meant too eager. That would send up warning flares. He corrected and relaxed his muscles into a softer expression but not too far where it would become a smirk. There was a sweet spot where it was a reassuring smile. He practiced again, going from a passive expression into a smile. It took a few times to get it right. There, that was it. He held it until his cheeks ached to build the muscle memory. Perfect.

Headlights shone down the dark country lane as her car curved around the bend. Right on schedule.

Exhilaration shot through him. He didn't need to fake that emotion. Even though she wasn't his perfect prey, she would do nicely for now. Perfection was out there waiting for him, and she didn't even know it. Soon. Soon he would have her, but first he would have some fun with this one. "Show time," he said aloud, smiling a genuine smile to himself.

CHAPTER ONE

Louisiana

FBI Special Agent Jessica Bishop slapped the back of her neck as a mosquito landed just above her collar. She examined the dead insect and streak of blood on her finger. Even before she had the chance to wipe away the remains, buzzing hummed in her ear as another mosquito zeroed in on her.

"Bug spray?" her guide offered, reaching into the deep pockets of his overalls. When he spoke, only the brown stumps of his bottom teeth were visible. His top lip was covered by a coarse auburn moustache that tapered into a straggly beard. At least the hair concealed the part of his chest not covered by the faded denim. He wasn't wearing a shirt under his overalls, and one of the suspenders had not been fastened so the long piece of material trailed down his back. Jess didn't know if it was a fashion choice or if the garment had seen better days, but when her guide moved, the outline of his rotund belly hung pendulously over his stained briefs.

Jess smiled as she accepted the green canister. She had already liberally doused herself in the stuff but it wasn't working. Every insect in the bayou was feasting on her exposed flesh. "When did you discover the body?"

The man had already been interviewed by Louisiana State Police and tentatively ruled out as a suspect, but Jess never ruled out anyone on the word of someone else. "Ezra is crazy as a box of frogs but harmless" was not an alibi in her book. If experience had taught her anything, it was that evil lurked in the most unlikely places: the seemingly devoted mother who drowned her children in the bath because her new boyfriend didn't want kids, or the pious clergyman who raped boys in the rectory. Evil was everywhere.

Ezra took a red bandanna from his back pocket and mopped his brow. Jess looked away so as not to focus on the myriad of crusted stains on the square.

"Wasn't as much me finding it as Cooter bringing her to my door. Well, not all of her, just a leg. Cooter had fair chewed it. Either that or the gators. I reckon that's what he was going for, cutting her up and feeding her to the gators. Makes sense to me, get rid of all the evidence. I suppose that's what I'd do."

Jess looked up from her pad, into Ezra's steel-gray eyes. His face was weathered from the sun but he looked younger than she initially suspected. Though deep lines fanned out around his eyes, his cheeks had not lost the fullness of youth and there was no hint of jowls competing with his double chin. "I suppose as far as counter-forensics go, feeding your victim to an alligator seems like a decent method, and the water might wash away some trace," she admitted. Jess gave the man in front of her a hard look. "But not all. There is always something left. Some clue, some trace, a witness, a trail. There is no perfect crime. Sometimes people think they have gotten away with it but they always make a mistake. And then we catch them."

Her impromptu speech was more for herself than Ezra. She willed her words to be true; it was the only way her life made sense. Sometimes the universe appeared disorganized and chaotic but it played fair. Like a giant karmic jigsaw that had been scattered across all four corners of the globe, all the pieces were there to be found. Her job was to find them all and piece it back together.

There was no magic to it, just simple hard work. Her process was iterative, boring even, far removed from the glamour of her TV counterparts, but she usually got there in the end.

She looked away, across the expanse of open water. The bayou was strangely alluring, like a world set apart, remote and rugged. The setting sun illuminated the murky film of pond scum. Algae glowed bright chartreuse with iridescent flashes, like slimy ham found at the back of the fridge, days past its prime.

Spanish moss hung like thick, fibrous drapes over the bare branches of oaks. It was beautiful and haunting the way the plant took over its host, merging with then dominating the tree until they both faded into each other, becoming one.

Ezra extended his hand to her, offering help into the airboat. Jess didn't need help but she took his hand anyway to be polite. Ezra took his place in front of the massive, encaged propellers that rose up ten feet. Airboats looked like giant electric fans stuck on tin fishing boats, but they got the job done.

Jess smiled when Ezra handed her ear protectors; she knew from experience she would need them. Last time she'd been on an airboat was when she was working a strangler case in Florida. Her ears rang for the rest of the day.

"What time did the divers get here?" Jess shouted over the roar of the engine.

"Round about lunch time. Still ain't found the body. Pulled out an arm. Still looking for the rest of her. I reckon she can't have been in there long else the gators would have finished her off."

Jess didn't bother nodding before she turned. Mist pelted her cheeks and arms as Ezra sped through the thick reeds. The bayou was funny, neither lake nor land but a swampy purgatory that straddled the line between the two.

This was the third body found in as many months, each dismembered, limbs and head severed clean from the torso. None of the heads had been recovered, which indicated they had been disposed of in another location or the killer was keeping them as a macabre trophy. Her gut told her it was the latter.

Water sprayed up as Ezra navigated through the reeds. Small droplets ran together to create a slick sheen on her arms. The sky darkened as they entered deeper into the bayou. Less and less sun penetrated the thick overgrowth, leaving the swamp in a perpetual cycle of twilight and complete darkness.

Ezra pulled up beside a worn jetty. The warped planks were held together by frayed rope. Her current partner, Alex Chan, and three uniformed troopers stood on the small platform.

Chan had caught an earlier flight in from DC, where Bishop and Chan were based. Even in the Louisiana heat, Chan managed to look put together. He was just shy of six feet, though he would tell you he was six foot one. His black hair swept over his brow with precision. Jess had never seen it out of place. Nor had she ever seen him with a crease in his suit or a scuff on his shoes. And she never would. He took Type A to pathological levels but as far as partners went, Chan was good. He worked hard, kept sexism to a bare minimum, let Jess choose the radio station, and apart from the time he had asked her out, there was no awkward tension between them.

Jess nodded her hello to Chan. She had been partnered with him for almost two years, but in her mind he was still her "new" partner or her "current" partner, like a placeholder while she waited for her real partner to return, which was ridiculous because Jamison Briggs was long gone. That bridge was burned; and they both still had the scorch marks to prove it.

"Hey," Chan said, holding up his hand in a stagnant wave.

"Hey." Jess dismissed the usual niceties like asking Chan how his flight was. He hadn't crashed so she would assume it was fine. She wasn't a big fan of small talk because it gave people the opportunity to ask personal questions. Her words were saved for coaxing confessions or social-engineering reluctant witnesses.

Luckily, twenty-two months paired with Chan bought her some grace. He no longer expected her to chat for the sake of it and he knew never to ask her anything more probing than where they should grab lunch. That wasn't to say they didn't have banter, just that none of it was coming from her. Chan could have good banter with a corpse.

"That is Officer Tibor." Chan motioned to the officer standing at the end of the jetty with a Colt M4 Carbine trained on the murky water. The rifle had been configured with a scope and night vision. The assault weapon was usually reserved for SWAT teams, but in this instance it was to protect the diver from alligators.

Jess didn't dare introduce herself and distract the sniper from his task. The water's surface was deceptively still but in an instant a gator could destroy the illusion of tranquility.

"And these are Officers Gates and Munro." Chan indicated to the troopers beside him. Both men looked near retirement. The department had sent senior investigators to oversee what the FBI was doing. Local police were only there as a formality. The FBI had jurisdiction but Jess always played nice. There were never any pissing contests on her watch. This particular crime scene may be in Louisiana but it was linked to a serial killer operating across state lines; that made it federal jurisdiction. Despite what the media would have people believe, most local law enforcement was grateful for the FBI's help. They were all here for the same reason: to catch a killer. In the rare instances of tension, Jess could always handle it. She knew how to read people. Every person was a mystery but every expression, every throwaway utterance was a clue to who they were and what they were really thinking.

The one who had been introduced as Gates eyed her up. His gaze narrowed into a hard stare. Her heart stopped for a painful moment when she thought she saw a flash of recognition in his pale stare. *Please don't recognize me*, she silently prayed. Even now, nearly thirty years later, her gut clenched when she met new people, especially law enforcement. It was stupid. The odds of someone recognizing her now were slim but every time the panic was real.

She ignored the clawing fear in her gut and stepped forward. If anyone recognized her, she knew how to deny and deflect. She had done it before. "Gentlemen. I'm Special Agent Jessica Bishop." Jess shook hands with both men before she reached into her breast pocket and produced two business cards. "I want to thank you in advance for your help. There is no way we could handle this without local law enforcement. Please don't hesitate to call. You know this area. You guys are the experts here." Jess chose her words carefully: "help" not "cooperation". You ask unruly children to cooperate; you ask peers or superiors for help. She had spent her entire childhood around law enforcement agents; she knew how they worked.

The tension in the pair visibly lessened, scowls turned into flat emotionless stares. They were no doubt trying to decide what to make of her. Physically, Jess was as non-threatening as they come. She stood barely five foot two and, with the exception of her disproportionately large chest, she was small. She always wore her long, curly brown hair in a ponytail but when she did take it down, she looked younger than her thirty-four years.

Gates eyed her up again. If he did recognize her, he had the good grace not to mention it, but his expression did not warm. In his mind they were supposed to have an adversarial relationship. That was how he had expected things to play out. But not today. Jess had turned that assumption on its head with a few well-chosen words and a timid smile. She often wondered if people knew how easily they were manipulated.

Munro was looking at her like a bunny he had saved from a snare but Gates was still suspicious. He was the holdout. She didn't need him on side but it would make things easier if he was. Cases were hard enough to work without ego and politics throwing up roadblocks.

Be vulnerable. Jess moved forward, pretending to trip. Officer Gates reached out his hand to catch her. It was instinct. Jess knew people and how to use it against them. When he moved closer, she could smell the stench of cigarettes and stale coffee that clung to him. "Sorry," she murmured, making herself sound just this side of pathetic. "I'm just not used to this heat. I don't know how y'all manage." Her voice dripped saccharin sweetness.

Gates visibly softened as he helped right her. *Job done.* Jess smiled to herself. Some days the master's degree in psychology paid for itself.

Jess turned to Ezra. The platform swayed under his weight as he stepped onto the jetty. This time when she reached out to keep from falling, it was genuine.

"Is this your house?" Jess asked Ezra. Nestled against the immersed trunks of cypress trees stood a one-room shack. The corrugated roof had oxidized to a powdery burnt red. The slabs that held the dwelling together were weathered and warped, which left large gaps. In some places they were large enough to fit a fist.

"Yes, ma'am."

A Bluetick hound ran down the jetty to Ezra and pushed his nose against Ezra's hand, begging to be pet.

"Cooter?" Jess guessed.

The dog looked up when he heard his name.

Jess reached down and stroked his head. She loved dogs. If she spent more time at home, she would have one. "So, you're the one who found our victim for us. Thanks for that, buddy." She scratched him behind the ears. Some woman's body had been reduced to a dog's chew toy but that wasn't his fault. There was no malice or intent with dogs. They didn't hurt people for the thrill of it. That's why she liked them.

"He doesn't take to most people." Ezra nodded at the dog who was now rubbing up against Jess's legs, eager for attention.

Jess gave him another scratch behind the ears before she stood. "Would you mind if I use your restroom?" She didn't have a warrant so Ezra was under no obligation to let Jess into his house. But this was the Deep South: even swamp dwellers had the manners to let a woman use the toilet.

Ezra hesitated for a fraction longer than he should have. He could be hiding something or maybe he was just ashamed of the state Jess would find his shack.

"Yeah, yeah go on," Ezra eventually said.

The smell of mildew hit Jess before she had even fully opened the door. The room was dark. There was no electricity in the small dwelling and the only window was overgrown with moss.

Jess turned on the flashlight on her phone. The shack was raised from the swamp by concrete blocks. The iridescent glow of water reflected through the gaps in the floorboards. Lucky Louisiana was warm because the house had no insulation and the only source of heat was a small wood-burning stove that doubled as the oven. A cast iron pot sat proudly on top, tomato sauce crusted on the lid.

There was a toilet in the corner. The cistern was not attached, nor was there any plumbing to it. Presumably the toilet itself was merely decorative to cover what it really was: a hole in the floor to shit in. Waste went straight out into the bayou, a worrying thought if the swamp was providing Ezra's drinking water too.

Jess turned her attention to the rusted iron bed. The sheets had come off the corner to reveal a stained mattress. Jess glanced through the window to make sure Ezra was not looking in before she pulled the sheet back further to examine the mattress fully. Faded yellow and brown marks covered the entirety but they were not fresh and more importantly none of them looked like blood splatter. They looked like Ezra had pissed the bed more than a few times, but this wasn't the crime scene.

"Bishop!" Chan shouted from outside. "Bishop, we have the torso."

Jess stood up straight. A bolt of electricity ran the length of her spine. A torso. That's why they had made the trip to Louisiana. The sad truth was the bureau's time would have been wasted if they had found the head attached. Every murder case was upsetting on a cognitive level. Jess knew the victim was always important to someone, but she just didn't have the capacity to care about every nameless victim. It would destroy her if she did. Jess saved her energy for the victim, the case in front of her. To that person, Jess gave her all.

She turned off the flashlight on her phone and joined everyone on the jetty. An open white autopsy bag lay at Munro's feet. In it was the torso and two of the dismembered limbs, including the one the dog had made a meal of. That was probably all they were going to find. The skin still had some areas of pink, and the flesh had not separated from the bone. She hadn't been in the water long. In this heat it would not have taken long for a corpse to turn into nothing more than rotting chunks in the soup that was the bayou.

Jess noted the large breasts of the victim. They stood too proud. Usually when women lie down, their breasts fall to the side, but the victim's didn't. Jess leaned in closer. The skin was mottled and streaked with purple and blue but across both breasts was the jagged line of a scar where there should have been an areola and nipple.

"Do you see that?" she asked Chan, pointing to the chest.

"Yeah, they look fake."

"Yeah, but look closer. She's had reconstructive surgery. If she had just had elective breast enlargement she would have a scar here." Jess pointed to her own armpit. "Or just under her breast. Sometimes there will be an anchor-shaped scar around the areola and down if a breast lift was performed at the same time. But no surgeon would remove the nipples unless it was a mastectomy." Jess's heart picked up speed. This could be their first solid lead. Until now they didn't have the identity of any of the victims. DNA had been taken so it could be compared to known missing persons but so far nothing had come up.

Munro glanced nervously from the torso to the horizon. He shifted his weight from one leg to the other like he was getting ready to dive off the jetty and swim as far away as he could. His face was like stone but under the hardened façade he was struggling with the proximity to a mutilated corpse. He really didn't want to be here right now but unfortunately the only way back was by airboat, and pride and/or duty would keep him from asking to leave even though every moment was torture. Jess wished he knew it was not weakness to admit it was too much to bear.

Despite being able to read people, Jess couldn't predict a person's reaction to a dead body. She suspected nobody could. She had seen hardened officers vomit while others wiped away tears they tried to pretend weren't falling. Some silently prayed over bodies, others cracked jokes. For most it was just a stunned silence but no matter how a person reacted, Jess didn't judge them. There was nothing worse than seeing death firsthand; it was like being violently assaulted by your own mortality. Whatever a person needed to do to deal with it was okay by her.

Jess knew people thought she was cavalier about death, but she wasn't. Nothing could be further from the truth, but she was hardened now. No corpse would ever impact her the way her first one did.

Sometimes she felt like she was going to cry, but she didn't. She wouldn't let herself because it felt like a violation of the victims. Tears were for the ones that knew them and loved them. She didn't have the right to cry.

Jess cleared her throat and brought her focus back to the case at hand. "This woman is a breast cancer survivor. Was a survivor,"

Jess corrected herself. "We'll be able to get a number off the implants from the medical examiner."

"What number?" Gates asked.

"All breast implants have a manufacturer's number on them. All medical devices like defibrillators and pacemakers and of course implants are required to have a serial number. The surgeon notes the number on the patient's records and a copy is given to the manufacturer. It's for safety and research purposes so if it ever becomes clear there is a defect in a product it can be recalled, but it also makes it possible to identify murder victims. I'm assuming the implants are either Mentor or Allergan because those are the biggest suppliers in North America. One of them will be able to tell us who our Jane Doe is."

"How do you know so much about breast implants?" Gates' mouth curled into a smile as he glanced down at Jess's chest, his tone too jovial for a crime scene, and his stare lingered far too long. He didn't even bother to try to hide it.

Her cheeks burned as annoyance crept over her. She was used to men openly ogling her in bars. She expected it there but not at work. She opened her mouth to speak, but before she could say anything Chan stepped in between them, anger written clearly on his sharp features.

"Special Agent Bishop knows a lot about most things. She's shit smart, that's why she's here."

Jess couldn't help but shake her head at the irony of Chan defending her honor. He had no problem objectifying women, and he had been known to say things to Jess that other people would think bordered on harassment, but the moment anyone else crossed that line with her he was all over them.

She really didn't need Chan or anyone defending her. Despite what he thought, Chan wasn't doing her any favors. She was more than capable of holding her own. She could handle this. If Jess wanted to, she could tear Gates down with a few words. There

were so many ways to subtly shame and chastise but she didn't
do it because this case, this victim, was more important than
point-scoring. If nothing else, she was pragmatic. In the grand
scheme of things, Gates didn't matter to her. She would forget
his face as soon as she got on the plane back to DC. She would
happily ignore the bullshit because nothing was as important as
solving a case and getting justice for the victims. That said, she
would break the fingers of any man who dared touch her without
her consent, but they could look all they wanted because while
they were being jackasses, she would be getting the job done.

Gates glared at Chan. The older man's mouth pursed like he
had a whole lot to say on the matter, but he had just enough
sense to keep his thoughts to himself. He stared down at the
algae-covered planks for a moment and then his head snapped up
again to look at Chan. Gates held out his finger, poised to attack.

"It's hot. We should get this body back to the morgue." Munro
jumped in. The comment was as much about brokering peace as
it was about the case.

Jess stepped forward. "Yeah it is. I'm not feeling all that great.
I should have brought water. I really don't know how y'all do it
down here in the heat." She smiled, a sign that she was willing
to ignore any previous indiscretions.

"Yes, ma'am, it is indeed hot. Best for everyone we get this
finished up sooner rather than later," Munro said.

After a long moment, Gates begrudgingly nodded his agreement.

Jess's shoulders eased with the small gesture.

Chan turned his attention back to Jess. "What about the
excision sites? Are they the same as the other victims?"

Jess glanced past him. Chan must have examined the torso
before she got back outside if he knew there were excision sites
on this body too. She stepped past him. When she knelt down,
water sloshed through the gaps in the planks, saturating her

pant leg. She examined the sites where sections of skin had been surgically removed. "I can see three. No four, each the size of a silver dollar. Maybe slightly bigger." The first torso they had discovered had made Jess stop dead in her tracks. She had seen cut marks coupled with decapitation before, but that was a long time ago. Panic had seized her as she noted the striking similarities between that case and the torso killer. In this case there were critical differences, particularly with victim selection, but her mind only saw the similarities.

This wasn't the same killer. Any connections she saw were because it's human nature to see patterns where none exist. The phenomenon was so widespread, psychologists even had a name for it: apophenia.

"Could he have cut out the skin to cover teeth marks?" Chan asked.

Jess shook her head. "No, he would have to cut out more flesh to remove bite marks." Jess demonstrated by opening her mouth as if she were going to take a bite out of an apple or, in this case, human flesh. She had seen firsthand the area that would need to be excised to cut out bite marks, and these were too small.

Chan sniggered. Jess could read his mind. He wanted to say something lewd but refrained because he had only just slapped down Gates for being inappropriate.

The diver propped his elbows on the edge of the wooden planks, goggles pushed up on his forehead. The weight of his oxygen tank pulled him back. "I'm going back under to look for the head."

Jess nodded. "Just keep looking until the light fades, but then I'm going to call it." Even with a sharp shooter it wasn't safe to have a man in the water. They weren't going to find a head. They were only looking so they could say they had tried. Jess didn't want a diver in gator-infested water any longer than absolutely necessary. They were lucky they had found one of the arms. The victim might have scratched her killer—so much good evidence could be found under a victim's nails.

She glanced down and examined the remains again. There were crude cut marks on the limbs where they had been disarticulated. She had seen the same on the other victims. Jess needed the medical examiner to confirm but she suspected it was done postmortem, as in the other two cases.

"It's for transport," Jess mumbled.

"Excuse me?" Munro asked.

"She does that. She talks to herself when she works."

Jess looked up. "Do I?"

"Yeah." Chan nodded. "I never told you because it's the only decent conversation I get out of you." The corners of his eyes crinkled when he smiled.

Jess stood up. "Sorry," she said, addressing Munro directly. "I was saying that cutting off the limbs isn't part of the ritual. The killer doesn't get anything out of it. He's doing it to make it easier to dump."

"How can you say that?" Gates eyed her dubiously, the coolness from before beginning to creep back in. "Seems to me you can't tell anything except you got yourself half a body. Anything beyond that is just conjecture."

The tension had not dissipated; it had merely gone from boiling to a simmer, ready to start again at any moment. But Gates would not focus the rage on Chan, who had already bested him; instead, Gates would go after her. In small, seemingly innocuous ways, he would question her competence, her very right to be here.

Classic kick-the-dog mentality. She knew the type well. He saw her as the weakest so he was going to take out his aggression on her. He wanted her to get defensive or petty, give him something to justify his hostility, so she pretended not to notice his demeanor. "Look at the cut marks at the hips. See all the tiny nicks and tears? Now look at her neck—that cut is clean, almost surgical. He didn't just want the head off, he wanted it to look good too."

Gates' eyes narrowed. "Are you thinking he keeps the heads? Like a trophy? What is he doing with them?"

Jessica stood again. "Yes. I think he is keeping them. I wouldn't want to speculate on why he chooses the head as a trophy. I don't think we will know that until we catch him."

CHAPTER TWO

The county medical examiner's office was a fifteen-minute drive from their motel. Chan drove, which gave Jess a chance to go over notes on her phone.

"You're even less talkative than usual this morning, which is saying a lot," Chan noted as he pulled into the parking lot. The morgue was located in the basement of a red-brick, colonial-style building. The thick hedge was cut in a severe box shape, not a single leaf out of place. Like every building in the South, the American flag took pride of place.

"Sorry. I didn't sleep well last night."

"You should have joined me at Pistol Pete's. These hicks know how to drink."

Jess looked up. "Is that what the sunglasses are about? What time did you get back last night?"

"I didn't."

Jess didn't respond. Any further questions would be an invitation for Chan to explain where he had been and what he had been doing. And quite frankly, Jess didn't care. She knew he hooked up with random women on most of their out-of-town cases. But that was his fiancée's problem, not Jess's.

"I need a coffee," Chan said.

"Do you want me to do this alone?"

"I saw a diner off the last exit—'

"That's fine." Jess spared Chan from making an excuse. They both knew he couldn't handle the smell of decomposition. He was completely cool around dead bodies until they started to smell. At that point Chan either vomited or made an excuse not to be there. The joke around the office was that when the blue bottles appeared, Chan split.

"I'll wait for you out here. You want me to bring you anything?"

"No thanks." Jess had already had three cups of coffee. She had woken up about four with the same persistent nightmare she had been having for months. Instead of trying to get back to sleep, she drank coffee in her motel room and watched infomercials.

Jess waited for Chan to pull away before she rang the buzzer. Thirty seconds later, a plump, middle-aged woman opened the door. The woman's frosted hair was secured to the side with a tortoiseshell clip. Jess didn't know any hairdressers in DC that offered frosted tips anymore. That had stopped being a sought-after look in the capital in the eighties.

"Hi, I'm Special Agent Jessica Bishop. I'm looking for Dr. Boaz."

"I'm Dr. Boaz. Call me Eliza." Eliza extended her hand to shake before stopping short and snapping off the surgical gloves she was wearing. "Sorry, Doris is off today. She usually answers the door so I am doing double duty."

"Of course. It's Labor Day." Jess remembered. It wasn't a holiday she usually celebrated, but no doubt Eliza Boaz would rather be at a barbecue or at the pool enjoying one of the last few days of summer. "I'm sorry you had to come in."

Eliza swatted Jess on the arm playfully. "Please, don't apologize. You saved me from my mother-in-law's potato salad. I'm sure that woman's trying to kill us all with salmonella."

Jess followed her to the elevator. Eliza pushed the button to the basement. "I almost forgot," the doctor reached into the pocket of her scrubs, "for the smell, though it's not too bad on this one." She produced a small navy tub of Vapor Rub.

Jess reached into her purse. "Thanks, I have my own."

She winked. "Not your first rodeo. Good, I like a gal who's prepared."

Jess smiled. Eliza Boaz was genuinely likeable; a rare attribute in the medical examiners Jess had worked with.

The steel doors of the elevator opened. Goosebumps rose on Jess's forearms. She had dressed for the heat of the Louisiana summer, not the air-conditioned morgue.

Three bodies lay covered on examination tables.

"Ignore my other friends," Eliza said.

Jess's eyes narrowed at the phrase. There were a few ways to refer to the dead people laying, ready to be dissected: victims, bodies, corpses, but not friends. It was an odd turn of phrase but maybe that was how Eliza was able to deal with death all day and still maintain a cheery disposition.

"Here we have your Jane Doe. We got lucky, she was found not long after her body was put in the water. My guess is less than twenty-four hours. If it had been any longer, decomposition would have masked the signs of trauma. She's in pretty good shape, all things considered." Eliza pulled back the blue sheet to reveal the corpse that had been pulled from the bayou. The body had been cleaned, which made the surgical scars more prominent. Because she had no nipples or areolas, she looked like a plastic doll that an errant child had taken a marker to.

The poor woman had survived breast cancer only to be murdered. And God only knew what had been done to her before she died. The world didn't really play fair. She told herself it did, but it didn't.

"The implants, do you think you'll be able to get a serial number off them?"

"Yeah, of course. I just wanted you to have a look before I started cutting her any more. I didn't want to interfere with the excision sites. They look interesting. I'm guessing they're important."

Jess gazed down at the four areas. Each one was along her sternum or on her breasts. Then Jess inspected the limbs. Luckily the diver had found one of the arms. Chunks of flesh had been eaten, presumably by fish or maybe birds. Most of the pinky and ring finger had been gnawed. The flesh around the missing digits was thin and almost furry in appearance. It had the same texture as the bubble-eyed goldfish Jess had introduced into her tank a few years ago. The other fish had taken an immediate dislike to him and chewed on and ruptured the fluid-filled sacks around his eyes, leaving dangling bits of skin, and because fish were bastards they continued to torment him, nibbling at his face until Jess took him out of the tank.

She glanced at the leg; other than the marks from scavenging animals, there were no cuts on either of the limbs. There were, however, mottled purple and yellow markings around the wrist and ankle.

"Ligature marks," Eliza said as if she was reading Jess's mind. "She was restrained. My guess is handcuffs. Some of the bruises had started to fade before she died but there are fresher ones on top. If you look here, you can see. Poor soul was held for a while before she was killed. She fought hard. I'm sorry, my friend." She directed the last words to the corpse. Her voice was a lilting whisper, like she was talking to a sleeping child.

"Any sign of sexual assault?" Jess asked.

"The water washed away any trace but I did notice a recent episiotomy scar."

Jess's head shot up. "She just had a baby?" An electric current ran the length of her spine. *Shit.* She hated when children were involved. Even when they weren't direct victims of crime, they suffered—the victim's children and the perpetrator's children too. Official crime statistics didn't reflect that fact but they really should.

"My guess is less than eight weeks before she was killed."

Jess's throat burned. *The thoughts that must have gone through her head. Did she try to barter for her freedom? Did she plead to live for her baby?* Jess rubbed at her temples. Her own thoughts were all over the place: lack of sleep.

"The excision marks…" Jess forced her mind back to the case. "What can you tell me about those?"

Eliza shook her head. The blond curl that had escaped its clasp bounced with the small movement. "Not a lot, I'm afraid: sharp instrument, perhaps a scalpel. Done postmortem. Most likely a counter-forensic measure based on the burns I am seeing along the sternum."

"Burns?" That was new. The other two victims didn't have evidence of burns.

"Look here. See that black line? My best guess is it's a brand. It burned through the skin and left the mark. The killer wouldn't have known he'd marked the muscle, too much trauma with the swelling. He would have missed it."

Brand. Jess's breath hitched. A cold chill descended on her.

Eliza glanced up at her. "You all right? You look pale. Is it the smell?"

Jess blinked a few times trying to clear her thoughts. It was just another coincidence. All crimes had similar elements. "I'm fine, thanks. About the swelling, I thought you said it was done postmortem."

Eliza snapped off her gloves and tossed them into biological waste. She turned to face Jess, her foot still resting on the push pedal. "The excisions were done postmortem but the burns were inflicted around the time of death. Your victim was alive when she was branded."

Again the word branded made Jess's pulse spike. It was not something she had seen very often. Only once before, actually. She cleared her throat. "Can you tell what the brand is?" Jess held her breath, worried what the answer would reveal.

Eliza shook her head. "No, but if you find me the instrument he used, I might be able to get a match."

Jess closed her eyes and let the sun warm her skin. The heat felt good but seeing sunlight was even better. There were never any windows in morgues. Jess needed natural light. Her first office at the FBI was in a windowless room. Every night she went home with a headache from the fluorescent lights.

"Jessie," a deep voice called. "Jessie Bishop as I live and breathe. Have you missed me?"

Jess's lids flashed open. Nobody called her Jessie except her partner—ex-partner—but Jamison Briggs had been gone a long time.

But here he was, leaning against a black SUV, wearing jeans and a white T-shirt that made his deep mocha skin look darker.

"A little birdy told me I'd find you here." There was a smile in his voice. The last thing Jess expected was a smile, not after the way they had left it. When Jamison smiled, his face transformed, softening him. And Jamison Briggs needed all the softening he could get. At six foot four, he dwarfed Jess. Most people were taller than her but Jamison was a mountain of a man, 230 pounds of solid muscle.

For a long moment Jess was too stunned to do anything more than breathe. She cleared her throat several times before she could finally speak. She hadn't expected to ever see Jamison again. Even if he returned to DC, she doubted he would be paired with her again, too much had been said. "You've cut your hair," was all she could think to say. An apology might have been better but she wasn't sorry. Everything she had said and done was to protect Jamison, to keep him from going undercover.

Jamison rubbed his head. The hair had been shaved to the skull. "Did you like my Afro?"

"You hardly had an Afro. No, wait, you did that once when we were working the college rapist case in Virginia." Jess couldn't help but smile. "Remember we had the agreement that neither of us would shave until we finished the case. And your hair kept getting bigger. Not even longer, just bigger." Jess smiled at the memory.

"Girl, that is what Afros do. You don't know enough black people if you don't know that. I think that's why they put us together. I'm your cultural sensitivity training." The corners of his eyes fanned out into small lines when he smiled.

Jess's breath caught in her throat. She had missed him. Even standing here in front of him she missed the way they were. She wanted that back. Jamison had been her best friend and that is why it had hurt so much when he'd left.

A car door slammed. Jess hadn't noticed Chan return but he was back and wearing a face like thunder. "What are you doing here?" Chan demanded.

Half of Jamison's mouth crept up in a lazy smile. "Good to see you too, man. Glad to see you still got that stick up your ass. Keeps you standing tall. Well, not tall but not too short."

Chan clenched his jaw. He and Jamison had never liked each other. They were polar opposites on every conceivable level. Chan was uptight and Jamison was as cool as they came. Nothing fazed Jamison. Even when he had been shot in the line of duty, he kept it together. He told the paramedics which side streets to take to avoid rush hour traffic. Jess had been a mess, she couldn't even speak, but Jamison had calmed her down by making jokes and teasing her about the latest guy she had been seeing. They had been a good team.

"You didn't answer my question." Antipathy dripped from Chan's words. "Shouldn't you be shooting up in some meth lab in Mississippi?"

Jess's face burned as anger and embarrassment shot through her. That's what she had said to Jamison before he left. In front of their entire team, Jess questioned Jamison's suitability to go undercover. She had gone for the jugular; nothing had been off limits. She used his family history against him, saying he was going to end up like his junkie mom and brothers. It was cruel and unprofessional but she would have said anything to make him stay.

"Alabama, man. I was in Alabama." Jamison turned his arms to expose the inside, presumably so Chan could check for track marks. "Still clean."

I'm sorry. The words formed in her mouth but she didn't say them. Now was not the time or place, not in front of Chan. But Jess owed Jamison an apology. The realization shot through her. He had been her partner and her friend. She had no right to tell everyone in earshot about Jamison's past.

Jamison was fiercely private. Only Jess had known about his family. The same way Jamison was the only one other than her bosses and the department psychologist who knew her past. They were bonded by secrecy and she had violated that.

Jamison's official story was that he was an only child, raised by his Grandma Patty in New Orleans. The uncensored story was far less pretty.

"Are you back? For good. Are you back on the team? Back in DC? No more undercover?" Her lungs burned as she waited for his response. She had watched him leave once before, she couldn't do it again.

"I'm back, Jessie."

Jess didn't realize she had been holding her breath until it escaped in an audible whoosh, tension easing from her with each molecule. She looked down, scared that Jamison would see the raw emotion on her face. "Good. Good." There was so much more she could say but the words escaped her.

"Wait, what?" Chan closed the distance between them. "Have you even been cleared? You can't just waltz back in. We're in the middle of a case."

"I can see Jess has been working a case. What have you been doing? The smell get to you again or was it just too much like hard work so you needed a coffee break?" Jamison gestured to the Styrofoam cup in Chan's hand.

"Fuck you." Chan threw the cup down.

Black coffee sprayed over Jamison's jeans. But the slight smile on Jamison's full lips never faltered. "You haven't changed a bit, man. Nice to know some things never do."

Chan turned back towards the car but paused before he slid into the driver's seat. "Are you coming?"

Jess stood frozen, momentarily paralyzed. Chan was her partner, her current partner.

But Jamison was Jamison.

"Um… I think I'll catch a ride back with Jamison. I should get him up to speed on the case."

"Whatever. I'll see you back in DC." Chan slammed the door shut and sped off.

CHAPTER THREE

The walls of the diner were painted blood red, or actually what people referred to as blood red, but real blood was darker, more blue. Either way, it was an odd choice for a restaurant. There was nothing soothing about the color scheme: red walls, gray laminate floors, and black vinyl booths with seats that creaked at the slightest movement. On second thought, it was probably intentional. The visual assault could cause mild dysphoria leading people to eat more and faster. *Smart.*

"So how the hell are you, Jessie? Or should I say Dr. Bishop? Have you finished your dissertation yet?"

"No, not yet. That's on hold."

Jamison raised a brow in question. "Why?"

Jess let out a stream of air. When Jamison left, she had just finished her second semester in the PhD program at Georgetown. She was studying forensic psychology. She quit when one of the inmates she was interviewing recognized her. That's when the nightmares had started. "I think my day job is dark enough. Any bandwidth I have left, I want to fill with song lyrics and cheesy movies. I can't read one more interview with a pedophile. Someone else can study them, I just want to catch them."

"I get it. You need hope. You need a place where you can pretend people are innately good."

Jess nodded, that was one way to put it. "So are you really back? For good? Are you back on the team?" She had to ask again in case she had misheard him or she had let her hope cloud her interpretation of reality.

"Yeah, I'm back."

"Good. We can use all the help we can get." What she meant was that she had missed him, but having an extra person didn't hurt either.

"Where are you at? What do you guys have so far?"

"A whole lot of nothing until today. The victim we found yesterday had breast implants, which is a stroke of luck because our Virginia and Maryland victims aren't giving us anything. Water killed all trace. They were in too long so I'm not sure we'll ever ID them, not that we haven't tried." Jess held her hand up. "Believe me, we've tried. I spent a day with a coroner in Virginia learning about the diatoms native to lakes in the Shenandoah Valley."

Jamison smiled. "Girl, don't play. I bet you loved that. You get way too excited about obscure knowledge. It's kind of your thing."

"Do I?"

"Do I? Listen to you. Jessie, you know more trivia than anyone I know. You're straight up the smartest person I have ever met. And I know a lot of people."

She considered telling him that general knowledge was not a true measure of intelligence as it only reflected crystalized intelligence and recall and not fluid intelligence and problem solving, but she realized that made her sound pedantic so instead she said, "Yeah, but most of the people you know these days are drug dealers and junkies so it's not exactly a salubrious sampling. I would hope I am smarter than all the addicts you know." Jess laughed.

Jamison's eyes lit up when he smiled. "Mmm, salubrious. You know I love your fancy words. But tell me, what did your diatoms tell you?"

"Sweet F-all," Jess admitted. "But last I heard the coroner thought he could get DNA from one of the victims. I'll chase it up when I get back to DC but I'm not going to hold my breath. Feels like we're chasing our tails with those victims. Hopefully we'll get a break and the manufacturer will give us a name. We just need one name, someone with a face, a history, anything that will bring new leads." Jess paused for a breath.

"You're at the point where you think you're never going to solve this, aren't you?" Jamison asked. "I can see it. You have that moment with every case where you get dejected."

"Just one moment? Lately it feels more like increasing levels of desperation punctuated by moments of hope until we finally get there. Meanwhile, you're always so calm and completely confident that we're one lead away." God, she'd missed Jamison's energy. She was a different person around him. Jess worked well with Chan but Jamison grounded her, kept her spirits up, and reminded her to relax.

Jess wrapped her hands around the steaming mug of black coffee and suddenly realized the coffee Chan had thrown earlier had been for her. He took his with cream and two sugars. Dessert coffee, she called it. A niggling sense of guilt clawed at her.

"You okay?" Jamison's voice brought her back.

"Yeah I'm fine. I'm just worried about Chan."

Jamison's dark eyes narrowed. "Grade-A douche. I know I've been gone a while, but I'm pretty sure you're the one who coined his nickname."

Jess shrugged. "He's… I don't know. He's not as bad as I thought. He has his moments. But he is a good partner."

Jamison was quiet for a long time as he tapped his long fingers against the rim of his mug. "I get it. No questions. No judgment."

"No!" Jess spat out coffee, nearly choking on the sip she had just taken. Hot liquid sprayed across the table. "No, I'm not sleeping with him. Good God, no. Christ, I have standards."

Jamison's dark brow rose, clearly dubious of her statement.

"Thank you," Jess said as she accepted napkins from him. "I admit I have had questionable taste in men in the past but even I know not to shit where I eat."

Jamison sighed. The corners of his mouth pulled down. He glanced up at the swirling blades of the ceiling fan as if he wanted them to splice through him. "Yeah, not all of us are that smart."

"What? What are you talking about?"

"That's why I'm here in Louisiana. There's something I need to talk to you about before we get back to DC."

"About your time undercover?" Jess put up her hand. She didn't want to know. On the drive over from the morgue she had skillfully avoided the topic. She was forcing the issue, trying to make it feel like they hadn't been apart. She spewed every minutiae of detail at him because she knew if she stopped talking Jamison just might tell her things that he had done. "Listen, I know how these operations go down. I'm sure you did things you're not proud of but I'm also sure they needed to be done."

Jess reached across the table, resting her hand on top of his. Jamison's role was to infiltrate the meth scene of the Deep South. Though she didn't want details, she'd needed to know he was okay so she had pulled some strings and seen all the reports that had been filed about him. He had been surrounded by drugs and violence. Nothing had been explicitly stated but Jess knew how to read between the lines. Someone had died and fingers were pointing in Jamison's direction. If he had done anything illegal or immoral, as Chan had implied, Jess didn't need to know. It was part of the job. And it was over now.

"You're not like your brothers. Even if you did things when you were undercover, you're not like them. You're a million miles away." She, more than anyone, knew that people should not be defined by their families. She hated that she had used his against him. If she could go back and take back things she said, she would a million times over.

"I'm getting married."

Jess pulled her hand away like she had just grabbed a red ring of an electric stove. "What?"

"Next Saturday. I want you to be there. You're the only family I got, Jessie." He tried to smile but it didn't reach his eyes. A sadness clung to him.

Jess's mind fired millions of questions at her all at once. Her head spun. This had to be a joke.

"Her name is Felicia. I met her in Alabama. I think you'll like her."

No. No she wasn't going to like her. "Are you kidding me right now? Because I don't think it's funny. I know you better than I know anyone else and you have never once mentioned marriage being in your plans." Jamison had explicitly ruled it out. He had said he had no idea how to be a husband and he had no desire to try to figure it out.

"Plans change, Jess. I'm going to be a dad."

Jess sucked in a sharp breath but her lungs refused to fill.

"Felicia's due on Valentine's Day. It's the right thing to do."

Jess shook her head again. "No. What are you talking about? Marriage? You knocked up your beat wife? Is that what this is?"

"Beat wife?" Jamison demanded, his voice incredulous. "Just who do you think you're talking about? I'm not Chan. I don't hook up with a random woman on each case."

"Lots of men do it. That is kind of why they have a name for it."

Jamison held up his hand. "No. No, lots of men don't do it. A lot of assholes like Chan do it. Don't tar me with that brush, Jessie. We have too much history for that bullshit. You know me better than that."

The bitterness in Jamison's tone silenced her. She had hurt him. He had the same desperate sadness in his eyes that he had the day he left. For a moment she couldn't speak, too scared to push him further away. But she couldn't leave this unsaid. "But you did do it. You met a woman on the beat and you got her pregnant. And now you're marrying her. You think you are doing the noble thing by marrying her. The noble thing would be to pay child support and be an active part of your child's life, maybe even get custody, but not marry a woman you met while you were scoring a hit. What kind of life is that? I know you don't want to be like your father. And you're not. You've proven that. Don't throw it all away trying to make a point you have already made."

Jamison scrubbed at his face. "Seriously, Jessie, you think I knocked up a crack whore? That's what you think of me. Felicia is a detective with the Alabama State Troopers. She was my colleague. Not some junkie."

The words sucked the oxygen from her lungs. His partner. Felicia was his partner and he was marrying her. For a minute she was too stunned to speak. "I need some air." Jess stood up. She struggled to breathe and every ragged breath she forced down was like acid corroding her from the inside.

CHAPTER FOUR

Washington, DC

Jess put down the phone. Finally they had a name. Lydia Steiner. Jess stared at the information she had just scribbled down. The torso in the bayou was no longer a Jane Doe. She was Lydia. She was someone's wife and she was someone's mommy. And now Jess knew her name.

Jess underlined Lydia's name again. As Jess suspected, the breast implants were the lead they needed. Now at least one of the victims had a name.

The keys on Jess's computer clicked as she typed in Lydia Steiner's social security number. Jess would leave most of the heavy lifting to an analyst—Tina Flowers, if she could get her. Tina was the most brilliant person Jess had ever worked with. Everyone wanted her on their case. The last she heard, Tina was still stuck on a white-collar case, lending her skills to combating insider trading.

Jess had been reticent to request Tina be pulled off that case when they hadn't identified a victim. It wasn't fair to other departments for anyone to be a prima donna. Resources were limited, but now that they had more to work with, Jess could really use her help. It would take a few days for the wheels to be put in motion but she had no doubt that her boss, Jeanie Gilbert, would make it happen. Jess played by the rules, always by the book. She worked the evidence not her gut instinct or office politics. Jeanie respected her for that, so if Jess really wanted Tina on the team, Jeanie would make it happen.

In the meantime, she could start a preliminary search now.

Jess's desk had four flat-screen monitors. Each was used for a different database. Seeing as much information she could at once helped her to spot things. She wasn't sure how Tina worked but this was what worked for her.

"Come on, Lydia, tell me who you are."

She glanced out the window while she waited for the pages to load. Jess was lucky enough to have an office with a view. A single oak tree stood proud. Soon the leaves would change and then fall but right now the thick branches were still covered in a thick blanket of green.

The top left-hand monitor flashed. "Okay Lydia Steiner, talk to me." Born October 7, 1984, Lydia Elizabeth Childs in Hartford, Connecticut. Father an optometrist. Mother deceased. Married Reuben Steiner, July 4, 2001. One child, Ava Rose. Reported missing by her husband eight days before her body was discovered.

Jessica wrote everything down longhand. Later she would amalgamate it all for her file, but right now she wanted every piece of information she could get because leads were hidden in plain sight.

She clicked to open a new tab to see Lydia's phone records. "Who have you been talking to?" More often than not, murdered women knew the people who killed them. They were their husbands, boyfriends, exes, people they thought they could trust. Jess scrolled through the numbers. She printed off Lydia's phone records for the past month and then took out a plastic tub of highlighters. Methodically, she identified every number and designated each a different color. Predictably, Lydia called and texted her husband Reuben Steiner the most, with an average of four calls or texts each day.

Jess needed to get back to Louisiana and interview the husband. Officers from the local parish would be delivering the news today that Lydia's body had been found. Today was going to be a shit day for Lydia's family.

All hope was gone now. In every case she had ever worked, the family survived on delusion: thinking, hoping, praying, begging that there were some other reason for their loved one to be missing. The final violation of a family was killing that hope and severing the last connection to their loved one. God, Jess hated that part.

Someone knocked on her office door.

"Come in," Jess said without looking up.

Lindsay Dixon walked in and sat down on the other side of the metal desk. Immediately Lindsay bent over, took off her heels, and pushed them under Jess's desk. "You have all your monitors going at once. You must have had a break in your case." Lindsay had been Jess's best friend — well, besides Jamison — for a long time. She knew her process well. Jess never had to explain herself to Lindsay; she just got it.

"I didn't know you were in the office today," Jess said, rolling her chair to the side so she could see Lindsay around her monitors. She had been meaning to call her. Jess had had to cancel their dinner plans when she got the call that a body had been found in Louisiana.

"Yeah I needed to finish off a report. He can't come back without clearing the psych evaluation." Lindsay pushed a lock of chestnut hair behind her ear. Even without mentioning his name, they both knew whom she was talking about.

Jess's back stiffened. *Jamison.* Lindsay was one of the bureau's most respected psychologists. She was also the most feared because Lindsay didn't profile killers; she profiled agents. Dealing with the worst humanity had to offer fucked with people. Lindsay's job was to make sure the damage left people the right side of sane.

"I don't want to talk about Jamison."

Lindsay smiled. She was the epitome of professionalism. She would never betray doctor–patient confidentiality but she would coax Jess to start talking. Jess knew the drill; growing up she had spent more time speaking to psychologists than other children. They all wanted to make sure she was okay, really okay. She had learned very early on how to fool them, give them just enough but never actually open up. That's also when she learned to not let anyone in. Nobody willingly got her secrets. Except Jamison, she had given them freely to him.

"Jess, I'm here as your friend, your best friend. Jamison knows I'm going to speak to you about his transitioning back to the team. He's back full-time on Monday and I think it will be awkward as hell for you both if you don't go to his wedding this weekend. I'll be there too. We can go together. It'll be fun. Or it won't but either way you should be there."

Lindsay was nothing if not a straight shooter. There was never any pretense or preamble with her, which is probably why they had become friends. And because at their first meeting when Lindsay interviewed Jess about her history, there was no pity in her eyes, no morbid curiosity or contempt, just acceptance. At long last Jess had found someone who saw her not her past.

Jess sat back in her chair. "He told you about that?" Part of her had hoped if she ignored the situation, it would resolve itself. She had her own special brand of delusional thinking when it came to dealing with life, another gift from her childhood. "So, you think it's a good idea that he's marrying a woman he's known for a few months—"

"Twenty-two months. That's almost two years. They didn't just meet, Jess, and that's not what you're objecting to."

Jess opened her mouth and then snapped it closed. Lindsay was baiting her. She could get anyone to talk, even Jess. Sometime it sucked having a brilliant psychologist for a best friend; like times when Jess wanted to stick her fingers in her ears and ignore the world.

"You would be upset no matter who Jamison was marrying. You were partners, best friends. You were the woman in his life."

Jess bristled, uncomfortable with the term "woman in his life." She wasn't the woman in anyone's life. She didn't want to be. That wasn't what this was about. She held up her hand to speak but Lindsay kept talking.

"Not in a romantic sense," Lindsay amended. "You have sex with lots of people. But you have very few close friends. People that you really trust to know you. You have Jamison and me. And now you feel like you're losing Jamison again. He's picking someone else over you to be the woman in his life. And it's his partner no less. That is going to sting."

Jess's back went rigid. "First of all, I object to 'lots.' I have sex with some men—"

"Lots is not a pejorative term unless you make it one. Do you want to discuss this tonight, maybe over margaritas and nachos? I really want to try the watermelon margarita at El Cartel."

"You interrupt people far too much to be a therapist. You know that, right?"

"Sorry. I only interrupt you. The rest of my day is spent listening intently and nodding. Go to the wedding. Smile, tell him you're happy for him—"

"I'm not happy for him. I'm scared for him. I'm upset for him. I'm—"

"Then tell him you're glad he's back. You are. So tell him that. Don't throw your friendship away because you're butt hurt."

"You're supposed to ask probing questions that lead me to the right answer, not give me explicit direction on how to live my life."

Lindsay wagged her finger. "Again, you're my friend, not my client. Besides, neither of us has the time to ask the questions to get you to the right answer. Girl, you just need told on this one. So, margaritas tonight at seven?"

Jess glanced at the monitors and sighed.

"You have to eat," Lindsay said.

"Yeah, but there's no biological necessity for margaritas."

"No biological necessity for margaritas?" Lindsay scoffed. "That's your policy not mine."

"I don't think I'm going to get out of here until late and I need to go for a run."

"Skip the run. I'll make you walk to the bar for all the drinks. That will be your cardio."

Jess smiled. "Okay fine but let's make it nine. That'll give me time to break the back of this."

The letters on the screen blurred and merged together. Jess gave her eyes a hard rub. She had been staring at monitors for too long. When her stomach rumbled, she realized she had worked through lunch. She glanced down at her watch; it was too late now. She was meeting Lindsay for dinner in less than two hours. She needed some fresh air, maybe a quick walk outside, and then she would finish going through Lydia's files.

What Jess did was such an invasion of people's private lives, analyzing phone records and reading messages. On an emotional level it felt like another violation of the victim, but it needed to be done in order to catch the killer.

She pushed back from her desk.

"Hey, Jessie."

Jess's head shot up when she heard the familiar deep voice. Jamison's muscular frame filled the doorway. It was surreal seeing him back in the office. It had taken more than a year for her to stop expecting to see him every time she turned a corner but now it was just as jarring to see him back. She was tempted to rub her eyes again to make sure he wasn't a mirage brought on from eye strain.

"Hey."

"Your eyes are red. Have you been crying?" Jamison frowned.

Jess shook her head. "No." Jamison had never seen her cry and he never would. "My eyes are just bloodshot from lack of sleep and too much screen time."

"Good." Jamison came in and sat down. "Not good that you're not sleeping well but I'm glad you're not upset."

"Yeah I'm fine."

"Here," Jamison said, handing her the paper cup he was holding. "It won't help with the sleeping but it is one of your healthier vices so I'm going to indulge it."

Jess pointed to the empty cup on her desk. "Chan brought me a cup about an hour ago."

"Of course he did."

"He seems to like to keep me caffeinated or else it's some Pavlov's dog type response, he sees me and immediately throws coffee my direction. I'm not sure what that's about but I'm not complaining."

Jamison's dark brow arched. "You don't know what that is about? Really, Nancy Drew, you can't figure out that mystery?" Jamison stood up and turned to go.

"Where are you going?"

"I'm throwing this away if you don't want it. It's too late in the day for me to drink coffee."

"Hold up. Nobody said anything about not wanting the coffee. I said I had just finished a cup, which means I'm ready for my next. Thank you. This will keep me going until I finish my spreadsheet."

Jamison's mouth hitched in a lazy smile. "You and your spreadsheets. I forgot about those. You really do like to see everything all at once."

"It drives Chan crazy, my need to write things down and make lists that I cross-reference with other lists, but so often the answer is right there in front of me. How many times have we seen it where the killer was hiding in plain sight?" Jess took a long swig of coffee. "This is nice. Thank you," she said again.

"You're welcome, just promise me that's your last cup of the day." Jamison sat down again. "What are you working on now?"

Jess returned to her chair and then swiveled her monitor so Jamison could see. "I have the name of our Louisiana victim: Lydia Steiner. I'll send you the files. I've spent all day getting to know her and compiling a list of every person she knows. That is what I'm doing on this screen." Jess pointed to the bottom right screen. "And this is every person of interest from the Virginia and Maryland cases. I'm not ready to give up on them. They still have something to tell us."

Jamison smiled. "What are they saying, Jessie?"

Jess sighed. "I don't know." She paused because she knew she sounded crazy but that ship had already sailed with Jamison so there was no use trying to hide it from him. "We don't know who they are but I still want them to help find their killer... you know, let them be part of this and know I haven't forgotten them even though I haven't been able to identify them. I still know they mattered to someone. It's batshit crazy, I know, because they're dead, but yeah that's my thought process right now."

"It's not crazy, Jessie. You honor people even in death, nothing crazy about that."

"Thanks. Right now, I'm one by one ruling out any connection between Lydia Steiner and the people of interest in the Maryland and Virginia cases. I'm more than ninety-nine percent certain there isn't one but I'm systematically going through just in case."

"Good. Leads are found in that one percent."

"Chan thinks this is an exercise in futility—"

"Chan's an asshole."

Jess pretended she hadn't heard him. "It probably is useless but at least by ruling people out, our suspect list is getting shorter. Though, of course, as Chan pointed out to me earlier, there are seven billion people on Earth. My strategy can't include ruling each of them out one by one."

"And again, I say Chan is an asshole."

This time Jess couldn't ignore him. "He's my partner. We have covered a lot of ground together. I know you two don't see eye to eye and I'm not asking you to but I can't be walking on eggshells around you. I'm going to mention him. We're all on the same team. He's going to come up."

Jamison gave a slow nod. "Was. He *was* your partner."

Jess's eyes widened. "What? What are you saying? Have you spoken to Jeanie?"

"A couple months ago when I was first talking about coming back. That was the condition. If I came back to DC I wanted to be partnered with you again. You're my partner. You and me, that's the way it works."

Jess's lungs constricted. She hadn't even let herself consider the logistics of Jamison's move back to the team. Of course she wanted to be with Jamison again, that went without saying. He was her partner. "Wait, Jeanie has known you were coming back for two months? She kept that one quiet. It's not like I don't have clearance; she could have mentioned that. Wait, what about Chan?"

"He is getting a new partner. Don't ask me who. You'll know when I do."

Jess had seen a lot of people come and go from the office. That was the transient nature of working for the government: you went where you were needed. She didn't care one way or the other who the new team member was, as long as they were competent.

"So, what do you need me to do? You want me to work all seven billion?"

"Thankfully it's a slightly smaller pool. Only just, though."

Jamison unbuttoned his sleeves and rolled them up. "What do we know about this guy? Start at the beginning."

"That question would have been much easier to answer last week. I would have sworn blind we were dealing with a local. Our Maryland victim was found in Rock Creek Park. That's practically in DC. Our Virginia victim was found off Skyline Drive. Everyone in DC has taken a drive up to Skyline. That's a go-to romantic road trip. These are both rural areas that locals know well. When Jeanie said a third body had been found, my mind went to Lake Anna, Great Falls, or the Potomac, certainly not in the middle of nowhere Louisiana."

"So, what are you thinking now? Copycat? Different killer?"

Jess shook her head. "It's the same killer. I know that. The decapitation, the excision sites, dumping the bodies in water: that's his signature. We haven't released any details to the media so we can safely rule out a copycat. It's the same guy. I'm just not sure he's from DC anymore. The bayou was so remote. I feel like he knows that area."

Jamison sat back in his chair. "He still might be from D.C. Thanks to Google Maps you can be an expert on any locale in the world. I don't think he needs to be from Louisiana to dump bodies there. What the three dumpsites tell me is that he travels. He can't be local to all of them but he could be familiar with all the areas if he has a job where he has to move around a lot. Like truck driver, pilot, salesman, military, something like that."

The hairs on the back of Jess's neck stood taut. A boulder formed in the pit of her stomach, the weight of it dragged her mind down with it.

"Jessie, what is it? What did I say?" Realization washed over his face in an instant. "Ah, shit. I wasn't thinking. I'm sorry."

Jamison's deep voice pulled her out of the past. She gave her head a terse shake to remove the last remnants of the memory. Her mouth felt too dry to speak. She was grateful for the cup of coffee. "No, it's fine. You're right. That is very likely the case. I mean it is the case obviously because we have dumpsites in three states. This man obviously moves around. We need to consider what profession he has that would lend to that."

"Jessie, I'm sorry. I didn't mean to stir up old demons."

Jess held up her hand. "Honestly, don't worry about it. You didn't." She lied. She pretended to look down at her watch. "Oh geez, I didn't realize it was so late." She could concentrate enough to make out the numbers on her watch but she needed to get out of the office, away from the case, away from the memory of the victims she had failed.

Jamison glanced at the clock on the wall. "Yeah I guess it is late. I have been mostly nocturnal the last couple of years. It's nice to be back on a normal schedule. Nothing good happens after midnight. I'm telling you that right now."

Jess paused before she shut down her computer for the night. "I'm meeting Lindsay for dinner. Do you want to come? I know your cooking is almost as bad as mine."

"Ah…" Jamison's face changed, his smile faded. "I… um… I can't tonight. Felicia will have already started dinner. Actually, I need to get going. She'll be wondering where I'm at."

The mention of her name sucked the air from Jess's lungs. She blinked a few times to regain her composure. Of course he would be going home to his fiancée. They lived together, why had Jess not realized that before? They were getting married, for Christ's sake. "Oh yeah of course," she said, turning back to pick up her bag.

"Maybe next time," Jamison offered with a weak smile.

Jess swallowed hard. They both knew there wasn't likely to be a next time.

CHAPTER FIVE

Jess pulled down at the hem of her dress. She probably should have bought something more appropriate for the occasion. She had work clothes, running clothes, and one ubiquitous little black dress she wore everywhere from funerals to dates. And now to a wedding.

She checked the address she'd written down. This is where they had picked to take the plunge into the great abyss called marriage? Jess had never contemplated marriage or even a wedding for that matter, but she was confident she wouldn't pick a run-down inner-city school.

Jess noted the various shades that peeked through under the cracked cream paint. At various points the building had been sky blue, canary yellow, and a pink which was the exact shade of Pepto-Bismol. Maybe the school district got a discount on the crappy colors no one else wanted. Or maybe the principal had read the study that found that brightly colored buildings could reduce the incidence of depression and substance abuse in urban settings. If that was the case, he or she should have kept reading because the benefits were short-lived and then you were left with an eyesore of a building.

She was stalling, thinking about pointless studies she had read in grad school. Shit, they were probably already married by now. Why was she even here? It was a Saturday night. There were at least a dozen things she would rather be doing.

"Jessie, you made it."

Jess spun on her heel. Jamison's dark eyes smiled. He was wearing a charcoal-gray suit with a white shirt and a blue paisley tie. The tie was new. Jess knew every piece of clothing Jamison owned. Or, at least, she used to.

Jamison leaned down and embraced her. Had he ever hugged her before? They had been friends for such a long time but she could not remember touching him like this, being this close. She inhaled his clean scent, nothing artificial, just fresh like soap.

"I'm so glad you came. It wouldn't be the same without you. You're the only family I have."

Jess cleared her throat. She didn't know what to say. She didn't want to congratulate him for making a mistake so she said, "It's good to have you back."

"Did you find the church okay?"

"Church?" Jess's eyes narrowed. "I thought this was a school."

"Yeah, it is that too. At the weekend it doubles as Grace Evangelical. Felicia's brother is the minister here. We wanted something small, just eighty of her closest friends and family. I'm not sure that woman is familiar with the word small."

"Oh wow. I don't think I know eighty people, at least not eighty people I would want to hang out with." Lindsay had been right—Jess only had two friends, her and Jamison. She didn't trust anyone else enough to let them get to the level of friend, so there was no way she could fill the pews of an entire church.

"I didn't say anything about wanting to hang out with any of them," Jamison laughed. "Is that for us?" Jamison pointed to the bag she was carrying. "I'll give it to Felicia."

"Yes, I mean no. It's for you. It's stupid. I bought it when you were undercover. It's nothing." Jess tried to put the bag behind her but Jamison's hand encircled hers.

"Let me see."

"It's really stupid. Just something I—"

Jamison reached into the bag and pulled out the gray T-shirt. On the front it read, "Black and Blue." He smiled. "I love it. It's perfect."

"Are you sure? Do you get it?"

"Yeah I get it. Black because I'm black and blue because I'm law enforcement. I love it. It's so you."

Jess shifted her weight from one foot to the other, not sure what *it's so you* meant. "I was really worried about you when you were gone. Every time I saw a police shooting on the news I had a small panic attack. I thought just your luck, you go undercover only to be killed by a police officer."

Jamison still didn't let go of her wrist.

"Thank you for worrying, Jessie. No one has worried about me for a long time. Just you."

Just you. Jess's gaze locked on his. All of the air left her body. *No, just no. I can't do this, not with Jamison.* She pulled her hand away.

She took a step back.

Every ounce of reason in her body demanded she tell him not to do it. This was a mistake, she knew it, and if he was honest with himself, he knew it too. But it was his mistake to make. She bit into her lip to keep from saying anything. She had already said everything she needed to say back in Louisiana. She needed to go home and commiserate with a bottle of Cabernet because she wasn't about to stay here and risk telling Jamison a few more home truths. It was time for her to hold her peace.

"Um… um I can't stay for the reception. I have a date." The lie rolled off her tongue. She didn't even have to think about it. "Oh, I almost forgot." Jess reached into her handbag. "You guys didn't register so I didn't know what to get you so I went with the safe bet and got a gift certificate. I even went to the mall to pick it up, which you know says a lot because I hate shopping even more than I hate large groups of people."

Jamison laughed. "That does say a lot. Thank you. And thanks for coming. It means a lot to me."

Jess looked away. "Yeah of course… I… uh…" Oh God, what did she want to say? She didn't want to say anything. She wanted it to be two years ago and she wanted to be able to stop Jamison from leaving. But that wasn't going to happen so she said the only thing she could. "I'm just really glad you're back. I missed my partner."

Jamison's face split into a broad smile. "Come on in and get a seat." Again, he wrapped his arms around her in a tight embrace.

She closed her eyes and breathed him in. She didn't put her arms around him to return the hug because she knew if she did she wouldn't want to let go. "Just give me a second. I need to make a phone call. I'll be right in." Her voice faltered but she coughed to cover it up.

"Cool. See you in a few."

Jess watched as Jamison went back into the building before she turned to stare into the setting sun. For a few long moments she watched the burning orange bleed into the purple sky. Her chest constricted. She couldn't breathe. *Get it together, Jess.* She could do this. He was her best friend. She would be there for him even if she knew he was making a huge mistake. She plastered on a smile she didn't feel and walked into the auditorium.

Behind Jamison, the altar was covered in white and cream roses. He wrung his hands together and looked up into the vaulted ceiling. A hot pink balloon had floated up and got caught in the rafters.

Jess chose a seat in the very back. The bride's side was overflowing with several of her guests seated conspicuously on Jamison's side. They had left the first row empty, presumably for his family, because they didn't know he didn't have any.

Behind them, Jess recognized several agents. Jeanie Gilbert was there with her husband as was Lindsay who turned and gave her a small wave inviting her to move closer to the front to sit beside them.

Jess shook her head. She needed to be in the back, by herself. She closed her eyes as she took in a deep breath. No matter what, Jamison would do this: marry Felicia. Jess knew him so well, his values, his personal code of ethics. For him this was the right thing to do and Jamison always did the right thing. He was as loyal as he was stubborn.

The first melancholy chords of the cellist filled the room. At the best of times the cello sounded mellow and contemplative; at the worst, sorrowful. A bridesmaid walked down the aisle. Her tan skin glowed against the fitted coral gown. Jess swallowed against the lump in her throat. This was real. Felicia would be coming down the aisle soon. The room started to spin. It was too stuffy. She needed air. She couldn't do this.

Jess bolted upright. As she stood, her gaze locked with Jamison's. Even from across the room she could see the question in his dark eyes. She couldn't be here for this. She had to go.

CHAPTER SIX

A trickle of blood dripped down her shin. She winced as she picked a pebble out of the gouge in her knee and threw it at the discarded bicycle on the ground beside her. She had begged for a bicycle for months. It was all she wanted for her birthday: a pink bike with tassels on the handlebars and a basket for her doll to ride along with her. Her mom refused, said she would get hurt, but her dad had bought her one anyway.

"Come on, princess. Try again. Randals never give up." Gently he wiped away the blood on her leg.

"I can't." Hot tears clouded her vision. She blinked several times to keep them from falling. She wanted to cry but she wouldn't let herself. Not in front of her dad. "I changed my mind. I don't want to ride a bike."

He stared at her knowingly. "Hmm," was all he said.

"Daddy, I can't, it's too hard."

He leaned down and kissed the top of her head. "Everything in life worth doing is going to be hard. But if you want it bad enough, you pick yourself up and keep going."

"I don't want to ride a bike." She hugged her hands tight across her chest.

He was silent for a long moment. "Okay," he said at last. "I'll never make you do something you don't want to do. But don't let fear hold you back."

Pressure built behind her eyes until she could no longer hold back the tears. "I am scared," she admitted through frantic gulps.

"It's okay to be scared. Everyone gets scared."

Her eyes widened. "You get scared?" The disbelief was clear in her voice. Her father was invincible.

"Of course I get scared. Everyone does but brave people keep going even when they're scared."

Salt from her tears nipped her cracked lips. She wiped her face with the back of her hands. "I want to be brave like you, Daddy."

"Princess, you are brave. You're the bravest girl I know."

Her cheeks warmed at the praise. "I'll try again. But don't let go. I need you to hold on." Even as she said the words, the fear mounted, wrapping around her, pulling her down.

He picked up the bike and helped her back on. "You can do it."

Her heart thundered against her ribs. The feel of the handlebars under her slick hands made her want to run away but her dad's smile made her want to try again even more. Tentatively she pushed down on the pedal. "Don't let go. Promise me you won't let go."

"I'm right here," he soothed. "That's it. Keep going. You're doing great."

She pushed down on the pedals, slowly at first, teetering along the cobblestone street and then faster as her fear faded. "I'm doing it," she said. "Daddy, I'm doing it!"

"You're doing great," her dad called from behind her. "Keep going."

Panic seized her when she realized he had let go and was now running behind her. "Daddy!"

"Just keep pedaling. You're doing great."

The complete confidence in his voice gave her the courage to keep going. She pedaled faster. The wind blowing through her hair made her feel like she was flying.

"You got it, princess. You don't need me. Always remember that: you don't need anybody."

CHAPTER SEVEN

Jess went straight to the bar. She didn't want to speak to anyone. She just wanted a drink or several drinks in short succession.

She wanted to be numb.

She picked The Waiting Room because it was close to her Metro station and she knew the area but she immediately regretted her decision when she saw the décor. Every flat surface was covered in mirrors: the walls, the ceilings, the table tops. Even the marble tiles on the floor were so highly polished she could see up the skirt of the woman next to her.

The mirrors were a big no for her. Jess didn't want to see her own reflection staring back at her. She didn't even want to *be* herself right now, why the hell would she want to look at herself all night?

After five minutes of not being served, Jess motioned to the bartender. "I'll take a Cabernet, whatever you sell by the glass. Thanks," she said when she managed to drag his attention away from his phone. When he looked up, disdain clearly marked his face, obviously disgusted at having to serve a customer.

He was the classic hipster type. His arms were covered in ironic tattoos, including a Tweety Bird holding a compass on his forearm. There was probably some symbolism to be found in the colorful inking but her brain was too fried to see it.

Jess resisted the urge to pull out her own phone. Usually she was happy with her own company but right now she didn't want to be alone and she did not want to make polite conversation with a brooding millennial. Lindsay had called twice but Jess had sent her straight to voicemail because she would rather shoot herself in the head than listen to Jamison's reception in the background. Besides, she didn't need to speak to Lindsay to know what she would say. Lindsay would tell her to sit with her feelings. Jess wasn't a fan of emotion at the best of times and she certainly didn't want to marinade in the shit ones.

Jess rubbed at her temples. No thinking about Jamison tonight, or the case, or the fact she had to head back to Louisiana to interview a victim's family.

A knot formed in the pit of her stomach. There was too much to numb tonight, cheap wine wasn't going to cut it. "No wait, give me the *best* Cabernet you sell by the glass."

"This okay?" He held up the bottle so Jess could inspect the label but all she could focus on was the raised translucent skin below his clavicle. The top buttons of his shirt had been left open to expose a brand in the shape of an arrow. The skin had healed to form a raised keloid scar.

An electric current ran the length of her spine as her case crashed back into the forefront of her mind. Lydia Steiner had been branded too. "Did you have that done locally?"

The bartender stroked the brand, a small smirk on his face. "My body modifications are for me. They're not a conversation starter. I'm not commenting on your body, don't comment on mine."

His response was well rehearsed. The smug look told her he enjoyed this conversation. He enjoyed chastising her for daring to notice and comment on his body. Righteous indignation got him off. He wanted her to apologize so he could berate her further, get her on the floor before he kicked her.

"You left your shirt open, not just the top button, the top two. You want people to notice. And your stretched earlobes, you can't even see them so you can't argue that you did it for yourself. You make no attempt to cover your arm sleeves. They are a sign to the world: I'm different, I'm special. Look how unique I am. I'm a snowflake. So yeah, I noticed. I commented. You got the reaction you wanted. Don't cheapen it by pretending you didn't want it."

The bartender turned, mumbling something under his breath that sounded suspiciously like "fuck you."

"I changed my mind on the wine. Give me a dirty martini."

She smiled when he returned with the drink, a visual clue that she was ready to let go of their previous interaction. If he wanted to go another round with the verbal sparring, she would, but she would far rather drink in silence.

He slammed the drink down on the bar hard enough for the clear liquid to slosh at the sides.

"Thanks." She slid one of the olives off the toothpick with her teeth as she slipped onto a white leather barstool. The worn material was soft against the back of her bare thighs.

Heat spread through her body with the first sip. Warm tendrils worked their way down her limbs with every drink until every part of her relaxed into the sensation. But too soon the glass was empty.

"Another, please."

The bartender glared but didn't comment. It was probably for the best. Jess had him swearing in seconds; a few minutes, she could have him crying.

"Jess?"

Jess turned to see where the unfamiliar voice was coming from. *Shit.* Someone had recognized her. She loaded the response she'd had in her arsenal since she was a child, ready to fire. *What? Who is that? I'll have to look her up.*

Her eyes narrowed as she tried to place his face. He was at least six feet tall with cropped blond hair, only just longer than a standard military buzz, and pale blue eyes that held her gaze long after the social norm. He had the thick, over-developed muscles of a football player. She had seen him somewhere but God only knew where. "Hi?" The word came out more like a question. She wracked her mind to place him.

The man's face split into a broad smile. "You don't remember me, do you?"

The bartender brought her another martini. Jess took a long sip before she replied. "Should I? Have you done something memorable?"

His smile deepened. "Clearly it wasn't that memorable. Internet Security and Compliance. Ringing any bells?"

"Ah, yes." That's where she remembered him from. He was the speaker from the seminar she was at last month about keeping crime files safe. She had overheard an agent say a little too loudly how fuckable he was. Standing up close now, it was hard to disagree. He had the chiseled jaw "All American Boy" thing going on. "Now I remember. Agent Mark something or other, wasn't it?"

"Close enough. It's Matt Ramsay."

"Matt, yes. Nice to meet you, Matt." Jess reached out to shake his hand.

"We met once before. At the Christmas party a few years ago at The Local Pour."

"Did we?"

"Clearly I need to work on my game if you can't even remember that." He laughed softly.

Jess's eyes narrowed as a flash of a memory played in her mind, dancing with a tall blond guy and singing out of tune. "Fairytale of New York. That was you!"

"That was me."

"Ah, that was a good night. So you're the hot agent I danced with? We did shots, didn't we? I almost thought I had made you up."

"Nope. That was real. What happened to you that night?"

Jess's smile faltered. The image of Jamison played in her mind's eye. She downed the rest of her drink before she said, "My partner happened. He put me in a taxi and sent me home before I could make a bad life choice." Jamison had always been there looking out for her. She had liked it, counted on it even, but not anymore.

Matt's gaze locked on hers. She couldn't tell if it was the alcohol or the intensity of his stare, but her skin flushed.

"Would it have been a bad life choice, you and me?"

Jess slid off the barstool. She left some cash on the bar to settle her tab. "Only one way to find out." She walked past him, her fingers brushing his as she went. She took a few steps before she turned. Her heart picked up speed. "You coming?" There was no one to stop her tonight.

In two steps Matt caught up with her. "Your place or mine?"

Jess laced her fingers through his. "Neither." This wasn't a date. This was about feeling good and forgetting. She wanted numb and only one thing could get her there right now.

Jess led him around the corner, following the signs down the stairs. She opened the door to the bathroom. Just like the bar, the wall was covered in a gilded floor-to-ceiling mirror but the tiles here were black.

"Here?" Matt asked. "My place is five minutes away. I have my car."

Jess didn't answer; instead she pulled off her underwear and then reached for his belt. She pulled up at his shirt to make it easier to reach his zipper. He was hard, ready. "Do you have a condom?"

Matt's hand encircled hers, preventing her from moving. "Slow down." He leaned down, his lips brushing hers in a soft kiss.

She turned her head away so he couldn't kiss her again. "No. That's not what this is about. This isn't a date."

His face changed; a flash of emotion gone as quickly as it appeared. Sadness? Anger? Regret? She couldn't read it and she didn't care because the expression was gone and the only thing left was desire.

"So, what is this about then? Just a hard fuck in a bathroom? Is that what you want?"

His tone was harsh but she didn't care because so was the sentiment. There was nothing tender about this, she had made that clear. Now they both knew where they stood. "Yes."

"Fine."

"Condom?" she asked again as she undid his fly.

Matt nodded. Seconds later he was unwrapping a foil packet and rolling a condom down his hard length.

He slammed her up against the wall. The small of her back hit the metal of the hand dryer. A biting pain ripped through her. She had to bite her lip to keep from screaming.

"Is this how you want it?"

His words were a challenge. He wanted her to ask him to slow down or stop, but she wouldn't. "Yes, just like that."

In an instant he thrust into her with enough force to lift her from the ground. He was big and as ready as she had thought she was, but her body wasn't. She held her breath as she let her muscles relax just enough to allow the sudden invasion but not long enough to ease the sting.

Jess closed her eyes and sighed. This was the part of sex she craved, when all emotion and thought drained from her. There was nothing, no pain, no worry, no shame, just… numb.

Over and over, he thrust into her. She was flying; nothing mattered. Each stroke sent her higher. Nothing numbed her like sex. The world went quiet. There was nothing, just sensation. *Don't let it end.*

Matt groaned as he thrust into her a final time. He collapsed against her, his chest against her face, his heartbeat strong against her cheek.

If he didn't move, it wouldn't end: the peace.

For a while they stood, her dress around her waist, his cock still hard inside her. But eventually he moved, pulling out of her.

And her eyes opened.

Her reflection stared mockingly back at her, partially obscured by the stranger fucking her. She needed to get out of here. "Thanks," Jess mumbled.

Matt's eyes narrowed in confusion, clearly not expecting her reaction. "Was I too rough? I'm—"

"It's exactly what I wanted. Thank you," she interrupted before he could ruin it by apologizing.

The tension in his jaw visibly relaxed. A small smile pulled at his lips. "Good. Let's do it again. But next time I'll buy you dinner first."

"No, we're good." Jess pushed past him and walked away.

CHAPTER EIGHT

Louisiana

Jess folded her boarding pass and shoved it in her pocket. She would shred it when she got home.

"Jessie, wait up." Jamison stood at the top of the stairs, one foot still inside the airplane, a blond flight attendant smiling up at him.

Of course she was smiling. Everyone liked Jamison.

"Hey," Jamison said when he reached the bottom of the stairs. "We good?"

It had been two days since Jess had walked out of his wedding. She had not spoken to Jamison on the flight from DC. She had specifically asked for a seat at the front of the plane because she knew Jamison was always given the exit row because of his size.

Jess pulled her sunglasses down from the top of her head. "We're good." They weren't yet but they would be, and Jess would fake it until then.

"I got an email from Tina to say that they found Lydia's car. I think we should check that out before we speak to the widower." Jess pulled out her phone to reread the message. Jeanie had come through faster than Jess had expected and got Tina back on the team.

"Do you like him for this? What's your read on it?"

"Smart money is always on the husband but his alibi checks out. He was at home with their baby. Computer records show him internet shopping the night she went missing. He bought rechargeable batteries and a video baby monitor. And then he bought the last season of *Sons of Anarchy* on Amazon Prime."

"So where did they find the car?"

Jess scanned the message. "In a place called Breaux Bridge."

"That's two hours from New Orleans and forty minutes from where she was found, give or take. What was she doing in Breaux Bridge?"

"I think she was having an affair. Tina found a second email address and social media profiles under a pseudonym. Lydia was talking to a man near Baton Rouge named Mike Snowberger. Chan and Milligan are going to interview him."

"Naw. Nobody goes to Breaux Bridge for an affair. You go there to watch high-school football and eat crawfish."

"So you know the area? Is that near where you grew up?"

Jamison didn't often speak of his childhood. When he did, it was never of his hometown. He only spoke about his time with his Grandma Patty and his regret at not being able to keep his family together after she died.

"It's not far. Same parish. Lived there until I was thirteen. And then foster homes in New Orleans."

"Well, if you know the area, you're driving. Which means I'm picking the radio station. You know the rules."

Jamison smiled. "It's been two years. I thought you might have new rules."

"Rules are rules no matter how long you're gone."

Jess's fingernails bit into the leather console as the planks of the wooden bridge whined beneath the wheels of their rental car. She held her breath as they crept along the creaking boards.

"Breathe, Jessie."

"I don't think this bridge is structurally sound."

Jamison shook his head. "Probably not but I've crossed it dozens of times and I'm still here. The water isn't even chest-high here. You'd be fine."

Jess closed her eyes and pushed the fear down. All humans were born with two innate fears—heights and loud noises—but they could be conquered. All fear could be with grit and determination.

"Of course they left their lights on. Let's count ourselves lucky they didn't keep their sirens on too." Jamison pulled the car over to the side of the road behind two police cruisers. "This is the most action St Martin Parish has gotten all year."

Jamison's voice brought her back into the moment.

"I hope they haven't compromised the crime scene."

"You know they have. I admire your optimism for holding out hope though."

Jess got out of the car and walked down a small embankment. Spanish moss collected at the edge of the road, fallen from the braches after it had murdered the tree. It looked like a postcard or the set of a horror movie.

Each step was heavy as her feet sank into the red clay soil. Every movement was met with the squelch of mud. Murky water pooled in her shoes, soaking her feet. She stopped for a moment to take in the surroundings; deep shades of green and brown, thick carpets of algae on the dark water mirrored the dense canopy above. Even now in the bright morning sun, very little light penetrated the darkness.

A tow truck sat at the murky edge of the water. Beside it were four uniformed officers, all middle-aged white men, each with a corpulent belly to rival the next. Louisiana must have lenient fitness standards because none of them looked like they could run a mile in less than twenty minutes.

"Morning, gentlemen. I'm Special Agent Jessica Bishop. This is Special Agent Jamison Briggs. I hear you found our victim's car."

Jess and Jamison took the time to shake everyone's hands as introductions were made, including the tow-truck driver.

"Yes, ma'am," the one with the nametag that read "Giboin" said. He was the thinnest of the four. He only looked like he was in the second trimester. "A couple of kids out necking stumbled across it."

Necking. Apparently people in the South still said that. Jessica looked up from her notepad where she was writing down everyone's names. Officers Giboin, Stevenson, Henderson, and Purdue, and Hal the truck driver from Hal's towing. He didn't offer a last name but he would be easy enough to identify. She would send the names of everyone back to Tina as soon as she was back in an area with decent cell reception. Tina could do a full check on all the men to rule them out as suspects.

"It's mostly submerged. But you can see it was burnt out good before it went under," Giboin continued.

Jess sighed. There went her last remaining hope for recovering any trace evidence. "Did you interview the people who discovered it? I'd like to talk to them. Ask them what they saw."

"Yes, ma'am. They're both juniors at Cecilia High School." Giboin turned to the man on his right. "Martin, put in a call to Mr. Dubois and have Ricky and Jennifer brought in this afternoon. I'll call their mamas let them know there is nothing to worry about."

"This woman was reported missing weeks ago. Has no one noticed this car here before?" Jessica glanced up to the dirt road. The dumpsite was off the beaten track but not completely cut off.

"No, ma'am."

Jess walked up the embankment to the road to see what motorists would see as they drove along the dirt road. She couldn't see the car. "They knew something was down here. They didn't stumble across the crime scene," Jess shouted down. She wasn't buying the story that some kids stumbled across the burnt-out car. "We need to speak to those witnesses."

"Milk and sugar?"

Jess glanced around the Breaux Bridge police station. Mahogany wall panels gave it the feel of a hunting lodge. A mounted animal would not have been out of place next to the American flag and the three-foot-tall, bronzed bald eagle perched at the information desk.

"No thanks."

Officer Purdue handed Jess a cup of coffee before pouring a cup for Jamison.

"Donut?" Purdue put down the coffee pot and opened up the pink cardboard pastry box. Grease stains where there used to be donuts marked the empty areas of the box. Half a dozen remained, including a maple old-fashioned with a bite taken out of it.

"No, thank you," Jamison and Jess answered in unison.

Purdue shrugged before he reached for a frosted donut covered in fruit loops. Two breakfast dessert items in one.

"Are we still waiting on counsel for the two witnesses?" Jamison asked.

Purdue wiped his mouth with the back of his arm, leaving white powder in the crease of his khaki shirt. "Jennifer Thomson's parents waived the right. They aren't happy about the way she came into contact with the law, you know what I mean?" His lips curled like he had just cracked a witty one-liner. "Shame, she always seemed like such a nice girl, honor roll, All-State for volleyball, sings in her church choir. Such a pity."

Jess's back stiffened. Purdue was shaming the girl for daring to have sex with her boyfriend. "No, I don't know. Explain it to me."

Jamison shot her a look telling her it was not worth an argument. "Yeah, we get it. What about the other kid?"

"Ricky. Just waiting on his lawyer. I think his parents hired Stephan Roux," he said like the name should mean something to them. Presumably Roux was a hotshot lawyer if Purdue expected them to know of him.

"So, Jennifer gets left out to dry and Ricky gets Johnny Cochran. That seems about right," Jess muttered under her breath.

"We'll go ahead and speak to Jennifer now," Jamison said.

Jennifer Thomson was sitting at the Formica table picking at her nail polish—navy blue with sparkles—when they entered the room. Her gaze darted up and then quickly back down, focusing on the chip on her index finger. Her thick, dark-blond hair hung down her back in a fishtail braid. The color was pretty in its plainness, no bleach or highlights to make it look anything other than what it was.

"Hello, Jennifer? I'm Special Agent Briggs, this is my partner Special Agent Bishop," Jamison introduced them. "Do you know why you've been called in this afternoon?" Jamison had adopted his interview persona. His tone was neutral but there was no denying the chill that settled. Jamison owned every room he walked into, but he was particularly potent in an interrogation.

Jennifer shrugged. Her shoulders crumpled inward like she was trying to disappear into the table. She glanced up at Jess and then quickly lowered her gaze again, never looking at Jamison.

Jamison's presence was intimidating to hardened criminals; it must be terrifying to a scared teenage girl. Some people had commented that Jess had resting bitch face. Admittedly she did, but Jamison had resting "I will murder you and no one will find your body" face. The fact that he was massive would do little to put Jennifer at ease.

Jennifer should have someone here for her. This wasn't right, leaving a minor alone to be interviewed by federal agents. Anger and disappointment collided in Jess. Jennifer's parent were punishing her, shaming her all because she had chosen to be intimate with her boyfriend.

Bile rose in her throat. It reminded Jess a lot of how her own mom had reacted when she found out Jess was having sex. Her cheeks heated at the memory of the smack across her face.

"Jennifer, you were down at Saw's Mill Road last night."

Jennifer didn't answer. There was not even a shrug to indicate she had heard her. The girl's mouth blanched as she bit into her bottom lip.

"Jennifer, do you know what obstruction of justice is? Do you know what happens to people who obstruct the course of justice?" Jamison's voice was just above a whisper but the question sounded like a threat. There were two distinct sides to Jamison: the carefree giant and the hardened investigator who took no shit and would do anything to solve a case. Jennifer was getting a glimpse at the latter.

Jess caught Jamison's eye and gave him a nod to indicate she would take over. Usually it took longer. They had their interview dance. Jamison would break them. He would ask lots of questions in quick succession while Jess took notes, then Jamison would hand it over to Jess to fashion the rope they had provided into a noose.

That wasn't going to work here. Jennifer was about to cry. Her parents had already broken her; she didn't need Jamison for that.

The girl was terrified and she was ashamed. Her shame was palpable. She couldn't even look at them. Her face was red and if she bit her lip any harder she would draw blood.

"Jennifer, I'm Jess." Jess put her hand on top of hers. "There is nothing to worry about if you tell the truth. You won't be in any trouble. But I need you to tell the truth."

Jennifer gulped and wiped at her eyes. "Will you tell my mama?"

Jess glanced up at Jamison. Jess's heart ached at the question. She knew too well what it felt like to seek the approval of a woman who would never give it.

"What don't you want us to tell your mama?" Jess was careful not to promise not to say anything. Jennifer was a minor; technically her parents had a right to know anything she disclosed.

"Is it a crime?"

Jess waited for her to keep going but she never did. "What? Is what a crime?"

Jennifer covered her mouth. Tears fell through scrunched lids. "I know it's a sin but I didn't know it was a crime." Her body convulsed as a sob tore through her.

Jamison shot Jess a questioning glance.

A sin. Jess's back went rigid. Sadness clawed at her. Jennifer was talking about sex. Christ, the poor girl thought she had been arrested for having sex. This was why Jess hated these backwards little towns. The things they taught their children. "Are you asking me if it's a crime to have sex with your boyfriend?"

Jennifer nodded. When she opened her eyes, bright blue irises sparkled in the watery pools.

"Was it consensual?"

Jennifer's eyes narrowed in confusion.

She didn't know what consensual meant. Oh God. If she didn't know what consensual meant, she was too young to be having sex. "Did you want to have sex?"

The tears started to flow again. Her breath came in small shallow pants.

Jess stroked Jennifer's hand softly. "Jennifer, did Ricky force you to have sex?"

"No!" If Jennifer had shaken her head any more emphatically, she would have risked ripping the muscles in her neck.

"Okay. It's okay. If you both wanted to have sex, no crime has been committed. As long as you wanted to do it, it is no one's business. Do you hear me? Don't let anyone tell you what you do is a sin." God, Jess wished someone had told her that when she had first started having sex. It took years to shake off the shame that had been heaped on her from her mom and even some well-meaning professionals that assumed she was using sex as a way to self-sabotage. God forbid she had sex because she actually enjoyed it.

Jamison's gaze warmed Jess's skin. He was staring at her too intently. Jess could feel it even before she looked up. What was he thinking?

Jess returned her attention to Jennifer. "You went down to Saw's Mill Road to have sex with Ricky. Is that when you found the car?"

Jennifer didn't answer for a few seconds. "Um… yeah."

Jess sighed. The hesitation was too long. She was lying. "Why did you go down there?" Jess knew from her own high-school experience, there were plenty of places to have sex: her bedroom, his bedroom, under the bleachers. There was no need to go to a muddy road in the bayou. "You have to be completely honest with me here, Jennifer. What were you doing on Saw's Mill?"

"I don't want to get in trouble."

"Then tell me the truth. How did you find the car?"

"Sunday before last," Jennifer gulped between tears. "It was Labor Day weekend, you know, so we didn't have school the next day. We heard there was a barn dance at Taylor's so we decided to check it out."

Jess nodded. "Who? You and Ricky?"

"Yeah."

"And what happened? Tell me everything. I can't help you if you hold anything back."

"We were on the bridge. There was a man."

Jess's gaze snapped up from her notepad. A chill crept up her neck. "You saw a man with the car?" Jess and Chan had been less than ten miles away at the time. That meant the suspect was still in the area when Lydia's body was found. He might still be. The killer knew this area well enough to evade law enforcement. Jess scribbled down the word "local" in her pad and underlined it twice.

Another sob tore through Jennifer. Her body shook with it like a wild animal succumbing to a fatal wound.

Jess rubbed Jennifer's hand again. "Look at me. No, not at your hands. Look right at me. Good. Now take a deep breath and hold it while I count to four. Good girl. Now slowly let it out. Slow as you can. Keep looking at me. Everything's okay. You're safe. Good girl. Now one more breath in and hold it for me." Jess talked her through the breathing exercise, repeating the cycle until Jennifer's hands stopped shaking.

Eventually Jennifer gave a timid smile. She really was a pretty girl with her big blue eyes and bow-shaped mouth. But, God, she was so vulnerable and naïve: a child in a woman's body. A sense of unease settled on Jess. She felt like a predator stalking easy prey. Jess had mastered the art of manipulation and that was exactly what this was. Jess knew people and she knew what would break them. What was happening now was trauma bonding. Jamison had scared the shit out of Jennifer. Jess was the hero swooping in to protect her from the perceived threat.

Jennifer was calm now, as at ease as she could possibly be given the situation. All it had taken was the stroking of her hand and a few calmly spoken words and now Jennifer was hers to use, she would tell Jess anything. This was another reason Jess hated working with kids. Professionally it was a victory, but as a human it felt more like a blow to the gut. Jennifer was too young to understand the consequences. Someone should be here for her. She needed someone really on her side.

Jess took a deep breath. She had no doubt Jennifer was about to disclose something. It might be nothing but it just as easily could be something that put her on the wrong side of the law.

Shit.

Jess closed her eyes and scrubbed at her face, trying to decide what to do.

She let out a stream of air. This kid needed a break.

"Okay. This is what's going to happen, you're going to tell me everything about that night. You're not going to leave out a single detail. Nothing you tell me will be used against you. I promise." Jess would do her utmost to make sure there were no legal ramifications for her. No doubt Jennifer's parents would be raining down their own form of misguided justice on her. Jess could not prevent that but she would do her best to protect her from the law.

Jamison's stare burned Jess's skin. She had no right or even authority to make such promises. They both knew it but Jamison would never call her out on it, not in front of anyone. Jess glanced up to see Jamison's mouth twitch down into a stern frown. His stare bore down on her, pinning her in place, but he didn't speak. He wouldn't. He would wait until they were alone to lay into her.

Jess turned her attention back to the case. "Tell me what happened. On Sunday night, did you see a man coming from the car?"

"Yes." Jennifer's voice was barely a whisper.

"Okay good. Can you describe what he looked like? Was he tall or short? Black or white? Any tattoos? Glasses? We'll get a sketch artist."

Jennifer shook her head. "We just saw him walking away. His back was turned. He was tall. Really tall, I think. It was hard to tell from where we were but he looked tall."

"What about his hair color? Dark or blond? Straight or curly?"

"It was really dark and he was wearing one of those things… what do you call them? They're like a really thin coat. Not for keeping warm, but like for keeping dry. Not like a big raincoat. Like a—"

"A windbreaker?" Jamison interjected.

"Yeah, like that."

"So, this man. How do you know he was with the car? The car has been there for weeks. Maybe he found it just like you. Why do you think he had something to do with putting it there?" Jamison pressed, the annoyance he felt at Jess seeping into his deep voice.

Tears brimmed in the corners of Jennifer's eyes. Her lip began to tremble again.

They were losing her. "You have to be completely honest. That is the only way we can help you. What was the man doing that made you think he was somehow involved with the car?" Jess asked.

Jennifer let out an unsteady breath. "We saw him put a purse in the glove compartment."

"What?" As far as Jess knew, no personal effects had been found at the scene. She scribbled down a note to check what contents had been logged. If they had found Lydia Steiner's purse, Jess needed to see it. "So you saw this man in the water? Help me out here because that doesn't make sense." The crime scene flashed in Jess's mind: the front end of the car completely submerged. The unease that had set in before was now tinged with suspicion and annoyance. Had Jess read the situation wrong? Was Jennifer playing her?

She continued, "There is no way he could have opened the door. The windows were all rolled open. The water pressure wouldn't have allowed him to open the door. It's impossible."

Jennifer shook her head. "It wasn't in the water. The car was on the embankment. Ricky and I were up the road. The car was already there. It had been there a week, I think maybe a little longer, just right off the side of the road right up from Hook Up."

"Hook Up?" Jamison asked.

"It's the little area on the side of the road, right by the bridge. Nobody from the road can see you so people go down there to, you know..."

"Hook up," Jamison finished for her.

Jennifer shrugged.

"So you saw him put the purse in the glove compartment, was that before or after he set it on fire and then pushed it into the bayou?" The incredulity was clear. "Well?" Jamison pushed. "Come on, keep going."

Jennifer covered her face with her hands. She looked like a small child, closing her eyes to block out the world because in the magical world of egocentrism, if she could not see what was going on, it did not exist.

Stop, Jess mouthed to Jamison. He was tanking the interview. He had been out of the game for a long time. Their dance was rusty; he wasn't reading her signs the way he once had, so now she had to spell it out. *I got this.*

"Do you?" Jamison said out loud, not bothering to whisper.

Jess ignored the disappointment in his voice. "Keep going, Jennifer. Tell us everything. You're safe. It's okay. You're not in any trouble. We just need the truth. Start again from the beginning. Tell us about the man. Tell us what he was doing."

Jennifer wiped the corners of her eyes. "It was close to midnight. Ricky and I didn't go to the dance because we decided to stay at Hook Up. I thought I heard someone, so we got out of the car and looked down. We had seen the car there before so we thought it was the owner coming back to get it, but he didn't get in the driver's side. He just opened the passenger side. He had one of those electric keys. It made this beeping sound and the headlights went on. He put a purse in the glove compartment and then closed the door and walked back up the road towards Mount Vernon Road." Jennifer gestured to show the direction. "We waited until he was gone and then—" Jennifer stopped abruptly. Her mouth hung open, frozen in place.

A sinking sensation engulfed Jess, like quicksand drawing her under. There was more to this story, something incriminating or illegal. That was why she stopped.

Fuck.

Jess glanced up to see Jamison's stare hard on her, pinning her in place but he did not speak. Behind his dark eyes, there was recrimination. The fine hairs on Jess's arms rose.

"What did you do, Jennifer?" She strained not to shout. Under the table, she balled her hands into tight fists.

"It wasn't me. I swear—"

"Just tell us what happened next."

"Please don't tell my parents." Jennifer whimpered. She sounded like a puppy that had just been smacked for pissing on the carpet.

"What happened?" Jess demanded. "How did the car end up burned out and stuck in the bayou?"

"It wasn't me. Ricky took the purse. I know it was wrong but we didn't think it was stealing. He left it there. And he didn't even lock the door."

Jess swore under her breath. Blood pounded against her temples, a surge of pain meeting every staccato beat. "So, let me get this straight. You took the purse—"

"Ricky. Ricky took the purse."

"Of course. Ricky. Your boyfriend, right? The guy you love? The one you were caught having sex with?" Jamison rubbed his knuckles against the stubble along his jaw. "Just want to make sure we're talking about the same person."

Jennifer nodded.

"Nope. I need to hear a yes or a no," Jamison pressed.

"Yes. Ricky took the purse."

"And then what did Ricky do?"

"Last night. We got worried that our fingerprints would be on the car."

Jamison's glance caught Jess's. He had caught it too. *Our.* Jennifer had just incriminated herself. She was worried about her prints being on the car too.

"So what did you do?" Jess had already put the pieces together but Jennifer needed to spell it out. "No, don't cry. We don't have time for that. Tell me what you did."

"Ricky brought some gasoline from his daddy's farm and he lit the car on fire. But then we, I mean he, thought that someone would see the car and start asking questions so we went back again and he pushed it into the water."

"Ricky did. All by himself? Wow he is strong. No wonder you like him so much."

Jess's lip twitched, a fleeting smile at Jamison's comments. Everyone in the room knew Jennifer was lying about her involvement now but Jamison wouldn't call her out on it because Jess was lead. "So that's when the police found you? Last night when you were pushing the car into the bayou?" *Destroying trace evidence and contaminating my crime scene.*

Jennifer nodded.

"Where is the purse now?" Jamison asked. "We need that purse. You asked before if what you did was a crime. The answer is yes. Theft and arson are a crime. Don't add anything to the list. Give us the purse."

"Rick—"

"Don't." Jamison held up his hand. "I don't care what he did. You're here right now. You. Not him. You took evidence from my crime scene. We need it back. Now."

"There was only forty dollars and some change. That's it. It wasn't a lot." Jennifer sobbed. Her pale blue eyes were now rimmed in smeared mascara. Tears and snot merged on the tip of her nose.

"Here, wipe your face." Jess took a tissue out of her purse. "Do you still have all the contents of her purse? Other than the money?"

"Yeah."

"Were there credit cards in her wallet?"

"Yeah."

"Did you use her credit cards?" Jess held her breath as she waited for an answer.

"No."

"Are you sure? I need you to be very clear on this. You have to be honest."

"No. We didn't use the credit cards. This is a small town. Everyone knows us here. We couldn't use them."

"Okay good." Thankfully neither Jennifer nor Ricky had figured out that the internet was made for credit card fraud. "This is what we're going to do. You are going to write down exactly what happened. And then you're going to give us back the purse, and all of the contents. Everything."

"But I don't have the money. I am supposed to babysit for the Smiths this weekend. I can get you the money. I promise. I have a little left over from my birthday. I'll give that to you now." Jennifer dove into her backpack, pulling out binders and an embroidered coin purse. "Here take this now. And I'll get the rest this weekend."

Oh God, she was just a kid. Jess's chest tightened, she thought this was about the money. She remembered all too well being young and stupid, making bad choices that could have ruined her life. Luckily people along the way had cut Jess some slack. Jennifer needed that same break right now. "We don't need the money, just whatever else was in the bag. Everything — cell phone, candy wrappers, keys. I need it all. Where is it?"

"Under my bed. I didn't mean to hurt anybody. It's a Coach bag and I've been saving up... I'm sorry."

"We're going to go right now to your house and get it. So whatever story you're going to tell your mama, you better get it straight now." Jess stood up. She didn't bother looking at Jamison. She already knew what he was thinking.

Jennifer's eyes widened. Fresh tears brimmed in the corners.

"I'm not going to tell your mother. The information you gave today won't go any further. You committed a crime. If the local police choose to investigate independently, you could be prosecuted. Ricky has a lawyer. You need one too. Don't ever speak to law enforcement again without a lawyer present. Do you understand?"

"Yeah."

"I never told you that. This conversation never happened. Right?" Jess said.

Jennifer nodded. "Thank you."

Jess turned down the car radio until it was just a low whine in the background. "Are you going to speak to me again at some point?"

Jamison rolled down the window and looked out at the horizon. The setting sun cast a haze on everything. "I don't think you want to hear any of the words I have for you right now."

Jess turned her gaze back to the road. They were headed to New Orleans to interview Lydia's widower. She had hoped to be there before six but the interviews had taken longer than expected. They shouldn't have bothered speaking to Ricky because after every question they put to him he looked up at his lawyer for guidance. After the third question it became obvious that he and his lawyer had a system worked out beforehand: if his lawyer shook his head, Ricky answered "no comment," when he cleared his throat, Ricky answered, "I don't recall," and a tap on the table with a ballpoint pen was the sign Ricky could answer freely. The latter only happened for Ricky to confirm his name and address. For every other question, they were stonewalled.

It would have been nice if Ricky had given them anything to work with, like a description of the man they saw leaving the scene, but since Ricky was denying even being at Hook Up, he was as good as useless as a witness. Not that it mattered; Jennifer had given them more than enough to make the trip to Breaux Bridge worthwhile. They had a timeline and even more importantly they had Lydia Steiner's purse and cell phone.

Jess glanced in the rearview mirror at the sealed evidence bag sitting in the middle seat. It had taken more than a little self-control not to pillage the purse and scroll through the phone. The items had to be processed before she handled them; the chain of command had to be enforced so they didn't give some defense attorney anything to work with when this went to trial.

Jess looked back up at the road. In the distance a sign for a diner chain peeked over the hill reminding her that she hadn't eaten since her protein shake at breakfast. "Are you hungry?"

"Nope." Jamison turned up the radio, indicating he didn't want to chat.

"Fine. I'll just stop at a gas station and get something."

"Fine."

"Fine."

Jess drove in silence for a few minutes but the pressure of enforced silence began to build again, like steam gaining a head just below the surface of her skin. Enough, this was ridiculous. Jess turned on her blinker to indicate she was pulling off onto the side of the road.

"What are you doing?" Jamison asked.

They were miles from anywhere. The diner sign had indicated that the next town was still a few miles away.

Jess turned on her hazard lights before she turned off the engine so no one would drive into the back of them. "Just say it. Whatever it is you're thinking, just say it. I don't want to drive in silence. If I wanted a moody asshole in the passenger seat I would have asked for Chan."

Jamison tugged at his tie to loosen it. "Just drive, Jessie."

"No. Not until you tell me what you're thinking."

"I'm thinking I'm tired and I want to get home to my wife."

Wife. The title cut through her like shrapnel. Jamison was bound to call Felicia his wife at some point; that is what she was. Jess stared down at the steering wheel, temporarily lost for words, subliminally tracing the geometric pattern of the car's logo. *Wife.*

Slowly realization crept in. Jamison knew how to play her. His words were chosen carefully, designed to distract her from their conversation. And it had worked. "I'm sure we can catch the red eye and you'll be home to your wife before you know it."

Jamison's gaze locked on hers. They could read each other. They both knew he had tried to play her. "You don't want to talk, Jess, you want absolution and I can't do that."

"We have offered deals to people who have done far worse."

"No. Don't pretend like you don't understand what you did. We made deals once we knew what we were dealing with, once we had all the cards in play. *We* made deals. *We.* We acted together. You went in blind and you made this decision unilaterally. There is no way you should have offered that girl anything. She lied, she destroyed evidence, she—"

"Exactly. She's a kid. She was in the wrong place at the wrong time."

"She committed a crime."

"So did he." Jess's voice broke under the strain of emotion. She wasn't even sure why she was upset, but she was. Seeing that girl get railroaded had triggered her. It wasn't fair. That is not what justice looked like.

Jamison shook his head. "What you did was straight up wrong. I'm not going to blow sunshine up your ass. You had no idea what she was going to confess to and you were tripping over yourself to cut a deal. She could have admitted to hacking up and burning a body and you would have pushed through an immunity deal."

"That's not true. I knew she hadn't really done anything."

"How?" he demanded. "How did you know? Don't clam up on me now, Jessie. You wanted to talk so now we're talking. You didn't know. You hoped. You had a hunch but you didn't know. So, your gut told you?"

Jess shrugged. "Yeah, maybe it did."

"No. That's not good enough."

"Why? You always go on your gut."

"You don't. You never have. You're by the book. You are one of the best agents I have ever known because you always play by the rules. But not with her. And you know why?"

Jamison's dark stare pinned her to her seat. Judgment and recrimination marred his features. Jess was getting the version of Jamison reserved for interrogations. There was nothing carefree about him now. There was no warmth, only a frigid distance.

Jess opened her mouth to speak, to say something to fill the painful void, make him understand, but the words didn't come.

"I saw when it happened. It was before we even went into the room. Purdue made a dumbass joke about Jennifer being caught having sex, and the switch was flicked. That's when you made the choice to cut her a deal. You hadn't even met her yet and you were defending her, and you want to know why?" Jamison didn't stop to let her answer. "Because this wasn't about a sixteen-year-old girl from Louisiana, this was about you. This was about every time someone tried to shame you. This was you telling them to fuck off. But here's the thing, Jessie, this was not about you. You had no right to make it about you."

Anger and indignation ignited her skin. Her cheeks burned with it. What was he saying? What shame? She wasn't ashamed of anything. How dare he imply that there was anything shameful about Jess's life?

Bile rose in the back of her throat. "Her boyfriend did the same thing and he's getting off scot-free. How is that fair?"

"It's not fair, but it's not our job to make it fair. Our job is solving cases. So whatever axe you have to grind, you do it on your own time."

She clenched the steering wheel until her hands shook. The words for a denial taunted her, coming into focus only long enough for her to acknowledge their existence but leaving again before she could grab hold of them and form a coherent sentence. Several times she tried to speak only for her mind to go blank.

Jess started the engine. Suddenly she had no desire to talk things through. This conversation was over.

CHAPTER NINE

It was nearly eight before Jess and Jamison pulled up outside Lydia Steiner's home in New Orleans. The house on St Charles Avenue was a palatial, three-story red-brick home, proudly held up with six ornately carved Doric columns. This was obviously where the money was in New Orleans. The lawn in front was larger than the plot of land Jess's apartment building was set on. There was nothing humble or understated about the home or the neighborhood. Each house was as grand and immaculate as the last.

Small stones of the winding path crunched under her feet as she approached the front door. Jamison's steps were loud behind hers. It was the first sound Jamison had made in over two hours. They had driven in complete silence. Neither of them had bothered to turn on the radio. Even when Jess pulled into a drive through, Jamison didn't speak, probably because she didn't ask him if he wanted anything. She ordered two bean burritos for herself. If he had wanted anything, he would have asked.

On either side of the porch hung a swing with plush throw pillows in various shades of blue and gray. It looked like the cover of *Southern Living* magazine, all posed and perfect. The swing must have only been for show because the plethora of expertly placed cushions left nowhere to actually sit.

Before Jess could reach for the doorbell, the door opened. State troopers had informed Mr. Steiner that the FBI would be visiting him tonight. Reuben Steiner stood only slightly taller than Jess, making him maybe five foot five or five foot six. His build was trim, slight even. His eyes were red, speckled in a sea of tiny, ruptured blood vessels, burst through crying. He didn't bother to wipe his eyes when fresh tears engulfed his caramel-colored irises. Liquid gathered in the corners threatening to spill over, but they didn't. Instead, when he blinked, they were sopped up by his dark lashes, like a spider's web catching rain.

He looked directly at Jess but his gaze was vacant.

"Mr. Steiner, I'm Special Agent Bishop, this is my partner Special Agent Briggs. We are so sorry for your loss."

He nodded. "Come in." His tone was flat, not even the smallest rise or fall to the slow cadence.

Jess had seen it before. Every reaction to grief was as unique as it was painful, but in the crudest, most general terms, people fit into broad categories and Jess had seen them all. Every emotion she could name, she had seen.

Some people were hysterical, screaming and crying, making primal sounds usually reserved for animals whose flesh was being torn clean off the bone by the jaws of a predator. Those people moaned and screamed until the agony brought them to the ground and then they shook. They always shook.

And some people acted like Mr. Steiner, flat, emotionless. Sometimes like Mr. Steiner their bodies might cry but they wouldn't even register it or they ignored it. The pain was too great so they ran from it even when it was smacking them across the face and pulling them under.

"If this is a bad time, we can come back in the morning," Jamison offered.

Jess looked away for a moment to focus her thoughts. A shadow of guilt tugged at her when she hoped Mr. Steiner would ask for them to come back tomorrow. If there was an emotion threshold, she had reached it.

"No." Mr. Steiner opened the door wider to let them in. "My mom will be back soon. This is the first moment's peace I have gotten since she got here. She's supposed to be here to help but all she does is ask questions, too many stupid questions. That's all she has done since Liddy went missing. 'Are you sure she isn't visiting her dad in Florida? Have you called the hospitals?' Like I wouldn't have thought to check the local hospitals."

"Liddy?" Jess asked. "Is that what you called your wife?"

Mr. Steiner nodded. "Yeah she was always Liddy to her friends." Without warning, he turned and walked away. His movements were slow, his feet barely lifting off the polished marble floor.

Jess and Jamison followed him through the entry hall. The massive room was dominated by two oak staircases. Each swept up in a curve, meeting at the top to create a balcony.

They continued into a family room. Like every other part of the house, the room was tastefully decorated, in this case with shades of cream and beige. Presumably they had a cleaner because the entire house was immaculate, nothing out of place, no dust gathering in corners.

"Please take a seat. I should have offered you a drink. Would you like a drink?" Mr. Steiner asked just as he sat down.

"I'm okay. Thank you," Jamison assured him as he sat down in a wingback chair.

Jess chose a seat on the other side of Mr. Steiner. "No, I'm fine. Thank you." Jess indicated to a framed picture on the table beside her. "May I?"

He didn't respond, just continued staring through Jess.

Jess examined the wedding photo. Lydia smiled back at her, beaming, her eyes fixed directly at the camera. Her husband on the other hand only had eyes for his new bride. It was a candid shot, Jess could tell by the fact Liddy was caught mid bite of wedding cake. On her fork was a buttercream rose, but it captured the complete joy of the moment. And the love. "She was beautiful." Jess wasn't just saying it. Liddy Steiner was stunning. Her long hair was corn-silk blond and her eyes a clear blue. Her cheekbones were high and chiseled, and even sitting down she had the posture and poise of a dancer. Jess hadn't noticed how beautiful Liddy was before because she had only seen her grainy passport picture and her body on an autopsy table. But she had been beautiful. And in this picture she had been happy. The incongruity was jarring. On one side was a beautiful woman, young and vibrant. And on the other side, the ugly side, there was the bloated torso of a murder victim—tortured, mutilated, burned, discolored, tossed in the bayou like garbage. But both sides were Liddy Steiner.

"Again, Mr. Steiner, we are so sorry for your loss."

Jamison's deep voice brought Jess back to the present. She pulled out her notebook. "Can you tell us about the night Liddy went missing? What was she doing in St Martin Parish?"

He shook his head. "I don't know. She was on her way to meet her sorority sisters in Baton Rouge. They would get together one weekend every year to catch up. Liddy didn't want to go. She didn't want to leave the baby. But…" His voice cracked. Fresh tears glistened. This time his eyelashes did not catch them and they rolled down through the stubble of his cheek. "I told her to go… have fun… she hadn't been out since Ava was born. She puts so much pressure on herself… put." He corrected himself. "She put so much pressure on herself. She wanted to be the perfect mom. That's all she wanted. She blamed herself for Ava's colic. She thought if she could nurse Ava it would be better."

Jess remembered the scars across Liddy's chest. "When did she have the mastectomy?"

"When she was twenty-eight. Her mom died of ovarian cancer at twenty-eight."

Jamison's eyes narrowed. "Your wife had cancer at the same age as her mother?"

"No. Liddy tested positive for the BRCA1 gene. She found out a few months before we got married. We almost didn't get married. Liddy said it wasn't fair to me because she was just going to die. She said she would never have children because she couldn't bear the idea of leaving them motherless." Mr. Steiner's lip trembled as he spoke. "I told her whatever time she had, I wanted to spend with her. But I never thought it would be like this." Another tear slid down his cheek.

Jess thought about giving him a tissue but the only thing she had in her pocket was a scrunched-up, hot-sauce-stained napkin.

"Liddy was obsessed with the statistics of dying. She could tell you more about the probability of death at any moment than any actuary. Her best odds were a prophylactic mastectomy. No breasts, no cancer. Only after that did she feel safe enough to have a baby."

"I'm sorry," Jess murmured. A woman willing to mutilate her body to prolong her life became the victim of a serial killer. The cruel irony was not lost on Jess. Nothing about Reuben Steiner's wife was screaming high-risk lifestyle.

"Did Liddy meet her friend's that night?" Jamison asked.

"No. She was lost. I knew I should have driven her. Liddy could get lost driving to the mall. She had no sense of direction whatsoever. We used to joke she only knew her left from her right fifty percent of the time." A feeble smile twitched on his lips at the memory.

"Was there a reason Liddy was in a rental car?" Jess asked.

"Her car was in the shop so we rented one. I made sure she had a full tank of gas and I printed off a map for her and programmed the address into the GPS so all she would have to do was tap a screen twice. I—"

"It's not your fault," Jess interrupted him. She knew where this was going. After he listed everything he had done to protect his wife he would start thinking of all the things he could have done and all the ways he had failed her. He would drive himself crazy. "There is nothing you could have done."

"She called me that night. She knew she was in trouble. I know that now. But I thought she was okay because the police came."

"What? What did she say? What police?" Jess's head snapped up.

"It was just before eight. She had reservations at a place called Latitudes for seven thirty. She realized she wasn't even in East Baton Rouge Parish when she saw a sign for Bayou Chene. So she pulled over and called me. She was in the middle of nowhere. She must have missed her exit. I should have told her to lock her doors and wait for me. I should have gone to get her. I shouldn't have let her go. She didn't want to go. I made her go. It's my fault."

"No." Jamison's voice was strong and deep, authoritative and commanding, and comforting. "You didn't do this. There is nothing you could have done to prevent it."

Mr. Steiner nodded. Jess had no doubt the recrimination and blame would start again but for a moment, Jamison had silenced them. When Jamison said something, people believed him. He was a natural leader because people looked to him. They craved his strength.

"What happened next?" Jess asked, gently bringing them back on topic.

"I was trying to figure out exactly where she was so I could give her directions back. I was going to map it out and send it to her phone. Then Ava started to cry. Liddy said not to worry because a police officer pulled up behind of her. She said she would ask him."

"Him? Not them?" Jess asked. "Did she say him? Was there only one police officer?" Jess wrote down a reminder to check with all law enforcement in the area to see if they had a record of contact with Liddy.

"I think so. Maybe. I don't know. She said the car had a flashing red light."

Jess's spine went rigid. The hairs on her arms stood taut. She looked at Jamison. He nodded, knowing what she was going to say before she even spoke.

"So, the car was unmarked." Jamison verbalized her thought.

"I don't know. She didn't say."

"If your wife had seen a marked car, she would probably have identified it as sheriff or police or a state trooper. That would have been the detail she focused on, not the flashing light. The fact that she focused on the light indicates there were no other markings on the car to designate it as law enforcement," Jess said.

Mr. Steiner narrowed his eyes in question.

"Special Agent Bishop's background is in linguistics and forensic psychology," Jamison explained.

"People convey information not only in what they say but how they say it, the words they choose," Jess added when the look of confusion did not ease on Mr. Steiner's face.

"Words help you solve crimes?" Based on his tone, he was clearly dubious of the assertion. Her own mother had a similar reaction when she had told her the field of study in which she was choosing to pursue her doctorate. The word "useless" had been bandied about more than a few times in the conversation. That was one of the many reasons she limited contact with her mother to Thanksgiving dinner. One meal a year was all Jess could take. It was enough to assuage Jess's guilt but not enough to let her mother in.

"Yes," Jamison answered for her when she didn't. "Agent Bishop is very good at her job. She picks up on things other people miss."

Jess's skin warmed at the small praise. Jamison had always valued her contribution and not seen it as a weird tangent like Chan had. Jamison's encouragement was why she had applied to the PhD program, and it had kept her in after she should have quit.

"So, you think that it's important? That is was an unmarked car?"

"It gives us a place to start. So yes, it could be important." Jess chose her words carefully. There was no reason at this point to tell a grieving widow that the person his wife reported could very likely be her murderer. "Did she give a description of the man she saw? Did she mention a race or a build? Anything of that nature?"

"No. I don't think so." Mr. Steiner closed his eyes as he rubbed at his temples. "Call the local precinct. They must have a log of it." His eyes were wide, hopeful.

Jess smiled, playing along. "Yes. We'll call them. Um… there is another thing we wanted to ask you about. I was going through Liddy's email and phone records. I saw she had another email address."

"Amelia Peregrine," Mr. Steiner said simply.

"Yes," Jess answered, struggling to keep the surprise from her voice. "You know about her accounts in that name?"

He nodded. "Yeah, I know about the accounts. Amelia was her mother's name. And Peregrine is the patron saint of cancer patients. That's the profile she used for online support groups. She said she liked to pretend that if anything bad happened it would be to Amelia, not to her. It was a game she played with herself to stay positive after she found out she was a carrier. She said when she closed the computer she put the worry away too. It didn't work that way but it was a nice thought."

"I get it." Jess wrote down the word hope. She stared down at the word, wondering why she had written it down; it wasn't pertinent to the case. And then she remembered what Jamison had said when she told him she had left the PhD program because she didn't want to intently listen to pedophile's spew bullshit to try to justify their crimes. He said she needed hope. He was right. Jess needed a place to go where she could pretend everything would work out and good always prevailed. Liddy Steiner had created that space of hope by inventing a pseudonym, a psychological whipping boy who took on the brunt of her emotional pain.

"The Amelia Peregrine account was fairly active." Jess stopped to think. There was no nice way to imply his wife was having an affair, but this was a line of questioning she needed to pursue. It was possible that the reason Liddy Steiner had got lost on the way to the restaurant was because she wasn't going to the restaurant at all. She could have been meeting the man she had been chatting with online.

Jess cleared her throat. "There was a considerable amount of email activity and even some video conferencing. In particular with a man in Baton Rouge named Mike Snowberger? Do you know anything about that?"

"Was she still doing that? I told her to stop. She promised she would after the mastectomy, but after Ava she started again." He ran a hand through his dark hair.

Jamison looked over at Jess. "Just to clarify, what was the nature of your wife's relationship with Mr. Snowberger?"

"Relationship? No there was no relationship like that. Is that what you think, that Liddy was having an affair?" His voice rose with indignation. His hands shook with rage or anger or maybe it was just grief because there was nowhere left for it to go.

Jess was careful in choosing her words. If Liddy was having an affair, her husband would soon find out. People liked to think they could take their secrets to the grave, but even the most expertly guarded secrets could be unraveled in death. "Mr. Steiner, we are looking into all of Liddy's relationships: friends, family, colleagues."

Mr. Steiner shook his head. "Liddy gave up work when Ava was born."

"Oh." Jess already knew that. She mentioned colleagues to distract and diffuse and thankfully it had worked. "Good to know. We will of course be looking into all of Liddy's sorority sisters. You wouldn't happen to have the contact details of the women she was meeting that night?"

Mr. Steiner nodded. His head moved up and down as quickly as a bobble head on the dashboard. "Yeah. Yeah. I can get those right now."

Jess put her hand on his. "It's okay, we'll get them before we go." The truth was Jess didn't need them. Tina Flowers could track them down from just their names. Jess had only asked to give Mr. Steiner something positive to focus on. Providing the contact information would make him feel like he was contributing in some way.

"You mentioned that you knew of Liddy's online friendships." Jess gently guided the conversation back to Mike Snowberger.

"Yeah, Liddy wanted me to meet him. Of course I refused. I wanted to be supportive but I didn't want to indulge her obsessions."

Jess glanced over at Jamison. He looked as confused by the conversation as she felt.

"Why did she want you to meet him?" Jamison asked.

"Liddy had been talking to him since we got engaged. Mike's wife died of cancer about… I don't know… a few years before we got married. Liddy wanted a widower's perspective. She wanted to know if he regretted marrying a woman with the cancer gene. Of course he didn't regret marrying his wife and he told her that. I was grateful to him because he convinced her that sometimes you got to just jump, not worry about what might happen."

"But you asked her to stop speaking to him when you got married?"

"Yeah. Not because I was jealous. It was never like that between them. I just didn't want to… I don't know. I guess I didn't want to indulge her paranoia. It was always a fine line. I wanted to be supportive of her fears but I didn't want to enable her to worry even more. Cancer, fear of dying was always there like a third partner in our marriage."

"But she kept talking to him. Did they have any contact offline?" Jamison asked.

"She wasn't having an affair." His voice was thin and brittle, no conviction left.

"That's not what we're suggesting. I'm asking if they ever met in person?"

"No. Not that I know of." He ran a hand through his dark hair again. His lip trembled. "I don't know... maybe... no... I don't know anything anymore..." His voice trailed off in an anguished whimper. He scrubbed at his face, wiping away the torrent of fresh tears before he looked down at his slick palms. A violent bellowing scream tore through the silence of the room.

Then he began to shake.

CHAPTER TEN

Washington, DC

"You're late." Chan was standing outside her office holding two Styrofoam cups. He was wearing a new suit. Like everything he wore, it looked expensive. When he walked, the shade of the material changed from dark blue to black. Jess didn't need to check to know the label was Italian. Everything was a show with Chan, from the perfectly coiffed hair to the silk socks the same shade of magenta as his tie.

Jess held up her travel mug. "They put in a new coffee kiosk at my Metro stop so I couldn't not try it. But I'm not late. I'm just not as early as normal." She checked her watch just to be sure.

Chan frowned at her cup. He followed her into her office. Only after he put one of the coffees down on her desk did she realize it was for her. She had assumed it was for his new partner.

"Have you met your new partner yet?" Jess asked.

"No, I got a brief about him, same as you. Apparently he was overseas somewhere, Accra maybe. Got back like three months ago or something."

"Algiers," Jess corrected. "He was based in Algeria. Glad to see you're paying attention to details as usual."

Chan smiled. "It would kill the small talk if I paid too much attention. This way he gets to tell me about his wife and kids and I get to pretend to give a shit."

"Kid. His wife just had their first baby, that's why they moved back to DC. Did you even open the email?"

"Not really. Team meeting in fifteen but Jeanie wants to see you first. She looked pissed. She was knocking on your door at seven."

"Great." Jeanie Gilbert never slept. Jess had never seen her enter the building in the morning or leave at night. The bureau was her life. Jess took a long sip of coffee. She needed caffeine to fortify her. Jess winced as the hot liquid scalded the roof of her mouth. The problem with taking your coffee black was there was no milk or creamer to cool it down.

"See you at the team meeting."

Jess nodded to Chan as he left. She took another sip of coffee. Hot or not, she would drink it. She would drink molten lava in the morning if it got her going.

Jeanie Gilbert's office was down the hall from hers. She had to pass Jamison's office but she did not stop to say good morning or even check to see if he was there. They hadn't spoken on the way home from Louisiana the previous night.

He was obviously still upset about Jennifer Thomson, but it would blow over, she hoped. She couldn't remember ever really arguing with Jamison. Having him back was an adjustment for the both of them. They just needed to find their rhythm again.

Jess knocked on Jeanie's partially open door.

"Come in," Jeanie called. Her voice, like her demeanor, was deceptively sweet. Jeanie looked more like a cozy grandmother than a federal agent, but she was one of the most capable and intimidating women Jess had ever met. Jess had never heard her swear but Jeanie Gilbert could cut any man down to size. Her intellect and fast reaction times were all the tools she needed. Her hair was a faded shade of mousey blond with just enough warmth to hint that she had once been a redhead. Her features were soft and her face round. Faded freckles mingled with deep lines. As always, her hair was tied in a loose bun at the base of her neck.

As the head of the team, everything went through Jeanie. The team was in constant contact with her, reporting everything back.

When Jess opened the door fully she saw Jamison seated across from Jeanie. He glanced up only enough to acknowledge another person had entered the room.

Jeanie Gilbert's office was austere, no ornaments or pictures to mark her space, not even a picture of her husband. Her private life was strictly private. Over the years, Jess had often speculated about Jeanie's life, piecing together fragments, trying to get a full picture, but there was still enough missing to leave Jess guessing. All she really knew after a decade she had learned when she met Jeanie's husband, Paul, at a Christmas Party. Paul was the chatty one of the pair. They had been married thirty-nine years and had no children but had two golden retrievers and lots of nieces and nephews that they doted on, apparently. When he reported they had no children, his mouth turned down, showing an obvious sadness about the situation. Jess suspected they were Mormon. Neither of them drank alcohol or coffee. It would make sense if they were Mormon; the FBI recruited heavily from the LDS church.

Jess's eyes narrowed in on the open file on Jeanie's desk. Unease crept up her spine when Jess read her name written across the top in caps.

"Please sit."

Jeanie lowered her bifocals to stare at Jess. For an awkward moment silence reigned. "Do you know why I called you in this morning?" she asked.

Jess shifted in her seat. She glanced from Jeanie to Jamison, who was sitting stony-faced, staring straight ahead. "Um… no. Should I?"

Jeanie's lips pursed into a frown, deep lines fanned out around her mouth. "I was reading through the report. There seem to be a few irregularities here. I was concerned enough to call Sergeant

Giboin to get his take on things. Make sure I wasn't reading this incorrectly."

What report? The impromptu meeting instantly felt suspiciously like an interrogation. Jess squinted to try to read what else was written in the file. Jess hadn't written up anything yet. She had this afternoon earmarked for catching up on paperwork. It was complicated; she needed time to think of exactly how she was going to document what had happened in Louisiana.

Jess turned to Jamison, silently begging him to look at her so she could get a read on him, but his stare remained fixed, staring straight ahead. All the warmth had been sucked from the room. The Jamison she saw was the version saved for suspects.

"Is it true Jennifer Thomson was told she would be given a deal?"

Ice tethered around her spine. That's what this was about. A boulder formed in the pit of her stomach as dread clawed at her. "Is th-that?" Jess stumbled on the words. She cleared her throat. "Is that what the report is about?" She clenched her hands in her lap to keep them from shaking. She knew Jamison was pissed but surely not enough to put something in writing that could possibly jeopardize her career. Jess was a good agent, he had said so himself. This was her first major transgression.

Jeanie's only response was a curt nod. With the small movement, the tenuous connection she felt with Jamison shattered. Jess couldn't breathe. The pain of betrayal stabbed her in the chest. Her heart ached with it. This wasn't about needing to find their rhythm. He had changed and so had she. They were different now, as people and as partners.

This wasn't the partner she knew. The man she knew would never throw her under the bus. And not like this, in such a cold, calculated way. Jess turned to look at him. Her gaze traced his hard features. There was no hint of a smile or kindness.

Maybe she had never really known him.

"Yes. Jennifer was told she would be given a deal," Jess admitted. She forced herself to look Jeanie directly in the eyes. She wasn't going to lie or run from the consequences. Nothing Jeanie could say would sting like the betrayal of having Jamison report her.

Jeanie pushed up her glasses. "Obviously, we can't honor that deal."

Jess ground her teeth together to keep from speaking. There was nothing she could say to mitigate the direction of the conversation. Right or wrong, Jess had made the deal to protect a scared kid. There was no way she could talk her way out of it.

Jamison held up his hand. "With all due respect, ma'am, I think we should try to honor the deal. Jennifer Thomson is a valuable witness. She provided us with some vital information. We would not have Lydia Steiner's phone if she hadn't led us to it."

Jess's head snapped to look at Jamison. Why? Why was he defending her now? He was like a cat toying with a mouse, swatting her about to revive her to make it more fun when he finally ripped into her.

"Well, you would say that since you were the one who offered her the deal," Jeanie said. "I'm asking Jessica what she thinks. Because, of the two of you, she appears to be the only one with good judgment."

"What?" Jess shook her head in confusion. Jeanie seemed to be under the impression Jamison was somehow to blame for what happened. "Excuse me, I don't—"

"It's in the report," Jamison interrupted her. "Jessie disagreed. She made it clear she objected to any premature talk of a deal. I made the decision to offer immunity. It was my call."

"Unilaterally? Without speaking to anyone to get the go-ahead?" One of Jeanie's sandy-colored brows arched in question.

"Yes, ma'am. And I stand by my decision. The witness was scared. It was the only way to get her to talk. I felt the information she could offer was time-sensitive and it was in the best interest of the investigation."

Jess stared open-mouthed at Jamison but he refused to even glance in her direction. Jeanie said something, but Jess did not hear the words, they were just sounds bleeding into the buzz of background noise. Jess could only focus on Jamison, watching his face, trying to read him. What was he doing? Why was he taking responsibility?

"Jessica."

Jess's head shot up when she heard her name. "Yes."

"I understand that having Agent Briggs back is an adjustment for everyone. You might not still be the best match. I'm always willing to shake things up. If you feel more comfortable working with Agent Chan, I can make the switch."

Jess sat paralyzed. *No.* Her mind screamed but the word did not come. She was too shell-shocked to formulate a coherent thought.

Still Jamison would not look at her.

"There's no need to make any decisions now," Jeanie continued, pushing herself back from the desk. "We can play it by ear but right now we need to get Agent Milligan up to speed. We'll see you there in a few minutes. I need to have a word with Agent Briggs."

Jess hesitated, not wanting to leave Jamison. If anyone was going to get reprimanded for this, it should be her. She opened her mouth to speak but Jamison silenced her with a terse shake of his head.

His stare was hard on her. *Don't,* he mouthed.

Jeanie Gilbert stood in front of the conference table. The room was dimly lit and for some reason the blinds were always closed even though there were no external windows, just one that looked out onto the hall. "I would like to welcome Special Agent David

Milligan. David was invaluable in solving the beach rapist case in Tunisia. He has a tremendous amount of knowledge. Use it."

Jess glanced over at David. He had a boyish face, clean-shaven with bright blue eyes and ruddy cheeks. If Jess had to guess his age she would have put him at mid-twenties, but based on when he graduated Penn State, he was thirty-four. Unlike Chan, David's appearance was far from pristine. His suit was pressed but the cuffs were frayed and there was a wet spot on his breast pocket where it looked like he had tried to wash off a coffee stain or spit-up from his baby.

David Milligan smiled faintly at the room. Jess hoped he had enjoyed the praise from Jeanie because that was likely to be the last time he heard any. As a rule, Jeanie did not offer praise beyond "fine." She did not feel the need to tell her team when she thought they were doing well. As she put it, she was not their parent. Her job was not to coddle them. Jeanie gave her agents a lot of freedom. Her expectation was that they were all professionals and she would treat them as such. She only reined them in when they needed to be reprimanded.

"I trust you read the file I sent you?" Jeanie asked.

David nodded.

"Okay. Then we can start with Bishop and Briggs. What did you find in Louisiana?"

Jess looked over at Jamison. When he didn't answer, she did. "As you know, we spoke to the husband, Reuben Steiner. He told us that his wife was on the way to Baton Rouge the night she was murdered. We are still not certain how she ended up in a parish an hour away. Mr. Steiner thinks she was lost."

"The wrong exit on the freeway is lost. An hour the opposite direction seems intentional," Agent Milligan said.

Jess smiled at him. Good, he was jumping in. It was always best to hit the ground running. "I think so too. She had a map and a guidance system. Tina, have you looked at her phone? Her husband said he programmed the restaurant address into her phone. Did he maybe get the address wrong?" Jess didn't want to ask Mr. Steiner about that possibility. He was already blaming himself for his wife's murder. It would be unconscionable for Jess to put it in his mind that a careless keystroke could have cost him his wife.

Tina entered something into her laptop, and the screen on the table illuminated. She used the arrow to point to the icon for the phone guidance system. Jess had forgotten how attractive Tina was. She reminded her of Snow White, flawless pale skin and dark hair. Her hazel eyes seemed to glow like they were lit from behind. She had no doubt Chan would hit on her if he hadn't already. "Here we go. The guidance system she used is called Shoshone. It's a relatively new one."

"Yeah I know it. I have it too," Jess said.

Chan chimed in. "Me too. I like the accents you can choose for the chick that gives you directions. And the landmark trivia option is good for long drives with a mute partner." He glanced at Jess to let the room know he was talking about her.

Jess remembered the drive through West Virginia well. Because they were near a Civil War battlefield, all the trivia had a military theme. "My life is richer for knowing the average Civil War soldier was five foot eight and weighed 143 pounds."

"So, about Chan's size," Jamison said.

Everyone laughed or at least smiled except for Chan, whose facial expression clearly said, "Fuck you." He glared across the table, his stare fixed on Jamison's neck like he wanted to jump across and rip out his jugular.

The hatred between the two was palpable. Agent Milligan looked at Jess, clearly confused and probably a bit worried about what he had walked into.

"Anyway, can you see if Mr. Steiner put in the right address?" Jess asked, bringing the conversation back to the case.

The keys clicked as Tina typed. "As you can see here, the address entered into Shoshone at 2:53 p.m. matches the address where Lydia Steiner was meant to meet her friends. And if you look here," Tina brought up a map of central Louisiana with red and blue lines over the top, "the red line indicates the most direct route to Baton Rouge from New Orleans. As you can see, Mrs. Steiner followed it until this junction here where she took a left towards St Martin Parish. The yellow here indicates where her last phone call was made."

"Chan, were you able to find out if any local law enforcement reported seeing her?" It was a long shot but worth checking.

"Checked with everyone right down to park rangers and border patrol, but nothing. Nobody reported seeing her or her car. Definitely nobody pulled her over or offered her assistance."

"Can we get a map of the area?" Jess asked. "I want to see exactly where she made the call from."

"Sure thing." In a few seconds a panoramic street view came up on the screen.

Instantly Jess recognized the road, the sharp bend, and the Spanish moss that hung like curtains. She had seen it driving into the location the body was found. "Can you show me how far it is from there to where we pulled the victim out of the water?"

Tina brought up another screen. "Less than half a mile."

"If she was found less than half a mile from where she went missing, chances are she was murdered there," David said.

"Yeah, but there is nothing out there, no houses, nothing. You've never seen anything like it. Only alligators and human filth come from there." Chan's lip curled as he hurled the thinly veiled insult at Jamison.

Jamison's response was an unfazed smile.

"That's not true," Jess said. "People live there. We met someone out there. It's not exactly a thriving metropolis but when I was in the boat going to the crime scene, I saw shacks. And they are definitely remote enough to kill and dismember a woman without arousing any suspicion. Remember, Lydia Steiner was tortured over a period of at least a week. The killer would have needed privacy for that. You don't get more private than the bayou."

"That doesn't explain why she was there in the first place," Chan argued.

"I think she was having an affair," Jess said. "Tina found an email address and social media accounts under a pseudonym. She had been speaking to a man called Mike Snowberger in Baton Rouge. I think she was meeting him."

"Yeah, but why would she not meet him in Baton Rouge?" Jamison asked. "If she was having an affair, which I don't think she was, she could have just met him in Baton Rouge. There is nothing particularly romantic about Breaux Bridge. It's hardly the Paris of the South. Nobody is going to go there for an affair."

"If he was meeting her to kill her, he's hardly going to invite her to his condo," Chan retorted, his tone smug. He was at the point where he would argue the sky was green just to piss Jamison off.

"What do we know about Mike Snowberger? Do we think he is a viable suspect?" Milligan asked, bringing them back on topic.

Jess liked David Milligan already. He stayed on topic and ignored Chan's baiting. The team needed that.

As if on command, Tina opened a screen with Mike Snowberger's picture. Across the top, "Suspect" was written in bold. Sadly, they were likely to add many pictures before they narrowed in on the killer. Tina glanced over at Jess and smiled. She must have remembered Jess was visual. She needed a face for every name.

Jess studied Mike Snowberger's picture. He looked like a typical good ol' boy: short beard, sunburned skin and a baseball cap with a frayed brim. He didn't look like a serial killer or even a bad guy, but they rarely did.

New research seemed to indicate that pedophiles tended to have more minor physical anomalies than the rest of the population.

On average they had higher palates and non-detached earlobes. At least in theory there were quantifiable differences in pedophiles to make them identifiable. The same could not be said for serial killers. There was no picking them out from the crowd because they looked like everyone else.

"Snowberger doesn't have an alibi, both his daughters are grown — a freshman and a junior at LSU. He was home alone but it's impossible to verify. He claims to have spent the evening watching television. His neighbors don't remember seeing him one way or the other," Chan said.

Jeanie Gilbert held up her hand to get everyone's attention. "Don't forget we have two other victims—one in Maryland and one in Virginia. We're not just looking at him for Lydia Steiner. Can you connect Mike Snowberger to the other victims?"

"He has a boat. He admits to fishing in the Shenandoah Valley. Though not in the timeframe we've established. I feel he's hedging his bets. Like he thinks if we find a witness that can place him there or a trace that connects him, he has probable deniability, but he doesn't want to fully commit."

Jeanie nodded. "How are we doing at identifying the other victims?"

Tina opened a new tab, a split screen of the two victims. In both cases the head was still missing and the limbs had been severed. Both bodies had been found submerged in water. Like Lydia there were excision sites on both bodies where the flesh had been removed. "The body on the left was found in Virginia. Her remains are too degraded to attempt a DNA match but the Maryland victim has been profiled. We have her DNA, we're just waiting for a match. We even have a partial print from the arm that was recovered."

Chan shook his head. "How can that be? Somebody knew these women. Someone would have noticed they were gone and reported them missing."

"Not necessarily. The Maryland victim's autopsy shows evidence of advanced pelvic inflammatory disease. She tested positive for hepatitis C, HPV, chlamydia, and gonorrhea," Tina pointed out

"She was a sex worker," David said.

"Most likely," Tina agreed.

"That makes sense. Prostitutes go missing all the time. A pimp isn't going to report it," Chan said.

Jamison shook his head. "If she'd been picked up, she would be in our system. If she had been working long enough to have that kind of wear and tear on her body, vice would have picked her up. She would have been printed."

Jess stared at the pictures of the women's remains. Her gaze was drawn to the Maryland victim. Just above her hip among the discoloration of decomposition there was what looked like a faded tattoo. Due to the extensive breakdown of tissue, it was hard to make out what it was. "Do you see that? What do you think that is?"

"It is brightly colored. A rose maybe?" Tina suggested.

"The color might be bruising or decomp," Jeanie said. "But the jagged line at the top is definitely part of the tattoo. Looks like a mountain range or the point of a star maybe."

Jess studied it. "If she had been arrested, there will be a record of this tattoo." Jails and prisons documented all tattoos for identification purposes and to monitor gang activity. "If we can tease out what the tattoo is and get a sketch, we might get a hit."

"Yeah but if she had been picked up we would have her prints in the system," Jamison reminded her.

Jess's shoulders slumped. He was right. "It doesn't make sense. The victimology is all over the place. One victim was a prostitute and another was a socialite. One was high-risk and the other the most risk-averse victim I have ever seen. She had a prophylactic radical mastectomy. This was not a woman playing fast and loose with her safety."

"But you think she was having an affair?" David asked. "Maybe that was their connection. They were both women of questionable moral character."

Jess's eyes widened as she dropped her pen. It slipped between her fingers and dropped to the floor. She looked to Jeanie to make sure she had heard him correctly. The tight slash of her pursed lips told her she had.

Jess cleared her throat. "Being a sex worker is not indicative of a moral shortcoming. Statistically, what it shows us is that she was most likely poor, uneducated, from an abusive or chaotic background. She was very likely a victim of rape and because of that she was more likely to be a substance misuser, but none of those things indicate she was a bad person. We know absolutely nothing about her moral compass."

Agent Milligan's eyes widened. Before he could say anything, Jeanie added, "We appreciate you are new to the team so it's important that you know, we don't judge our victims. Women with high-risk lifestyles are no less worthy."

David held up his hand. "I didn't—"

"The only person who we know is morally lacking is our killer. It's best we all remember that." Jeanie's tone was saccharin-sweet but she established a boundary he would be smart not to cross again. "Now back to our case. Let's dig deeper into our Jane Does. Think outside the box. Chan and Milligan, you're on our Maryland victim. Keep working missing persons. Start interviewing pimps, known Johns, and other working girls, see if one of them knows about a missing sex worker. Once we've identified her, we can establish a connection with Lydia Steiner if there is one. Tina, I want you to find out everything humanly possible about Mike Snowberger. Let's work the affair angle. What do we have to support the theory?"

"It's all circumstantial," Jess admitted. She wasn't even sure she still believed Lydia was having an affair but it was the only line of inquiry they had. "There are plausible reasons for Lydia to have had a pseudonym. Her husband was aware of it and her correspondence with Mr. Snowberger."

"You're right to question the relationship."

"Should we question him again?"

"No. Not yet. Let's watch him like a hawk. I'll organize full surveillance. And Tina, I need transcripts of all their correspondence. Bishop and Briggs, I need you back in Louisiana. Milligan is right, if Lydia Steiner's body was found less than a mile from where her body was found, that's most likely where she was murdered. Find the crime scene."

"What about the flashing lights Lydia reported?" Jess asked. "That sounds to me like the killer could have been impersonating a police officer."

"But why would Snowberger need to impersonate a police officer if they were having an affair? Surely he would just call her up and tell her where to meet him? And how do we know Lydia Steiner saw an unmarked car? She could have made that all up to buy time. Create a plausible excuse as to why she wasn't where she said she would be," Jamison pointed out.

"True," Jeanie said. "There are too many unknowns at this point. Time to start crossing things off the list."

"I almost forgot," Jess said. "I called the coroners for the two Jane Does. The Maryland coroner confirmed her victim also showed signs of being branded. She couldn't say with 100 percent certainty but it appears the victim had burn marks on her sternum." Jess paused, waiting for some sort of reaction from Jeanie when she mentioned branding. She was the only one who would put it together. She knew that case almost as well as Jess. If there was a connection between the two cases, Jeanie would spot it. Jess relaxed when Jeanie didn't react. "The cuts could be a forensic measure to cover up what he is branding on them or part of the torture. Either way, we're dealing with a sadist."

"Yes, we are. And that's why we need to catch him. Does everyone know what they're doing?" Jeanie pushed herself back from the conference table. It was clearly a rhetorical question because she was halfway across the room by the time she finished asking. "Any question, my door is always open. Let's find him."

Jess waited for everyone to leave so she could speak to Jamison alone, but he closed his computer and left without a glance in her direction. Jess blew out a stream of air. He couldn't avoid her forever. The idea of another silent drive through the bayou left her cold. She shoved her laptop back into her satchel.

"It's Jessie, right?"

Jess looked up to see Agent Milligan standing over her. She stood so she was not eye level with his crotch. "Jess," she corrected. Only Jamison called her Jessie.

"OK, sorry, Jess. I'm sorry about what I said. I think I got off on the wrong foot."

Jess shrugged. From the read she got from him, he seemed like a decent enough guy. She didn't want to give him a hard time. She had made her point and he had heard her; that was all she wanted. "It's all right. Welcome to the team."

"Are things always so heated between Chan and Briggs?"

"Well, that's a loaded question." Jess smiled. She didn't want to influence David's opinion of his new partner. He would figure out who Chan was for himself soon enough. He was either going to love him or hate him but she had no intention of trying to sway him either way. "They're both great agents and they're both great guys… in their own ways." She walked away before David could ask her another question. The polite thing would be to stay and make small talk and ask about his time in North Africa and his new baby and how he was adjusting to life back in DC. She would make herself do all those things at some point but right now she just needed to clear the air with Jamison.

She walked down the hall to Jamison's office. His door was shut but she didn't bother knocking.

Jamison glanced up from his keyboard. "I'm just looking at flights to Louisiana. The area where the body was found is rural as it gets. You were right—people live there but they're off the grid. They're not going to be paying taxes or registering to vote or doing anything else that would make it easy to locate them in a database. We're going to need local knowledge. I think we speak to the sheriff's department, get their read on things. Maybe get a short list of suspects."

"Yeah," Jess agreed. She didn't have much to say on the subject beyond that because her mind was still focused on what had gone down in Jeanie's office. She sat down across from him. She was waiting for Jamison to say something but he kept working. "J, what happened this morning—"

Jamison sighed. "Do we really need to talk about this? I think it's pretty clear what happened. Let's just get back to work."

Jess held up her hands in question. "No, I don't know what happened. We haven't spoken since we left Breaux Bridge. I have no idea what you're thinking or what happened. I can honestly say I'm thoroughly confused."

Jamison ran the back of his hand along his jaw as he thought. "Look, Jessie. I don't agree with what you did. I straight up told you you were wrong. You didn't see the big picture. You saw a kid you could rescue. There were consequences and I took them. I wrote up the report to keep you from falling on the sword."

"Why? Why would you—"

"You're my partner. I will always call you out on your shit but I will always have your back."

A lump formed in the back of her throat. This was her Jamison, the one she knew from before, the guy who always looked out for her. "Thank you."

Jamison shrugged. "Girl, don't thank me. Just don't do it again."

"I won't," she promised.

Jamison smiled. "Stop playing. We both know you would do it again in a heartbeat. That's why I love you."

Jess's heart stopped with a painful thud. All the air in her lungs left with an audible whoosh. Time stopped, trapping her in the moment. It was a throwaway comment, her mind knew it, but her body reacted like it was what it had been waiting to hear, which was insane.

What the hell?

That was twice she had reacted to him like that and it wasn't okay. That was not who they were. Jess didn't see Jamison like that. She never wanted to see him like that. He was her partner. Those two worlds could never collide. She knew better than to shit where she ate. Jess blinked, suddenly confused and embarrassed by her body's response.

"Felicia will kill me if I don't ask you today. She wants to know if you can come to dinner on Friday."

"I… um…"

"She wants to meet the famous Jessie Bishop. She was hoping to meet you at the wedding but you had a date. How was it?"

Jess's cheeks burned. "Um… yeah, fine." The date was actually a hard fuck against the wall of a public bathroom. Jamison was one of the few people who knew that side of Jess. She wasn't ashamed but she kept it private. Her sex life was nobody's business. She didn't set out to be promiscuous, she just didn't have real relationships. The harsh reality was that every time she had sex with the same person more than a few times, it became perilously close to something that resembled a relationship and Jess could not go there. Relationships came with the expectation of emotional intimacy and Jess wasn't willing to share anything more than her body with another person. Jamison knew and he didn't judge her.

"So, can you make it Friday night?"

"I don't know."

"Come on, Jessie. She's my wife. You're my partner. You really should meet."

"Sure," Jess said just to end the conversation. It would be easier to call and cancel than make an excuse now.

CHAPTER ELEVEN

Jess jabbed her index finger into the groove of her temple, rubbing until the tip ached, but still the throbbing in her head would not stop. She'd been staring at her arsenal of computer screens for too long. She'd barely left her office for the last three days.

She was convinced she would find something, a smoking gun to tie Mike Snowberger to the case, or at least enough to definitively say he was having an affair with Lydia Steiner. Jess would have really loved to have found a police light but Mike had never purchased one or even visited a website that sold them. That didn't mean he hadn't purchased one. It just meant that if he had, he was smart enough not to leave a paper trail.

Tina had downloaded every message they had exchanged and there was nothing remotely romantic, nothing that would indicate a sexual relationship at all. Mike wrote about missing his wife and Liddy wrote about loving her husband and child and never wanting to leave them. In theory, they could have saved romantic chats for video conferencing but it seemed unlikely because there was nothing in their messages to support a romantic relationship. Jess had read over every email and private message at least twice looking for something, only to come to the conclusion she'd been wrong about their relationship.

Jess sighed as she admitted defeat on this one: Mike Snowberger was looking like a dead end. He could still be connected to their Virginia victim but it was looking more and more unlikely. She was wrong more often than she was right but that was the nature of the beast. It was an iterative process. She went over things, over and over, collecting more information, chasing leads, making wrong guesses, taking wrong turns, until she finally got it right. The beauty was she only had to be right once. She could take as many bites of the apple as she could muster as long as she got there in the end.

Jess's phone vibrated on her desk. She squinted down at the unknown number. The only people who texted her were Tina, Jeanie, and Lindsay. She opened the message.

It was great seeing you again, although briefly. Maybe next time I can take you to dinner. Call me if you want to get together. Matt

It took several seconds for her to work out who Matt was—the guy from The Waiting Room. Flashes of the night played in her mind. It wasn't her finest hour but it was still miles away from her worst. She shook her head. Why? Why did he text her? What did he want? How did he get her number?

Jess leaned forward to consider the situation. Matt Ramsay was an FBI agent so it wouldn't have been hard for him to track down her number, but why he wanted to contact her was a different question entirely. Why would he want to see her again? Did he expect her to call him? She had made it abundantly clear that was not what the night had been about. Did he find out about her past when he was looking for her number? She shook her head. Her mind always went there. She needed to stop. It wasn't healthy. At some point she needed to let it go. The inmate who had recognized her was a one-off. Before then it hadn't happened since she was in high school, and it was unlikely to happen again. *Just let it go.*

Jess dropped her phone, suddenly not sure what she was supposed to do. Matt was a fellow agent so it would be hard if not impossible to fully ghost him. Their paths were bound to cross again at some point.

Jess was pulled out of her thoughts by a knock on the door. "Come in."

"Any joy on the Mike Snowberger front?" Jamison came in. He'd taken off his jacket and tie and rolled up his shirt sleeves to just below his elbows.

"Nope. What about you? Any leads in Louisiana?"

"A whole lot of nothing. Local police have been great, they've done door-to-door searches of every shack they can find on the bayou. There's nothing that looks good for our crime scene. They did find a nice little shooting gallery though. They made an arrest."

"Oh well, at least there's that." Jess's shoulders sagged. "Shit. It's gone cold again, hasn't it? I hate this part of a case."

"I know. Something will turn up. It always does." Jamison sat down across from her.

Jess scrubbed at her face. "Don't say that. We both know once it's cold, there's nothing we can do until there is another victim. New murder, new clues. I hate that. I don't want to be waiting for another woman to die."

"I know. I can't believe I'm saying this, but maybe Chan will come through with something on the Maryland victim."

"A prostitute Jane Doe? I'm not holding my breath for an ID."

"You never know. Stranger things have happened. Chan might come through."

"Hold up. Are we putting our hopes in Chan?" Jess laughed.

Jamison smiled. "I mean he is still a douche but he must have some redeemable qualities if you like him."

"Past the douche, under the thin layer of womanizer is a pretty decent guy."

"I'll take your word for it."

Jess hesitated for a second, reticent to say anything about Chan because Jamison already disliked him. "But there is one thing, his favorite ice cream flavor is vanilla. That's weird, right?"

Jamison's eyes widened. "Are you serious? Vanilla isn't even a flavor. It is the base you add flavors to."

"I know, right?" Jess smiled as she remembered the summer before Jamison left. Every Friday they went for ice cream at a shop boasting it offered the most varieties in the continental US. They were systematically making their way through each flavor to determine the best. They both agreed from the start to not even bother trying vanilla because it wasn't a real flavor.

"So, what's your take on the new guy?"

"Milligan?" she asked as if there was another new guy. "Yeah I guess he seems nice. What about you?"

"Yeah, he seems okay, slightly awkward, but you know I kind of like that type now after a decade of you."

"Thanks."

"You're welcome. Now grab your stuff."

Jess's eyes narrowed.

Jamison rolled his eyes. "Don't tell me you forgot. Girl, awkward doesn't even start to cover it with you sometimes. It's Friday." He paused waiting for her to figure out what he was talking about, but when she didn't say anything, he said, "Dinner. My place. You're finally meeting Felicia."

"I-what-was that a definite?" She remembered agreeing to the nebulous concept of meeting Jamison's wife at some point. Nothing concrete had been arranged. She didn't put it in the calendar on her phone. Nothing happened in her life without being documented in her phone.

"Yes, it was. Grab your stuff. I'm driving. I'll take you home after dinner."

"I have my card. I can just take the Metro."

When Jamison smiled, she realized what he had done. He had distracted her into agreeing but carrying on with the premise she had already agreed.

Before Jamison had gone undercover, he had rented an apartment in the West End, but since he returned he had bought a house in Forest Hills. The neighborhood was too leafy and suburban for Jess. All the streets were tree-lined and all the sidewalks had moms in yoga pants pushing jogging strollers, the kind of place where neighbors knew everyone's name and stopped to chat. Jess preferred the anonymity of urban life, where she was never more than a stone's throw from a coffee shop or Metro station. She had a car but she rarely used it.

"I think you're going to like Felicia."

Jess didn't answer. It was the fifth time he had said that to her. She wasn't sure whom he was trying to convince. "Is this it?" Jess indicated to a sage-green bungalow with an arched entry over a brick porch.

"Yeah."

"It's nice."

Jamison unlocked the door and dropped his keys in a wooden bowl on a side table near the front door then led her into the living room. Jess looked around. The house was done in shades of gray and the same muted green of the exterior. It was tasteful and understated and decidedly feminine with all the subtle touches like the monogramed pillows, the candles arranged in the open fireplace, and the faux fur throw hung over the side of an overstuffed chair.

"Baby, we're home," Jamison called.

Jess glanced at the door, suddenly claustrophobic. She should have made an excuse. She didn't want to be here doing this, not tonight. Jess had never introduced Jamison to any of her bad life choices. She didn't see why she had to meet his.

"Hey, baby," came a velvet voice from the other side of the house.

Jess turned to study the tall African-American woman who entered the room. She was wearing charcoal trousers with a black blouse and a magenta sweater that complimented her mahogany skin. Tight curls fell to just below her shoulder blades.

Her heels clicked on the walnut floorboards as she walked over to Jess. "Hi, I'm Felicia." Her face beamed. When she smiled, two rows of the straightest, whitest teeth Jess had ever seen were exposed. She looked like she could be a toothpaste model... or a runway model, any kind of model. The woman was gorgeous.

Jess hadn't allowed herself to picture what Felicia looked like or to think about what Jamison's type was. Maybe coming face to face with her would be less awkward if she had.

"Jess, this is Felicia. Felicia, this is Jess." Jamison introduced them. As he was speaking, Jess noticed that Felicia had already extended her hand but Jess hadn't noticed because she had been too busy studying her. Jess realized her palms were slick, so she wiped her hands on her trousers before she reached out to shake Felicia's hand.

So this was Jamison's type. Jess stared down at Felicia's French manicure, struck by how different they were. Felicia was tall and polished, poised and perfect. And Jess was... She shoved her hands into her pockets. She would stop biting her fingernails on Monday. No point in pretending she would do it tonight. She couldn't expect herself to be social with Jamison's wife and not bite her nails within the same twenty-four-hour period.

"I hope you're hungry. I made risotto and I always make too much. I can never get the amount just right. Luckily JB likes when I turn the leftovers into arancini." Felicia smiled up at Jamison adoringly.

JB? Who was this person? It was like Felicia was talking about a stranger. Jamison never went by anything other than Jamison, or Briggs, or occasionally J when Jess was in a hurry, but never JB. No one called him that except Felicia apparently.

"Felicia is an amazing cook. You're in for a treat."

Of course she was an amazing cook, because being tall and supermodel-beautiful weren't enough. "Great, I love risotto." Jess had never had proper risotto but she had put cheese on leftover takeout rice many a time. It was her go-to hangover meal and the extent of her cooking abilities.

"Please go on through to the dining room. I'll be out in two minutes. I just need to open a bottle of wine. JB and I found this great Pinot Grigio on our trip to Napa."

Jess's eyes narrowed in confusion. How had he had time to go on trip to the West Coast? Being undercover was not a nine to five. It didn't come with vacation time.

"We went out to California before I came back to DC," Jamison explained.

"JB wasn't sure he wanted to go back to his current job. He had an interview at the San Francisco office. It's gorgeous out there."

Jess waited for Felicia to leave the room before she spoke. "What?" The muscles in her neck tightened. *Jamison had considered not coming home?* The realization hit her like a ball bearing to the gut. All that bullshit about them being like family… saying that Jess was all he had left…

"I didn't take it," Jamison said.

Jess couldn't look at him. "Clearly." She clenched her hands into fists behind her back to keep them from shaking. Would he have even contacted her to tell her he was leaving for good or would he have just left?

"Jessie, I was just looking for a fresh start."

Jess studied the crack in the corner of the ceiling, tracing the thin line as it fanned out when it collided with the crown molding. "Yeah, I get it. It's fine."

"Jessie—"

"Y'all going to come in? Dinner will get cold," Felicia called.

Jamison tried to grab Jess's hand to keep her from leaving but she pulled away and went to the dining room. She would have dinner, make polite conversation, and then leave.

"This looks great." Jess forced a smile. She pulled at her collar. It was too hot in here. She couldn't breathe. A flash of a memory played in her mind. Usually she only dreamed about her past but apparently she was no longer playing by those rules. Now memories appeared at will, insidious and stealth, she never knew when they would invade. She closed her eyes and focused on her breath, concentrating on the sensation of her lungs filling to the point they burned.

"Wine?" Felicia asked, but her voice sounded far away like Jess was listening from under water.

"Sorry, what?" Jess shook her head to dislodge the unwanted thoughts.

"Jessie only drinks Cabernet," Jamison said.

Jess rubbed her eyes. This had to stop. She needed to get her shit together. "No, thank you. I'm not drinking tonight." Alcohol and anxiety were an unpredictable combination.

Jess sat down at the table and laid the linen napkin over her lap. "This looks great." Shit she had already said that. She probably should have brought index cards with bullet points of socially acceptable small talk. She could have crossed things off as she said them. Wouldn't have been any more awkward than this. How could she analyze every utterance of others for meaning and not even be able to make polite conversation with this woman without a considerable amount of effort? It was pathetic.

"Thank you." Felicia stood above her, filling her wine glass with ice water. When she turned to fill Jamison's glass, her cardigan opened enough to see the pronounced curve of her belly. Jess sucked in a sharp breath. She had to look away. She focused on the red line of dried blood around her index finger. She usually stopped biting before she drew blood, but not this time. There was nothing left on her finger except a pathetic facsimile of a nail.

"Bon appétit," Felicia said, inviting them to start their meal.

She didn't have to ask Jess twice. If her mouth was full, she wouldn't be expected to talk. The risotto was good, nothing like Jess's equivalent of cheddar on white rice. This dish was creamy rather than congealed and it had plump peas mixed through rather than remnants of Szechuan chicken.

"Jamison has told me so much about you, I feel like we've already met."

Jess swallowed. "Um… yeah." What was she supposed to say to that? If this was on an exam, what would she say? She always aced tests. *Treat this like a test.*

But no words came.

"Are you from the DC area?" Felicia asked when the silence became awkward.

Jess groaned inwardly. She should have tried hard to think of something to say so she could have steered the conversation as far away as possible from her family and childhood. Without a shadow of a doubt those were her two least favorite topics. She took a deep breath. She had no idea what, if anything, Jamison had told Felicia about her life, and being caught in a lie would take this experience from awkward to unbearable. "No, I'm not local. I was born in Germany. I'm an army brat so I've lived a lot of places. My parents divorced when I was eight. It wasn't amicable. I haven't seen my dad since. My mom married another army officer. He retired a couple of years ago. They live near Houston." Jess breathed a sigh of relief. That was the most concise and censored encapsulation of her life she could give without outright lying. If Jamison had told Felicia anything more, that was on him.

"Houston is nice." Felicia smiled.

"Yeah," was all Jess could think to say. She hated going home because it was like stepping into an episode of *Hoarders*, complete with the high-level denial and the stench of cat piss. "Oh… and I have no siblings," Jess blurted. That was the usual follow up question so it was best they cut that one off at the pass so they could move swiftly on to another topic.

"An only child, just like JB then."

Jess coughed, choking on a spoonful of rice. She grabbed her wine glass and gulped down mouthfuls of ice water to push it down. "Excuse me," she coughed. "Sorry, what did you say about Jamison's family?" Jess glanced over at him. His face was impassive but he clenched his spoon so hard his knuckles drained of color.

"It's interesting that both of you are only children and you both haven't seen your dads since you were children. Obviously it's different because both of Jamison's parents died in a car accident and your dad is still living."

Jess's heart stopped mid-beat. For a long moment she forgot to breathe as she waited for Jamison to correct his wife, tell her she had gotten it wrong, but he never did. A glacier settled in the pit of Jess's stomach, preventing her from eating or even breathing too deeply.

Ice spread through her. She stared down at her bowl, pushing a pea through the rice, navigating it with the back of her fork, trying desperately to make sense of what she had just heard.

Felicia was speaking but Jess couldn't concentrate on what she was saying. She had heard one too many home truths for one night. Jess sat just staring at her food, wishing she could be anywhere but there.

Suddenly she realized she didn't need to be there. She wasn't chained to her chair. She had only come out of consideration to Jamison. And right now she wasn't sure she wanted to be around him. She needed some distance to process the day.

Jess reached into her pocket for her phone. "That's the office," she said, pretending to read a message. "Tina has some… things she wants me to go through." She couldn't think of an excuse quick enough. She just needed to get away.

"Oh no, that's such a shame. I made crème brûlée for dessert."

"Sorry. Thank you for dinner. It was nice to meet you."

Jamison pushed back from the table. "I'll take you."

Jess couldn't look at him. "No, it's fine. I'll get an Uber." She already had the app open so he couldn't object.

Jess got up. "Thanks again."

Felicia's eyes were wide. She glanced from Jess to Jamison.

"Sorry," Jess mumbled when she brushed by Felicia as she made her way to the front door. She couldn't get out of their house fast enough.

She knew Jamison was behind her when the front door didn't close. She glanced down at her phone. Apparently Raul was 3.8 miles away. She really wished the app told her the color of the car that was coming so she didn't get excited every time a hybrid drove past.

"Jessie—"

Jess spun on her heel to face him before he could try to explain away what she had just heard.

"I know I hate my past so I refuse to talk about it, but I never outright lie. And I certainly would not lie to someone I was married to, someone I was about to have a baby with. Your mom was a junkie. One of your brothers died in a drive-by shooting, and the other is serving a life sentence for murder. And your sister, we don't know where she is, but we certainly know she exists." She didn't bother whispering. If Felicia heard, she heard.

"I needed a fresh start."

Jess shook her head. "I'm not talking about San Francisco. I don't give a shit about that. I'm talking about the fact your wife doesn't even know the first thing about you." Jess turned to walk down the steps. She would wait on the corner. All those times

Jamison told Jess not to be ashamed of where she came from. *Such bullshit.*

Jamison grabbed her shoulders and spun her around to face him again. His fingers bit into her arms, keeping her in place. He stared directly into her eyes. "I needed a fresh start," he enunciated each word.

"What? What does that even mean?"

"I hate that you know my past. I can't get away from it with you. It's who I am. But not with Felicia. I'm just me. There's no baggage there. I need that, Jessie."

His words fell on her like concrete blocks, crushing her under their weight. Her chest tightened until it was hard to breathe. How could he possibly think that, after the things she had confided in him? "Is that how it is? You think people will assume you're a thug because your brother was? That must be how you think. So what about me? What do you see when you look at me?" Jess pulled away. "No. No don't tell me." She couldn't take anymore.

"No, Jessie. It's not like that. Come on, don't go."

"Go back in and lie to your wife some more. My ride is here."

CHAPTER TWELVE

The rough border of her bonnet nipped at her forehead when she turned to look at the field of hidden treasure just beyond the rope. Every time she moved even a fraction, a piece of straw poked her right between her eyes. She pulled at the purple ribbon that kept her hat anchored. She would not be able to get any eggs wearing the silly hat.

"Leave your hat on. You look pretty."

"Daddy, I can't bend over to get any eggs with it on. I don't want to wear it. Nobody else has to wear a silly hat."

Her dad glanced around at the sea of children. At least fifty kids were huddled behind the rope, waiting for the mayor to sound the horn and start the Easter egg hunt. Most of the girls were wearing similar bonnets, but instead of pointing that out, he said, "Okay, princess. Let me get a picture of you for your mommy first before you take it off. And if she asks, you wore it the whole time and I only let you have one piece of chocolate."

She bristled at the mention of her mother. She should be here. "She doesn't need a picture. She could have come if she wanted to see me."

"You know she would have loved to be here but she has a headache. Come on, stand up tall, let me see that pretty smile."

She shook her head and pursed her lips into a frown so her dad could not take a picture. Her mommy didn't deserve a picture. For a minute that morning she had let herself hope that her mommy would actually come, but in the end, she had gone back to bed. She would rather sleep than spend time with her daughter.

"Well that is not the best smile I have ever seen. This is a better smile." Her dad crossed his eyes and stuck out his tongue.

A giggle welled inside her. She tried to fight it, but when her dad puffed out his cheeks, a laugh bubbled over. He held up the camera and snapped several photos in a row, the bulb flashing with each picture.

"No, daddy," she protested. A sudden sadness tugged at her. "If she loved me, she would be here."

His mouth opened in surprise. He fell to his knees in front on her. "Oh princess, she loves you. Don't ever doubt how much you are loved."

She shook her head again. "She never spends time with me. She hates me."

He took her hands in his. "No. That isn't true. She loves you more than anything." He stared out onto the horizon like he was trying to decide what to say next. "Your mother is not as strong as us. You and I are the same. I can't explain it but we're strong. We have a strength she doesn't have. But she loves you. And we love her because we're family and family is there for each other no matter what."

Pride swelled in her. She was strong. She was just like her dad.

CHAPTER THIRTEEN

Jess didn't want to go home. She wanted to clear her mind… be numb. Only one thing did that for her.

She stared at the brass-plated number on the door. She didn't need to check to make sure she had the right house. She had stared at the address the entire ride. This was the right house. But something stopped her from knocking.

What am I doing?

He hadn't invited her. He didn't know she was coming. He might not want to see her. She closed her eyes and took a deep breath. If he didn't want to see her, he could tell her, and then she would find someone else.

Jess knocked before she could talk herself out of it. She didn't want to be alone and she didn't want to find someone in a bar.

"Jess?" Her name came out more like a question than a salutation.

"I misused a federal database to get your address," Jess blurted out as way of an explanation.

"I did the same thing to get your number. So, I guess we're even." He smiled and a single dimple appeared on his right cheek.

How had she not noticed before that he had a dimple? Probably because she hadn't spent much time looking at his face, but looking at it now she was reminded how handsome Matt Ramsay was. If she was going to make a bad life choice, it may as well be with someone she found attractive.

"Do you want to come in? Can I get you a drink?"

She wasn't here to drink or to talk. "Do you want to have sex?"

Matt's mouth dropped open. His eyes widened, clearly surprised. His square jaw was covered in dark stubble. "Um… yeah. My answer to that is always going to be a resounding yes."

Jess stepped over the threshold. "Now. Are you free? I don't know if I can come back later."

"I get the feeling that if I said I was busy, you would find someone else."

"Yeah," Jess admitted. She would. Just like the night they had hooked up. If Matt Ramsay hadn't approached her, it would have been another man she screwed against the bathroom wall.

"I also get the feeling there's someone you'd much rather be spending the night with."

Jess shrugged. She didn't know the answer to that and she didn't want to think about it anymore. "I just want to spend the night with someone. So, are you free?"

Matt answered by pulling her hard against his chest and kissing her.

Jess sat up looking for her underwear. It was somewhat of a shame that she had to take off clothes to have sex. Leaving after would be much quicker if she didn't. Matt stood beside the bed naked except for the argyle socks he hadn't taken off. He was still wearing less than Jess, who still had on her bra and blouse, though the buttons were undone.

Matt pulled at the condom on his now flaccid penis. His body was strong and lean, deep ridges defining the individual muscles of his abdomen. When he walked, the muscles in his ass tensed, making them even firmer. He reminded her of a statue of a Greek god.

"Do you see my underwear?"

"You don't have to go." He tied a knot in the top of the translucent rubber.

Jess's eyes narrowed. "Why? Did you want to have sex again?"

"Um… I don't know, maybe. But I thought we could talk."

Jess smoothed down the hairs that had escaped her ponytail. "I… um… I…" She hadn't planned for the eventuality of conversation. "I'm not much of a talker."

"Okay. You want to watch a movie and not talk? Maybe have some wine? Or we could go out for a drink."

Jess stood up to look for her underwear. "Um…" It wasn't the end of the world if she couldn't find them. This wouldn't be the first time she had left clothing behind. When you left in a hurry, things were bound to get left behind.

"Never mind." The corners of his mouth pulled down. The light behind his eyes darkened. "Here's your underwear." Matt pulled back the comforter. "You want to let yourself out or can I show you to the door?"

"I can show myself out. Thanks."

CHAPTER FOURTEEN

Jess waited in the corridor while the cleaner emptied the waste-basket in her office. All of the other offices were dark. It wasn't even six, but Jess couldn't get back to sleep. The Metro didn't open until seven on a Saturday, so she ran to work, stopping at a twenty-four-hour gas station for a cup of coffee.

She had managed almost five hours of sleep before she woke up in a cold sweat, a personal best for the month. For a change, it wasn't her usual nightmare that pulled her out of a deep sleep, it was a niggling feeling about the case. Her subconscious mind kept going back to the mottled tattoo on the Maryland victim. Though she couldn't even make out the marking, there was something eerily familiar about it.

Jamison was right: if the woman had been picked up for prostitution, there would be a record of her fingerprints in the system, so chasing down the woman's tattoo in hopes that a jail had documented it was an exercise in futility. But there was one angle they hadn't considered, and Jess could not let it go until she had exhausted every possibility.

Prostitutes were often branded by their pimps to mark them as their property. The most common tattoos for trafficked women were crowns, barcodes, or simply the pimp's name. If Jess could figure out the tattoo on the victim, she might be able to trace it back to a pimp. It was a long shot but the victim deserved for Jess to take it.

"Buenos dias, Rosaria." Jess gave a small wave when the cleaner came out of her office.

Rosaria jumped back. Her eyes widened in surprise, clearly not expecting anyone in the building so early. "Señorita Jess!" she squealed as she pulled out her earphones.

The way she pronounced her name, like she was saying "yes," always made Jess smile.

"Lo siento." Jess apologized for scaring her. She had hoped that by staying in the hall she would not startle her.

"Why you so early?" Rosaria asked, switching to English. "You drink too much coffee. I see." She pointed at the trash. Thankfully caffeine abuse was not a crime because Rosaria had enough evidence in the form of takeaway cups to secure a conviction. "Is not good for you."

Jess nodded. "How are your grandchildren?" she asked, skillfully moving the topic away from her. Before she even finished asking the question, Rosaria had taken her phone out of the case strapped to her arm and started scrolling through pictures.

Jess oohed and awed as Rosaria talked her through every picture she had taken or been sent in the three months since Jess had last been in the office early enough to catch her. Jess frowned to herself when she realized her initial reaction to seeing the plethora of happy snaps was that it was good the family had so many up-to-date photos of the children in the eventuality one of them went missing. She wished she could say the cynicism was an occupational hazard, but the truth was more sinister.

Jess had to close her eyes for a second as a memory assaulted her. She fought to push it back under, but the macabre vignette would not stop playing. Rosaria continued talking but Jess only caught every few words.

Eventually Rosaria threw her arms around her in an embrace to say her goodbye.

Jess's back stiffened. She wasn't a hugger but Rosaria was, so each time they had a conversation it ended with Jess on the receiving end of a bear hug.

"Remember not so much coffee," Rosaria said as she pushed the trolley of cleaning supplies down the hall.

Jess smiled rather than lie and say she would commit to anything. She flicked on the light switch. It took a second for the bulb to warm up. She switched on her computer. While she waited for the file to open, she pulled out a pen and a fresh pad of paper.

Jess clicked on the autopsy photo, and a picture of a mutilated torso filled her screen. She clicked again to zoom in on the tattoo on the hip. The monitor filled with various shades of green and purple with flashes of black lines running throughout. Her eyes narrowed as she tried to determine what was bruising and decomposition and what was tattoo. She pulled out her highlighter pens and tried to recreate the tattoo, but the result was a formless mess of color.

Jess sighed. Her limited artistic abilities and the advanced state of decomposition made it difficult to tease out anything. She needed to ignore the color and just focus on the lines.

She printed out the autopsy photo and then took out a piece of tracing paper from a store cupboard and laid it over the top. Carefully, Jess traced each of the lines she could make out.

The placement of the lines was inconsistent with any crown drawing or tattoo she had seen. "Stars?" she said aloud to the empty room, remembering Chan's comment that she talked to herself when she worked. She filled in the rest of the lines, trying to complete the star pattern, but the pitched angles were too obtuse for the point of a star.

Jess crumpled the paper and started again. Jeanie had suggested the jagged lines looked like a mountain range. She could sort of see it but it looked more like a pattern—like triangles within triangles. A flash of recognition shot through her. Her heart pounded against her ribs. That's where she had seen it before. Surely it couldn't be the same. Fear and anticipation mounted in her as she pulled up the bureau's Tattoo Recognition Database.

Jess refined the search parameters and instantly the screen filled with the familiar markings. The hairs on her arms stood taut. "Ah, shit." Panic seized her. First the decapitation, then the branding and excision sites, and now this. That couldn't be a coincidence.

Someone was fucking with her.

Jess closed her eyes and took a deep breath. It took several moments for her to form a coherent thought. She was being ridiculous. She was seeing patterns where they didn't exist. That's what it was, it had to be, because the alternative was unthinkable.

Jess filled her lungs to capacity and held the breath until it burned. She needed to think. It didn't make sense. The tattoo could be random. People got all sorts of meaningless tattoos, like the bartender with the Tweety Bird holding a compass. Just random meaningless images. They meant nothing.

But no woman would have that image. There had to be a reasonable explanation for it.

Jess opened her eyes and examined the photo again. It was just clumps of color punctuated by dark lines. She took a long, hard look, asking herself what she saw. It was like a Rorschach test. If a dozen people were presented with this, there would be just as many interpretations. She still saw continuous interlocking triangles. But were they there? She couldn't tell anymore.

A lump formed in the back of her throat. No matter how hard she tried to swallow past it, she couldn't.

Jess needed to tell Jeanie. She should have told Jeanie her suspicions about the brands. That's what this was about. It was just guilt messing with her. Jeanie was the team leader. She was running this investigation; Jess reported everything to her. Jess should have flagged up the similarities between the cases as soon as she spotted them.

But if Jess told Jeanie, the entire team would have to know. And what if she was wrong? Then she would have outed herself and shown she was a raging lunatic chasing ghosts.

No. Jess couldn't go there, not for some insane hunch.

She needed to be rational, think it through. The chances of the tattoo being related to Jess's past or even meaning anything were overwhelmingly small. There was nothing to gain from reporting her suspicions and everything to lose.

She turned off her monitors and shredded the autopsy photo and tracing paper. She glanced up at the door to make sure no one was watching even though there was no need to hide what she was doing. She wasn't destroying evidence but guilt clawed at her just the same.

CHAPTER FIFTEEN

The Metro was busier than usual for the weekend but Jess was fortunate enough to have a seat. A twenty-something with a man bun and a month's worth of patchy auburn stubble stood in front of her holding on to the overhead bar with both hands. Most people managed to hold on with one hand but apparently he needed to hang over her with both arms outstretched. Usual Metro etiquette was to stand at an angle so the person sitting did not have an eyeful of crotch to contend with. Unfortunately, man bun had not got the memo, so Jess had been treated to the elastic band of his briefs for the last three stops. She tried being subtle and asking him to turn his head and cough but he either didn't get it or really did not give a shit about personal space because he shook his head and rolled his eyes.

Before the train left the station, Jess's phone rang. She glanced down to see who was calling. "Hi, Tina. What's going on?"

"Good morning, Jess. Where are you?" Her words were rushed.

Man bun scowled down at her, clearly annoyed she was taking a call and disrupting the serenity of his commute. He made a dramatic whoosh sound, somewhere between a sigh and a gasp.

"I'm actually on my way in now. I'm almost there. What's going on?" Jess raised her voice just to remind the man he was in her space. He'd lost the right to be annoyed twenty minutes ago when he stuck his crotch in her face.

"We have another body. Call came through this morning from Alabama. Torso was discovered in a dam along the Coosa

River. Preliminary reports say she matches the identity of missing New Jersey native Hannah Henderson. Still waiting to see if we can get DNA but the tattoo on her lower back and the nipple piercings are a match."

Tattoo. Jess's heart stopped. Guilt and shame assaulted her from every angle. Grief palpable and real settled on Jess like she was responsible for the latest victim because she had concealed things from her team. It wasn't logical but Jess could not shake the familiar feelings of culpability. It took several seconds for her to speak, and when she did her voice was paper thin. "What… what was the tattoo?"

"Um, let me check. Okay here we go, says here it is a butterfly. Does that mean anything to you?"

Jess let go of the breath she was holding. Relief washed over her. "No." She closed her eyes and told herself again the latest victim wasn't her fault. She was not responsible. It was crazy and egocentric to think the case had anything to do with her. She needed to let it go. She was no use to the investigation if she couldn't get her shit together and let go of the past.

"I'm almost at my stop. I'll see you in fifteen minutes. And Tina, thanks." She remembered her manners just before Tina cut the call.

Jess ran up the stairs to her office, skipping every other step. She spotted Tina by the water cooler filling up a red metal bottle. "Tina," she said, holding up her hand to indicate to give her a minute to catch her breath. Jess had sprinted from the Metro station, not even stopping at the coffee kiosk.

"Hi. Were you running?" A bemused smile settled on Tina's full lips.

"Yeah," Jess panted. "You said we have another victim. Tell me about her. Please."

"Oh but the morning meeting is in half an hour. You want a cup of coffee first?"

Jess got her meaning. Tina didn't want to explain it again to the rest of the team. Unfortunately for Tina, when it came to leads, Jess had the patience of a hyperactive toddler mainlining E numbers. "What do we know about the victim? Where exactly was she found? Who found her? Who reported her missing?" Jess fired questions at her in rapid succession. "Can I just see the file?"

Tina sighed, "Everyone's already here. I'll just call the meeting now."

"Everyone? Even Jamison?" He had never beat Jess to the office.

Tina didn't answer because she was too busy typing. "There," she said when she looked up. "Team meeting in two minutes. Want that coffee I offered?"

Jess took a deep breath. "Yeah, I think I do." Jess reached for the only mug in the cupboard without a chip or a loose handle. She had no idea whose child was an honors student at Oakmont Middle School, but God bless them, they had contributed a sturdy mug to the arsenal of coffee cups in the office kitchen.

Jess followed Tina into the conference room. They sat on opposite sides of the table and waited for the others to join them.

Tina smiled over at her. "I think you have an admirer."

Jess's eyes widened. "Excuse me?"

"Matt Ramsay. He called me to get your number and ask me about you. Is it all right that I gave it to him?"

Jess swallowed past the lump in her throat. The walls of the conference room crept in by several feet as Jess's two worlds collided. She shouldn't have gone into The Waiting Room to pick up a guy. Too many agents drank there. She should have picked up a stranger. *Never shit where you eat.* That was her motto. Shame she hadn't adhered to it. "Yeah it's fine. We… um… we went for a drink."

Tina's smile broadened. "I knew you two would get along. You're a lot alike."

Jess stared down at the fresh blood on her index finger where she had tried to bite a fingernail that had not grown back yet. So, she and Tina had reached the banter level of a relationship. She wasn't sure she wanted that; not that Tina wasn't great.

"You're both crazy smart and super intense," Tina continued.

Jess sipped her coffee. It tasted like the pot was dirty. She would have stopped at the coffee kiosk had she known being early only meant making small talk. Her morning coffee was a ritual and a treat for enduring rush hour.

"He didn't need to call me. Matt has crazy IT skills. I think he just wanted the scoop on you." Tina paused, presumably so Jess could jump in, but when she didn't Tina added, "There wasn't a lot I could tell him really."

Jess blinked. Tina was reaching out, offering the first brick in the foundation of friendship. It took her a second to decide how to proceed. "Yeah, we really should organize a team night out, properly get to know each other." She left it vague and didn't offer anything concrete that she would have to call and cancel later when she got anxious about having to be social for a solid block of time.

"Hey," Chan said as he entered the room. David Milligan was two steps behind him.

"Good Morning," Tina said.

The tension in Jess's shoulders eased when Chan jumped into a play-by-play of his weekend. The pressure to make conversation immediately disappeared. There was no need to speak when Chan was around. Maybe that was why Jess liked him. Even when he asked questions, he was quite happy to answer them himself.

Milligan hung on every word. Chan was like a one-man show and David his attentive audience. They were going to make a good team because he either found Chan amusing or he was fabulous at faking it. Chan would never know the difference, so it was all good.

"Good morning," Jeanie said as she entered the conference room. Jamison was two steps behind her. He caught Jess's glance and smiled.

Like nothing had happened.

"Thank you all for coming in. I know this is not the way any of us would like to be spending our Sunday but as you all know by now, we have a new victim. So let's dive in. Tina, can you get us up to speed?"

"Yes. Agent Briggs, can you hit the lights."

Jamison turned off the lights before he walked around the table and sat beside Jess.

Tina typed on the keyboard and an image appeared of a New Jersey driver's license. "I would like you to meet Hannah Henderson. She was a thirty-two-year-old drugs rep from River Edge, New Jersey. She worked primarily with physicians in Manhattan."

At first glance Hannah looked like just another pretty blond, but when Jess looked closer she noticed the dark roots and the eyes set too far apart to be considered conventionally attractive. She was not someone Jess would describe as pretty but it was obvious she put a lot of effort into her appearance. Her nose looked like it had been done, and her makeup was flawless.

"Hannah's neighbor reported her missing last month. According to her boss she hadn't been at work for over three weeks before that."

"But they didn't think to check on her or report her missing?" Milligan asked.

"Nope. Her boss said she hadn't been happy at work and he assumed she'd quit. New York police have spoken to her colleagues and she was not well liked. No one cared when she didn't show up to work. They were just glad she wasn't there."

"Ouch," Jamison said.

"Oh, it gets better. It's widely rumored that Hannah Henderson made her sales the old-fashioned way, and by that I mean sex.

According to one of her co-workers, she was sleeping with at least three of the doctors she was selling to."

"Can we get their names? The men she was reportedly sleeping with?"

"I'm already one step ahead of you. I've sent you the names with some other interesting facts about the men in question." The room was dark but Jess was almost certain Tina winked at her. "There is one man in particular that caught my eye."

Tina clicked to open another screen and a picture of a middle age man in an embroidered lab coat appeared. "This is Dr. Joel Nester. Until six months ago he was a psychiatrist at Bellevue. He also had a thriving private practice specializing in soccer moms with a penchant for muscle relaxants."

Jess squinted at the screen. Hannah Henderson was not conventionally beautiful but she appeared to make a considerable effort with her appearance and general presentation. Dr. Nester was seventy pounds overweight. He had thick salt-and-pepper hair that fell awkwardly on his forehead, like he had forgotten to get it cut. It was too long to be tidy and too short to be a style choice. His jawline was weak. His small, rounded chin melted into the curtain of neck fat to create a continuous wall of billowing, gelatinous flesh, and his left eyelid drooped like he had had a stroke.

"They were a couple?" Chan voiced the question everyone in the room was thinking.

"Logic and eyesight would say no, but credit card statements say yes."

"Gross," Chan muttered.

"Oh, we haven't even begun to get to the gross part yet."

"It gets grosser?" Chan asked, clearly dubious.

"It certainly does. Wait for it…" Tina clicked on a new screen. An image of a pretty brunette filled the screen. She looked mid-thirties, maybe forty. "This is Paige Dooley."

"That's not gross. She is pretty cute," Chan said.

"Yes, she is, but the things Joel Nester did to her were anything but. You see, Dr. Nester is no longer practicing medicine in the great state of New York and she is the reason why. Miss Dooley is a big fan of methamphetamines, namely Ritalin, which Dr. Nester provided her with when she was his patient. She began seeing Dr. Nester in a professional capacity shortly after the birth of her second son. He was treating her for postpartum depression. According to court documents they started having sex a few months into her treatment." Tina paused to look around the room. She was like a showman working the stage, extending the silence to maximize anticipation.

Jess had to smile. Tina was genuinely likable. If they ever did arrange a night out, Jess was going to make herself go.

Tina took a deep breath. "Granted it's not that unusual for doctors to sleep with their patients—unethical, yes; unheard of, no. But what sent up little red flags for me was what the not-so-good doctor was into. In a word: coprophilia, or as it's also known, scatophilia."

David's mouth fell open. "Scat? As in shit?"

"That's the one." Tina pointed at David with both index fingers for emphasis.

David chewed on the corner of his mouth. His glance darted around the room before it settled on the table, and he examined the laminate top like it was the most interesting thing he had ever seen.

"It's okay," Jess said, guessing why he was uncomfortable. She had given him a hard time at the last meeting when he dared to speak up. No doubt he had no idea what was safe to say, so he was trying to silently process what he had just heard. "It's disgusting. We don't judge victims but feel free to judge people who are sexually aroused by fecal matter. It's revolting."

David let go of the breath he was holding. "Right? That is nasty. I almost threw up."

"Be careful. People are turned on by that too. It's called emetophilia," Chan said.

Everyone turned to look at Chan.

"What? Don't look at me like that. I'm well read. Don't be jealous because I know my way around a paraphilia."

Tina gave a nervous laugh. "Um, moving swiftly on from how you became so *au fait* with sexual fetishes, let's get back to Dr. Nester." She looked at Chan with a mixture of pity and contempt.

For the first time since Jess had met Chan, he looked embarrassed. She could honestly say that he did not have a snowball's chance in hell of sleeping with Tina. The woman was going up in her estimation by the minute. Jess might need to go ahead and arrange that girls' night out herself.

"Anyway. As I was saying, what is particularly worrying is that Dr. Nester enjoys doing the shitting and he is not above forcing it on his sexual partners. Miss Dooley claimed she endured months of emotional and sexual abuse at the hands of her therapist. She began seeing another therapist to whom she disclosed what was happening, and charges were brought against Dr. Nester."

"Why isn't he in prison?" Jamison asked.

"Because it appears his crime was well thought out. Before he started abusing Paige Dooley, he diagnosed her as paranoid and put it in his notes that she made similar claims against several men in her life. Paige denies this, and her current therapist says she shows no sign of paranoia or delusional thinking. Long story short is Nester paid her off and got out of dodge. He left NYC and bought a small practice outside of Montgomery, Alabama."

"Tell me he wet the bed, set fires, and abused animals as a kid, and I would put money on him being our killer," Milligan said, referencing the homicidal triad.

Tina shook her head. "I'm good, but I'm not that good. But I can tell you he is left-handed, which as you know is another indicator."

Jamison nodded at Chan, "So is our boy."

Chan clenched his fist so hard the pen in his hand shook. As always, the antipathy he felt for Jamison could not be suppressed.

David cleared his throat. "So, where does that leave us? Is Nester a viable suspect? Does he have an alibi?" he asked, successfully bringing the conversation back on topic.

"I really can't do all the work. I need to leave something for you guys," Tina said with a laugh. "Just kidding, I'm still working. He lost privileges at Bellevue mid-March. He bought a practice in Montgomery in July. I don't know what he was doing in-between."

Jeanie stood up and switched on the lights. "I think we need to pay Dr. Nester a visit, don't you? Bishop and Jamison, I want you to interview him after you've visited the morgue."

CHAPTER SIXTEEN

Alabama

Every morgue Jess had ever been in could have been designed by the same architect. Even for elements like tile and color choice, where there was room for some individuality, none of them strayed far from the template. Tiles were always medical green, the color of scrubs, and they were always the same three-inch square.

Jess unscrewed the cap from her small tub of vapor rub and dabbed it liberally under her nose before offering it to Jamison, who did the same.

The coroner, Dr. Stevenson, stuck his clipboard under his arm as he reached down to open the second door from the bottom in the five-high body locker. The doors had white laminate covers over surgical steel. The cooler was state of the art, definitely as good as, if not better than, anything Jess had seen in a major city.

How often were all twenty-five slabs of the refrigerated storage cabinet in use at the same time? It seemed like overkill to have the capacity for so many bodies in such a small rural community. Fair enough if it were Montgomery, but Ophir Springs had a population of 5,206. It was very much doubtful that twenty-five people would die in mysterious or violent circumstances at the same time, thus requiring autopsies. The set-up screamed budget surplus – use it or lose it. Shame that they hadn't re-done the color scheme and tiles with the windfall.

When the door opened, the stench of decomposition ambushed her senses. The menthol did nothing to stop the brutal attack on her olfactory receptors. Bile rose in the back of her throat as she fought the reflex to vomit. On instinct, her body betrayed her by sucking in a sharp breath to quell the attempted coup in her stomach. Immediately, she regretted the traitorous breath—her gut cramped in a painful spasm as it tried to rid itself of the little she had in her belly. Her eyes watered and her throat burned. The smell of death was not just an odor; it was a full-body assault.

Jess turned and took in small, shallow breaths, just enough to keep her from passing out. She closed her eyes and allowed her body to adjust to the stench. She would never be used to it but she knew from other cases that the need to vomit would pass in a few minutes. She would compartmentalize the smell and her body's visceral reaction like she did with every other unpleasant or painful thing in her life.

"Where was she found?" Jamison asked, pointing down to the covered remains of Hannah Henderson.

With a surgical-gloved finger, Dr. Stevenson pushed his glasses further up his nose, but as soon as he let go they fell again. He glanced at Jamison for only a fraction of a second and then his gaze went to the side, fixed like he was speaking to an invisible person. "The torso was found by a plant worker at the Logan Martin, one of the northernmost dams on the Coosa River."

The coroner was tall and lanky; his forearms and fingers long, almost alien-like. His hair was cut so close to his head that he almost looked bald but the glow cast by what was remaining marked him as ginger. "Her head and limbs have not been found," he added quickly, again glancing at Jamison for only a fraction of a second before returning to stare past him. There was a point on the wall that his gaze always went back to. Jess had turned to see what it was that captured his attention before she realized he wasn't looking at anything. He simply couldn't force himself to look directly at people.

Jess took out the map of the Coosa River. Most of the river had been developed for hydroelectric power by the Southern Company. The dams were an ecological disaster for the flora and fauna of the area but they made narrowing down search parameters easier. "If the torso was discovered in Logan Martin, it had to have gone in either at Weiss or H. Neely Henry. We're not going to find the head, but if we find the limbs, it looks like that is where they would be."

"No. There are too many trash gates at the powerhouse in Weiss. No way any body part is getting through those gates," Jamison said.

"Hmm." Dr. Stevenson made a sympathetic noise. "True." His voice was soft and gentle, almost contemplative. "You know this area?"

This time Dr. Stevenson didn't even attempt to make eye contact with either of them. He just looked straight ahead. It was a bit disconcerting to speak to someone who never looked directly at them.

Jamison nodded. "I worked in the area for a while."

"In the Montgomery office?" There was a lilt to his voice, excitement that he had made a tangible connection to another person. He probably rarely felt that, so he celebrated when he did.

"No." Jamison didn't expand or explain that he had been undercover.

"In Birmingham?"

"No." Again Jamison didn't offer an explanation. It was clear he didn't want to disclose he had been undercover because inevitably that would lead to more questions.

Dr. Stevenson's shoulders slumped, clearly dejected. He wanted social interaction but he didn't have the skills. Maybe that was how he had ended up in a morgue: he simply did not have the people skills to deal with living patients.

"I think she was dumped no higher than H. Neely Henry," Jamison said.

Dr. Stevenson continued to stare at his safe spot on the wall.

"Ever been out there? The fishing, man, it's great. The biggest catfish you have ever seen. Do you fish?" Jamison asked him.

"No." He shook his head. He looked disappointed in himself that he had nothing to contribute to the conversation. "The bass are good too," he blurted. "I heard someone say that once. There are two types of bass in the Coosa: striped and largemouth." He smiled, clearly back in his element of facts and figures.

"Is that right? I'll have to check that out. I do like bass. Nice mild flavor. I love catfish but you got to be careful with the bottom feeders."

Dr. Stevenson nodded so energetically his glasses slipped to the tip of his nose. "People erroneously believe all fish are good for you. In actuality it's fish high in Omega-3 fatty acids. As far as health benefits, the same cannot be said for fish high in Omega-6 like catfish. And then of course you have the nematode risk associated with catfish."

Jess couldn't help but smile as Dr. Stevenson explained the parasites found in fish and the relative dangers of infection based on geographic location. A few times he seemed to forget himself and actually looked away from the fixed spot on the wall.

The interaction was so Jamison. He listened intently to everything Dr. Stevenson said. If he was bored or didn't care about what the coroner was saying, he didn't show it, and he would never tell anyone, not even Jess. He had the unique ability to make people feel valued and at ease.

"Our victim went missing about a month ago. Do you think she was in the water the entire time?" Jamison asked, gently bringing the conversation back to their case.

Dr. Stevenson pursed his lips as he considered the question. "Aquatic decomposition is a peculiar one. Back when I was in training, the rule of thumb was one week of decomposition on land was the equivalent of two weeks' decomposition in the water: that's to say bodies decompose twice as quickly on land as they do in the water. Unfortunately, it's not nearly as straightforward as that. New research indicates that submersion in fresh water can actually accelerate decomposition in certain circumstances, which could be the case here."

"How so?" Jess asked.

"As you may know, the weather we have been having in Alabama has been unseasonably warm. At temperatures this high maggots can die before they can pupate, which slows down the decomposition process. Water is cooler, thus allowing for blowflies. Then of course there is the other end of the spectrum where fresh water can actually preserve bodies." Dr. Stevenson glanced up from his fixed spot on the wall long enough to look at her. "I read about a case in Minnesota—Duluth, I believe—where two bodies were pulled out of the lake after five years almost completely preserved. There were no visible signs of decomposition, no discoloration, no odor. Fascinating case really. Adipocere occurred and preserved the bodies. That's when the fat turns to soap in a process of anaerobic bacterial hydrolysis."

"Human soap?" Jamison asked.

Dr. Stevenson nodded vigorously. "Oh yes. It's not a common occurrence but it has been well documented as early as the seventeenth century. Scientifically speaking, the process isn't difficult. During World War I the British press reported Germans using the bodies of their own fallen soldiers to produce glycerin and soap. Later this was disproved, though the rumors started again during World War II. Again there was no proof of it happening on an industrial scale but at the Nuremberg Trials evidence was provided that German scientists had indeed developed a process for rendering soap from the human remains. The extent to which the technology was used is still wildly debated. Fascinating stuff…" Dr. Stevenson's voice trailed off.

Jess stared at him blankly. Between his story and the overwhelming stench of the corpse beside her, she couldn't think of a single thing to say.

"So, was this body preserved by being placed in water?" Jamison asked.

"Oh no, quite the contrary." Dr. Stevenson pulled back the white sheet to expose the remains of Hannah Henderson. "The decomposition in this case is advanced as you can see by the green discoloration."

Jess's eyes widened when she saw the mutilated corpse. The torso didn't even look like it belonged to a human. The skin was dark green and bloated. From the open wounds where her lower limbs had been disarticulated, organs protruded, a long-coiled section of her bowel trailed under her. At the gaping hole beneath her hip, her stomach strained to escape.

"Usually in fresh water, the abdomen will rupture from the pressure of the gasses. In this case they were able to escape through the wounds."

Jess examined the body. There was so little left to identify her as human. The remains could pass as the rotting flesh of any large animal. Her gaze went to the sternum. Though the skin was dark and sloughing off she could still see the tell-tale straight edges of excision sites. She counted four, each roughly the same size. "Are there signs of burns on the musculature where the flesh has been removed?"

"Here, look here," he said, pointing. "Muscle has been excised here, not just the skin. It is possible there was a burn here. I cannot say that with any certainty, but it is well within the realm of possibility."

Jess nodded. She just needed it to be a possibility.

"Oh, one more thing. It's rather peculiar. I've never actually seen it before or read about it, come to think about it. That's not to say that it is entirely unique."

"What's that?" she asked, preparing herself for another "peculiar" tale from the coroner. It was a shame that he disliked human interaction so much because he would be captivating at dinner parties. He could offend and intrigue guests in equal measure.

"Right. What was I saying? Oh yes, peculiar. I found something unusual in her blood." He riffled through the pages on his clipboard. "Oh right, here we go. She had higher than therapeutic levels of methylphenidate."

"Yeah? What does that mean?" Jess asked, excited they might have something concrete to work with.

"Well it means she either accidently or purposefully ingested more methylphenidate—or Ritalin as it is more commonly known—than is currently recommended by the FDA. I can't say with any confidence if it was intentional."

Ritalin? Jess couldn't keep from rolling her eyes, though she did have the manners to look away before she did it. Dr. Stevenson's idea of what constituted an exciting development differed considerably from her own. "I'll check and see if she had a prescription."

"All right. I suppose that could be useful information for you," Dr. Stevenson said but his mouth pulled down into a frown.

Social skills were not his forte. Jess more than got that. But at least she had the skill set required to fake it when needed. It was oddly comforting to speak with someone who struggled with human interaction more than her.

"You don't think it is relevant information?" she asked.

"I suppose it could be, but I was actually thinking you would be more interested in the other compounds I found in her system."

Jess sighed. "What other compounds?"

"Let's see here. We have formaldehyde, glutaraldehyde, methanol and of course some humectants."

"Of course," Jamison said. There was a smile in his voice. The man had the patience of a saint. He would happily let Dr. Stevenson bumble his way through the entire day.

"What does that mean? Obviously, I know what formaldehyde is, but the other things?"

"Oh yes, my apologies." Dr. Stevenson pushed his glasses up again. "They're embalming agents. This one is a rather concentrated one. Most have formaldehyde contents ranging from five to thirty-five percent. This one was on the higher end."

"What? Do you mean she was embalmed?" Jess stared down at the torso. That didn't make sense. There were signs of decomposition on the body, namely the maggot infestation along the open wounds where her legs had been sawn off and in her bowels. "Are you certain?"

"Yes. Look just here on the neck. See that small bruise about the size of a pencil lead?"

Jess had to squint to see the tiny dark pinprick just below where the head had been decapitated. Her entire neck was mottled shades of green and brown, making it hard to see a single small discoloration. "Yes, I see it."

"That's where she was injected with embalming fluid, directly into the carotid artery. Based on the bruising it was done before death."

"He started to embalm her before she died?" Jamison said incredulously. "Wow."

"She was most likely unconscious at that point though. Her hyoid bone was snapped from repeated manual asphyxiation. If you look at the pattern along her neck, you can see the assailant changed hand position several times."

"Like he was getting tired and needed a rest?" Jess asked.

"Or he was stopping to resuscitate her so it lasted longer." Jamison shook his head. "Sick son of a bitch."

Dr. Stevenson nodded. "Yes, either of those are possibilities."

"The head is all he cares about," Jess mumbled to herself. "The carotid artery goes straight to the brain, right? He's keeping the heads. That's why he preserved them. That's why the cut marks on the neck are precise. He wants the heads to be pristine. It's not about counter-forensics. They're his trophies."

CHAPTER SEVENTEEN

Jess glanced around the waiting area. The walls were covered in silk wallpaper, a cream background with an intricate swirling gold pattern. The gold was picked up throughout the room from the door handles and light fixtures to the tacks on the upholstered chairs. Above them hung a crystal chandelier, dropping down at least five feet from the vaulted ceiling. Dr. Nester's office was opulent. Jess counted no fewer than four arrangements of fresh flowers, lilies and roses mainly, the same pale shade as the walls. That wouldn't be cheap.

From somewhere in the ether came the sound of a bubbling brook, presumably it was meant to be calming. Every few minutes a bird chirp would join the gentle cacophony.

Jess picked up a magazine from the pile on the glass-topped table. She and Jamison had been assigned the honor of interviewing the "Shitting Doctor." She really hoped if Nester was their guy, the media would run with that name. Serial killers didn't deserve cool names like Zodiac or Night Stalker. They deserved to be called Piece of Shit or Ass Licker.

"This woman is anorexic." Jess put down the magazine and pointed to another cover. "And this chick is a narcissist. How can a psychiatrist keep magazines like this in his office? Shouldn't he have things that promote a healthy body image and mental wellbeing?"

"Remember this is a guy who shits on women for fun," Jamison said.

"Yeah, fair point. When do you think he's going to see us?"

Dr. Nester's secretary had confirmed he had finished with his last patient at seven. It was now seven fifty-three and he still hadn't come out to the waiting room to find them. They had watched his last patient, a thin, thirty-something blond woman, leave almost an hour ago, so there was no doubt Dr. Nester was alone in his office.

Jamison shook his head. "It's a power play. The key is to pretend we don't even notice he has wasted our time. It's not like we have anywhere else to be, right?" Jamison winked.

Jamison would have had to actually lie down to look any more relaxed. His fingers were laced behind his head, creating a hammock, and his feet were resting on the coffee table. After twenty minutes of waiting, Jamison had taken off his tie and propped up his feet. It was his own power play. To the casual observer he just looked relaxed or even rude but for Jamison it was neither; it was calculated. Jamison wanted Dr. Nester to find him like this because it was likely to knock him off his stride.

"I still smell like death." Jess sniffed at her blouse. She opened her tub of vapor rub and dabbed some on her neck like a make-shift perfume. She would have liked to change her clothes after their trip to the morgue but she hadn't packed anything. They were scheduled for the red-eye back to DC, so she didn't need an overnight case.

"Yeah, I didn't like to say."

"I hope it washes out."

"It will. Grandma Patty always said, 'Everything comes out in the wash.' Pretty sure she wasn't talking about decomposition but the sentiment remains the same."

Jess was quiet for a minute as she stared at him intently. "Jamison?"

He looked up, his dark gaze locking on hers. "Yeah?"

"Can I ask you something?"

Jamison smiled. "I've never known you to ask permission first. You always just dive in."

Jess tucked the piece of hair that had escaped her ponytail behind her ear. "Yeah, I know. That can get me in trouble sometimes."

"Not with me, Jessie. What do you want to know?"

Jess paused, suddenly realizing there were so many questions she wanted answered. Like why he had left to go undercover. Why he picked Felicia. On second thought, she didn't really want the answers to those questions. She might not be able to compartmentalize them and keep going with the fragile new normal they had. "Does Felicia know about her, about Grandma Patty?" Some of Jess's favorite things about Jamison were his Grandma Patty stories and sayings.

Jamison sighed. "Nah. I can't tell her about the good without telling her about the bad. It's all in the past now."

The warmth of relief spread through her chest. That was one of the many things she had that Felicia never would. Jess knew who Jamison really was; that was something.

Jess's phone buzzed in her jacket pocket. The vibration pulsated against her ribs. She pulled it out to read the message that had come through.

"What is it? You're frowning," Jamison said a minute later.

Jess looked up. "It's a message from Tina. Hannah Henderson has a brother in Texas. He's her only living relative. The coroner's office contacted him about her remains so he could arrange a proper burial for her. And he refused to take responsibility."

"Wow, that's harsh. Were they estranged?"

"No. He's just a dickhead and doesn't want to pay for the funeral cost. He told them to just keep the body because it's not his responsibility. According to Tina he makes plenty of money. He's just not willing to spend it on this."

"What an asshole."

"Yeah," Jess agreed. "It's not all bad news though. Tina discovered that Hannah rented a car at the airport in Montgomery last month. She is currently running background checks on the employees at the rental company. And get this, the car was found in Ashville that day close to Neely Henry Lake. Local police noticed it was a rental and called the company, who picked it up. No report was filed because no one thought a crime had been committed."

"Everyone just thought Hannah dumped her car in Northern Alabama?"

"Apparently. And with her handbag and luggage still in the front seat. The rental company tried calling her to pick them up. Her stuff has been sitting in lost property at the airport since she went missing. They have now sent her things to the Montgomery office for processing. Tina will let us know what they find."

"Cool."

"There is still one thing I can't wrap my head around: the victims. I'm not seeing any striking similarities between Hannah and Lydia beyond the fact they both rented cars before they died. That's it. That is the victimology we have at the moment. And then we have the other victims. God only knows where a prostitute fits in. There are absolutely zero similarities in their lives other than that. Hannah was a risk-taker and by all accounts pretty vile. She had zero friends. Even her own brother won't claim her remains. On the other hand, we have Liddy Steiner: risk-averse, mother of the year, everyone loved her. Add on to that our victims lived in different states and their bodies were found hundreds of miles apart. If you presented me with just this information, I would say they were unrelated."

"Except the bodies," Jamison said what she had been thinking.

"Yeah."

"Ahem." A nasally voice whined from the opposite end of the room.

Jess's head snapped up to see Dr. Joel Nester standing in the doorway. Where he came up to on the doorframe made his short stature obvious. He was less than five foot six, which made the girth of his belly even more prominent. Charcoal suit trousers were pulled high over the crest of his stomach. There came a point in every obese man's life when he had to choose to wear his pants above his gut or below. Dr. Nester had chosen the former.

His eyes narrowed into tight slits. Anger contorted his face, flattening his brow and pushing his ruddy cheeks up until they appeared to engulf his dark eyes. He glared at Jamison's feet propped on the coffee table.

Jamison was slow to get up, taking his time to unroll his sleeves and button his cuffs. All the while Dr. Nester became more and more visibly agitated. His lips flattened to a straight white line against the scarlet background of his flushed face.

Well played, Jamison.

Jess crossed the room. "Thank you for seeing us tonight, Dr. Nester. Your secretary said you're busy so we we'll try not to take up too much of your time."

Dr. Nester couldn't look at her. He was too busy watching Jamison crumple up a disposable paper cup and toss it in the trash, or near the trash to be precise. It hit the side of the wicker wastebasket before falling onto the cream carpet. Missing was intentional. Jamison never missed.

Nester's nostrils flared so briefly few would have caught it, the micro expression came and went in an instant then was replaced just as quickly with a confident smile.

"Yes, I am indeed very busy. I'm not entirely sure I can be of any assistance in this matter."

"Why don't we go into your office and I'll decide how helpful you are." Jamison smiled but there was no denying the challenge in his low voice.

Nester's smile faltered only for a second before he quickly recovered. "Please, follow me."

Nester turned and walked down the windowless hall. The floors were carpeted in the same short cream pile of the waiting room. The walls were covered in a coordinating wallpaper of beige and gold stripes. Recessed spotlights lit the area. Like the waiting room, the décor was sophisticated and high-end. All the paint was fresh and the wallpaper was not peeling back anywhere, which indicated it had all been done recently.

Nester opened the double doors to his office. The room was a large hexagon with a double height ceiling that rose to a point high above them, creating the feeling of a church, fitting since this was a place where people came to disclose their darkest secrets.

Behind a polished mahogany desk were Nester's credentials, displayed in gilded frames: an undergraduate degree in organic chemistry from MIT, an MD from Harvard and postgraduate training from Johns Hopkins and Boston University. The diplomas were not just framed, they were matted to increase their size. The display was not to assure his patients he was qualified, it was boastful and intimidating. The intention was not to soothe, but to subtly subjugate: Nester was better, smarter, more powerful; what he said was the truth. From where patients sat there was no way they could avoid looking at the wall of greatness.

All three stood in the doorway for a moment. Nester didn't invite them in; instead they stood surveying his kingdom. He wanted them to compliment him on his office. It was important to him that everyone recognized his achievements and stroked his ego. For that reason, Jess said nothing.

She let the silence hang between them, awkward and acute. The only sound was Nester's labored breath. Then Jess walked in and took a seat on the sofa. She wouldn't wait to be asked to take a seat. That would give Nester too much of the control he craved.

The supple material brushed her arm. She had never felt leather that soft. The stitching was so intricate with no discernable seams, just a continuous blanket. It was no doubt designer and probably cost as much as her car. Such luxury was completely unnecessary to the therapeutic experience. It was just another way for him to show off.

The couch dipped as Jamison sat beside her.

She waited for Nester to waddle into the room and take a seat behind his desk. She couldn't tell if it was corpulence or posturing that slowed him down. Either way, he took his time to sit down and get comfortable, and he arranged some notes on his desk. He had had almost an hour after his last patient to sort out his paperwork. The show was simply another subtle way to assert his dominance.

Jess smiled knowingly at Jamison. Nester was trying to smoke them out, make them act hastily and show their hand before they were ready. He was relying on the fact that as a rule people were uncomfortable with silence. One psychologist had actually worked out how long it took for a silence to become awkward: four seconds. Four seconds without someone saying something in a conversation was enough to invalidate a person and make them feel rejected. No doubt Nester used silence as a tool and a weapon when he worked with patients. Little did he know that Jess preferred silence with most people and Jamison knew the game and he wasn't going to play.

Nester looked up at them, first staring at Jamison and then Jess. When he turned to her, something in his face changed. The smugness was replaced by disbelief, shock even, as he studied her face. "Jessica Randal?" His nasal voiced dipped low in question.

A jolt of electricity darted down her spine. Every muscle in Jess's body tensed, recoiling at the moniker and the knowing look in Nester's small, rodent eyes.

Oh God, he recognized her. Jess closed her eyes.

Fuck. Not him. Not now.

The room spun, the walls inched in. She couldn't breathe. She gasped but it was like someone was holding her underwater. She tried to give her rehearsed response but her throat closed, not even air was getting past.

Of course it would be this cretin who recognized her. He was the right age. He would have seen the story unfold on the nightly news, the hunt for The Headmaster. Nester would have watched as they recapped the highlights from the trial. He would have relished every disgusting, vile fact. He would have seen the cover of the magazine with the picture of her reaching out to try to hold his hand.

Jess's throat burned the way it did that day from screaming so much. If she hadn't been sitting, she would have collapsed. She clasped her hands together. She used the thumbnail of one hand to press into the sensitive nail bed at the base of her other thumb. The result was excruciating. It was an old trick used by medical staff to rouse drunk patients. She pressed until the pain was great enough to drag her out of the nightmare and bring her back to the present.

This is what a panic attack felt like. She took in a long, fortifying breath before she said, "As I… I… I told your secretary, I am… I'm Special Agent Bishop, this is my partner Special Agent Briggs."

"You're not Jessica Randal?" Nester eyed her with a feral interest like a cat preparing to take its fatal swipe against an injured bird. "My apologies. But the similarities are striking: your coloring, the dark curly hair, and the…" he paused for effect as he scrutinized her features, "beauty mark above your mouth. Just like her. It was a fascinating case. If you haven't already read about it, I strongly suggest you read up on The Headmaster case. Absolutely riveting. What I wouldn't give to interview Jessica now. I bet she is an absolute mess. Are you sure you have never heard of her?" His dark eyes challenged her. He didn't believe her and he wasn't going to let it drop.

Jess forced herself to keep her hands by her sides even though her instinct was to cover her face to keep Nester from inspecting her. She had no doubt that had he been closer he would have reached out to stroke her cheek.

She opened her mouth to speak, to refute his assertions, tell him she had no idea who or what he was talking about, but nothing came out.

Jamison must have sensed her distress because he slid closer to her. "We're here about the death of Hannah Henderson. Her cell phone records indicate she was in contact with you around the time she went missing. Were you in a romantic relationship with her?"

Nester laughed, a strangled forced sound. "Romantic; such a quaint turn of phrase, very parochial, dare I say narrow-minded, immature even." Condescension dripped from his tone. He spoke to Jamison but never looked away from Jess. His gaze was everywhere: her mouth, her breasts, her legs, finally settling on her crotch.

Jess sank back further into the couch, desperate to sink into the cushions and disappear, be far away from here. Her skin burned with shame. She felt dirty and exposed.

Jamison reached out and touched her arm. His long fingers gently tapped against her, so soft she wasn't sure she was really feeling it. Only when she looked down and saw his hand did she know for sure she wasn't imagining it. Too soon he moved. He only wanted her to know he was there, that he had her back. He was trying to give her strength because he saw her struggling, but the small gesture nearly undid her.

"I was just trying to be polite. But if you're up for forgoing civil discourse, I'm in. Were you just fucking Hannah Henderson or were you shitting on her too?" Jamison asked.

Nester's beady eyes widened. "There seems to be rather a lot of judgment coming from you. Are you perhaps triggered by unconventional sex?"

Jamison stood up and walked across the room, closing the space between the couch and desk in three long strides.

"Quite honestly, I'm just impressed you find anyone to screw you. I don't care that you shit on women and call it foreplay. I do care if you were abusing her or anyone else in any capacity."

"Why did you immediately go from avant-garde to abuse? That is very telling."

Jamison leaned over the desk. His large form blocked Jess's view. All she could see was the broad expanse of Jamison's back. "Cut the shit. No one cares about your sex life except you. Now back to Hannah Henderson. She came to Montgomery on the fifth. Was she coming to see you?"

For a long time silence reigned. This time it wasn't about dominance; it was about Nester thinking of a response that would soothe his battered ego. He was no doubt unused to people questioning his authority.

"Hannah was scheduled to come down for the weekend. She never arrived." The bravado had gone from Nester's voice.

"She never showed up, and you what? Thought she got a better offer? She realized screwing you was akin to bestiality? What? Talk me through your thought process."

Nester cleared his voice. The wheels of his swivel chair squeaked as he shifted in his seat. Jess couldn't see him but she could imagine him repositioning himself to create distance between Jamison and himself. When Jamison chose to be, he was the most intimidating person Jess had ever met. He reserved that persona for situations that required it but it was always there, lingering close to the surface, another layer.

"We weren't exclusive. I assumed she had changed her mind about the weekend we had planned. Our relationship was quite intense. That's to say our sex life was extreme. We were always pushing the envelope. I just assumed she had reached her limit."

"More extreme than shitting on her? What exactly were you planning on doing to her?"

"I wasn't going to do anything *to* her. We were exploring her limits. Everything we did was consensual. It always is."

"Except when it's not," Jamison reminded him. "We've read all the transcripts from the Paige Dooley case."

"Those files are sealed."

"We're the FBI. There is no such thing as sealed. We know what you did. You're lucky you're not in jail. Though that can change. Miss Dooley dropped her civil case; a criminal case is another matter. What will the district attorney find when he has a look into your past? How many other women will tell the same story? I need to tell you, buddy, all these fancy degrees won't help you where you're going."

"I haven't committed any crimes." His voice broke. All his earlier confidence had abandoned him.

Jamison shrugged his shoulders. "Here's the funny thing about the South. It doesn't matter if what you're doing is legal or consensual or—what did you call it? Oh yeah, avant-garde. None of that matters. What matters here is a big-city doctor moved into their town with his immoral, perverted ways. They won't take too kindly to that. Your proclivities become common knowledge and you're going to be at the receiving end of angry men in white hoods. Southern folk don't care about consensual; they care about you being a pervert. Something tells me having a pitchfork pointed your direction is a hard limit for you. Shame there won't be any safe words for you. Now cut the bullshit."

"Are you threatening me?"

"Nope. I am straight up telling you that if you piss me off I will make sure it is common knowledge you were chased out of New York for having sex with and shitting on your patients. No threats here, just giving you my plan of action. So, are we cool?"

Jamison took Nester's silence as an affirmation. "Great. Let's start at the beginning. Hannah Henderson was coming to see you, right?"

"Yes."

"Look at you being all helpful. See how easy that is? I ask questions, you answer them. Beautiful. Now we're getting somewhere. Hannah's flight landed at 7:15 p.m. You could have picked her up at the airport. I checked with your secretary. She was super helpful. Said your last patient was at five that day. See, if my lady comes to town, I'm picking her up. But not you. Why not?"

Nester didn't respond.

"Naw. A shrug isn't working for me. I need words," Jamison pressed.

"It was important that she knew her place. Picking her up at the airport would have influenced the power dynamic."

"Power dynamic? Is that code for you're an asshole? Seems like a dick move to me, but yeah let's go with power dynamic. We know the plane landed on time. She picked up the keys to her rental twenty minutes later. We have her on CCTV leaving the airport and then nothing. Did she say she was meeting someone before she came to your house? Was she going to make any stops?"

"Absolutely not. She was instructed to go straight to my house. She would have not made any stop."

"Instructed? Like you told her what to do and she did it?"

"Yes, that was part of our—"

"Let me guess," Jamison said. "Your power dynamic?" He shook his head. "But she never showed up. What part of your power trip was that? It must have pissed you off that Hannah changed her mind. You had a big weekend of shitting ahead of you, probably stocked up on your stool softener and whatnot. I get it, you had plans and she stood you up, that hurts."

"She did not *piss me off*. She re-evaluated her limits."

"How do you know?" Jamison demanded. "What did she say?"

"She texted to say she was on the I20 coming out of Birmingham. She obviously had changed her mind because she was driving north back to New York."

An uneasy feeling clawed at Jess. The conversation with Reuben Steiner played in her mind. Liddy Steiner had been lost when she was murdered. If that was the case with Hannah Henderson then they had the connection between the victims they had been looking for. Spurred by the new information, she bolted up. "Show me your phone. I want to see the text," she demanded.

She stood beside Jamison, looking down at Nester. From this angle, with Jamison by her side, Nester wasn't scary, he was just a pathetic man who abused his power in the worst possible ways. It didn't matter if he knew who she was because she knew exactly who he was too.

"You don't have a warrant." Nester's one good eye, the one that didn't droop, widened in surprise.

He thought he had intimidated Jess into silence. That alone was enough to give her back her voice. "Nope we don't. But you're going to let me see your phone because you're very helpful and you want to help us find Hannah's killer. I'm assuming you cared for her."

"If you don't want to show Agent Bishop your phone, I would be happy to make a few calls. I have lots of connections with law enforcement down here. As a courtesy, I think I should give them the heads up that they might want to keep an eye on you. Got to do my civic duty and make sure you're on their radar."

Nester made an agitated noise. He breathed heavily as he opened his breast pocket and pulled out a phone. His stubby fingers drained of color as he clung onto the black case.

Stony-faced, he punched at the code with his index finger. "Here. Not like this is any of your concern." He thrust the phone at her.

Jess read the messages.

I'm on the I20 just past Birmingham. Is this right?

An hour later Hannah texted:

In Odenville. This doesn't seem right. Call me.

Jess looked up from the screen. "You moron. She was lost and she was asking for help." She handed the phone to Jamison to read the messages.

Nester's face contorted in disbelief, his rubbery features closing in on one another.

"You're an idiot. A woman is dead because you didn't pick up the phone and give her directions. What an asshole." Jamison shook his head.

"No." Nester's voice was paper thin.

"Did she know anyone else in Alabama who she could have gone to meet?" Jess asked.

Nester shook his head.

"Then I have to agree with my partner. You're an idiot."

CHAPTER EIGHTEEN

"Mass has ended. Let us go in peace to love and serve the Lord," the priest announced from the altar, making a sign of the cross.

Everyone started to sing. This was her favorite part of Mass. She loved the songs and she could even read all of the words now so she could sing along, but she didn't sing as well as her daddy, nobody did. They kept singing until the very end of the song, all five verses. Most people left as soon as the priest walked through the door, but not them, they always stayed to the end to finish the song.

She knelt down to cross herself, and her special red dress brushed the pew, rippling in shiny waves. Her mommy didn't want her to wear it because it was a party dress and she might ruin it, but her daddy said every day was a celebration so there was no need to save her clothes for a special occasion. Mommy just nodded and then took some of her pills and went back to bed with a washcloth over her eyes.

She stood up and reached for her daddy's hand. She had to squint when the doors of the church opened. The sun was so bright but the heat felt good on her back. The leaves had just changed color and were getting ready to fall but it was still so warm, a perfect day.

"Do we have to go home yet?"

"Where do you want to go, princess?" He swung her hand with each step as they walked.

She shrugged, she just wanted to walk with him, it didn't matter where they went as long as they didn't have to go home.

"How about ice cream? I seem to remember my best girl had a perfect report card and we have not celebrated yet."

She beamed up at him. Pride swelled in her. He was proud of her. "Can I get sprinkles?"

He nodded. "Of course. What is the point of ice cream without sprinkles? Oh and hot fudge. Oh and don't forget the whipped cream and cherry. You can't have ice cream without those."

She giggled as they walked to the shop. It was the best day, just the two of them. She felt so safe and loved.

And then the sirens blared and her world collapsed.

CHAPTER NINETEEN

Jamison took the keys from Jess's hand. "I'll drive. You don't look like you're up for it."

Jess didn't say anything. She was too busy replaying that conversation with Dr. Nester. Jamison waited until she had buckled her seat belt before he closed the passenger door.

Jess looked out at the night skyline. The sky looked ominous. At the horizon black melted into hues of pink and orange around the sliver of setting sun that had not yet been engulfed by the night. The air was charged, an electric current coursed through the warm breeze. A storm was coming.

In the distance the Alabama capitol building was lit up, grand enough to rival the White House. The lawns were immaculate, blankets of dense green grass and thick box hedges. Not a single piece of litter marred the pristine grounds. Begrudgingly she admitted it was pretty. She didn't want to like Alabama because it had taken her partner from her.

Jamison turned on the engine and pulled out of the parking lot of Dr. Nester's office.

A pickup truck pulled up beside them at the traffic lights. A gun rack with two shotguns hung in the rear window. "Does that bother you?" Jess indicated to the Confederate flag on the license plate. Her skin prickled every time she saw one.

"As a black man? Nah, I like it when racists identify themselves. Saves me a lot of trouble."

The truck pulled away, gray smoke billowed from the tailpipe. Jess watched as it trailed off and the offensive emblem blurred into an orange and blue dot.

"He knows you're Jessica Randal."

Jess winced at the name. She wasn't Jessica Randal anymore. She was Jessica Bishop now. She had taken her stepfather's last name and not looked back. Somehow hearing her old name from Jamison's mouth made it worse, like the worst kind of betrayal. That was a lifetime ago. Jess wasn't that person anymore. Her heart hammered violently against her ribs. She looked out the passenger window so Jamison couldn't see her reaction.

Jess cleared her throat. She couldn't think about her past right now, so she would bury it. Work was what she needed.

"Hannah Henderson was lost when she was murdered. Her texts say as much. Liddy Steiner was lost. She called her husband to tell him. That's what they have in common: both women were lost. We wanted to know what they had in common and that's it. And it makes sense a sex worker would get lost. They travel to see clients all the time. I really think this is the connection. He's preying on lost women. Their guard is down; they're confused. If he presents to them as law enforcement, they're not going to question it until it's too late."

"So, we're not going to talk about what Nester said? Okay, I'm down with that." Jamison switched on the turn signal before glancing over his shoulder and pulling into the middle lane.

"They also both had rental cars. Tina is running background checks on the rental company employees. I think that is where our killer works. If we cross-reference employees with people who have purchased police lights and embalming fluid, that's how we're going to find him."

"A car rental employee? And what? He followed our victims hoping they would get lost and he could strike?"

Jess sighed. When Jamison said it aloud she realized it was far-fetched. "Maybe. I don't know. Both women were unfamiliar with the area so it isn't a leap to assume they might get lost. He could have followed them, waited for them to pull over and then he would strike. Maybe he follows lots of women and these were the unlucky ones who happened to get lost."

"Okay, assuming that is his MO. How would you explain the fact that the victims live in different states?"

"I don't know," Jess said, her mind drifting. The Headmaster had had victims in different states too, different countries even. That's why he got away with it for as long as he did. "Maybe he got transferred. Maybe he has a partner. Maybe—"

"Jessie, what's going on?"

"What? I'm working the case. It's an iterative process. You know that. You taught me. You go over things again and again until you get there."

"Nester has obviously riled you. I've never seen you like that before. You looked scared."

Jess shifted uncomfortably in her seat. Suddenly her seat belt was too tight. She felt like she was being suffocated; there may as well have been fingers wrapped around her throat. "You said you were okay not talking about him."

"I am. But I'm not okay with you being this upset. He's a piece of shit. Nothing he says matters."

Jess put the tip of her finger to her mouth to chew on her nail but there was nothing left for her teeth to latch onto. She tried the next nail and then the next but they had all been bitten down to the quick. It hurt just to try to find a bit of nail to attack but she kept going anyway. "I know. Nester is an asshole. That's it."

"Yeah, he is. He's also a prime suspect. He doesn't have an alibi for Liddy Steiner's or Hannah Henderson's deaths," Jamison pointed out.

"He also has no known connection to Liddy Steiner. We've checked. They have never crossed paths. We will have Tina look into his credit card history and see if he's ordered police lights or embalming fluid and mortuary equipment. If he has, we can go from there. But I really think Liddy Steiner would have mentioned it to her husband if she saw a deformed troll pull up behind her that night. That would have stood out for me."

Jamison was silent for a while. He turned to look at her. His stare burned into her. He opened his mouth to speak but he didn't, instead he returned his attention back to the road. Traffic was a sea of red lights inching forward. He wanted to say something but he held it back. The tension of holding it in was written in the tight muscles of his jaw.

"You really don't want it to be him, do you? Because you don't want to have to see or speak to him again. You would rather it be a random guy at a car rental than Nester because he knows who you are."

Jess sucked in a sharp breath. She pulled at the collar of her blouse. She felt exposed and vulnerable. No one could read her like Jamison, not even Lindsay and she was a psychologist. "You said we didn't have to talk about it."

"We're working a case and he's our prime suspect. How can we not talk about it, Jessie?"

"The same way we don't talk about you living a lie," she blurted before she had the chance to think about it. This was not how she had imagined broaching the subject but it needed to be said. "You have no right to lecture me when you have created a past for your *wife* that has no basis in reality and we're ignoring that. We're also ignoring the last two years. We have never talked about your time undercover. Ever. I've read the reports. I know everything you did. I know that a high-level dealer died and lots of fingers were pointed at you. Your life was pretty fucking bleak. I know it because I read it, not because we talked about it. You've never confided in me."

Jamison's expression darkened. "You read the files?"

"Yeah," Jess admitted. She didn't have the right or authority but there was no way she couldn't. She had to know what was happening.

Jamison's eyes narrowed. He took his hand off the steering wheel and ran his knuckles against the hard line of his jaw. "All right, Jessie, what do you want to know? You want the redacted version? Or are we going all in? The incriminating stuff too? The parts that will make you question our friendship? You want those details too?"

Jess studied the outline of his features, his wide expressive mouth and his thickly muscled jaw. "Nothing could make me question our friendship. You can tell me anything, Jamison. You know that. You don't have to pretend with *me*." She wasn't Felicia; she didn't need a storybook version of him.

"Nah, you can't say that," Jamison scoffed. "There are deal-breakers. There have to be. Everyone has a line; where they draw it is the only difference."

The dark undercurrent in his tone caused a chill to prickle her skin. His voice did not sound like his; he was like a stranger, cold and detached. For a moment she sat paralyzed, unable to speak or even think. What if he was right? What if she was so utterly repulsed by his actions that it damaged her feelings for him? There were very few people she trusted, and even fewer she could call a friend. She couldn't lose him.

Maybe she didn't want to know. "We all have darkness inside us. And we've all done things we're not proud of. I don't need to know your secrets. I know you and that's what matters."

They drove in silence the rest of the way to the airport. The only sound was the rain hitting the roof and the whine of the broken wiper struggling over the screen.

They dropped the car off at the rental company and then sprinted the distance to the entry hall of the small airport. There were no covers over any of the walkways so by the time they made it to the check-in desk, they were both soaked. Water dripped from her ponytail. Her clothes were soaked through and plastered to her. She needed to go wring them out before she got on the plane.

"Do you want to go try to dry off and I'll see about getting us checked in?" Jamison offered.

"Yeah, thanks. Apparently, some physicist worked out that you actually get more wet running in the rain than you would if you just walked normally."

"Girl, you know more random stuff than anyone I know." When he smiled at her his gaze dropped lower to the thin material of her blouse. The glance was quick, over as soon as it began, almost like it hadn't happened.

She looked away. She didn't want him to look at her like that. And she didn't want to want him to look at her like that. That was not who they were.

She needed some space.

Jess made her way to the bathroom. She looked at her reflection in the floor-to-ceiling mirror next to the hand dryer. Her mascara had run down her face in watery black lines and her hair looked like it had not been brushed in a few days. The water weighed down her tight curls, pulling them low on her back, showing the true length. There were no paper towels so she used toilet paper to dab at the smudges under her eyes.

Jess unbuttoned her blouse and slid it over her shoulders. She wrung out as much excess water as she could before she put her shirt under the hand dryer. It might not actually dry the shirt but at least it would warm it enough to put it back on.

Jess looked like a homeless woman who slept in bus stations and showered in public bathrooms but there wasn't much she could do about that now so she settled for washing her face and drying her shirt. As the hot air of the dryer warmed her skin, realization crept slowly over her, igniting every nerve ending. That wasn't the first time she had seen Jamison look at her that way. Over the years there had been moments when he had held her gaze too long, or his hand brushed hers, or he would touch the small of her back when he held the door open for her. How had she not seen it before? She was a goddamned FBI agent. She read people for a living.

Her mind blanked, not knowing what to do with the new information. She couldn't deal with this now.

For a while she just stood with her back to the wall, watching people file in and out of the bathroom, checking their tickets, shoving souvenirs in already overly full bags. Observing other people provided a blissful moratorium but eventually she had to rejoin her own life.

She found Jamison sitting on a bench near a cinnamon roll kiosk. He was holding a brown paper bag in one hand and two bottles of water in the other.

"I got some good news and some bad news," Jamison said. The moment was gone. He had returned to her cool, no-nonsense partner. She could almost fool herself into thinking she had imagined it. Almost.

"Give it to me," she said. If Jamison could pretend there was nothing going on, so could she. He might be the king of compartmentalization but she was the queen.

"Our flight is cancelled. We can't get one until ten thirty tomorrow morning."

"Seriously?"

"Yep. But the good news is there's an airport hotel at the other side of the parking lot."

"The other side of the parking lot? I didn't see a hotel. Oh, do you mean the one we passed on the way in? That's like a mile away. That is not good news."

"Yeah but we get to test your theory and see if we get less wet walking than we do running."

Jess took one of the bottles of water, unscrewed the lid, and took a long swig. "I've yet to hear any good news, J. You suck at the good news/bad news game."

He held up the brown paper bag. "I got you a turkey and Swiss sub with everything plus jalapeños."

Jess smiled. "Now we're talking. I love jalapeños. They should be considered their own food group on the pyramid chart. You should have led with the sandwich." She took the bag and unwrapped her sandwich. "Didn't you get one?" she said once she had swallowed a mouthful.

"I already had it. You were in there a long time."

"Sorry."

"No worries. I got some quality people-watching in."

"I can eat and walk if you want to get to the hotel," Jess offered.

"No, take your time. We have all night."

Jess's skin heated at the turn of phrase. It was a throwaway comment that meant nothing but there was nowhere else she'd rather be right now.

Her phone vibrated in her pocket. She pulled it out to see if it was a message from Tina but instead it was a message from Matt Ramsay, asking if she wanted to go for drinks. She deleted the message and returned the phone to her suit jacket. Matt had messaged her three times that week to ask her about her day or invite her to dinner. She ignored each of them. She didn't have the time or inclination for a relationship. He was nice enough and she liked having sex with him. If he could just message her that he would like to have sex again, she would probably text back.

She finished eating her sandwich in silence while Jamison read the magazine he'd taken from Nester's office. "Okay I'm ready to brave the elements."

"You want a cinnamon roll or a frozen yogurt? Perhaps a churro? Girl, we are in food-court nirvana. Does not get much better than this."

"No, I'm good. It's getting late. It's probably best we go check in."

CHAPTER TWENTY

The hotel lobby was decorated in burgundy velour, black leather, and polished brass. The décor was more in keeping with a Victorian brothel than an economy airport hotel but it looked clean, which was all Jess cared about.

They looked around the lobby, trying to locate a member of staff to check them in, but it looked like the building was empty. On closer inspection they found the night clerk watching the Texans/Redskins game on a grainy portable TV, hidden behind the high wall of the front counter.

"Can we please get two rooms?" Jamison asked the man seated behind the desk.

"Sorry, what?" The man took off his headphones and jumped up. "Did you want to get a room?" He looked mid-twenties with thick sandy hair. He wore a blue and red jersey that marked him as a Texans fan. Clusters of angry red spots of adolescence still marred his fair skin.

"Yes, two, please," Jamison said.

"Two rooms? I'm not sure we have two. A few flights have been canceled 'cause of the storm." He banged on the keyboard as his voice trailed off. His Adam's apple bobbed up and down just beneath the skin of his thin neck. "Let me see. Hmm… no, not there. Give me a second. We're in the middle of a massive refurbishment. All of the bathtubs are being replaced with walk-in showers." He stroked his fingertip over a whitehead on his chin as he thought.

Jess turned away to look around the lobby. If she was in charge of the makeover she would have started with the foyer that looked like a bordello. The only thing that kept the room from looking like it was transplanted from the Wild West were the two vending machines in the corner.

"I can give you a king-size on the fifth floor."

They waited for him to tell them what else was available, but when he didn't follow up with another room, Jamison asked, "And?"

The man was no longer paying attention to them, his gaze had returned to the game. The Texans were on the fifteen-yard line with possession. He would be focused on the game until the Texans scored or fumbled.

"We'll take it," Jess blurted. They were adults; they could share a room. There was bound to be a sofa she could sleep on. It would only be weird if they made it weird. She took out her credit card and laid it on the counter.

Without taking his eyes off the television screen, he ran her credit card and handed her the receipt and room key. "Elevators are at the end of the hall. Swimming pool is closed because—"

"Let me guess, the refurbishment," Jamison said.

He didn't respond. He was too busy wincing and clenching his fists above his head. The Texans quarterback had just been sacked. The stadium erupted, Redskins' fans screaming and jumping up and down.

Jess sighed. "Ooh, that's going to hurt. They finally get a decent quarterback and they leave him wide open. Right there is why they will never make it past the playoffs."

The man frowned but didn't say anything because she was right.

She followed Jamison down the hall and into the elevator. From waist-level up, the back wall was mirrored. Jess grimaced when she caught a glimpse of her reflection. Even after cleaning up she still looked like she had been dragged backwards through a hedge. Her hair had dried into tight matted curls. She took out the packet of antibacterial wipes she carried in her pocket and wiped down the buttons before she pushed the number five. "The ground floor button is the dirtiest because everyone who leaves pushes it. Not that the other buttons are clean, just less dirty."

Jamison smiled. "Girl, the things you know. You could provide the interesting facts on the GPS program you and Chan were going on about."

"Shoshone? It's a good app. Have you downloaded it?"

"Yeah. It seemed a bit glitchy, but I like the trivia. It was cool. It was like having you beside me."

Jess's cheeks warmed. Every clipped beat of her heart pushed blood higher to the surface, until her cheeks burned. She kept her focus on the panel of buttons until the elevator stopped and the doors slid open.

"Um… I think our room is this way." Jess indicated down the hall.

Jamison followed through the corridor. She slid the card into the door and waited for the light to flash green.

The room was tastefully decorated in shades of beige. The floors and doors were walnut and above the bed hung an obligatory non-descript modern-art painting. It may have been a skyline or a sunset; it was hard to discern shapes under the thick layers of acrylic paint.

"Our lucky day—the bathtub has been replaced so looks like we got ourselves a refurbished room," Jamison said.

There were white paint splashes along the edge of the door. "Yeah, it looks fresh enough." Jess put her bag on the desk. In the mirror she caught a glimpse of Jamison looking at her. She snapped her head up so their gaze would not meet.

"There really is only one bed."

Jess turned to face him. "Um… should we call downstairs and ask if they have a rollaway or something?"

Jamison shook his head. "They won't have anything. I'll take the chair if you're bothered." He gestured to the upholstered tub chair in the corner.

The chair was more ornamental than functional. Even Jess, who was half of Jamison's size, would struggle to get comfortable in it. "No, it's fine," she said a bit too eagerly. "It's late. Let's just get some sleep. I'm going to take a shower and go to bed. Unless you want to have the first shower?"

"Nah, I'll shower in the morning, thanks."

Jess slipped off her shoes and headed for the bathroom. Her toe caught in the groove of the wood-effect floor tiles. They looked and felt like real walnut. Complementary stone-effect tiles lined the walls from floor to ceiling and a granite worktop with a bowl sink spanned the wall of the niche opposite the toilet. Out of habit she locked the door before she turned on the shower. She had lived alone her entire adult life but she always locked the door on the bathroom and bedroom even when no one was in the house.

She stripped off and folded her clothes before laying them on the worktop. She was going to have to wear them tomorrow so she didn't want them too wrinkled for the flight home.

There were five jets embedded into the tiles in addition to the square showerhead above her. She sighed when she stepped into the shower. A powerful stream ricocheted off the tender flesh between her shoulder blades and her neck. Her body coiled and burned as the pressure battered the knot in her trapezius muscles. Some days she really did feel like she carried the weight of the world on her shoulders. She knew from experience if she didn't release the tension she would wake up with a migraine. Her eyes watered from the pain as the hot water pulverized her skin but she forced herself to stand under the unrelenting torrent until the throbbing sting dulled to an ache as the knot loosened.

Long after she had washed and rinsed her hair, she stood under the water. The glass screen on the shower clouded over and tear-shaped drops beaded the mirror in thick condensation but Jess didn't move. There was still too much to wash away. This case was getting to her, which didn't make sense because she had dealt with worse. Maybe it was Nester recognizing her, or the similarities she kept seeing that weren't really there, or maybe because she wasn't sleeping properly anymore. More often than not, she woke up, shaking, drenched in sweat, nightmares and memories still playing. There was no going back to sleep after that. She pushed the vision away. She didn't want that in her head before she went to sleep.

She tried to think about something else but the only thing that came to mind were the autopsy photos from this case, so she thought about every detail. The macabre pictures were preferable to the tangents her mind could create. She stood in the water until her skin wrinkled.

Turning off the water, she wrapped a towel around her head to dry her hair and then pulled the terrycloth hotel robe off the wooden hanger. The crown logo was emblazoned on the breast pocket in gold thread.

She unlocked the bathroom door. The room was black, only a sliver of watery light peeked from under the door. Everywhere else was engulfed in darkness. She considered turning on the light but the even cadence of Jamison's breath told her he was asleep. Sliding into bed next to him would be considerably less awkward if he stayed asleep.

"Ah shit." Jess winced as her shin collided with the side of the desk. She gave her battered leg a rub and then tentatively shuffled the rest of the way, never lifting her feet, so she wouldn't run into anything else. Once she reached the edge of the bed she stood for a long moment. Even in the darkness she could tell Jamison was lying on the side of the bed closest to the window.

She held her breath like she was about to dive into a pool and gently eased down the cover so she would not wake him. The bed sank under her as she sat. She pulled the sides of the robe closer. Thank God for the small mercy of the coarse, waffle-print fabric.

Only when her head hit the pillow did she exhale the breath she had been holding. Slowly she turned her head to face Jamison even though she couldn't see anything. His breath was strong and steady, like him.

She closed her eyes and willed herself to sleep. Her head ached from forcing back memories. She was going crazy. She needed this case to be over. At every turn she was faced with reminders of her past. She thought she had kept it all bottled up so well but she was kidding herself. He was everywhere, in every decision she made, every suspect she interviewed, every case she solved. She could not think about these victims without seeing his.

CHAPTER TWENTY-ONE

Goosebumps rose on her arms. It was so cold. The first snow of the season would be here soon and then she could make snow angels with her daddy and then drink hot cocoa. He always gave her the pink marshmallows. He picked them out of the pack, especially for her. She pulled down on the sleeves of her sweater. There was a hole near the cuff on the left side. Her mommy would be so mad. That was why she always rolled up the sleeves before she went to school. She would have to roll them up again before her mommy saw it. Her mommy was always crying or in bed with one of her headaches.

The stair creaked under her. Daddy told her never to come down into his shop. It was dangerous, he said. She could hurt herself with one of his saws. "And that would make me sad, princess. I never want anything bad to happen to you because you, my princess, are the one perfect thing I have done." He would always say that and then kiss her on the top of her head in the exact spot she would have worn a crown if she really were a princess.

She shouldn't be down here. She knew to wait upstairs and draw pictures and listen to the radio while she waited for daddy to finish his work in the basement but the fire had gone out and it was cold. She wasn't allowed to play with matches. Mommy would smack her face if she did. She needed daddy to start the fire again.

The high-pitched whine of the saw blared. It got louder with every step until by the bottom she had to rub her ears because they were sore.

"Daddy!" she shouted over the saw. "Daddy!" But he couldn't hear her because he was wearing earmuffs. His arms were stretched high above his head, the blades spinning so fast it looked like a blurry haze.

He leaned over and then she saw it, his work, but it wasn't really work; it was a little boy.

His small, crumpled body was naked on the concrete floor. His eyes were closed like he was sleeping but there was a pool of black red blood oozing from the back of him. Where was he hurt? There were no cuts. She needed to go get the Band-Aids.

"Daddy?" her voice cracked.

This time he heard her. Slowly the blade stopped and he turned to face her. The pain and shame in his eyes scared her.

"Daddy, what's wrong with him?" She started to cry. Hot tears rolled down her face faster than she could wipe them away. He fell to his knees in front of her like he was praying.

"Oh, princess," he wept.

"Don't cry, Daddy. Don't cry."

"I'm sorry. I'm so sorry." He lay at her feet and wept, his body convulsing as violent sobs tore through him.

"It's okay," she said over and over rubbing his back. She could barely see him through her own tears.

"It was an accident," he gulped. "But they won't believe me. You know it was an accident. You know, princess. You know I would never hurt anyone. Say you know."

"I know, Daddy," she cried as they held each other.

CHAPTER TWENTY-TWO

"Jessie, wake up! Jessie, come on. It's okay. You're safe. I got you."

"I knew." Her voice broke. She shivered. Her robe stuck to her, drenched through with sweat that had long since turned cold. The icy material clung to her, stopping her from escaping its frigid embrace. She wrapped her arms around herself trying to get warm but she couldn't stop shaking. "I knew. I always knew but I lied to protect him." Her voice was hoarse and her throat ached from screaming. Her body shook as memories tore through her. "Why? Why do I still love him?" Her cheek was pressed against his chest. His heart pounded with the same frantic cadence of hers.

"Shh, it's okay. Let it out. It was just a nightmare. I got you."

Jamison's arms tightened around her. He rubbed her back, holding her. Warmth from his body slowly spread to hers. "I got you," he repeated over and over. "Do you want to tell me what it was about?" he asked, his voice a whisper, nothing demanding or threatening, just a simple question. His chest was slick from her sweat.

"Sorry. I got you wet."

"It's all good." Jamison pulled just far enough to turn on the lamp beside the bed.

Jess squinted as her eyes fought to adjust to the sudden onslaught of light.

"What was the dream about, Jessie?"

Jess pulled away, suddenly aware of how close Jamison was. She didn't want him in any way tarnished by the ugliness of her past. This was the part of her history that shamed her. She could remove herself from what her father did but not the lies she had told to protect him. She had never admitted it to anyone, not her mom or the army of social workers and psychologists that paraded through her life and certainly not the law enforcement officials and lawyers that had interviewed her. Lindsay didn't know, nor did Jamison.

For so long this was her burden to bear alone. She had created a narrative where she had no idea what was happening with her dad until he was ripped out of her life. But she was in good company; her mom had piggybacked on her lie. Jess had no doubt her mom knew something. Her dad had raped, murdered, and decapitated thirteen boys in their house. She must have known but it was better to be another victim rather than an accomplice after the fact. "I don't want to talk about it."

"I know and that's why you probably should."

Jess was quiet for a long time. Deep down she knew Jamison was right; she should speak to someone. So many times she had considered telling Lindsay but every time she stopped herself because she didn't want to dive deep into her psyche and analyze it. Jess was scared Lindsay would see exactly how fucked up she really was. The best-case scenario, she would lose a friend; the worst, she would lose her career.

She took a deep breath. "It's the same dream every time. They started just after you left."

Jamison flinched, his entire body tensed.

"No, it's not like that. It's not because you left. I'm not blaming you." Jess sat up. She didn't know where to start. "You know how I quit my PhD program? I think I told you I stopped because I was busy or I can't even remember what excuse I gave you. I tell different people different things. They're all lies. I stopped because of the nightmares. During the day I can control what I think about but at night my subconscious screws me over hard."

"You started having nightmares because of the men you were interviewing. The sex offenders?"

"Pedophiles. Yes." Jess pulled the sides of her robe together. "Yeah, that's where it started but it's not really about that, not really. Do you remember reading about the Mathew Sims case?"

Jamison's eyes narrowed as he considered the question. "Yeah, I think so. He's the principal who raped boys from his boarding school. He killed one of them too, didn't he? The crime scene was staged to look like a break-in so at first everyone thought the perpetrator was someone from outside?"

Jess nodded. "Yeah that's him. He's on death row in Texas. His school and his wife stood behind him until he was convicted. No one could believe he did it. All the character reports from his friends and colleagues said he was a nice guy, the last person you would suspect."

"Were you dreaming about him? About his crimes?"

"No." If only it were that simple. "I was dreaming about something else... but to understand, you need to know the reason I interviewed him was because he reminds me of my dad; a nice guy who was actually a horrible man." She put the tip of her finger into her mouth, ready to bite it, but Jamison stopped her. He pulled her hand down so it rested in his. Her hand looked pale and frail against his dark skin. Jess was silent for a long time. She wasn't sure if she could bring herself to tell him the rest.

"Jessie, come on, talk to me."

Jess shook as she tried to contain an assault of memories. "I was dreaming about my dad. I dream about him most nights... about something I saw."

"Oh Jessie, I'm so sorry. I didn't know you witnessed anything."

"Yeah, I did. I did see something. Nobody knows though. I never told anybody. All the times I was interviewed as a kid, I always said the same thing, that I saw nothing and knew nothing."

It wasn't even hard to remember the lies because she told them so often.

"But you did see something," Jamison said.

"Yeah. I think I was six, maybe seven. I've pieced it together based on where we were living at the time to figure out it must have been the tenth victim. There were three more after." Just saying the words aloud shamed her. There were three boys who would be alive today if she had told someone, anyone, what she had seen. The secret was like a vice wrapped around her, squeezing. She was going to go crazy under the pressure. "I went into the basement and I saw my dad above his body. I knew... I knew something was wrong but when he said there had been an accident and he asked me not to say anything, I didn't. I never did. If I had told someone, I could have saved the others."

He reached for her. "Oh God, Jessie. No. You can't think like that. You were a child. You bear no responsibility for anything he did. Of course you didn't tell anyone. You were a scared little girl. It's not your fault. You got to let this one go." When he spoke, his lips brushed her forehead. The soft caress of his mouth made her skin burn. "You did nothing wrong. Never let anyone, including yourself, question that."

She hadn't told him the most shameful part. She didn't want to but she couldn't carry it alone any longer. Even if he hated her for it she had to get it out.

"I loved him so much, Jamison. I still do. I miss my dad." She closed her eyes because she could not bear to see his reaction. She shouldn't still love her dad but she did. He was not a sadistic killer to her; he was her daddy: the man who taught her to ride a bike and carried her on his shoulders. He had never hurt her and he never would. He made her feel safe and loved. She couldn't admit that to anyone. For over twenty years she had had to fake apathy. She figured out quite quickly what emotions were acceptable and she emulated those, but deep inside she still loved him.

"Of course you do. He's your dad. You're a good woman, Jessie, and you're a damn fine agent."

His assurance was too much. Rather than make her feel better, it unleashed more emotion, darker and scarier. It felt like a dam straining, about to break.

She couldn't let that happen. She would drown in it. She needed to be numb.

Only one thing could do that.

Voices in her head screamed at her to stop, told her not to go there, not with Jamison. But the need to be numb was stronger. It muted the voices. All she could hear was her frantic pulse. Each frenzied beat pushed her further, drowned out all reason. He would make her feel better. If only for a few minutes, the memories would stop. Her mind spun, craving the oblivion. She needed the blackout that only sex could bring.

She could not stop herself to think. She needed him, needed this. She pulled his head down until his lips brushed hers. For a fraction of a second he paused but then his mouth captured hers. Her lips parted for him. Frenetic energy surged in her. There was no conscious thought. Her body knew what to do. His hands were on her, everywhere, firm and skilled. He pushed her against the bed and deepened the kiss. Desire and urgency propelled them. With frantic need she pulled him closer, needing more.

From somewhere in the haze she recognized the distant ringing of a phone. She pushed the thought away, it had no place in her reality. Finally, the ringing stopped only to start again.

"Fuck," Jamison said, sitting bolt upright. "I can't do this."

Jess blinked. Her robe had fallen open, leaving her breasts exposed, not that Jamison was looking at her. His face was in his hands. She reached out to touch his arm but she stopped herself.

Jamison stood up. His boxers, the only thing he was wearing, were slung low on his hips. The deep ridges of his oblique muscles formed a pronounced V shape above the elastic band. His erection strained against the thin blue material of his boxers. He held out his hand to stop her from trying to speak. "I'm married, Jessie."

Jess swallowed past the lump in her throat. "I know."

"I'm married," he said again. "I can't do this. I can't be the person that makes you feel good for a few minutes."

"Because you love her?" Jess whispered. She took a deep breath and braced herself for the answer.

"It can't be me. You just want someone, anyone to make you feel good. I've seen it before. I've known you for a very long time. I know how you work. You don't care who it is, you just want somebody to screw. I can't be that guy for you."

Jess winced at the harsh words. The truth of the sentiment slashed her. She tried to object to the portrayal but Jamison was right. That was who she was. She had never tried to pretend she was anyone she wasn't. Sex for her had always been about getting numb. "Yeah that's who I am. At least I'm honest about it. Now your turn to be honest. Do you love her?" He hadn't answered, and the detective in her needed to be appeased.

Jamison pulled on his trousers, fastening the button but not bothering with the zip before he put on his shirt and his shoes. "I got to go. I need to get out of here."

"There aren't any other rooms."

"I can't be here right now. I'm going back to the airport. I can't do this."

Don't go. The words stuck in her throat. She would never shame herself by saying them out loud. She wouldn't beg him to stay, not again. She had done it before and he had left then too.

CHAPTER TWENTY-THREE

Washington, DC

Jess straightened her suit jacket. She had gone home to get changed before coming all the way back into the city. For most people, four o'clock would mean the workday was almost over, but normal business hours didn't apply during an active investigation.

There was nothing she couldn't do from home, but Jeanie had called and texted to say she wanted to speak to her about something in person. Jeanie refused to give any specifics but her clipped tone and the urgency in her voice told Jess that it was unlikely to be a pleasant conversation. It was about her father. It had to be. Jeanie must have figured out the similarities between this case and her father's crimes, or Jamison had told her that Nester knew she was Jessica Randal.

She spent the entire flight considering what Jeanie was going to say, going through every permutation of what it might be. At least worrying about what Jeanie had to say kept her from worrying about the fact she had made a complete ass out of herself with Jamison. She knew she had to apologize to him but he hadn't been at the airport that morning. She had expected and dreaded seeing him at the gate but he wasn't there. He had not made their flight home.

His office door was closed. She hesitated a second before she knocked because she didn't know what to say to him. An apology was probably the best place to start, just rip off the Band-Aid and clear the air so they could get back to some semblance of normality. She had crossed a line and it wasn't okay. Sex was how she coped with the ugliness of her life but she knew better than to let that part of her anywhere near her professional life. She had messed up and she needed to hold up her hand and admit it. Thank God Jeanie's call had stopped them before Jess could properly fuck up the one healthy relationship she had with a man.

"He's not here," Tina said.

Jess looked up. "Oh… I… uh… um… do you know where he is?"

She shook her head. As usual Tina looked effortlessly beautiful. She was one of those women who could pull on something from the bottom of a dirty hamper and look like she was ready for a red-carpet premiere. Her purple wrap dress intensified her hazel eyes, almost made them glow. "I thought you might. He called this morning to say he was taking a few personal days. Apparently there was some sort of family emergency and he had to leave town."

"Oh. Did he happen to say why?"

"No. You guys need to work on communication." Tina smiled.

Jess sighed. If only she knew the half of it. "Oh okay. I'm going to try to catch Chan and Milligan before they head home. I want to see where they are on their end."

"Seriously, this team really is the worst for communication. I think I'm going to set up a planner on your phones so you can keep track of each other. Chan and Milligan are away in Louisiana to—" Tina stopped herself mid-sentence. Her mouth dropped to form a perfect O. Her glance darted from Jess to Jeannie's office and back again before she settled on the seam in the carpet tiles.

"What? What are they doing in Louisiana?"

"Have you spoken to Jeanie?"

"No, I just got in. What's going on?" She hoped that by feigning ignorance Tina would give her a clue about what was going on. Jess needed to know what, if anything, Tina knew about her past.

"Yeah maybe you should speak to Jeanie. I think she is in a meeting right now but um… yeah, she'll be out soon I think. Maybe."

"What's going on? Is this about the case? Why do I need to speak to Jeanie?" she pressed, searching Tina's face for clues.

Tina shifted her slight weight from one foot to the other. "I don't want to overstep. I like this team. I don't know if it's confidential. Jeanie just said to leave it with her."

The hairs on Jess's arms rose. Her eyes narrowed. "If it was confidential, Jeanie would have told you that. Now what's up?" Her voice was terser than she would have liked.

Tina's lips pursed like she was considering if she should say anything.

"Do you have information on my case? Did you find something on Hannah's phone? What is it?" It took all the energy she possessed to not shout.

Tina's expression looked pained, like she was trying to decide if she would rather have her eyes burned out with acid or a blowtorch. "You didn't hear this from me, okay?"

"Yeah sure."

"No really. I like this job. I don't want to go back to white collar."

"Okay. I won't say anything."

"Do you promise?"

Jess pushed down the scream that formed in her belly. "Yeah. Yes, I promise."

"Yesterday you asked me to look for people who have purchased embalming fluids and mortuary equipment." Tina stopped to look down the hall. There was no one in earshot but she still looked around to make sure.

"Yeah, and?" Jess demanded, unable to contain her growing exasperation. "Did you get a hit?"

"Yes."

Jess sighed. "Well, who is it? Is it someone we have interviewed?"

"Um… yeah, that's what Jeanie needs to speak to you about."

"Just tell me."

"Okay, but you can't tell Jeanie I told you. There is a storage unit and a PO box just outside Baton Rouge. That's where the equipment was sent. Not just mortuary equipment, there were surgical saws and scalpels and a whole lot of stuff that looks like it belongs in torture porn."

That's it? Relief washed over her. Maybe Tina thought Jess would be embarrassed because they had had a potential suspect in Baton Rouge, Mike Snowberger, but they had essentially ruled him out when Joel Nester became a person of interest. A lot of times the assailant turned out to be somebody they met early on in an investigation and dismissed as a possibility. It sucked but it was the nature of the game; they got it wrong a lot more than they got it right. Luckily they only had to be right once per case.

"In Baton Rouge? Okay we need to have a closer look at Mike Snowberger. He isn't far from there. Can you check his records? See if he has an alibi for the time Hannah Henderson went missing. He doesn't have an alibi for Liddy and we know they had a connection. And we can connect him to the Shenandoah Valley. Let's bring him in, see what he has to say for himself." Jess could only really get a read off him in person.

Tina swallowed hard; her throat bobbed up and down in a pronounced movement. "Yeah, of course. I'll look into him again but there's something else you need to know. The credit card for the storage unit and all the equipment are all registered to… um… you."

Jess's heart stopped with a painful thud. For a moment everything in her body paused, her breathing, her pulse. Every synapse failed to fire and then just as quickly they began again, playing catch-up. Her heart vibrated with a pace just shy of atrial fibrillation. "What?"

"That's what Jeanie needs to speak to you about."

"To me?" She shook her head. *How is that even possible?* "Like to a Mr. Bishop? Or a J Bishop?" Her last name wasn't especially unique. Later she would calculate the probability of having the same surname as an assailant, much later, when he was behind bars and she was sleeping properly again.

"The credit card is registered to Jessica Elizabeth Bishop of the District of Columbia, born December seventeenth. Mother's maiden name is Ralph. First pet was Waldo. Kindergarten teacher was Mrs. Emerson."

Her mind spun. "What the actual fuck?" She held on to the wall for support. "How?" she whispered. "How could he know the answers to my security questions?" Someone really was fucking with her. She didn't even remember her actual Kindergarten teacher. She picked those names for answers to security questions because they were made up. No one could research them. Her favorite coffee cup, which she had had since she was a freshman in college, had a picture of a sunset below a Ralph Waldo Emerson quote. Her passwords were a nod to the writer, and to coffee, mostly to coffee.

"Chan and Milligan are there now. They're looking through surveillance videos to see if they can see anything. Forensics are there too now, dusting for prints. There's a lot of blood there. And a cage with shackles. It's definitely looking like our crime scene."

"Shit." A realization hit her. "I need to change my passwords." If this guy had the answers to her security questions, who knew what else he had access to.

"Yeah, and I'm going to do some diagnostics to see if anyone has tried to access classified information under your name."

Her gut clenched in an icy spasm. "It's someone close to the case. There hasn't been media coverage yet. I haven't done any press conferences. My name and face aren't out there associated with this." There was always a possibility with high-profile cases that media coverage would attract unwanted attention for the family and for the law enforcement involved but this case wasn't at that level. No doubt it would be once they connected all the dots and caught the guy, but for the moment they were all still flying blissfully below the radar.

The hairs on her arms stood on end. "I think it's someone in law enforcement. We thought it was someone impersonating an officer because of the unmarked car with the police lights but it is just as likely it is an actual officer. Shit, we need to look at the officers we've liaised with."

"All the files have time stamps. I can see when everyone looks at them."

"Who? Who is looking at them?"

"Just the team." Tina hesitated for a moment. "But you're accessing them four times as often as anyone else."

Jess's eyes widened. "I mean, I like to read over the files. Everyone knows I do that. I read over interviews. Sometimes I don't catch things the first time. I'm more of a visual processor. It helps to see it written down." Shit. She was defending herself. She shouldn't have to explain that she was doing her job.

Tina's expression was tight; there was something behind the faint smile but Jess couldn't read it. "Last night they were accessed remotely. It was your login but it bounced off a proxy server."

Jess's heart sank. Disbelief: that was the emotion Tina was trying to hide. She thought Jess was lying or at least hiding something. "No, that isn't possible. Jamison and I were in Alabama but I would never use an unauthorized or unsecure device. We interviewed Nester and then—" She stopped herself from saying what happened next, sharing a hotel, a bed with Jamison. "I

emailed you and Jeanie from my phone but nothing classified. I
didn't access any files. Not last night. And I certainly have never
used a proxy server to access my own files." Jess pulled her phone
from her pocket and thrust it at Tina. "Look at it. You want my
laptop too? Check it." Jess opened her bag.

"I wasn't asked to confiscate your phone."

"Take it and check it." Jess would spare herself the indignity
of official procedure. She had nothing to hide.

"No. I don't need to look at them."

Jess refused to put the phone back in her pocket. She would
clear this up once and for all. "Obviously, I have an alibi for
Lydia and Hannah. I was here. You can't get a firmer alibi than
a room full of FBI agents. If we ever ID the other victims, I'm
sure I'll have an alibi for those murders too. As for the storage
unit, you obviously have my prints on file. Check them against
any you find there."

"Put your phone away. No one thinks you have anything to do
with this. The storage unit was rented over a year ago. We need
to figure out who set this up and why he targeted you."

Jess took in a sharp breath. "We didn't even get this case until
two months ago. How is that even possible? There was no way of
knowing I would be assigned this case. None of this makes sense."
A blinding pain shot between her eyes. Jess pinched the bridge
of her nose. Fuck, what was happening? Her head pounded with
each frantic beat of her heart. The room spun, the walls inched
in. She was having another panic attack. She was losing control.
It needed to stop. Now. "Sorry, I can't talk right now. I need—"
Jess didn't finish the sentence.

She was going to be sick. She ran down the hall to her office.
She threw open the windows. Unfortunately, for safety reasons
the panel only opened a measly six inches. She sucked in frantic
breaths. The grass had just been cut. The fresh scent hit her but
rather than quell the nausea, it added to it. Shit, she really was

going to throw up. She hadn't been sick in years and now she was about to vomit all over her office. She frantically rubbed at her temples. The pain was causing the queasiness. If she could get on top of that, she would be okay.

No, she wouldn't. She wouldn't be okay until she caught this son of a bitch and figured out how to take her life back. She needed help. She hated to admit that to herself. It felt weak to admit she couldn't handle this on her own. She was strong and she was persistent. She had to be. That is all she had going for her. Her resilience was all she really had.

Jess opened her top drawer and took out a bottle of ibuprofen. She swallowed two without water and then smoothed her hair back, tucking in the stray curl that had escaped the rubber band. She walked down the hall to Lindsay's office.

The door was open. She always left it open if she wasn't in a meeting as a way to encourage agents to stop by and chat, to make speaking to her seem informal and friendly rather than what it really was: an evaluation of the agent's mental health and capacity to safely perform their job. The walls of her office were painted in a soothing mushroom color that straddled the line between gray and beige. All the other offices were painted in standard, government-issued white but Lindsay had come in one Saturday and redecorated her office. She hadn't asked permission and no one questioned it. Most people were scared of Lindsay, some because she was intimidating but the majority were just straight-up uncomfortable with mental health professionals. People assumed every conversation with her was an evaluation. In a lot of ways Lindsay was isolated because people were reticent to speak to her but that was precisely why Jess liked her, or at least why they had found each other. They were both outliers in their own way.

"Hey, Lindsay, you got a minute?"

Lindsay looked up from her desk. "Hey, stranger, I was looking for you this morning. Come on in and shut the door."

Jess went in and sat down on the sofa across from her. She picked up a gray satin cushion. Metallic sequins were sewn into the delicate material. When Lindsay started, the furniture in her office was the same metal and navy blue burlap used in the conference rooms. It was functional but cold and uncomfortable so she had immediately gotten rid of it and had it replaced with a soft leather couch and a coordinating wingback chair. By the time Lindsay added the window treatment, her office looked more like a living room than an office and somehow she had managed to get the bureau to foot the bill; meanwhile Jess was still waiting on the payment for the charger she'd invoiced.

"So, what's up? I feel like I haven't seen you in ages. You missed quiz night last Thursday. The team needed you," Lindsay said. By "team" she meant the two of them and whatever guy Lindsay was dating at the time. Currently the guy was an accountant from Virginia. They really didn't need Jess's help. Lindsay had an eidetic memory. Jess was only on the team because Lindsay insisted on forcing her out of the house once a week for socialization. Jess was the shy puppy the owner kept dragging to the park hoping it would eventually learn to play with other dogs. She hadn't yet, but God bless her, Lindsay kept trying.

"Did you win?"

Lindsay made an are-you-kidding-me face. "Of course, but we would have won by more had you been there. It's not really winning without total annihilation, we both know that."

Jess managed a smile. To the rest of the bureau Lindsay presented as the consummate professional. She radiated quiet confidence and empathy. But the other side of her, the one that Jess got to see, was cutthroat competitive. She would shove a granny into a ditch to win.

"So, what do you want to talk about? You being in love with Jamison maybe? I don't know, I'm just throwing out ideas."

Pain seared her temples when she tried to shake her head. "I'm not in love with anyone."

"You know therapists have a name for this. It's called denial. We could work through this. First step is admitting it."

"You're not my therapist. You're my friend. Possibly the only one I don't want to sleep with," Jess admitted, squeezing the pillow on her lap closer. Her wrist nipped where the rough edge of the sequin scratched below her cuff.

Lindsay's eyes widened. "I knew it!" she shrieked in victory. "I told you you were into Jamison."

"I'm not into Jamison. You said it yourself, I sleep with a lot of men. It doesn't mean anything. Attraction means nothing. Sex means nothing."

Lindsay stared at her, her face completely impassive.

"Don't try that on me," Jess scoffed. "Now is when you will leave a pregnant pause to create a vacuum so I start spewing my innermost thoughts. But that only works on people who are uncomfortable with silence."

"Normal people, you mean." Lindsay smiled.

"Yes, those ones."

"Remember the first time we went to lunch? I'm still impressed that you were able to sit across from me in silence for nineteen minutes without saying a single word. You just ate your Caesar salad, no awkwardness, no looking around the restaurant. That's when I knew we were going to be best friends. At that moment I knew you were either more secure in yourself than anyone I had ever met or you were very much on the autistic spectrum. Either way, I was in."

A smile tugged on the side of Jess's mouth. "No, I had just figured out what you were doing and I wasn't going to cave. And by the way, I was totally uncomfortable."

"See, that's why I like you. You're smart and iron-willed. The world needs more women like that. Jamison needs a woman like that."

It hurt when Jess rolled her eyes. "Are you for real bringing this back to Jamison? You do realize that you totally fail the Bechdel test."

"Screw the Bechdel test. I was with her when she said that writers should include more female characters. But then she lost me when she specified that for those women to be valid they have to do more than discus male characters. How dare anyone say that interpersonal skills and friendship aren't as important as other contributions? A woman helping another woman navigate any aspect of her life is a positive thing. She claims to be a feminist but then cheapens the importance of female friendship. Women kick ass at emotional intelligence—don't be devaluing our contributions, especially on things where we outperform men." The color in Lindsay's cheeks deepened as she spoke. Jess half expected her to start wagging her finger. Few things got Lindsay as fired up as equality.

Jess's vision blurred as the pain from her temples radiated. When would the damn painkillers kick in? She couldn't think with the pounding. "Agreed. But sometimes there are... um... you know, bigger problems than men, and women should be discussing those too." How she wished her feelings for Jamison were her biggest problem. That bullshit paled in comparison to her crumbling sanity and the pressure to find a serial killer who she quite possibly knew or had at least met. She had worked with a lot of police officers over the years and had no doubt pissed off a fair few with her curt nature and militant adherence to rules. There was no way to quickly compile a shortlist of potential suspects. She would have to go through all her old cases.

Lindsay leaned forward in her chair. A slight frown pulled down on the corners of her mouth. "I'm sorry. I totally missed that you were being allegorical. There is something you want to talk about." Her tone changed, softened, as did her body language. "Tell me."

Her voice was so soft, she sounded nothing like her bombastic best friend. She had only heard Lindsay like this once before. They had taken a wrong turn and ended up in Brentwood. There had been a woman on a street corner. She was pulling chunks of her own skin off with her bare hands, huge bloody wounds covered her. The poor woman had been in a full psychotic episode and was convinced the Russian government had had her microchipped. Lindsay talked her down enough to give paramedics time to arrive and dose the woman with enough tranquilizers to topple an elephant. Lindsay cooed platitudes, telling the woman she was safe and they would find out what was happening and help her. She never once challenged the delusions; she just listened and made the woman feel safe. She had been amazing. No doubt she would be amazing again now if Jess opened up to her. Lindsay would help her no matter what she disclosed about her childhood. Jess could tell her everything she had seen as a child and how it still affected her today. She would help her work through it.

But their relationship would change.

It would be the professional Lindsay she saw in the hallway. Jess would get to hear her sweet, soft therapeutic voice, not her unbridled cackle. Jess couldn't bear that, to lose her friend, to have Lindsay look at her with compassion and pity. She needed her friend.

Jess stood up. She winced at the pain from the sudden movement. An invisible vice had been fastened to her head, and every time she moved it tightened. "No, I'm fine. I... I... uh just wanted to apologize for missing quiz night. I'll be there next week hopefully. I don't know. There's a lot going on right now. I mean with this case. So, let's just play it by ear."

"Jessica—"

"Look, I got to go. I'll catch you later," Jess interrupted her before she could say anything else. It had been stupid to come here. That was not the relationship she had with Lindsay. She couldn't go there, not with her. No more feelings. She couldn't handle them today.

She needed to get numb.

CHAPTER TWENTY-FOUR

Matt Ramsay smiled when he opened the door. His blond hair was damp like he had just had a shower. It was slightly tussled as if he had used his fingers rather than a comb to brush it to the side. He was wearing a red "kiss the chef" apron over a white T-shirt and jeans.

His house was immaculate, not just tidy with everything in its place but military clean. Even the polish on the walnut floors glistened.

The smell of garlic and thyme permeated the hall. Jess glanced past him to the open door of the dining room. The table had been set with crystal wine glasses. Candlelight gave the room a soft glow. "Shit. You're busy." Her cheeks burned as embarrassment settled in. Matt had dinner plans with someone else. She thought she had been clear when she had texted:

I'm free from seven.

Matt had replied:

cool.

In her mind that meant they were good to go. They were hardly elaborate plans but as far as hookups went it seemed concrete.

"Sorry. I'll go." Jess took a step back, if she was quick she could catch her taxi driver before he pulled away, but Matt caught her arm and prevented her from moving.

His eyes narrowed in confusion. "What are you talking about?"

"Sorry. You have plans. I misunderstood. Look, I'm sorry."

"Please stop apologizing." Matt's hand was still locked around her wrist. "Yeah I have dinner plans with a hot agent who I have been asking out for a while. I finally wore her down."

"Oh… cool. Have a good time. I guess… I'll see you around." She tried again to pull away but he wouldn't let her. She should have asked the taxi driver to take her to a bar. Anonymous sex was easier with actual strangers.

Matt's smile deepened. "Seriously? You think I have a date planned with another woman. Wow. I'm not sure if that is more of an indictment of your character or mine."

Jess stared at him blankly.

"It's you. You're my hot date, Jess. You said you were free tonight from seven. I made dinner. Coq au vin. I didn't know what you liked but you ordered Cabernet once so I figured chicken in red wine was a safe bet."

Jess looked again at the candlelit dining room. In the center of the table there was a glass vase filled with peach roses. They were tied with a satin ribbon the same shade as the blossoms. She swallowed hard against the lump in her throat. The pain in her head turned to hot pressure behind her eyes as her frustration mounted. That's not what she wanted tonight; not what she needed. "I think you have the wrong idea. I'm not that woman."

"I don't even know what that means."

"Can I have my hand back?"

Matt's eyes widened when he glanced down and found he was still holding Jess by the wrist. "Christ, I'm not very smooth at this dating thing either. Promise to not run when I let you go?" It was a rhetorical question because he released her before he had finished speaking.

Jess winced at the word dating. She tried to swallow again but her mouth was too dry. "Look, Matt. I don't need any of this.

We don't need to pretend. I know other women need this." She gestured to the dining room. "But for me this is about sex. I like having sex with you and I think you like having sex with me."

Half of his mouth crept up in a lazy smile. "Um, yeah I like having sex with you."

"Then say that in your texts. Say you want to have sex with me and ask to arrange a time. Let's not pretend we're dating or that you give a shit about my day."

"How was your day?" Matt asked.

"What?"

"Your day. How was it? I want to know. I give a shit about your day. I have given a shit since we first met. I think I have made that clear."

Jess rubbed at her left temple. The searing pain had eased to a dull ache. She just wanted to have sex and forget about everything.

"Do you have a headache? I have Excedrin in the bathroom."

"No, I'm fine. Thanks." She looked around again—the flowers, wine glasses, candles, it was too much. The muscles in her legs twitched to run, far away, anywhere but here.

"Have you had dinner?"

Jess shook her head. She had planned on ordering a massaman curry from the Thai place that had just opened across the street from her apartment. Based on the traffic, she was fairly certain the restaurant was a cover for money laundering and the police would be raiding them any day but until then she was going to enjoy the best roti she had ever had.

"Good. Do you like coq au vin?"

Jess's palms were suddenly slick. It was too hot. "I don't know. I don't think I've ever had it."

"Good. Then you have nothing to compare it to."

Jess shifted from one foot to the other. The need to run overpowered her, but manners kept her in place. She was intense and awkward but she was never knowingly rude. "Look, Matt. I…

uh appreciate your…" She stopped herself from saying "pretending." That would sound too accusatory. "I appreciate your efforts. But this…" She gestured to the room. "It's unnecessary. I know that usual protocol is for the man to make an effort to show his interest and is rewarded with physical intimacy if the woman is interested and duly impressed."

"Wow, I have never heard romance explained so clinically."

"That's my point. This isn't romance. I don't want a relationship so you don't have to pretend to be interested in anything other than sex. I'm a sure thing so I would actually prefer if you would just be honest."

"Honest? Huh." Matt ran a hand through his blond hair. "I honestly don't see what part you're not getting. I like hanging out with you."

Jess made an exasperated sound.

"What?" Matt asked. "What is so hard to believe about that?"

Matt studied her, his stare scrutinizing as his gaze swept over her features. "In what way have I given you the impression I wasn't interested? Was it tracking down your number like a stalker? Or was it using all the data on my phone plan to text you and ask you out?"

Jess bit into her lip as she considered her answer. He was staring at her too intently for her to form a reasoned response.

Matt shook his head. "You honestly don't believe that I would want to hang out with you, do you? Is it all men you have such a low opinion of or just me? Seriously what kind of fucked-up relationships have you been in?"

The sadness in his voice cut her. She had been holding it together so nicely, and now some guy was going to undo her with his bullshit make-believe. Matt took a step towards her. Her body went rigid as he wrapped his arms around her and pulled her against his chest.

"What are you doing?" she asked.

"I'm hugging you. You look like you've had a really shitty day and could use a hug. We can continue our discussion about why I couldn't possibly really like you later."

Jess tensed. Physical touch was something she usually reserved for sex.

"Seriously, woman, have you never been hugged?" There was a lilt to his deep voice. "It helps if you lean into it, there you go. Yep that's it, stop fighting it."

Jess relaxed against him. It felt good to be held. God, she hated to admit it but it felt good to have strong arms wrapped around her, and a man that was not going to change his mind in a few seconds and push her away.

"Screw it, I will tell you now because you are so incredulous about me actually liking to spend time with you. The reasons include but are not limited to: you're smart, and complicated, and beautiful, and you have great tits. Yeah, I said it, you have great tits and sitting across from you for an hour will give me a chance to stare at them."

Jess laughed. She wasn't beautiful; attractive maybe, but not beautiful. He didn't need to tell her she was.

"Have dinner with me and let me stare at your breasts."

There were a million reasons to leave but one to stay: she felt wanted, right then in that moment, someone wanted her. No doubt the feeling would prove ephemeral and it would hurt more in the long run that she had allowed herself to give in to the illusion of connection. But right now, it didn't matter.

"Yeah, that sounds nice."

Matt led her through to the dining room. Like the rest of the house, the room was tastefully decorated. The dining table was made of reclaimed wood with a chunky iron base, and polished rivets adorned the sides, giving it an industrial, almost steampunk feel. The leather chairs had matching embellishments of polished studs. On the cream walls there was a collection of framed antique maps.

"Your house is beautiful."

"Thanks. I'm still finishing things off. I came back from Germany almost five years ago but I still haven't really gotten to the place where DC feels like home."

Matt pulled out a chair for her.

"You worked in Germany?" Jess asked as she sat.

He nodded. "I was in the Berlin office."

"I was born there, not in Berlin but in Frankfurt," she let slip out before she realized it would open the door to a conversation about her childhood.

Matt's face lit up. "Really, how long did you live there?"

"Um… for about a year I think. We moved around a lot."

"So, your dad was military? What was that like moving around? You must have met a lot of interesting people." Matt opened the bottle of red wine on the table. The label looked like one of the antique advertisements that had recently become popular.

The hairs on the back of her neck stood taut. The mention of her dad made her stop cold, immediately her defenses were on high alert. She looked over at him. "Yeah, he was in the Army. My parents are divorced. I lived with my mom and stepdad though," she said tentatively. She scrutinized his reaction, searching for the slightest flicker of recognition. If there was even the slightest possibility of Matt knowing her true identity, or if he followed up with another question about her dad, she would leave and never come back. There were reasons she did not have relationships, and get-to-know-you sessions were high on the list.

Matt poured her some wine, filling the glass just enough to cover the bottom before he offered it to her. "If you don't like this, I have a Merlot in the kitchen."

She took a sip. Dark fruity flavors warmed her tongue. "Mmm, it's great."

Matt filled up her glass. "So how was your day? I really do give a shit about that, by the way."

Jess bristled, still uncomfortable with the pretense that this was anything other than two people using each other. Even at the best of times people didn't really care, they only asked out of habit and societal norms. "My day was great, thanks."

He gave her a dubious look. They both knew she would not have been on his doorstep if her day had been great. "You're working on the body in the bayou case, aren't you?"

"Is that what they're calling it? There have also been three bodies found in lakes but that doesn't sound as cool, does it? Everyone loves alliteration: body in the bayou, that has a nice ring to it." She realized she sounded callous when Matt's eyes widened. "Sorry. Yeah that's my case."

"Any new leads?"

"Tons, I just haven't found them yet."

"I like your optimism. Give me a second. I'll just go get dinner. Promise you won't run away while I'm gone." He winked.

Jess sat back against the high-backed chair and took a long sip. The fullness of the bouquet played on her palate, subtle rich flavors: sweet like ripe black cherries and savory like licorice. When she swallowed, heat spread down her neck and over her arms. Only after Matt had left the room did she remember that she should have offered to help in the kitchen.

A few minutes later Matt returned with two plates.

"This looks delicious." Jess didn't even need to remind herself to compliment him. It really did look amazing; as good as anything she had ever been served. Creamy mashed potatoes were topped with a chicken breast in a rich red wine sauce and served with tender herbed baby carrots. "Wow, and it tastes even better," she said after she swallowed the first mouthful.

Matt beamed at the praise. "Thank you. I'm somewhat of a foodie. I love to cook. What about you?"

"Nope, but I love to eat."

"My mom was the best cook. Every Friday she would try a new dish. No cuisine was off limits—Ethiopian, Thai, Brazilian. You name it, we tried it. I think that's where I got my love of food. What about your mom, does she like to cook?"

Jess must have made a face because Matt laughed. "Why that reaction?"

Jess took a long sip of wine to fortify herself before she answered. "Sorry, it was just the idea of my mom doing anything remotely maternal or domestic. The cognitive dissonance was just too much for my face to control."

"That bad, huh?"

Jess sighed. "That's a loaded question."

"Sorry. I'm nervous. I really didn't think you were going to ever text back."

"Don't apologize. My mom is difficult. Aren't they all?" she half-joked as she took another sip of wine.

Matt shrugged. "I guess. I mean mine always insisted on drawing hearts on the napkins in my lunch box with little notes of encouragement. Insufferable woman," he laughed. "No, my mom was, is actually, great. My biggest complaint from childhood is that she wouldn't let us get a dog because my dad was allergic and apparently him breathing was more important than us having a pet. Oh, and she didn't always make chocolate chip cookies. Half the time she made oatmeal raisin because those are my brother's favorite. That's not even a cookie, that's a congealed breakfast."

Jess laughed. "I agree. What's the point of a cookie without chocolate?"

"I know, right?"

Jess smiled as he regaled her with anecdotes from his childhood in Michigan, his time at MIT, and his most recent posts with the FBI. "Sorry, I'm boring you," he said.

"No, you're really not," she said honestly. Matt had an effortless nature that put her at ease. He was sweet and self-deprecating with just enough quiet confidence to make him sexy. As they continued to eat and chat, she could not remember a time she had felt so uninhibited. He asked her enough questions about herself to seem interested in her opinion but never crossed the line into nosy. If she were in the market for a boyfriend she would definitely consider him. She almost laughed out loud at the idea of contemplating a long-term relationship.

"Do you have room for dessert?" Matt asked after the second bottle of wine.

Jess held up her hand. "No, I'm stuffed. It was great." She pushed back from the table and stood up. The night had wound down and it was time to go home. There was a niggling sadness that it was over. She hadn't achieved the numb she had set out to find but Matt had provided an unexpected distraction. She felt almost chagrined for it to end but it had to. She had talked too much and no doubt bored him. Embarrassment would take hold once the buzz wore off. "Thanks for dinner." She didn't follow up with "I'll see you later" because she wouldn't. That would definitely be crossing into relationship territory. Matt was a great guy and a great screw. No doubt he would be a great boyfriend for someone else.

"You're welcome. Thanks for the company. I didn't want to eat alone tonight."

Jess nodded, realizing she felt the same. She left the dining room and turned down the hall towards the front door.

Matt caught her hand, pulling her back. "The bedroom's the other direction." He gathered her against him.

Jess's eyes widened. Her heart pounded against her ribs. She really should go home and not complicate things further. The right thing to do would be to remember all the reasons this was a bad idea… and she would… but not until he made her feel good.

"Wanting to talk to you doesn't mean I don't want to sleep with you. In fact, it means I want it more." He leaned down and captured her mouth in a kiss.

Jess's phone vibrated on the bedside table. Light from the screen reflected off the discarded foil condom wrappers. She squinted, trying to make out the numbers on the phone, but her eyes could not focus enough to read the caller ID, let alone the time.

"Ignore it," Matt rasped. "You're off the clock." He was lying behind her, his arm draped across her, their naked bodies pressed together.

Jess hadn't planned on staying over. She never spent the night with men she had sex with but she had fallen asleep, probably because she hadn't really slept the night before. She had woken up once during the night and tried to leave, but Matt had pulled her back to bed, refusing to let her leave until the morning. Not that she had offered any resistance. She was exhausted and it felt good to have a warm body against her. "I think it's my boss." She widened then narrowed her eyes several times to try to clear her vision.

After several failed attempts, she slid the button across the screen. "Hello," her voice croaked.

"Jessica, this is Jeanie Gilbert."

Jess's heart picked up speed. Jeanie rarely called her at home and never in the middle of the night. "Hi, is everything all right?" She sat up in bed. The sheet dropped to her waist. She tried to tug the material up higher to cover herself but it would not reach. She pulled again before she realized Jeannie couldn't actually see her.

"Sorry to call so late but I knew you would want to know as soon as I found out. Louisiana State Police have found another body. Preliminary reports are that it's Jennifer Thomson. You interviewed her in relation to the Lydia Steiner murder."

Her gut clenched in a painful spasm. "Yeah, I know who she is. Oh my God," she whispered. She was so young and naïve, just a kid with her life ahead of her. "Are you sure?"

"Yes. Breaux Bridge police are on the scene. They think it's her. They haven't asked the family for a formal identification because it would be too upsetting. They will have DNA confirmation this week."

Jess's mind spun. "What happened?"

"Initial reports are that she cut class yesterday. The school principal notified her parents. When Jennifer wasn't home by dinner, they called it in. She was found just after midnight."

Jess swallowed past the lump that had formed in her throat. "Is it—" Jess couldn't finish the sentence. Her lungs tightened. Guilt punched her square in the chest. "Is it our guy?" She squeezed her eyes shut and willed Jeanie to say it was unrelated, an accident maybe, something, anything unrelated to the case. "Is it our guy?" she asked again.

"That would be speculation."

"Please just tell me." She had to know if her actions had killed Jennifer Thomson. Whoever had hacked into the FBI files would know that she had cut Jennifer a deal as a material witness. Jess had documented that Jennifer had seen the killer and could identify him even though she couldn't. She put it in the report to justify the deal but it had made Jennifer a target. Shit, why had she spoken to a minor without a lawyer or guardian? Jennifer would have never confessed and she might still be alive.

Jeanie sighed. "I really don't want to speculate until we have more information. But I will say that she was found in her car. Her body was burned."

"That's not our guy." Jess hadn't killed her with her mistake. Relief rushed through her, but the initial reprieve was drowned by a tsunami of grief. She was still dead. A kid was dead.

Jeanie was silent for a few seconds like she was reticent to say anything else. "She had been decapitated. We haven't yet found her head. And there are several incision sites on her torso."

All the air left Jess's body. Her lungs burned as they constricted. She couldn't speak. Jess had killed her. Jennifer's name and address were in the file. Jess had led the killer straight to her, to a young, scared girl. *Oh God.*

"All reports are preliminary. We need to keep an open mind. Chan and Milligan are already there because they were investigating the storage unit and the PO box."

"The ones that were set up in my name." Jess acknowledged the elephant in the room. She had left the office before Jeanie had the chance to speak with her about it. "I hope you know I had nothing to do with this. I understand that Tina will have to do diagnostics on my devices to prove I'm in no way involved. I understand if you need to pull me until this is resolved. Whatever the protocol is, I understand."

"Jess, we need as many boots on the ground as we can get. No one is suggesting this has anything to do with you beyond a deranged killer taunting law enforcement. Can you be at the airport for 6 a.m.? I can get you on the first flight to Louisiana. I'd like you to work the crime scene but I understand completely if you think you're too close to the situation. I can have Chan and Milligan—"

"No. I can do that." Jess owed it to Jennifer. "Um… what about Jamison?"

"Agent Briggs is taking a few personal days to deal with something. Chan and Milligan will stay in Louisiana."

"Okay," was all Jess could manage to say. She wanted to ask where Jamison was and when and if he would be back, but she was scared she might not be ready for the answer.

CHAPTER TWENTY-FIVE

Louisiana

Louisiana was starting to feel like a second home, a home she wanted to burn to the ground. She had spent far too much time here and come up with nothing. She hated the state now. Gone was the eerie beauty. That illusion had died with Jennifer Thomson. This place was just a backwater swampland ghetto.

Jess didn't need a map or satellite navigation to find the crime scene. She had been here before. This was where Liddy Steiner's body had been pulled out of the bayou. She would definitely be visiting Ezra and his dog Cooter again because the odds of two bodies being found on one man's doorstep and him not being involved was astronomically small.

Four police cruisers were parked on the side of the road. Jess recognized most, if not all, of the officers that were lined up talking. A lot of police work at murder scenes in rural areas involved standing around discussing how to proceed because mercifully they did not have a lot of experience with violent crimes. A white tent had been set up to protect forensic evidence, so they were learning; sad that their small community needed this knowledge.

Jess sank into the red mud when she got out of the car. Her feet tensed as murky water seeped over the top of her feet and into the crevices between her toes. The high heels she was wearing

were entirely inappropriate for this terrain but she hadn't had
time to go home to change. She had just enough time to shower
before leaving for the airport. Matt had insisted on driving her
because he didn't have to go into the office. Most of what he did
with compliance could be done remotely. It should have been
awkward because only really good friends brave DC traffic in the
morning to do an airport run, but it had been okay. They had
listened to talk radio and Jess had sipped the coffee Matt made
her from a travel mug.

"Hey," Jess greeted the officers lined up around the entrance
to the tent. There was no need for introductions; they all knew
each other. Their chatter died down, replaced by somber silence
like they suddenly remembered why they were all there. "Are my
colleagues in there?"

The thinnest agent, Giboin if she remembered correctly, shook
his head. "Just Agent Milligan. Agent Chan isn't here yet."

Jess's eyes narrowed. "By himself?" Annoyance mounted in her.

She didn't wait for an answer. She pulled back on the thick
vinyl curtain that acted like a door at the entrance. Milligan was
bent on one knee, his back to her, examining something on the
ground next to a white Volvo Saloon.

"What the hell are you doing?" she demanded. Irritation
simmered just below the surface of her skin. "Tell me you did
not come into a crime scene by yourself to collect evidence. Are
you on retainer for the defense attorney or something? When
we catch this guy, his lawyer will use shit like this to get him off.
I don't know what they're doing overseas but back home we try
not to create a case for the defense." Jess tore into him. She tried
to keep her voice down because they were in earshot of a half
dozen law enforcement officials, but her annoyance got the best
of her. The vast majority of their training was focused around
building strong cases. Had he forgotten that? Catching killers
wasn't enough; they needed to be put behind bars.

David stood up. "I just got here." His shoulders pulled back, pushing out his chest in a subtle show of physical dominance. No doubt it was subconscious but it pissed her off just the same. Jess was small; there was no need for any man to demonstrate superior strength. It was redundant and screamed of insecurity and or hostility. Either way, she didn't have any interest in it.

"Don't touch anything. You didn't find anything. You didn't see anything. You didn't even think anything until I got here."

Milligan's mouth flattened to a white slash but he didn't speak. At the best of times Jess couldn't be described as laid back, but when it came to adherence to procedure she was tyrannical. There was nothing she hated more than a maverick. Rules were in place because they were good practice. They worked, that's why you stuck to them.

"Where the hell is Chan?"

Milligan's nostrils flared. He looked away briefly as he sucked in a deep breath, trying to calm his anger. He was trying not to snap back at her. Too right he needed to keep his cool because she wouldn't hold back if he tried to defend his actions with verbal aggression. "He said he would meet me here. I just got here myself."

"And you thought you would start collecting evidence without him? Please talk me through that thought process. That's not how we work around here."

A flash of confusion darted across his face and then disappeared just as quickly, but Jess clocked it. "What? Please tell me you and Chan didn't do something stupid like divide and conquer, each of you take a different scene."

Milligan didn't refute her assertions; instead, his gaze turned to the ground like a cashier who had just been caught with his hand in the register.

"Oh my God, you did. What the actual fuck?" She clamped her hands into angry fists. "Are you kidding me right now? Like seriously are you joking? If I have ever given you the impression I was up for a laugh about this sort of thing, I sincerely apologize because I don't mess about with my work."

"Chan said—"

"I don't give a shit what Chan said. Did you graduate from the academy? Have you worked a crime scene before? You do understand chain of custody, don't you?"

When Milligan tried to speak, Jess held up her hand to keep him from saying anything else. "When you make a mistake, you acknowledge it, you don't make an excuse." She looked away so she could think. She clenched her teeth until her jaw ached. A few times she opened her mouth to speak but she quickly snapped it shut when she realized she was too angry to continue the conversation. She counted to four as she filled her lungs to capacity and held her breath for the same time before slowly letting out the air. She repeated the cycle a few times until she was back in control. "Did you or Chan go to any crime scenes alone yesterday?"

"Yeah but—"

"'Where? Where were you?"

Milligan shrugged. "I went to the post office and had a look at surveillance at the PO box registered to *you*."

He stressed the final word, implying this had something to do with her to deflect from his own actions, but Jess would not be thrown off the scent.

"And Chan? Where was he?"

"He was at the storage unit and I think he was going to interview Mike Snowberger. I'm not sure. I looked at footage all day and then went back to the hotel about eight o'clock. I had dinner and then called my wife and went to bed."

"So, neither of you has an alibi for Jennifer Thomson's murder."

David's face contorted in shock. He could not have looked more upset if she had smacked him across the face.

"That's what any good defense attorney will ask. And he will have a field day with your answer. Any evidence you recovered is compromised. You fucked up." Jess looked away. There was so much she could say but there was no point in belaboring it. She would save her real vitriol for Chan. What were they thinking? It wasn't even a rookie error: it was downright stupid. He knew better. He had tried this kind of shit before. She let it slide when it was just him sneaking off in the middle of the day to screw random women, but when it involved her case, she made sure Chan toed the line.

God, she hated when people cut corners or went off script, it was dangerous and myopic. They did it for the quick fix, an instant hit because they were too focused on catching the guy, but that was only one side of the coin. None of it mattered if the evidence they gathered did not secure a conviction. This was not an academic endeavor, it wasn't good enough to know who committed a crime if the person wasn't stopped and punished.

"Here is what we're going to do. We're going to have the nice officers outside hold our hands for the entire process. You're not going to shit without someone in a uniform standing beside you, handing you toilet paper. And Milligan, you're never going to pull this crap again. You have a kid who needs a dad with a job." She left the threat hanging above him.

"Officer Giboin," Jess shouted over her shoulder. "Can I see you for a second?"

A few moments later, Officers Giboin and Purdue entered the tent. Good, the more the merrier. "We need an extra set of hands. Would you mind giving us a little help?" She handed Officer Purdue one of the fresh notebooks she always carried with her. "Can you please take notes?" Asking him to be her scribe was a pathetic excuse to cover the fact she was asking for a chaperone, but it was all she could think of on short notice. She had never been the creative type.

They all slipped on gloves and shoe covers before Jess opened up the back seat to have a look at the naked torso. "Is this how everything was found? Doors closed? Body in the back seat? Her purse in the driver's seat?" She had to ask because it would have been a natural reflex to close doors or unbuckle seatbelts.

"Yep," Giboin said.

"Good," Jess nodded. "The purse needs to be processed and then we need to see what's on her phone." A teenager's entire life was on social media. That was the best place for them to start to figure out where she was yesterday.

She leaned in to examine the body. There was no need for the vapor rub because the victim hadn't been dead long enough to smell. The skin was in near-pristine condition except for the three excision sites along her breasts. She would have a closer look once the ME had her on the slab but she wanted to see the body in situ. Because the corpse had not been submerged in water, it was easier to differentiate between the crude cuts of the disarticulation sites of her limbs and the pristine cut along her neck. There were definitely two different instruments being used, something primitive to get rid of the arms and legs, and something surgical in nature to remove the head.

Jess squinted. "Can I borrow your flashlight?"

Purdue took his light out of his belt and handed it to her.

Jess clicked the button and shined it into the car. A thin band of light illuminated a pattern burned into the charred flesh between her breasts. Jess gasped when she saw the familiar symbol. "He left one of the brands. He didn't cut that one out." Her stomach clamped in a painful spasm as the voices she had been fighting so hard to silence screamed at her in a brutal chorus. Even though she knew before that this had something to do with her, the brand pushed her over the edge. She was going to be sick.

Jess couldn't open her eyes. If she did, she would vomit. Her head would not stop spinning. For a moment time stopped, trapping her with her thoughts. She should have told Jeanie her concerns about the brands as soon as the coroner pointed them out on Lydia Steiner. Maybe Jennifer Thomson would still be alive. They would have figured it out sooner that this was about Jess and they could have protected Jennifer. This was her fault.

All three men inched forward to peer over her shoulder. Someone's breath was hot on her neck. "What is that?" Giboin asked. "A triangle?"

Jess took a deep breath. They would all know soon enough but she wasn't going to be the one to tell them. She would leave it to Jeanie to explain what the signs meant. "It's a delta sign. Can you write that down please? Delta sign on sternum, midline between the breasts." She tried to sound unaffected but her voice faltered.

One of the most recognizable signs for pedophiles was an interlocking triangle, a continuous line that created a small triangle inside a larger one. It was a symbol for "boy lover." The inmates at Central Prison in North Carolina could not get their hands on a boy lover brand but one of them did manage to smuggle in a fraternity ring with a delta sign, which was close enough for them. After her father was sentenced, a group of prisoners had held him down and branded him with a delta sign, to mark him as a child rapist, one sign for each of his victims, thirteen in total.

She could not look at anything that looked remotely like a triangle and not see her father's crimes.

Jess pushed away the thought as she stood up. She could not think about anything besides finding this killer. "Where are her limbs? I was under the impression all of her limbs had been found and her body had been burned." She had been half asleep when she'd taken the call from Jeanie so she wasn't sure which things Jeanie had told her and which she had assumed. "This torso hasn't been burned." Come to think of it, neither had the car, though it did smell of bleach. Counter-forensic measures appeared to have been taken but not the ones she expected.

"In the corner. They're all there. They were set on fire," Milligan said.

Jess snapped around to see what Milligan was referring to. It was the pile she had seen him standing over when she came in. It took all the willpower she had not to scream out loud. Instead she shot him a look that encapsulated her feelings. From his response, she knew he read her correctly.

Jess walked over to the pile. The limbs had been wrapped in what looked like Spanish moss and then set on fire. Jess glanced down at the damp ground. "Did it rain yesterday or last night?" Jess asked. Because this was swampland it was impossible to tell what came from precipitation and what was the natural state of primordial ooze that leached out of the bayou.

"Showers off and on throughout the day."

Jess looked back at the car. "He wanted us to find the torso so we could see the brand. He's giving us a clue. And he didn't burn the car for the same reason, because he wanted us to know whose car it is. So why did he burn her limbs?" she asked out loud.

"Because his DNA is under her nails," Giboin said.

"Exactly." Jess nodded. "And luckily Mother Nature smiled on us and stopped the arms being completely incinerated. We might be able to get a match." Her heart slammed against her ribs as it picked up speed. The killer thought he was being clever, taunting her with clues, but he wasn't clever enough to make sure he had destroyed all the incriminating evidence. Maybe just maybe this would be the break they needed. *Not so smart after all, are you, asshole?*

Chan handed Jess a cup of black coffee. He was still trying to make up for the stunt he pulled with Milligan. She got it; they just wanted to get out of the purgatory of the Deep South, and back to DC. The irony was that they were still stuck in Louisiana because

Ricky's parents refused to let him speak to anyone without counsel, and Stephan Roux hadn't been available until the following day. Ricky and his lawyer were still in the interview room of the Beaux Bridge police department prepping. Roux would be going over what to answer and how to answer it. Based on the Rolex Roux sported, his services couldn't have been cheap and these were all billable hours. They could take as long as they wanted, because they had already missed the last flight home and Jess wasn't in any hurry to get back to the motel. The seats here at reception were comfortable, the coffee was hot, and she had taken to the bald eagle statue on the front desk. There was something noble about the tacky, rustic, all-American décor.

"Any news on your prodigal partner?" Chan asked.

Coffee scalded the top of her mouth as she swallowed. "He's taking some personal time. You know as much as me."

Chan opened two packets of sugar and mixed them in with a wooden stirrer. "I don't like that guy."

She didn't need to clarify that he was talking about Jamison. "Shocking. You have always done such a great job hiding your true feelings."

"I'm serious. There's something really not right about him. He was weird even before he went undercover but now he is seriously messed up. We're in the middle of a case. Where does he get off going on a vacation?"

Jess didn't answer. Instead she took another sip of coffee.

"I'm serious, Jess. I don't trust him. He is not right in the head. I don't know how he got cleared to come back. Undercover work can mess with you. You know he murdered someone, right? Just be careful, okay?" The normal bravado was gone, replaced with what sounded like genuine concern.

This was neither the time nor the place to be having this conversation. "Why don't you worry about your own partner?" Jess glanced over to Milligan.

He was sitting in the corner texting with one hand, stroking the razor cut on his cheek with the other. He was giving her a wide berth. She was ready to let bygones be bygones but he was still nursing a grudge. He hadn't even come to dinner with them. She and Chan had found a decent steakhouse just off the highway but Milligan had sat in his motel room with basic cable and a protein bar. If he was waiting for an apology from her, he'd be waiting for a long time. She had said what needed to be said. She probably could have said it without swearing, but Milligan had gotten off lightly compared to Chan, and Chan wasn't still acting butt-hurt.

"He's fine. Just pussy whipped, though I don't know why. I've seen a picture of his wife. She is not hot, like not even a little."

Jess just stared at Chan blankly, giving him no emotion. He said shit like that for a response so the best way to deal with it was not to respond, give the fire no oxygen.

Officer Purdue rounded the corner. "They are ready for you."

"About time," Chan muttered. "I hate when lawyers dick about, wasting time."

Usually Jess would agree but the stall tactic had actually worked in their favor because it had given them time for an analyst to process Jennifer's things and for Jeanie to arrange for a warrant for Ricky's phone records. Had they interviewed him yesterday, it would have been a whole lot of aimless digging; now they had direction and lies to catch him in.

Jess waited for Milligan to stand up, but when he didn't she did. She wasn't going to invite him to do his job. "Let's go." She nodded to Chan who followed her lead.

The plan had been for Jess to watch behind the glass while Milligan and Chan interviewed Ricky, but she would rather be in there anyway and let Milligan lick his wounds for a while. If he was going to be on their team he needed to learn to roll with the punches. There wasn't time for ego during an investigation. Yes, she had snapped at him but it was time for him to get over it.

Jess tensed when she entered the interview room. The last time she was there it was Jennifer Thomson she was interviewing. She had sat where Ricky was now, her hair in a thick braid down her back, but there was no hotshot lawyer looking after her best interests, just a scared girl at the mercy of two federal agents. Jess swallowed against the lump in her throat and pushed all the emotion down. She would be useless to anyone if she gave in to what she was feeling. One blessing from her childhood was her ability to compartmentalize. She acknowledged the pain, but pushed it down to process later. Once the case didn't need her full attention, she would let herself grieve and she would fully acknowledge her own culpability.

"Hello, Ricky, we meet again," Jess said from the doorway. Ricky was sitting forward, his elbow resting on the table as he fidgeted with the string of his maroon hooded wrestling sweatshirt. On the left arm, CAPTAIN was written down the side. Jess glanced briefly at Stephan Roux but did not acknowledge his presence. If she did, it might knock her off her stride. She was here to speak to Ricky not his flashy lawyer. "You haven't met my colleague yet. This is Special Agent Chan."

Ricky raised his head briefly in what could have been considered a nod.

"I'm sorry about your loss. I know you and Jennifer were close. She was your girlfriend, right?" Jess said, waiting for him to refute it, but he just nodded again. His lawyer scribbled something down on a yellow pad. He was probably just doodling because no one had actually said anything of interest.

"Your girlfriend, huh?" Chan said. "Was she really?" He made an exaggerated expression of disbelief. "Because I got to say, from where I'm sitting, things were not looking good on the puppy-love front."

Ricky looked up at his lawyer, who was still staring intently at his legal pad. Stephan Roux looked up over his wireless glasses. "I'm sorry, was there a question?" he asked Chan.

"Was Jennifer Thomson your girlfriend at the time of her death?" Jess interjected. If Roux was going to be pedantic and want things to adhere to a strict question-and-answer format, she was happy to comply and leave Chan to go off on tangents. Chan was a natural showman, and interviews were a chance for him to perform.

Ricky shrugged. "I don't know."

"It's a pretty easy question," Jess said. "Was Jennifer Thomson your girlfriend at the time of her murder?"

"Her *death*," Roux interjected. "I don't believe the coroner has determined a cause of death."

Jess's eyes widened. What a stupid thing to say, even for an attorney. Lawyers really were some of the biggest assholes she came across. She wished she had a crime scene photo with her to shove in his face, watch him try to engage in verbal gymnastics while looking at the mutilated corpse.

"Her head and limbs were cut off and then set on fire. I'd put my money on that not being accidental or self-inflicted. But sure, we'll rephrase. Was Jennifer Thomson your girlfriend at the time of her death?" Jess asked.

Chan waited a few moments for Ricky to reply but when it became clear no response—verbal or otherwise—was forthcoming, he said, "Do you know the trouble with kids today?" Chan asked rhetorically. "They live their lives on social media. You can't even shit without it being documented and hashtagged. It's just not normal, is it, Bishop?"

"Nope, it's not," Jess agreed.

"People don't talk the way they used to," Chan lamented. "In my day, if I was having a problem with my lady, I would call her or I would hop on my BMX and I would pedal over and see her. Remember riding around until you got your license and could afford a car?" Chan asked Jess.

"Yep, spent a lot of time on my ten-speed." Jess played along. Interviews with Chan were a lot about improv skills. He never

Jess shook her head. "No, they most certainly are not. That is not going to play well for you."

Two angry red flags of color anchored on Ricky's cheeks. She couldn't tell if he was embarrassed or angry. He was a teenage boy so chances were he couldn't identify the emotion either.

"Here's the thing, that's really not going to play well in court. Over the next week you ignore all of her messages but when you do finally respond it is to tell her you hate her because she tried to ruin your life by speaking to the FBI. You say, and I quote, "*You stupid bitch. You say you love me, but if you loved me you would have lied to the police. You tried to fuck with my scholarship. I hate you. I wish you were dead.*"

"Ooh." Chan winced. "That is going to hurt. The jury is going to see you're not above perjury. That's not a great start. And then wishing her dead, there isn't a big leap from there to murder. It's not looking good for you, man."

"That's conjecture," Roux said. "It's pure speculation—"

Jess held up her hand to stop him. "Just wait. It gets even better. In addition to calling her a bitch thirteen times, a whore seven, a slut another seven, a dirty slut twice, you cap it off by calling her a stupid cunt."

"Ouch." Chan shook his head. "Ladies really do not like that word."

"No, we don't," Jessica agreed. "It's not a nice word. And it is not something you should be calling any woman." Jess gave him a hard stare. There were a few names she wanted to call him right now. "Now here is where it gets interesting. Turn the page." Jess waited for everyone to flip through the pages. "Your tone changes here, does a complete one-eighty. Three days ago, you said, "*I miss you, babe. Things have been so messed up. I'm so messed up without you. I am so sorry. Please let me make it up to you. I need to see you in person.*"

Jess looked up to gauge his reaction. "As you can see, the messages go back and forth with you working out how and when

got straight to the point; everything was allegorical. He loved to create a narrative and her job was to play along. At first it drove her crazy. They would rehearse what they were going to say, but then they'd get into an interrogation and the script would go out the window. She had hated it but eventually she learned to just play along because it worked. This was Chan's specialist skill: he was the most proficient liar she had ever met. To this day she couldn't say which of his stories were real and which were bullshit.

"Hmm, those were the days." Chan sighed. "But," he smiled, "I have got to tell you that as an FBI agent I love text messages. Those are pretty much the best things ever. I mean, did you know that phone companies keep every message you send for up to three months? Just sitting there on a server waiting for someone to get a warrant and look at them. Do you want to know how easy it is to get a warrant? I bet you do. I can tell, Ricky, that you're an inquisitive guy, so I'm going to tell you. It is pretty easy. Well, for me anyway. Judges just seem to like me. I'm kind of like the warrant king. Tell them, Bishop."

Jess had to bite her lip to keep from laughing. "That's right, Chan, you're the man."

When Chan smiled at her, she couldn't help smiling back. If nothing else he was entertaining.

"You know what I like even better than text messages? Social media. I know I said it was the downfall of civilization, and it is, but I love that everything is just out there for the world to see. People forget to secure their privacy settings and then everyone and their Aunt Ida knows when they get in a fight with their girlfriend. And is there anything better than when people change their relationship status? I mean, pop some popcorn because we have got a show."

"It is pretty great," Jess agreed.

"I know, right? Chan nodded. "My favorite is actually the private messenger programs. Though it is a complete misnomer because there is nothing private about them. They're not even encrypted. They are scanned constantly for information. That's why if you write about a car you suddenly get all sorts of advertisements from dealerships in your newsfeed."

"Is that right?" Jessica played along. Actually the major social media sites had recently added an option to encrypt conversations, but she didn't correct him. Most people didn't even realize it was an option and rarely utilized the feature because it was a big pain. People had to manually select the option for each individual conversation.

"Yep. It is all fascinating stuff but not half as fascinating as what I found when I looked at your messages, Ricky boy." Chan winked.

Ricky sat bolt upright like an electric current had been applied to his backside. "Wait what? They can't do that, can they?"

Roux adjusted his glasses. He cleared his throat to speak but Chan interrupted him.

"Can and did. I'm telling you, my IT skills are on point. Just a little something I do." Chan shrugged in a show of false modesty.

"I told you. He really is the man," Jess said. In reality the warrant had been secured by Jeanie, and Tina had done all the heavy lifting with phone records and computer profiles. Jess pulled out four copies of the messages Tina had recovered from Jennifer's phone. Chan hadn't even made the copies but she was going to give him his moment in the sun. He lived for this shit.

"This will all need to be verified," Roux said.

"Of course it will. Just curious, how much do you charge an hour?" Jess didn't wait for a response because she wasn't expecting one. "This is not going to be cheap for your parents. My parents would have been pissed if I had not one but two run-ins with the feds in less than a month. I'm so glad yours seem to be so chill." Jess had clocked his parents on her way into the station and they looked anything but *chill*. Jess had picked a seat in reception

where she could watch them. Mom's eyes were red-rimmed, her complexion splotchy. Dad kept wringing his hands together and readjusting his position. They were sad and anxious like any parents would be. Dad owned a struggling farm and mom drove a ten-year-old minivan; they were hardly living the high life. This would be putting a financial strain on his family and it was important for Ricky to know that.

Jess pointed to the first line on the packet she had handed Ricky. "As you see right there, everyone knows you broke up with Jennifer after she spoke to my partner and me. There is your relationship status update with a timestamp. It was just about twenty-eight hours later. Now if you turn the page, can you read me the first message from Jennifer?" Jess waited for Ricky and his lawyer to turn the page.

"Come on, Ricky, don't be shy," Chan said. "You're going to have to read this out at your trial anyway and it's always better to have a dress rehearsal and work out the kinks. You don't want to be stumbling over words. It won't make a good impression on the jurors."

Ricky's head snapped up. "What?! What trial? I didn't do anything!"

"No spoilers," Chan said. "We will get to that part in a second. But we need to set the scene. You can't just go barreling in; you need to lay the groundwork. So, go ahead and read Jennifer's message to you. No wait, let's have Agent Bishop do the honors. It will sound better in a woman's voice."

Jess cleared her throat. "*Ricky, please. I know you're mad but thought we were ok. Why did you ask me to sneak out and see you you were still mad? Why did you have sex with me? Did you kn last night you were going to break up with me?*"

Chan shook his head. "That was harsh. You called her ov have sex one last time before you broke up with her. That dick move, bro. The jury is not going to like that, are they Bi

to meet up. You made plans to both cut school and get together at a farm in Evangeline Parish."

Ricky's head snapped up. "I didn't say that. I never wrote any of that. I don't even know anyone in that parish!" His entire body recoiled at the suggestion. His cheeks went from scarlet to a color that bordered on purple. He swallowed several times. "I didn't send those messages." He pulled on the sleeve of his lawyer's jacket, trying to get his attention. He looked like a small boy who had found out the boogeyman was real and was living under his bed. "It wasn't me. It really wasn't me."

Jess tapped her pen on the desk. She had strongly suspected the latter messages weren't from Ricky even though they were sent from his account, but she needed to see his reaction to make sure he had nothing to do with it. The sentence structure and lexical choices were off. They were close—the killer had obviously read through Ricky's previous messages and tried to emulate his style but what had given it away was the killer's use of "you're." Ricky consistently incorrectly wrote "your" when he meant "you're." Jess very much doubted the Louisiana State Educational system had rectified his grammatical shortcomings in the few weeks between the messages.

"I don't know what to say to you, Ricky. I would like to help but those messages came from your account. The best technical minds in the country will testify to that fact. From where I'm sitting it looks like you lured your ex-girlfriend and then murdered her."

"That is premeditation, isn't it?" Chan said.

"Indeed it is. And you just had your eighteenth birthday. That's a shame, Louisiana is a death penalty state."

Ricky's jaw trembled. His face crumpled into a pained grimace and the corners of his eyes glistened.

"I'm sorry, kid. This isn't looking good for you. It is your profile, though," she stressed again hoping he would take the bait. *Come on, Ricky. Give me some names.*

"What if someone hacked my computer?" he blurted.

"I don't know. I mean that's why we have passwords on computers and phones to protect people from getting hacked." Chan sat back and stroked his chin like he was thinking.

"Lots of people have my password. My little sister because she plays games on my computer. I think my parents have it. Yeah, my dad does! My dad has the same password on his computer!"

Bingo. He took the bait. Jess smiled. That's what she needed to hear. "I need you to write that down for me, please. That will clear things right up and you can go home. Just write down all the people who you know have access to your password."

Roux opened his mouth to speak. Understanding flashed in his narrowed, gray eyes.

Jess shook her head. "It is best to remember who your client is. You need to have his best interests at heart," she said to Roux pointedly. They both knew he had been played. Jess had spent the day checking Ricky's alibi and it was ironclad. He had been at school and then a wrestling tournament the entire day. Seven teachers vouched for his whereabouts. This interview had never been about Ricky. This was about confirming that Andy Sutton had access to his son's social media profile.

Stephan Roux was friends with Mary and Andy Sutton. He played golf with Andy and Andy was the one paying Roux's bill, but Ricky was his client and his only loyalty had to be to Ricky.

Andy Sutton didn't have an alibi for Hannah Henderson, Lydia Steiner, or Jennifer Thomson's murders. Tina had discovered that he and his wife had separated around the time of the first murder and he was living in a trailer fifteen minutes from where Jennifer's and Lydia's bodies were found.

All the evidence they had so far was circumstantial but if Andy Sutton was the guy they were looking for, the first thing he was going to do when he got arrested was start pointing fingers. She had seen it before. There may be honor among thieves, but a killer and his defense attorney would blame absolutely anyone to create doubt.

Jess just wanted to make sure the fingers weren't pointing at Ricky. One kid had already lost her life because of this investigation. Jess was going to make damned sure another kid wasn't hurt too.

CHAPTER TWENTY-SIX

Washington, DC

"Are you sure you don't want to get dinner?" Chan pulled up in front of Jess's apartment building. He had brought her home from the airport even though he lived on the other side of the city. Despite what he said, her apartment wasn't on his way home. He had just added over an hour to his journey. He was stalling because he didn't want to go home to his fiancée. He hadn't said anything but Jess was pretty sure there was trouble in paradise. She wasn't surprised. First of all, Chan was the man in question and he had a pathological need to screw as many random women as would let him; and second, while the rest of the country had a fifty percent chance of failing at marriage, law enforcement officers had anywhere from a sixty to seventy-five percent chance of divorce. Any way she looked at it, she couldn't see any of his relationships lasting.

"No thanks. I really need to call Jeanie. I have some things I need to discuss with her but first I'm going to go over my notes and speak to the office in Baton Rouge, see how the surveillance is going on Andy Sutton. If he's our guy, I'm confident we'll be able to build a case against him for Jennifer's death. He certainly had the motive; he was pissed that she implicated his son in a crime. Plus, he had the opportunity."

She was putting off calling Jeanie. In fairness, the conversation should probably happen in person, so it would have to wait for the morning because Jess had reached her limit. She had dealt with enough for one day.

Jeanie would have to tell the team about Jess's past. It was part of the case, there was no hiding it anymore. She knew it had to come out but she wanted one last night to come to terms with it.

"But?" Chan said. He switched on his hazard lights and flipped off the taxi that beeped at him for stopping on a red line. "Go around, asshole," he shouted at the driver.

"We'll see where the evidence takes us. I would feel better if we could establish a connection between the other victims." *And me.* She wasn't going to rule anything out until she had a full report back on Andy Sutton and she established his connection to her. Why had he targeted her and how did he know about her dad? None of this made sense. "I just can't get my mind around how our guy managed to ensure all three of the known victims ended up lost. The message that was sent to Jennifer asked for her to meet at a farm in Evangeline Parish but there is nothing to suggest she ever made it there. She ended up at the same place Liddy Steiner was found. I thought before that maybe he followed them, hoping they got lost."

"Who's to say she didn't go to Evangeline Parish?"

"No. How could he get her car and her body back? It's forty miles. He couldn't have walked it and there is hardly a reliable taxi service out there. We will check with local car services and have a look at his friends to see if anyone gave him a ride that day, but it makes more sense that Jennifer drove herself to the spot where she was murdered. But then that doesn't make sense because we saw the map she had downloaded to her phone and she had the guidance system app open." Jess shook her head. She was missing something. She was sure there was a glaring piece of the puzzle sitting right in front of her but she was missing it. She would find it. She would go over and over her notes until she saw it.

"Thanks for the ride. I'll see you in the office in the morning."
She got out of the car and shut the door. She watched Chan pull
away before she headed to her apartment.

She took the stairs to the sixth floor because she needed the
exercise. She hadn't gone for her usual run in a few days because
the motel in Louisiana didn't have a gym and she didn't feel safe
attempting a street run in an area she wasn't familiar with. After
she looked over her notes she would have a date with her treadmill
and a cheesy movie.

The door to her apartment jammed on the avalanche of mail
behind it. She gave an extra push, moving the pile out of the way.
It would all be catalogs and junk mail. She bought everything
on line, so she was on the mailing list of every major retailer in
America. She would shred everything with her name and address
on it and then recycle it but first she needed to feed her fish. Thank
God for the once-a-week feeding bricks because otherwise PETA
would be calling about her mistreatment of animals.

Jess opened the lid on her tank and put in what looked like a
denture tablet. "Hello Kraus, hello Hitchens, hello Harris. Did
you miss me?" She waited for the food to start to dissolve and the
fish to swim up for their meal before she closed the lid. And then
she turned to the smaller tank with its single inhabitant. "And
don't think I forgot about you, Mr. Dawkins, because I didn't.
You look so lonely on your own. It's a shame your friends want
to eat your face." Water splashed up as she slipped in his food.
The real shame was she wasn't home enough to have a dog. It was
acceptable for owners to have conversations with their dogs but
chatting with fish was sad and slightly worrying.

"Okay, time to get to work," she said to Dawkins the fish.
She pulled out her computer and waited a second for the screen
to light up. When it didn't, she pressed the power button a few
times before she realized the battery was dead. She glanced over
at the coffee table where she kept her charger but it wasn't there.

"Shit." She knew exactly where she had left it: Matt Ramsay's house. She had taken her hand luggage with her to Matt's because she hadn't gone home before she'd gone to his house. There was reason number 583 why she was not a fan of relationships: people always ended up leaving stuff at their partner's house or vice versa. The idea of that made her skin crawl. Everything in her house had a spot. She didn't want other people's stuff messing up her place and she didn't want to be trailing across the city to get back her things when she forgot them.

She hesitated for a fraction of a second before she reached for her phone. She could just go buy another charger but it was after six and she would have to figure out where the nearest electronic store was. Screw it. She hit the button to call him.

On the second ring, he answered. "Hey Jess. I was just thinking of texting you but I couldn't actually bring myself to text, '*Want to get together and have sex?*'—I know you said you would prefer if I was more direct but when I typed it out it looked a bit creepy. A lot creepy actually. So then I tried, '*Want to have dinner and then sex?*' but that just made me sound like a hungry pervert so I deleted that too. And then you called me. I'm realizing now there was no need to tell you about my creepy attempts at text messages. Shit. Oh good now I am swearing at you. Okay let's try this again. Hello, Jess. I'm just sitting here at the office being cool because that is what I am: super cool."

Jess smiled. Matt had no idea how sexy his inept attempts at conversation were. She would take that over cocky arrogance any day of the week. "Hi, Matt. I'm just sitting here at home also being super cool, you know chilling with Richard and the boys."

Matt cleared his throat. "Um, Richard?"

"Yeah, Richard Dawkins is one of my fish, my favorite actually. The other fish are kind of jerks and pick on him. We're all chilling here trying to get some work done and I realized I left my computer charger at your house." She surprised herself with how easily the conversation flowed with Matt. She wasn't renowned for her levity but something about him helped her tap into that part of her.

"See, my cunning plan of stealing your stuff while you're sleeping so you have to come back is working. I'm telling you I have all the moves."

"You really do." She laughed. "So, can I have it back?"

"Yeah of course. I'm just about to finish up for the night. Want to meet me at my house? I can make you dinner and then maybe that sex I was going to text you about. Or I can run home and then bring it to you."

"And maybe then have some of that sex you were texting about?" Jess's skin burned. She was flirting. That is what this was. It felt like flirting. She couldn't be sure because she hadn't ever knowingly done it before.

"Yep, we could definitely do that."

Jess's cheeks ached from smiling. He made her forget. She liked Matt, not just for a quick screw. She liked to talk to him and every time she pulled out her phone, she secretly hoped he had texted her. She groaned inwardly. She couldn't like him. That is not what this was supposed to be about. He was a nice guy, a really nice guy. He deserved a really nice woman or at least a woman who could not best be described as caustic and detached.

"I live the opposite direction. How about we meet for dinner. Let's say Pentagon City."

"Did Jessica Bishop just ask me on a date? A real date? Um… yeah I'm in."

She opened her mouth to contradict him but technically it was kind of a date. She had picked the location because it was a neutral territory where she was unlikely to try to have sex with him; not that she was above having sex in public spaces, it was just less likely. She knew that if she had sex with him again it would start to look and feel too much like a relationship and she couldn't go there, not with everything that would entail.

"I'll see you in an hour. There's a great hole in the wall Mexican place called La Comida. It is one of those places that will either give you food poisoning that will land you in the ER or the best meal of your life. There is no in-between."

"I think you missed your calling as a food writer," Matt said, laughing.

He thought she was funny. No one thought she was funny. Heat crawled up her neck; her skin was on fire. *Oh shit.* She was really falling for him. She was going to have to shut that down hard. She would get her charger and that was it.

"I'll see you in an hour. Text me if you can't find the restaurant," she said.

"Or to remind you I want to have sex with you," Matt retorted.

Jess smiled. If her grin got any wider, her face was going to break. The muscles were not used to this sort of overuse.

Jess took her car because she hadn't driven it for a while and the battery would go flat if she left it much longer. Plus, she wouldn't be tempted to drink if she knew she would be driving.

She was used to taking the Metro or a taxi everywhere in DC, and she wasn't sure how to find Pentagon City from her new apartment. Once she got on the 395 there would be signs, but she couldn't be sure she would find the interstate from memory so she pulled out her phone and entered the address of La Comida and then sat her phone in the cup holder in the console.

"Guidance will begin when you join the indicated route," a chirpy voice called out. Jess pulled out of her building's underground parking structure and followed the guidance system's directions to the freeway. The traffic was bumper to bumper but she didn't mind because it gave her more time to respond to the instructions.

Jess relaxed as she merged onto the freeway. She knew where she was going from there. From the corner of her eye she saw a message flash up on her screen. She groaned, knowing what the message would be: she had used all her data for the month. "Damn it." That was the third time it had happened in the last two weeks. Each time she had topped up her plan and now she felt stupid for flat-out refusing to upgrade to an unlimited plan, because if she topped it up again she would have paid more than if she would have just committed to the premium service.

What was using all her data? When Jess reached the parking lot at the mall she pulled out her phone. The parking gods shined their love down on her and she found an end spot right near the entrance.

She glanced down at her phone. This was driving her crazy. Clearly her skill set did not extend to technology. How could she be going through data this fast? Usually Chan helped her out with this sort of thing. Before that it was Jamison rescuing her when she accidently deleted a file or when her wireless printer was acting like the spawn of Satan that it was.

Suddenly she remembered she had the best IT specialist on the Eastern Seaboard on speed dial. She rang Tina's number and then put the speaker on so she could hear her while she fiddled around with her phone.

"Hi, Jessica." Tina's voice was bright as always. Jess could imagine her smiling.

"Hey, Tina, I have a quick question totally unrelated to the case but I thought you might know how to fix it. I know you're off the clock and—"

"Fire away."

"My phone keeps running out of data and I hardly ever use it to search the internet or anything. I have no idea where my megabytes are disappearing to."

"Ah yes I can help you with that one. Are you video conferencing on it or streaming movies? That kills data fast."

Jess shook her head before she realized Tina could not see her. "No, I really only use it to call and text. The internet is more for backup."

"What about social media? Do you access those from your phone?"

"Nope, I don't use social media."

"Of course you don't." Tina laughed. "Any dating apps?"

"No, but you're just asking that to be nosy, aren't you?" Jess could not help smiling. Tina was a good laugh. If Jess could relax a bit they would probably be friends.

"Pretty much, but apps can use a lot of data, even when they're not open they can be running."

Jess stared down at her phone. "The only apps I have downloaded are ParkMobile to pay for parking and Shoshone for guidance." Electric darts fired through her skin as a zing of recognition bolted through her. "What was the guidance system Jennifer Thomson and Hannah Henderson had on their phones? I know Lydia Steiner had Shoshone, what about them?"

"Um… I'm not at my desk. I was just walking out the door. Can you give me two minutes to get upstairs and I'll call you right back?"

"Yeah. Thanks," Jess said before she cut the call. Less than ninety seconds later her phone rang. "Hey, Tina. Did you find it?" she asked.

"Yes. All three were using Shoshone," Tina confirmed.

Jess's heart pounded frantically against her ribs. "They all got lost using the same guidance system."

"Do you think that's significant? Couldn't it be a coincidence?" Tina asked.

Jess tapped her fingers on the steering wheel as she considered telling Tina what she was thinking. The idea was so off the wall she was scared to ask if it was possible because despite the adage, there really were stupid questions. "It's crazy, I know. This sounds insane but Liddy Steiner and Hannah Henderson were lost. Like really lost. We can confirm that with phone calls and text messages, and Jennifer Thomson was found nowhere near where she agreed to meet her ex-boyfriend. Let's say she was lost too. We have three women all lost while using the same satellite navigation system. What if that's how he's luring them to the kill sites. They are literally driving to their deaths and they don't even know it."

"Oh shit," Tina whispered.

"Am I crazy? Is it even possible for someone to hack into that?"

"Yes," Tina blurted. "I mean, yes that is possible and no you're not crazy. And this is all making sense. Oh God, I know what's happening with your phone. Delete the app right now. I need you to take it off your phone right now." Her voice was a panicked whisper.

"What? Why? What's going on?"

"It's the God View. Another company just got busted for it. Shoshone must have it too."

"What?" Jess's heart thundered. "I don't know what that is."

"Just delete the app," Tina shouted. "Where are you?"

"I'm in a parking lot at the mall. There are hundreds of people here. I can see a security guard. I'm fine. And I am deleting the app now."

"Good. Okay sorry about the freak-out. You can see now why I'm not a field agent. I don't do well under the pressure of dangerous situations," Tina apologized. "Wait what? You're at the mall? Since when do you go to the mall?"

"I… um… I…"

"You're on a date, aren't you? With Matt! Is it with Matt? I knew you would like him," Tina exclaimed, clearly delighted.

"Yes, I'm meeting Matt but it's not really a date. We're just meeting so he can give me back my charger and then having a quick dinner."

"Um that's the definition of a date."

Jess rolled her eyes. "Anyway, can you tell me why I needed to delete the Shoshone app right now?"

"Oh yes, sorry. I got distracted with your love life. We will be going back to that by the way. The God View means that anyone with access can see where any user is at any time, even if the app isn't open. That's why your phone was running out of data. It was constantly sending updates of your location."

"Who would have access to the God View?" Jess asked.

"In theory it should just be the back office at Shoshone. So, with a company that size maybe 100 people. They would also have the capability of overriding the destination someone put in. They could put in another destination and guide them there just like you said about your killer."

Jess squeezed the steering wheel. This was the piece she had been missing. "Okay 100 employees is better odds than we started with. Can you please find out who at Shoshone has access to the God View? If we can get their names we can do full background checks and then move into surveillance with anyone who fits. Maybe we'll get lucky if we cross-reference with people who have bought embalming fluids. That's got to narrow it down. Also we need to see if our three potential suspects could somehow have access. Can you please check if Mike Snowberger, Joel Nester, and Andy Sutton have any connection to Shoshone?"

"Okay I'm on it. I'll call you back if I find anything."

"We need to let the team in on this. Can you call everyone in?" Jess glanced down at her watch. "I can be back in less than an hour." Jess knew she should ask Tina to check the suspects' connection to her father's crimes too, but she couldn't bring herself to do it. She would let Jeanie tell everyone at once so she would not have to repeat the same story over and over.

"You're on a date. Besides you just landed. Give yourself a few hours to catch your breath. I can handle things on my end. I'll just be doing computer searches. There is nothing for you to do right now anyway. Have dinner. You need to eat."

Jess sighed. She itched to get back into work but Tina was right and she didn't need Jess staring over her shoulder while she worked. "Okay but call me as soon as you find anything. Anything, like I mean absolutely—"

"I'm hanging up now, Jess. Enjoy your date."

Jess didn't even have time to thank Tina before she cut the call.

Her heart would not slow down. They were close. She could feel it. She closed her eyes and took a deep breath to try to calm her nerves. Her pulse was so fast the beats ran together so it felt like her heart was vibrating. *Oh my god.* The number of times she had used her satellite navigation… alone at night. She never questioned it. It was safe. It was a tool to get her home. She scrubbed at her face. Thousands of people use the app every day, probably hundreds of thousands, more likely millions.

A loud thud on her window made her jump. A piercing scream tore her throat. "Fuck, you scared me!" she screamed. Her entire body shook. She held onto the steering wheel to try to quell the shaking, but all of her vibrated with adrenalin.

Matt opened the car door. "I'm so sorry. I thought you saw me. Hey, what's wrong? I'm sorry I scared you, Jess." He leaned in to unbuckle her seat belt so he could gather her against his chest in a bear hug.

"I'm sorry. I can't stop shaking," she whispered.

"I know. I got you." He pulled her in closer. "Are you okay?"

Jess blinked a few times before she could answer. "I keep losing it in front of you."

"I know. I'm starting to think it's me."

She smiled. "No, it's not you. You don't upset me."

"Good. I never want to hurt you."

She smiled at his response. "Thank you," she said after a few moments when her body had stopped shaking and her pulse had returned to baseline.

"For what?"

"For letting me lose my shit with you."

"Anytime. Did someone upset you? You want to tell me what you're upset about?"

She did actually. For the first time ever she wanted to talk about her feelings with someone. She didn't feel the need to pretend she was okay. "Yeah, I'm sad. And I'm scared and excited and a little stressed and happy. I'm happy to see you," she admitted. She realized she wasn't making sense so she explained further. "The first stage in emotional regulation is teaching kids how to identify and name emotions. The second step is teaching them how to deal with them. I don't think I ever made it to the second step so right now I am feeling a lot of emotions and I'm not really sure what to do with them, but my endocrine system seems to know what to do, so it's doing its thing and throwing adrenalin at me. I'm just along for the ride."

"Okay. I'm happy to come along for the ride too if you'll let me. I like you, Jess. I like how analytical you are, even now about your feelings. I like that." He pulled back so he could look at her. "I like a lot about you actually."

I like you too. The words hung between them but she couldn't say them. Instead, she picked up her phone and started texting.

"What are you doing?"

"I'm texting you my address because hopefully at some point in the future you're going to text me to say you want to have sex and I'm going to text back, *'Come on over.'*"

★★★

"I only order a main course here because I need something to put the salsa on. When the waiter comes and asks you which salsa you would like, the correct answer is either the hottest one you have or all four please. Either answer is acceptable," Jess said as she picked up the menu. She glanced over at Matt. It was hard to be stressed around him. He was so laid back and unassuming. She liked the way he made her feel at ease, made her forget to worry.

Their waiter, Javier, came up just then with a bowl of sliced serrano peppers. "For you, Miss Jessie, because the cook never could get it hot enough."

"Ah, you remembered. Thank you, Javier."

"Do you come here a lot?" Matt asked when Javier had left.

"Jamison, that's my partner, and I, we used to come here about once a month. I haven't been in a while."

Matt's smile flattened. "Yeah, I remember Jamison. I'm fairly certain you and I would have hooked up three years ago if it wasn't for him."

Jess nodded because she didn't know what to say to that. Chances were they would have hooked up then and that would have been the end of it.

"I wondered that night if he stopped us because he was in love with you."

"No." Jess shook her head a bit too emphatically. "He was looking after me because we're partners but that's all it is, all it ever was." *All it ever will be.*

"It seemed like more. The way he looked at you. He was way into you."

"I like the steak fajitas but the chicken burrito is also great."

Matt laughed. "You're very subtle with your topic changes."

"Yeah, it's a gift," Jess said just as her phone rang. She glanced down at Tina's number. Her heart picked up speed. She didn't think Tina would get back to her so quickly. "Sorry, I need to take this. It's work. Give me two minutes. If the waiter comes back I'll have the steak fajitas." Jess stood up and walked outside to take the call. "Hi Tina, what do you have?"

"Okay, well I've been doing a bit of digging. Shoshone does indeed have the God View feature but more importantly it has a few other insidious features. The first is that in the terms and conditions you basically sign your life away. They should have called themselves Rumpelstiltskin because you may as well be promising them your firstborn child. Second of all, you know how you can sign in with your social media account? Well, you don't because you don't actually have one, but for the rest of us this part matters. Shoshone keeps a record of your password, and because most people use the same password for multiple things, anyone with access to the God View has access to your social media, including private messages. That's how your guy is getting information and picking targets."

"Wow."

"I haven't got to the wow part. The wow part is the killer has had failed targets. Not every woman has fallen for it. I went on a few internet forums and I found three women in the DC area complaining that Shoshone gave them the wrong directions. In each case, they figured it out and downloaded a map instead. You were right, Jess, this guy is using satellite navigation to lure women to him. The whole system is compromised. As long as this guy has the password, no one is safe."

"Shit. This is big." Jess's hands shook from the adrenalin surge. "What are we going to do? There are millions of people who use this app."

"We need to get it pulled from the market. Women are at risk."

Jess shook her head. "It's too big. This is a public company. We can't force them to shut down and they won't do it voluntarily."

"Then we take it to the media. Women need to know about this," Tina said.

"I know but that's not our call to make."

"How can you say that? We can make a call. I can make a call. Like I will literally pick up the phone and do that."

"No," Jess said. She got where Tina was coming from, but knee-jerk reactions would not make anyone safer. "This is above our pay grade. Any decision to go public can't be made at our level. It will start a panic and he will get lost in the mayhem. If he knows we're onto him, we'll lose him. I know your gut says to blow the whistle on it but that won't catch him. I'm going to call Jeanie. We need her to make the call."

There was a heavy sigh on the other end of the phone. "You're right," Tina said. Her words said she agreed but her tone said she was not happy about it. "Jeanie's still here. I'll speak to her."

"Thanks, Tina. And really good work today. I'm glad we were able to steal you from white collar."

"Thank you. See you in the morning."

Jess hung up the call. Without hesitating, she called Jamison. It was her body's natural reflex. Good news or bad, she always wanted to share it with him. The phone rang six times. On the seventh ring she thought the call was going to go through to voicemail but Jamison picked up. "Jessie, it's really not a good time." Siren's blared in the background.

"What's wrong?" she demanded. Something was wrong; she could hear it in his voice.

"That's the police on their way. They're coming to interview me. Felicia is missing."

Her hands were suddenly slick. She almost dropped the phone. "I'm coming. I'll be right there." She cut the call before he could tell her not to come.

Jess ran back into the restaurant. She threw what little cash she had onto the table. "I'm sorry. I have to go. It's work. Please stay and have dinner."

Matt stood up. "Are you okay? What's going on?"

She didn't have time to explain. "Yeah I'm fine. My partner needs me."

"Your partner." The corners of Matt's mouth pulled down into a frown. "The one who isn't in love with you? The one who you don't have a history with? That partner?"

Jess didn't know what to say. "I'm really sorry. He needs me, but text me later," she said, hoping he would get her meaning. Jess liked Matt and she wanted to spend time with him but this was Jamison. Her career, her partner would always come first.

CHAPTER TWENTY-SEVEN

Jess made it to Jamison's house in a time that would have bested any Grand Prix qualifying time. Luckily she had not been pulled over for speeding but she had every intention of showing her shield if she had. Nothing was going to stop her from getting to Jamison.

Jess pulled in behind one of the three police cruisers that were lined up on the street in front of Jamison's house. *Slow night, boys?*

An officer was standing on the front porch chatting with another who stood in the open doorway. Jess flashed her shield as she walked past. "I'm Special Agent Jessica Bishop."

The officer at the door, a young African-American man, nodded and allowed her to walk in. Jamison was on the couch, his head in his hands. He was wearing jeans and the "Black and Blue" T-shirt Jess had bought him.

"Hey," Jess said.

Jamison looked up at her. "Jessie." He tried to smile but it faltered at the grimace line. "You came."

"Of course," she said, slightly offended that he could contemplate an eventuality where she would not be there for him. They had not left things well between them in Alabama but that didn't matter now. They could deal with any awkwardness later. "What's going on?" She glanced around to see four officers walking around the house like they owned it.

Before he could answer, one of the officers she had passed on the way in came in and sat down across from them. The man was tall with sandy hair and hazel eyes. Faded freckles blended into what could almost pass for a tan. "I'm Officer Lewis. Can you tell me, when was the last time you saw your wife?"

"Um… I think it was two, no three days ago," Jamison said. "I can't remember. Jessie when were we in Alabama?"

Jess's eyes widened. She turned so the police officer could not see the shock that she knew was written plainly on her face. *He had not seen his wife in days?*

"It was four days ago," she said once she had regained her composure.

The officer wrote down her answer in his notepad before he looked up. "Sorry, I didn't catch your full name."

Jess gave it to him again.

"Thanks, and in what capacity do you know Mr. Briggs?" he asked without looking up from his notepad.

"Special Agent Briggs is my partner," she said, hoping his title was enough for them to award him professional courtesy as fellow law enforcement.

When Officer Lewis looked up, she noticed the deep cleft in his chin. "Partners as in romantic?"

"Partner as in he has been my colleague in the FBI for over a decade."

Officer Lewis nodded again as he wrote down her answer.

"So, Mr. Briggs. Your wife has been missing for four days and you just called it in tonight?"

Jamison shook his head. "She wasn't missing. I knew she was leaving. She was going to stay for a few days with her sister. I saw her when I got back from Alabama. She was supposed to be back today because she had an appointment with her ob-gyn. When she missed the appointment, I called her sister. When her sister said she hadn't seen her, I called it in."

Officer Lewis tapped the end of his pen on the cleft of his chin. "So the day of the domestic disturbance was the last time anyone heard from your wife?"

"Domestic disturbance?" Jessica demanded. "What domestic disturbance?"

Jamison rubbed at his eyes. "It's nothing, Jessie. We just had a disagreement."

Officer Lewis flipped through his notes. "Two neighbors reported hearing a woman screaming at around 3:15 p.m."

"It was just a disagreement. I didn't hurt my wife. I know where this is going. You see a domestic disturbance with a black man and you think the worst. I get it, man. But that's not what is happening here. Felicia is missing, not hurt, not dead, missing. And your job is to find her."

Jess sat petrified, unable to talk or move. Unease crept along her skin, alarm bells rang in the distance, but she tuned them out so she could listen to every word as Jamison repeated his story time and time again as Lewis subtly rephrased the questions. He was trying to catch Jamison out. Jess employed the same technique herself. He was looking for any small slip-up to seize upon. If he wasn't stopped, he would pick at the same spot until it unraveled or Jamison snapped.

Jess stood up. "This isn't an interrogation. You haven't arrested him. You haven't read him his Miranda rights. You have enough information to go on. Agent Briggs has been more than compliant but it is late now. If you have any more questions you can come back in the morning."

Officer Lewis gave her a hard stare. She turned to Jamison. "You're done talking. Show the officers to the door," she commanded. Jamison was not in the right state of mind to be calling the shots right now. "You're done," she repeated.

"Yeah. It's late," Jamison agreed. He got up and saw the officers out.

Jess stood at the window and watched as they huddled on the curb, talking and glancing back at the house. Officer Lewis pointed to the houses on either side of Jamison's. They must have been the ones who called in the domestic disturbance. He was making plans to interview them, if he hadn't already. Jess knew exactly how it would play out.

"Don't speak to them again without a lawyer. Don't even confirm your name," Jess said when Jamison came back. Her voice was flat. There was no emotion to express what she was feeling. She was numb. "Don't say anything incriminating to me. I don't want to have to testify against you."

"Jessie." Jamison took a step toward her.

She held up her hand to stop him. "You need a lawyer," she repeated.

Jamison's eyes pled with her. He couldn't have looked more hurt, even if she had punched him in the gut. "Jessie, I didn't—"

"Don't. You can't tell me anything. Nothing. I don't want to know. I never want to have to testify against you. I can't do that. If you need money for a retainer I will tap into my savings."

"Fuck, Jessie. You think I killed her."

"Don't!" Jess screamed. Her whole body shook with the force of it. "I have been here before. Don't say anything. Don't cry and tell me you're sorry. Don't protest your innocence. Just don't fucking speak. I will do whatever needs to be done because you're my partner but don't fucking speak to me about it."

"I didn't kill her. I don't need you to cover for me, Jessie. I'm not your dad."

"Fuck you, Jamison." She lunged forward and slapped him across the face. Her hand screamed in pain from the force of the blow but she hit him again and again until her arms burned. He didn't raise his hands to stop her or thwart the attack. "Fuck you," she whimpered when she could not raise her hand another time.

Betrayal stabbed her deep in her chest. Her heart ached with it. Jess grabbed her bag off the coffee table. She couldn't be here. Jess would do everything within her power to help Jamison but she could not look at him right now.

CHAPTER TWENTY-EIGHT

The buzz of her doorbell pulled Jess out of sleep. The room was black except for the sliver of light around the blind. She sat up and rubbed her eyes and waited for the tinny sound to chirp again so she would know she wasn't dreaming. She had fallen asleep researching Shoshone. Their investor relations page was a wealth of information with everything from employee bios to presentations, and a letter from the founder espousing the company ethos. The words "safety and wellbeing is paramount" stood out as particularly ironic given the spate of murders the app had facilitated.

When the doorbell chimed again, Jess grabbed her Glock off her bedside table before she went to the living room and pressed the intercom. "Hello?"

"Jessie, it's me. Can I come up?"

"I can't do this." Jess's voice cracked. "I can't see you right now." Her hand still ached where she had hit him but that sting paled in comparison to the ache in her chest. She had trusted Jamison with her darkest secret, that she had lied to protect her father, and he had thrown it back in her face. No one had ever made her feel so small or dirty as Jamison had.

"Please give me five minutes, I need to explain. They found Felicia. They spotted her car in a hotel parking lot near the Washington Monument. She used her credit card to check in after our fight. A police officer is going to interview her in the morning."

Jess didn't respond. There was nothing to say. She should probably feel relief that Felicia had been found, but she felt nothing.

"I told you I didn't hurt her," Jamison said. His voice was raw; the pain was still there. His deep tone scarred with an undercurrent of grief telling Jess she did not have a monopoly on betrayal. There was plenty going around.

"Five minutes," she said as she buzzed him in.

Jess put her gun on the coffee table and then unbolted the door and waited for the elevator to arrive at the top floor, but it didn't. Instead, Jamison rounded the corner from the entrance of the stairs.

"Hey," he said.

"Hey." Jess stepped to the side to let Jamison in. The glow of the fish tank was the only light in the room. She closed the door and then turned to face him. "I'm glad they found Felicia. That's great." It was the right thing to say so she said it even though she had no idea how she really felt about it.

"I made a mistake, Jessie. You were right. I just wanted to do the right thing, be a good man, but I shouldn't have married Felicia. I don't love her. I never have. It's over."

Jess waited for the relief and vindication the words should have brought, but they didn't come. They were empty words; none of them mattered now. What was done was done.

Jamison took a step closer. "She left because we had a fight."

"I know. I figured that out with the domestic disturbance report."

"We were fighting about you."

Jess's eyes widened. "What? Why?"

"Because she figured it out when she met you."

She shook her head. "What? What did she figure out?"

"She said again that she wanted us to move to San Francisco and I told her I couldn't do that. And she asked why and I told her the truth. I can't leave you, Jessie. I can't do it again. I never should have gone."

His stare was hard on her, the desire palpable. Heat radiated off him. She recognized the look in his eyes, had seen it in countless men, but never had it been so acutely mirrored in her.

Jess swallowed hard. So many thoughts fired at her but no accompanying words. Jamison's proximity made it hard to think. There were so many reasons she should push him away but the attraction was too strong. She was too tired and raw to rationalize. She knew he would make her feel good. If only for a few minutes he would make her forget everything.

"Are you going to say something?"

"I don't know what to say." She bit into her lip until she tasted blood. This was a line they shouldn't cross but she didn't have the resolve to stop. She wanted him too much. She needed Jamison to see sense and stop this insanity while they still could. "In Alabama you said—"

He put his arms around her waist and pulled her against him. "I know what I said and I was wrong. Yeah, you're messed up but I'm messed up too. I think that's why we work. I do want to be that man for you, the one that makes you feel good and the one that helps you forget. I've always wanted to be that man."

All the air left her body in an audible whoosh. If she was dreaming she didn't want to wake up.

"We both have a lot we want to forget tonight. Let me be that man for you, Jessie."

She didn't need words or promises. They meant nothing to her. They both knew what this was: two people finding comfort and pleasure in each other. It could never be anything more than that because they were like two negatively charged magnets: they could only get so close before they violently repelled each other. "Jamison—"

He silenced her with a kiss. His mouth was hot and needy on hers. As soon as his tongue touched hers, all her resolve was gone. She wanted him, she always had. She had ignored it, pretended the attraction was not there. They both had. They had fought it hard but in the end, they'd lost. She tugged on his shirt, pulling it out of his jeans so she could get her hand under it. She needed to feel him. Her hands were everywhere, mapping each muscle, every hard plain and deep ridge.

Her need was frantic. She had to have him now before one of them came to their senses. She needed him inside her, just once, an experience that no one could take away or undo. This might be all they got so she was going to take as much as she could.

Suddenly she felt like she had been doing it wrong all these years. With Jamison there was no desire to get numb. She wanted every sensation, every sight, and every feeling.

Jess tore at his clothes. She couldn't get them off him fast enough. If he was naked he couldn't leave. She unbuttoned his jeans and pulled them to the ground, followed by his boxers. She tried to pull off his shirt but he was too tall so she gave up and took off her shirt instead. She stripped naked in front of him. She felt vulnerable and exposed but more alive than she ever had before. "Please don't stop this time," she whispered.

"I'm not stopping." He pressed her hard against the door and pushed into her with a single hard thrust. "I don't think I could even if I wanted to."

Her eyes watered at the sudden invasion "Don't stop," she begged when he hesitated. He was giving her time to adjust but that was time where he could change his mind and she could not bear that tonight. Even though she knew it was a mistake, she needed to be with Jamison just once.

She held onto him. She never wanted to let go because in that moment the world felt right. She held onto him, savoring every touch and kiss, willing them to memory so that later when she told herself it meant nothing, she would know she was lying.

Don't let it end.

But eventually it did. Jamison carried her into her bedroom and laid her down on the bed.

"Please don't go yet." She hated how needy she sounded; it wasn't her, she didn't need anyone but she wasn't ready for things to go back to normal. Her normal wasn't happy.

Jess wasn't a doe-eyed girl looking for love. She knew how this worked. He was right—they were both screwed up in their own way but that wasn't enough. Her alarm would be going off in a few hours and it would be like this never happened, but for right now she wanted to pretend.

The mattress dipped as Jamison climbed in bed beside her. He pulled her against his chest and he kissed her temple. "I'm not going anywhere." He kissed her and then they had sex again, this time slower. There was no need to sprint to the finish just to make sure it really happened. Jamison was there, in her bed, and he wasn't going anywhere.

Jess slammed her hand down on the snooze button of her alarm. It was too early. She needed ten minutes to lay in bed with Jamison. His weight was heavy on her back as he cuddled her, almost pinning her to the mattress, but she didn't want to move. It felt good: right, like her body was made to have his beside her.

The buzzing went off again. She hit the snooze button again before she realized it was her doorbell. "Shit," she muttered when she realized whoever was ringing the bell wasn't going to stop until she answered. It was probably a delivery. Deliverymen had a bad habit of ringing every apartment number until someone answered and let them in. Maybe if she ignored it long enough some other schmuck would answer it.

"Jessie, I think there's someone at your door." Sleep took the timbre of Jamison's bass voice to impossibly deep levels.

"I know. But if we ignore it, it will stop. It's not for me anyway. Nobody has my address." Jess's eyes widened as she remembered.

Shit. She struggled out of Jamison's embrace and sat up. Someone did have her address. She had given it to Matt. Oh God, and he had texted her last night but she hadn't responded because she was too upset to deal with human interaction of any kind. Oh God, this was awkward.

"Where did I put my sweatpants?" She opened her top drawer and pulled on a fresh pair of underwear and slipped on a T-shirt and the suit trousers she had worn the day before. "I'm coming already. Stop." She jumped when the buzzer blared again.

She ran to the intercom at the front door. "Hey," she said as she held down the button.

"Jessica Bishop?" an unfamiliar voice asked.

"Who is this?"

"This is Officer Cervetti from the Metropolitan Police. We're looking for Jamison Briggs."

"Why?" Jess stared at the grainy video of the monitor. Two Caucasian police officers stood at the entrance to her building.

"Miss Bishop we are looking for Mr. Briggs. Is he in there?"

Jess ran back to the kitchen and grabbed a pad of paper and a ballpoint pen off the counter. "Hold up your badge," Jess said.

Officer Cervetti complied.

"It's too close. Pull it back a little," Jess said. The pen wouldn't work when she held it horizontally so she put the paper on her bent knee and scribbled down the shield number. She examined the shield. It looked authentic.

"Jessie, who is it?" Jamison rounded the corner from the bedroom still stark naked because he had left his clothes at the front door last night. There was no self-consciousness there at all, like it was perfectly natural for him to be undressed in front of her. Though no man would be self-conscious about taking his clothes off if he looked like Jamison.

"The Metropolitan PD sent some officers to speak to you."

Jamison's dark brow arched in question. "What? Why?" He pulled on his boxers and jeans. "Okay let them in," he said as he pulled his T-shirt over his head.

Jess opened the door and waited for the officers to make their way up. Thirty seconds later the elevator doors slid open and eight uniformed officers came up, all wearing bulletproof vests.

What the hell? Talk about overkill. No wonder they were always complaining of budget problems if this was the way they wasted manpower.

"Jessica Bishop?" the one who identified himself as Officer Cervetti asked. He was young, looked fresh out of the academy. He had the slim body of a boy, not yet filled out. His hair was cut nearly to the scalp on the sides but the top was a mop of dark curls. His eyes, which were the same espresso shade, were thickly lashed, which made his rapid blinking all the more apparent. His partner didn't identify himself and Jess didn't care to ask. If possible, he looked even younger, like a fairer version of his partner. Behind them were another six officers of varying ages. She didn't bother to get names because it was too early to care.

"Yes, I'm Agent Bishop. Come on in. Is there a problem?" Jess stepped to the side to allow them into her apartment. This was the most people that had been there at once since she had moved in.

The officers stood in her living room, silently surveying the surroundings. The youngest-looking one swallowed several times; his Adam's apple bobbed up and down as his gaze darted around the room. He was nervous. He was trying to ascertain the risks to himself.

The hairs on the back of Jess's neck prickled. This was not a routine follow-up for a domestic disturbance or even a missing person.

"Gun!" one of the officers screamed, pointing to the Glock on her coffee table.

Jess jumped. On reflex her hand went to her hip for her own gun but of course it was lying on the table where she had left it last night.

"Gun! Gun! Gun!" he screamed again. Every officer drew their weapon. "Put your hands up. Now! Now! Get them up over your head," he screamed again.

"That's my service weapon. I'm FBI," Jess shouted, but words were swallowed by the chaos.

"Get your hands up, asshole!" one of them shouted.

Jamison moved in front of Jess to shield her. "Take it easy, boys. Nobody pulled a gun." His hands were already raised above his head but the officers kept shouting. "My hands can't get any higher, man. It's all good. Come on. Just dial it back. It's all good." Like always, Jamison was cool as ice. "Nobody wants to draw their weapon on you. Take it easy."

"Don't tell me what to do, asshole," Cervetti shouted. His hand shook with rage or adrenalin. "Turn around. Get on your knees."

Jamison slowly shook his head but he complied. Cervetti slapped handcuffs on him.

"What the hell are you doing? Why are you putting cuffs on him? Is it because he's twice your size or because he's black? Seriously, what the hell is your problem?" Jess demanded. "That is my service weapon, which I have every right to have in my home. Don't forget I have your badge number, jackass." She would be going in personally to file a report. She had a shitload of vacation time she needed to take and she couldn't think of a better way to spend it.

Jamison's eyes pleaded with her not to say anything else but the rage boiled too hot for her to contain.

"Jamison Briggs, you're under arrest for the murder of Felicia Briggs and her unborn child. You have the right to remain silent. Anything you do say can and will be used against you in the court of law."

Jess gasped. *No!* Surely, she had misheard him. She lunged back and hit the bookcase. The one picture on her shelf, of her shaking hands with the director of the FBI at her graduation ceremony when she received her marksmanship award, fell. Glass shattered. A shard ricocheted and embedded in the top her foot. "No," she whispered. "No, not again." Instantly she remembered the feeling of her dad being pulled away from her, her hand slipping out of his, his palm sliding over hers as she clenched onto his fingers. And then he was gone. The memory galvanized her. *Not again.* She stepped forward to reach Jamison. Glass crunched under her bare feet but the pain did not reach her. "Don't say anything. I'm calling you a lawyer. Don't speak to anyone until he gets there."

She would do what needed to be done. He was her partner, she had his back.

Jess watched from her window as Jamison was led outside and put in the back of the police car.

As soon as Jess had hired a lawyer, she drove straight to Jamison's house. She wasn't even sure why she was there but she needed to see it for herself. If this was the crime scene, she had to see it.

Jess looked over her shoulder before she opened the door. The bureau had taught her many things, including how to pick almost any lock.

The house was eerily quiet but reminders of Felicia were everywhere. On the hall table there was the latest copy of a parenting magazine and pair of purple reading glasses. By the door was a polka-dot umbrella and Wellington boots like she had just returned from a walk. This wasn't just a crime scene, this was a family home: her home. Felicia should be here. Jess half expected her to round the corner with a tray of cookies in her hands.

What the hell am I doing? Why was she even here? Was it to find evidence of Jamison's innocence or his guilt? She didn't know.

And what if she found something? What then? Would she destroy the evidence? Is that why she was here? She was too afraid to let herself answer that question.

Jess pressed her back against the door for support. It was hard to breathe. She tried to compartmentalize and push everything down but vignettes kept playing in her mind. She saw Felicia smiling and the gentle swell of her pregnant belly.

Oh God, Jamison. Why? How did it happen? She could not imagine an eventuality where Jamison would hurt a woman, any woman, and especially not his wife and his unborn child. It just wasn't him. It must have been an accident.

It didn't matter. No matter what happened, Jess couldn't tamper with evidence. And she couldn't lie, not even for Jamison. Her stomach ached. It was like feral cats trying to claw their way out. She couldn't do it. She scrunched her hands into fists to keep them from shaking. How fucking pathetic was she that she would even consider tampering with evidence?

Jamison was right about one thing: she was screwed up. She had been willing to sacrifice who she was and everything she believed in because she was scared of losing someone she cared about again.

She shook her head. No, not again. She wouldn't make that mistake. She was an adult now and she wouldn't break the law for anyone. She was a child then with no control or real comprehension of the world. What happened with her dad wasn't her fault. Realization struck her like a blow to the gut. All the years with social workers and therapists trying to help her find absolution and she couldn't because she didn't get it, the guilt wouldn't let her. "It wasn't my fault," she whispered as she slid down the door.

She had actually considered destroying evidence.

She was going to be sick. Jess propelled herself forward and ran to the bathroom. She reached the toilet just as bile began a vicious assault on the back of her throat. Her gut clenched as she heaved over and over. Even after her body had nothing more to offer, her stomach cramped. Her eyes watered from the force. Jess held on to the cool porcelain until her head stopped spinning enough for her to stand up and wash her face. A dusting of purple-red blots covered her cheeks and eyelids where blood vessels had burst. No concealer was going to cover that up. She looked like shit but it was fitting because this was probably the shittiest moment of her life. Shame fell heavy on her. *But I didn't do it.* She repeated the words over and over.

She had savings; not a lot but enough to fund Jamison's defense, and she could tap into her retirement if she needed to. She would do this properly and have faith in the system.

From the corner of her eye, the glint of metal reflecting in the mirror caught her attention. Jess turned to examine a large gold ring nestled between two stacks of folded hand towels. She picked it up to look at the tarnished face. A delta symbol stood proud, black like soot, like it had been burnt.

Jess gasped. The ring slipped through her fingers, falling on the tiles and bouncing against the wall before it finally landed between the toilet and the vanity unit.

Jess's pulse spiked. *That shape.* Identical to the delta sign branded on her father and Jennifer Thomson. *Oh God! No!* Her mind screamed. Why? Why did Jamison have a burned ring? Come on, there had to be an explanation. *Oh shit. No. Oh God, no.*

Jess dropped to her knees. She was wrong; she had to be. She pulled her phone out of her pocket and switched on the flashlight. The light illuminated the black lines of the triangle. She stared at it for several minutes, examining every facet without moving it. Forensics would have to match it to the burn on Jennifer Thomson but Jess knew.

It was a match.

Jess collapsed against the wall. She pulled her knees up to her chest. Her mind fired accusations at her, compiling evidence and mounting a case. In her mind she heard Chan's voice warning her. *I don't trust him. Undercover work fucks with people. He's changed. Just be careful.* She shook her head to dislodge the thoughts. This was Jamison. It couldn't be him. She couldn't reconcile the brutality of the crimes with the man she knew.

But even as she made excuses, the timeline flashed in her mind. Jamison didn't have an alibi for Jennifer Thomson's murder and he was in Louisiana when Lydia Steiner's car was found abandoned. Oh God, Jennifer saw him. That was why she was murdered.

Her body shook as she tried to keep a sob from bubbling up. This wasn't the time to break down. She took a deep breath and held it until it burned. She needed to be rational. She was too close to see anything clearly; she had go back to the elements: means, motive, and opportunity.

She would never see the motive, she just wouldn't. She never saw it in her dad and she would never see it in Jamison, so that left means and opportunity. Her skin went cold as she played through the timeline.

Jamison didn't have an alibi for any of the murders. She shook her head. Why? Why would he do it? And why bring Jess into the depravity. Was it to punish her for the things she said when he left? Or was he just so messed up from his time undercover? The things he had seen, the things he was forced to do. Guilt pierced her thoughts. She had known something was wrong with him, but she ignored it. That was why she didn't let him tell her the details of the drug dealer's death. Murder. Jamison admitted to killing a man, that was murder, no two ways about it. He had killed someone and Jess had accepted that as normal. He had excuses and she was more than happy to believe them; hell, she would have made up the excuses for him.

She couldn't do this. She was too close. She would just drive herself crazy. She stared at the ring. She didn't realize until that moment it was possible to hate an inanimate object, but she did.

She wanted to throw it in the trash, or flush it down the toilet, or bury it: anything to make it disappear. She could easily enough put it in her pocket and no one would ever be the wiser. But destroying the evidence would not destroy the truth. She would always know.

How could she love a man capable of such sadistic violence? Twice.

CHAPTER TWENTY-NINE

Jess had never felt worse. In a lifetime punctuated by shitty days, this one stood out, taking pride of place. She couldn't kid herself that it was going to get better anytime soon either. The worst days were still to come but she couldn't think about that now. She contemplated not going into the office. She had nothing positive to contribute to her team today. They would figure things out faster without her. Even at the best of times she didn't consider herself indispensable; she was just another foot soldier in the war against crime, but now she would be actively hindering an investigation. She couldn't point anyone in Jamison's direction; this was a death penalty case after all. She knew now she could not destroy evidence but she sure as hell would not be putting the needle in his arm.

At some point she needed to speak to Jeanie. She owed it to her boss to be upfront about her relationship with Jamison. It wouldn't be fair for the prosecution to blindside her; it would undermine the credibility of everyone on the team. Jeanie deserved better than that so Jess would tell her that she had slept with Jamison.

But not until her team named him as a suspect.

Jess found Tina in the break room eating a lemon yogurt and reading a dog-eared paperback. On the cover was a shirtless cowboy with more abdominal muscles than human anatomy deemed possible. She was so engrossed in the book that she didn't take her eyes off the page as she ate.

"Hey," Jess said from the doorway.

Tina was startled. "Sorry, I didn't see you there. Chrishell is about to tell Chase the baby is his not his brother's after all, hopefully in time for a bone marrow transplant to save Gunner. By the way, I called all of this on page eleven."

"Oh," was all Jess could think to say. She had never read a romance novel so she wasn't sure if the melodrama and odd names were integral components for the genre.

"I know it sounds ridiculous but I'm a sucker for a happy ending. Torture the hell out of the characters but at the end I want them holding hands as they walk off into the sunset."

"I like the sound of that too," Jess admitted. "But I don't think I have the willing suspension of disbelief required." She opened the cupboard and pulled out a chipped mug with a picture of a cat hanging from a limb, and poured herself a cup of coffee.

"That has been on the warmer since this morning. It'll be burnt by now."

Jess took a sip. It wasn't great but it was still coffee.

"We postponed the morning meeting for you. Lots of new developments." Tina scraped around the edge of the carton to get the last spoonful of yogurt.

Jess's head snapped up. She thought she had missed the meeting. She had specifically told Chan to make sure they went ahead and had it without her. She obviously couldn't tell them but she was bowing out of the investigation. They were good; they would piece everything together. All Jess could do was sit and watch.

"There. I just messaged everyone. Meeting in five minutes."

Tina was always so genuinely happy and friendly. Maybe it was the romance novels. Jess needed to try one, or she could take up binge-drinking. It wasn't too late to develop alcoholism and fully embrace the stereotype of a lonely maverick detective. She was already halfway there.

Jess threw back her head and downed the rest of her coffee in several hurried gulps before she poured herself another cup. "Okay, let's do this."

Jeanie, Chan, and Milligan were all in the conference room when Jess and Tina arrived. Jess chose the seat opposite Chan. Milligan still wasn't giving her eye contact but she didn't have the time or energy to worry about that.

"What the hell happened to you?" Chan said pointing to her face.

She had forgotten about the broken blood vessels on her face. "I… uh," Jess sputtered to come up with an excuse. She had planned on going home to try to cover it with powder but she had forgotten.

"Don't be a jerk," Tina said. "Nobody points out your crimes against hair gel."

Jess smiled her thanks to Tina. If Jess's life were ever less of a mess she would definitely consider hanging out with her out of work.

"Okay, that's enough of that. Let's get started." Jeanie sounded like a school teacher rounding up her errant pupils. "First of all, it has been brought to my attention that Agent Briggs has been taken in by the Metropolitan Police. I know we're all shocked by this and I will keep you updated as things develop. I have a call in to Lieutenant Ogilvie." The way she glanced at Chan made it seem like he had been the bearer of bad news. The looks on Tina and Milligan's faces told her this wasn't the first time they were hearing the information. No doubt it had been the hot topic that morning.

"I don't think any of us are really that surprised. When my buddy down at the two seven called me, shock was not what I felt. I'll tell you that. I'm just surprised it didn't happen sooner. He was always weird."

"Agent Chan, Agent Briggs has not been charged let alone convicted of a crime, it is best you remember that." Jeanie looked over her red-rimmed glasses. Her voice was soft but the message was clear.

"Good money is on him getting charged tonight." Chan did not heed her warning. He was too far gone in his celebrations. Only then did Jess fully appreciate the animosity he held toward Jamison. He wasn't going to let it go. "He killed his wife. You know where they arrested him?" Chan paused for effect. His eyes trained on her; hatred hardened his stare.

Jess swallowed hard. Electricity coursed up her neck and over her cheeks as shame flushed her skin. The muscles in her legs coiled, ready to bolt. This wasn't the way she had anticipated telling her team. Damn it, this was no one's business. He had no right to say anything and certainly not like this.

"He was shacked up with some Badge Bunny. He was cheating on his wife. That's why he killed her. Most people would just file for divorce but—"

"Agent Chan, that is more than enough," Jeanie warned. It was the first time Jess could remember hearing her raise her voice.

Jess cleared her throat. "Who was he found with?" She had to know what he knew. The uncertainty was unbearable. If he knew, she would rather have it out in the open rather than hanging above her.

Chan shrugged, "I don't know. Some bi—" He stopped himself before finishing the sentence. "Just some random woman, not his wife."

Jess let go of the breath she was holding, an invisible weight lifted.

"I know we're *all* very concerned about Agent Briggs but we have a case," Jeanie reminded them. She stressed "all" to let Chan know he had better fake concern if he couldn't really muster any. "We have had a tremendous number of developments over the last twenty-four hours. Firstly, well done to Agent Flowers and Agent Bishop. Through some very impressive work they have managed to uncover the MO of the killer and narrow our pool of potential suspects."

"It was mostly Tina," Jess blurted. Praise was in very short supply from Jeanie. Normally Jess would have basked in it, but it felt wrong delighting in closing the noose around Jamison.

Tina smiled. "Thank you."

"I have spoken directly to the management of Shoshone. After a bit of persuasion, their CEO saw things my way and he is eager to help. Originally we believed that only around 100 employees would have access to the God View; unfortunately the number is six times that amount. We are running background checks on all the employees as we speak."

"But you're not shutting them down?" Milligan asked.

"No. The product is not defective and has not led directly to the deaths of anyone. There are no legal grounds for pulling the product," Jeanie said. It was impossible to tell what she was thinking because she played her cards close to her chest. If she were chagrined, they would be the last to know.

"But it's not safe for the people who use it. Five women have been murdered," Milligan pressed.

"The killer also used a saw and formaldehyde. Would you suggest having those pulled from the market too?" Jeanie didn't give him time to answer before she said, "We also have another development. Tina, can you tell them about the call you received from the field office in New Orleans?"

"Sure. Yes, I received a call about an hour ago. They were able to recover DNA from under two of Jennifer Thomson's fingernails. It looks like she scratched her assailant. They have typed it and are running it through CODIS, so hopefully we might have a match today."

Jess's mouth dropped open. She wasn't ready. She thought she had a few days or weeks to figure things out. Who was she kidding? Even if she had years she would not know how to deal.

"Before anyone asks," Jeanie said, smiling, "no, we cannot compel all 600 Shoshone employees to submit to a DNA test, but fortunately their management realizes it would be advantageous to deal with this quickly and so have implemented a voluntary program. Naturally, as a voluntary program, certain individuals may choose to opt out. That is of course completely within their right. And it is completely within our right to have a closer look at those people."

Well played. Jess had to smile. As always, Jeanie's face was a picture of placid serenity. No doubt Shoshone thought they had the upper hand when they were dealing with Jeannie, but she hadn't even dealt them into the game. She always managed to end up on top, and a lot of the time people didn't even realize because they were too busy underestimating her. More fool them because under the unassuming demeanor was an iron will. She was bridled strength, calm, focused, and always in control. Jess had learned so much by watching her.

"Right. I think that is us. Unless anyone has anything else to add?" Jeanie looked around the room. When no one said anything, she said, "Jessica could you hang back so I could speak to you for a second?"

Jess blinked. "Um… yeah sure."

Jeanie waited for everyone to clear the room. "How are you?" Jeanie stared at her over her glasses. She was wearing an olive-green cardigan with tiny mother of pearl buttons down the front. It looked hand-knit. Jess could imagine Jeanie curled up by a fire listening to music and knitting, or whatever normal, wholesome people did.

Jess shrugged. "Fine." Jess didn't know what she had expected Jeanie to say but it wasn't that.

"You may notice I didn't mention the similarities between the brand used on Jennifer Thomson and the one used on your father."

Jess sucked in a sharp breath.

"I think it's best for everyone if that aspect of the investigation is handled with discretion. I will personally be handling that. I am checking every suspect's links to you and/or your father."

"Thank you." Jess didn't ask how and when the team would be informed of her past. She didn't want to know.

Jeanie nodded. "You have a lot going on right now. You only just got your partner back and now that partnership faces an uncertain future. That alone is a lot of upheaval for any agent."

Jess didn't know what to say. From the way Jeanie was studying her she sensed that Jeanie knew something. When Jeanie looked at her she felt like she really saw her, and that scared Jess. "I'm worried. If that is what you're asking." She was going to find out soon enough, and Jess owed it to her to be the one who told her. She shouldn't have to read it in a police report.

Jess licked her lips. Her mouth was suddenly dry. More than anyone in her life, Jess cared what Jeanie thought of her. She didn't realize it until that moment how much of her career was based on wanting to make Jeanie proud. In a lot of ways she was the mother she had always wanted. "Jamison was arrested at my apartment." When Jeanie didn't react, Jess added, "He spent the night with me last night." She couldn't bring herself to look her in the eye. She couldn't bear to see disappointment or anger there.

"I see. Did his wife know you were having an affair?" There was no surprise or judgment, just a question.

"No!" Jess's head snapped up. "It wasn't like that. It only started. Last night was the only time."

"The first time since he came back?" Jeanie pressed.

Jess shook her head. "No ma'am. That was the first time ever. Jamison and I were never more than friends."

Jeanie smiled. "You were always more than friends, Jessica. Whether you were intimate was another matter, but your partnership went beyond friendship."

She nodded. She wished she had the insight into her life that the people around her seemed to have. Not that any of that mattered now. "Is he going to be charged today?"

"I don't know. I wish I could tell you more. But that is what I wanted to talk to you about. You are going to need another partner for the foreseeable future so I wanted to get your thoughts. Obviously we are going to need someone to fill in for Jamison. You worked well with Chan. If you would like to be paired with him again, you can be. Normally I would like to pair the new person with—"

"Yes. Please partner me with Chan. I would appreciate that. Thank you." Her lungs squeezed at the thought. She didn't want any partner but Jamison, but that wasn't in the cards for her. At least with Chan she had familiarity on her side. They had worked well together before.

"All right. I will take care of that. Is there anything else you want to discuss?"

Jess bit the corner of her mouth. There was more to say but now was not the time. "No. Thank you." She gathered up her stuff and stood up.

"All right. My door is always open, Jessica. And well done with the Shoshone app. That was really good work. You should be proud."

Jess just managed something that looked like a smile before she opened the door to leave.

Chan and the team were waiting for her at the end of the hall. "What was that all about?" Chan asked.

Milligan still wouldn't look at her. Before she could reach them, he walked away. Annoyance tugged at her. He needed to get over himself. Thank God Jeanie hadn't recommended Jess be partnered with him because she would have had to rain down some home truths.

"Oh nothing. She wanted to touch bases about a report I filed," she lied. Lying was becoming second nature. If she kept it up, she would soon be as good as Chan.

"Okay, cool. Tina was just saying it was about time we had a night out so we're heading to The Local Pour after work for a drink. Do you want to join us?"

"Um no, sorry. I have plans." Another lie tumbled from her lips. She was truly excelling. "Next time," she said, knowing she would have an excuse then too.

"Plans like a date? With Matt?" Tina grinned. "I knew you two would hit it off. I'm so happy."

"Yeah, with Matt."

The corners of Chan's mouth pulled down into a frown. "Next time."

"Yeah, next time."

CHAPTER THIRTY

Jess stepped over the shards of glass from the shattered picture and collapsed onto the couch. The day had crept by in slow motion. Every minute was excruciating as she pretended to work. She stared at her monitor and even faked a phone call when she heard someone in the hallway. The entire afternoon all she wanted to do was come home, but now that she was there she couldn't understand why she had been so desperate. There was nothing here for her, and the frantic need to run away hadn't changed even though her location had.

Jess sighed. She had better clean up. She needed to sweep up the glass and strip the sheets off the bed. She couldn't sleep in a bed that smelled of him. She wanted to; that was the sick part. Even now, knowing everything, she still wanted him. God, she hated that about herself. She wasn't one of those pathetic women holding her hand up to the glass at a prison visit, pretending to hold hands with her incarcerated lover. She hated those women. They were weak and pitiful, everything that Jess detested.

She made a move to get off the couch but she couldn't. She didn't want to clean up. The glass reminded her of what had happened. She needed to fully process it this time and make a clean break. No more living in hope and denial. She closed her eyes. It physically hurt. Why did it hurt so much? Why did her body ache with it? She knew how to press things down better than anyone else but this refused to shift from the center of her chest. She couldn't keep going like this. She was going crazy. This is what insanity felt like. A scream formed in the pit of her belly but she knew if she gave into it she would never stop.

Jess needed to run. That always cleared her mind. She dragged herself off the couch and changed into shorts and a purple tank top. She laced up her shoes and then strapped on her running holster. Most people didn't carry while they ran, but most people had not seen the body of a runner that had been pulled off a path, raped for three days in a makeshift camp and then set on fire while she was still alive.

Jess plugged in earphones and picked her favorite running playlist: Absolutely No Love Songs. She strapped her phone to her arm and put her keys and a twenty-dollar bill in her pocket before she grabbed a bottle of water from the fridge. A gun, keys, phone, water, and money; she had no idea where she was going but wherever it was, that was all she needed.

She ran down the stairs and then hit the street. The streets were a blur of people. A mob trickled out of the Capital South Metro station. She kept her head down and plowed on. People could move out of her way just as easily as she could move out of theirs. By the time she ran past the Library of Congress she had hit her stride. Her muscles were warm and her heart was pulsating strong in her neck. Her speed felt good, fast but not insane, just below eight minutes a mile. She could keep this up forever or until she felt better, whichever came first. She had done this run so many times she barely registered all the landmarks that drew thousands of tourists to the city every year. She ran past the National Air and Space Museum and then past the Smithsonian and along the Mall before she turned up Pennsylvania Avenue. She picked up speed as the White House came into focus. Tourists were gathered at the gates along with a group of protestors. There were always protestors at the gates. Reading their signs was usually a highlight but today Jess kept her head down and kept running. This was where she usually turned around and ran home. If she paced it right the loop should take just over an hour but she wasn't feeling anywhere near ready to go home. The endorphins hadn't even begun to take the edge off. Nothing was quieting the voices. Every emotion she had pushed down was now pushing back. Every situation she had compartmentalized was fighting to break free from the forgotten crevices she had shoved them into. She always said she would deal with things later but in truth later meant never.

She just needed to keep running. Jess headed down a side street. She had never taken it before. The cafes with open-air seating made it look like the bistros of Europe she remembered from her childhood. People were just sitting down for dinner. She glanced in the window of a restaurant with exposed brick walls and hundreds of filament bulbs hanging from the ceiling. It looked romantic so Jess looked away and changed direction. She ran all the way down Dumbarton to Wisconsin. When she reached Canal Road she realized she had run to Georgetown, to Matt's house actually.

Jess stopped and wiped the sweat off her brow. Her breath came in labored pants. She had sprinted the last mile but no matter how fast she ran she couldn't outrun her feelings.

What was she doing? Matt had texted her to ask her for dinner but she had ignored it because she would rather spend time worrying about her propensity to love serial killers than spend time with a perfectly decent man. What the hell was wrong with her? She shook her head.

Jess couldn't just show up at his house again. If nothing else, it was rude. But she was empty and broken and maybe he could help her get numb for a while or even just take the edge off. The way she used sex was destructive and maladaptive, and judgmental people would say sinful. She knew it; she had just enough self-awareness to see it, but it worked and that was all that mattered right now.

She pulled out her phone and texted Matt:

Hey. Are you free?

She took a long swig of water.
Seconds later he texted back:

Yes. Want to get together?

Her phone was almost dead so instead of texting back she took another drink of water and then ran down the street to his house. She pressed the buzzer. She didn't let herself stop to think about what she was doing. If she thought about it she might stop, and she needed this.

A few moments later Matt opened the door. The surprise at seeing her here at his house was written on his face. "Hi. This is a nice surprise. Do you want to—"

"I don't want to talk. I can't." She hated herself so much right now but she needed the pain to stop. She stood on her tip-toes and kissed him. He wrapped his arms around her to pull her in to deepen the kiss.

He pulled back, a strange expression on his face. "Are you carrying?" Before she could answer, he undid her holster and laid it on the hall table next to his keys, then he picked her up and carried her upstairs to the bedroom.

She closed her eyes. She didn't want to see him, his face, or what he was doing. She just needed to do this and make the pain stop.

★★★

Matt collapsed on top of her. His breathing was heavy in her ear. He kissed her temple. "I'm glad you came over."

"Thanks." She kept her eyes closed. There was a mirror on the back of the bedroom door and she didn't want to see herself right now.

When he kissed her again, she winced.

"What's wrong?" he asked.

No lies would come so she didn't say anything.

"I don't have any food in the house. Do you want to go out for dinner?" Matt stood up and pulled on his pants.

Jess pulled up her shorts. They were still around her ankles. She had not even taken off her running shoes or tank top. When she stood up she glimpsed herself in the mirror. "No. I need to take a shower. I'm a mess."

Matt leaned over and kissed her. "You always look sexy. You can take a shower here. Stay over tonight. I'll take you home in the morning to get dressed for work and then we can drive in together."

"I don't—"

"Indian or Thai? I know you like it hot. Let's do take-out tonight. It's been a long day. I don't want to cook. I have seen the vindaloo from the place down the street make grown men cry. Shall I ask them to kick it up a notch for you?"

Before Jess could let herself think of an excuse, she nodded her head. She didn't want to be alone with her thoughts.

"Okay, great. Here, you can wear this after you get out of the shower." Matt pulled out a blue T-shirt from the top drawer. On the front it said New York City Marathon Finisher. She had a matching one in a smaller size.

"Did you run this?" she asked.

"Yeah, last year."

"Me too." She smiled and wondered if she had seen him there.

"What was your time?"

"Three hours, fifty minutes."

"Wow. That's fast."

Jess shrugged. Anything that looked like a compliment made her feel uncomfortable. "It was all right. I mean I was hardly keeping up with the Kenyans."

Matt smiled before he leaned down and kissed her again. "Beautiful, brilliant, and modest. That is the trifecta. And I'm dating her. I'm living the dream over here, boys."

Jess was going to correct him and tell him they weren't dating. That's not what this was. No one had talked about a relationship or commitment. If they had she would be the biggest ass on the planet because she had slept with another man less than twenty-four hours ago. She opened her mouth to object but he silenced her with another kiss.

Eventually he pulled back and said, "Take a shower and I'll order dinner. You need energy for what I have planned for you."

"Please don't say it's another run because my feet are sore. I think I have a blister on my toe."

"And you're funny. You won't be needing use of your toes for what I have planned," he laughed. "But there are Band-Aids and antiseptic cream in the top drawer if you need them."

"Thanks."

"You're welcome. Do you want rice or naan bread? There is a correct answer to this, by the way," he said, quoting her from when she had been talking about salsa.

"Um… rice please."

"Ooh, wrong answer. The correct answer is both."

"That's what I meant." She smiled.

Matt left to go order dinner while she took a shower. She loved how clean his house was. Everything was in its place. It was like a luxury hotel but if she took the soft furnishings to the lab she would not get body fluid samples from fifty individuals.

She washed and conditioned her hair and used the mandarin body wash to get rid of the last remnants of her run. Her foot did indeed have a burst blister so when she got out of the shower she put on a Band-Aid to keep it from rubbing against her other toe.

She gave her hair a quick pat dry and slipped on the T-shirt Matt lent her. She didn't have any underwear but the shirt reached to just above her knees. She still looked bad but at least she looked clean.

Jess went downstairs to find Matt paying a delivery driver. "Ooh, I have money upstairs in my shorts. Let me pay half."

Matt shut the door. "I got it. What would you like to drink? I have a bottle of Cabernet in the kitchen or I have beer. Beer goes well with curry."

Jess shook her head. "No, I'm not drinking tonight. I'm giving my liver a rest. Just water for me, thanks."

Matt took the paper bag into the dining room. He had already set the table. "I asked for the hottest dish they make."

"Bring it." Jess smiled.

Matt served a plate for her and then one for himself. He tore off a piece of naan bread and handed it to her.

Jess's mouth burned with the first bite. Even her lips were warm where they had touched the fork. Her eyes and nose watered. She swallowed and then smiled appreciatively. "That's what I'm talking about."

Matt dipped the prongs of his fork into the sauce, held it to his mouth for a tentative bite, and then went in with a forkful. He winced and grabbed his glass and chugged a mouthful of water. "How can you eat that? Oh my God, that is hot."

"Ooh, don't drink water, that will just make it worse. Capsaicin is what causes spicy food to be hot. It binds to the pain receptors on our tongues and because it's oil-based, water just spreads it around your mouth. Fats and sugars keep it from binding. That's why people add yogurt or drink soda with spicy foods."

"I would be more impressed right now with your knowledge of the science of mouth-burning food if I wasn't in physical pain. That will teach me for trying to impress you." Matt grimaced as he downed the rest of his glass of water and then started on hers.

"I'm sorry. Not many people like food as hot as me." Only one actually. Chan could match her chili for chili. He seemed to get off on pain.

Jess finished off most of the curry on her own while Matt stuck to the milder side dishes. When they were done, Jess helped him clear away the leftovers and wash the dishes.

"Are you sure you don't want that glass of wine now?" Matt asked.

"No. I'm okay." Jess knew better than to drink when she was feeling this raw. That was a recipe for alcoholism. "I just want to sit and watch really mindless television."

"I can do that."

Jess followed Matt back upstairs to the bedroom. A flat-screen television dominated the wall opposite the bed.

"Are we thinking action or comedy?" Matt asked.

Jess pulled back the covers and climbed in. "You pick."

CHAPTER THIRTY-ONE

A buzzer was ringing somewhere. Jess opened her eyes to the darkness. Rain pelted off the windowpane. Disorientated by sleep, it took her a few seconds to remember where she was, but then her day came back to her like a slap in the face.

"Matt?" she called. His side of the bed was empty. "Matt, I think there is someone at the door." Jess got up. The bathroom light was off and the door was open but Jess checked in there anyway. "Hey Matt, where are you?"

The buzzer went off again. Jess walked to the top of the landing and looked down. All the lights were off. She gripped onto the rail to keep from falling down the stairs. "Matt!" she shouted again louder. "Matt, where are you?"

Jess flipped on the switch at the bottom of the stairs, and light flooded the hall. "I'm coming," Jess called when the buzzer went off again. She stood on her toes to look through the peephole. When she saw who was standing on the other side, her heart stopped with a painful thud. "Jamison," she gasped.

Without hesitating she opened the door. All sense of self-preservation disappeared when she saw him because she knew he wouldn't hurt her. The dichotomy was there, the same one in her father: killer and protector, and Jamison was the latter to her. The monster was caged but she knew it was still there, lurking in the shadows. "How did you get out? Did you post bail already?"

Jamison's shirt was soaked through. It clung to the solid outline of his broad chest. His eyes narrowed when he saw her wearing nothing but a T-shirt. He had to have known if he found her at a man's house in the middle of the night, it was not likely for a tea party, but still he looked surprised… and sad. The corners of his mouth pulled down into a frown. Betrayal and disappointment were written plainly on his dark features. For a second he could not look directly at her. "I wasn't charged. I didn't do it, Jessie."

Jess winced at his protestations. Even after the verdict, her dad would tell anyone who would listen that he was innocent too, even Jess. Even after everything, he persisted. "How did you find me?" Jess asked. She hadn't told anyone she was spending the night with Matt. She didn't even know she was going to until she got here.

"I wanted you to know before you… well, before you did something like this. Do you even know this guy's name? Ah Jesus, Jessie." Again, he looked past her. He couldn't even look at her. His hands clenched into fists and then flattened again. "Sorry. I shouldn't have said that. It's none of my business what you do."

Her shoulders dipped under the weight of her shame. She hated that Jamison was finding her here or maybe she hated that she still cared what he thought. "How did you find me?" she asked again.

"You still have the Find My Friend app on your phone. Remember the time we got separated in Maryland and I installed it on our phones so we could always find each other?"

She swallowed hard. His words sent a glacier pumping through her body; shards of ice ripped through her veins. Jess took a step back, away from Jamison.

"Jessie, I had nothing to do with Felicia's murder. Her body was found by a maid this morning. Her credit card was used to check into a hotel. But she was never seen going in, just a man with a suitcase. When he left, he put on the "do not disturb" sign. And nobody did, not until early this morning. She had been decapitated and her limbs removed. She had the same excision sites. It's our killer, he killed Felicia."

Jess took another step back. *Stop!* Her mind screamed. Who were the lies for? The world would soon know the truth. Would he keep lying then too? Yeah, he would, the same way her dad did. Jamison reached out for her hand but she pulled away.

"Jessie, there is CCTV footage of me at an ATM across town when she checked in. There is no possible way I could have had anything to do with it. Shit, why aren't you looking at me? Are you scared? You're scared of me. Oh Christ." Jamison scrubbed at his face with both hands. He held out both hands, palms up. "I don't know what I can say."

"Jess, what's going on? Is there someone at the door?" Matt called from the back of the house. She turned to see him. He was barefoot, wearing low-slung jeans and a T-shirt. He walked up behind her and put his hand on the small of her back. "Can I help you?" he asked Jamison.

Jamison's eyes narrowed. In a flash his face changed, a potent mix of anger and recognition. Rage radiated off him. Jamison lunged forward. "You!" he shouted. "You're the one I saw coming out of my house. Jessie, get away from him." Jamison wrapped his hand around her wrist and tugged her hard. If his solid chest had not stopped her, she would have fallen flat on her face. "Jessie, get out of here."

"Jamison, stop! What are you doing?" Jess pulled away from him. "Go home, Jamison."

"I need you to listen to me. I saw this guy lurking near my house. You need to get out of here." Jamison's eyes pleaded with her. "Please trust me on this one, Jessie."

Jess shook her head. She couldn't do this anymore. No more games. Her whole body ached. No more lies. Jamison was incoherent the way her dad was. He had blamed everyone else too: soldiers, priests, teachers, the man who owned the shop at the end of the street, anyone but him. And Jess would have believed anything her dad had said if she hadn't seen the body. "I know, Jamison. I know everything."

"You know what? What do you think you know?" Jamison demanded.

Matt stepped in front of her to shield her from Jamison. "Hey, buddy. I think you need to leave."

"Move." Jamison pushed his way into the house. "I'm not leaving without my partner."

Matt shoved Jamison hard but Jamison did not budge. He outweighed Matt by at least forty pounds of muscle.

"I said move," Jamison growled.

"And I said leave." Matt lunged forward and leveled a blow to Jamison's jaw. His lip split open, dripping blood on his white shirt. Matt swung again with his other hand but this time Jamison was ready and blocked the punch.

"Jessie, get out of here. This is the guy we're looking for. Come on, girl. You need to believe me on this one. If you don't trust me, call Chan or Milligan. Have them come pick you up. Wait at the end of the street. Just get out. You just need to get out of here."

"Don't!" Jess screamed. God, she wanted to believe him. In a perfect world, it would be true and there would be an explanation for everything. She didn't even care if the explanation implicated Matt. She would sacrifice him a million times over to make things okay. "I can't deal with this bullshit. I love you, Jamison, and I will put every penny I have to my name into your defense. But don't do this to me."

Jamison's eyes widened at her admission. They had never talked about feelings but there it was. It was out now and she wouldn't take it back. She loved him still. It was all sorts of fucked up but she loved him.

"Jessie, please for me, get out."

Matt reached for her hand, pulling her back to him. "I'm going to call the police. I want you out of my house." Matt slammed the door against Jamison, pushing with all his might, but Jamison thwarted his efforts and shoved the door open, sending Matt crashing against the wall. Jamison came in and reached for her.

Matt staggered to his feet and lurched for the Glock Jess had left on the entry table but Jamison got there first. He knocked it to the floor and then dove at Matt, pinning him to the wall by his neck. "What did you do to her?" he seethed. Something in Jamison had snapped. His body shook.

Matt's eyes bulged as his face went from red to purple. "Is this what you did? Did it feel good, big man?"

"Stop!" Jess screamed but Jamison didn't listen; if anything, he squeezed harder. "Stop it!" she screeched again, this time pummeling her fists into Jamison's back. She swung at his kidneys. She hit him over and over. Any other man would have been brought to his knees but Jamison didn't even register the blows.

Matt's eyes glassed over and rolled back. He was about to lose consciousness. Jamison was going to kill him.

"Jamison, stop!" she screamed again. She couldn't watch him murder a man.

Jess dove to the ground and grabbed the Glock. She took the safety off. *Oh, Jamison. Don't make me do this.* "Stop!" she cried, pleading with him not to make her do this. "Stop or I'll shoot."

Jamison was too far gone to hear her. The rage had taken over. He wasn't the partner she had been in love with for over a decade. He was a stranger, someone capable of murder. Her instinct was to close her eyes because she could not bear to watch, but she forced her stare to lock on her target.

Jess squeezed the trigger until the recoil jolted her hand. The shot ripped into Jamison's right shoulder. Instantly his shirt was a sea of red. Jamison's arm dropped to his side. The impact pushed him into Matt. They both collapsed onto the floor. Blood continued to pour from Jamison's shoulder. The wound wasn't fatal but he would need surgery if the bullet had not gone straight through.

Jess crawled over to Jamison. She knelt beside him, cradling his head. "Why?" she whispered. "Why, Jamison, why?" Holding him now, she was overcome with the desire to kiss his temple and tell him everything was going to be okay, even though it clearly wasn't. His breath came in shallow pants.

Only when Matt groaned did she remember he was in the room. Her head snapped up. The poor man had just been assaulted and she was busy comforting his assailant. She was a special kind of disturbed. "Matt. I'm sorry. Are you okay?" She crawled over to him. "Are you hurt?"

He shook his head. He used the support of the wall to stand.

"Here, let me help you."

"I'm fine." He glared at Jamison.

"My phone is dead. Call an ambulance."

Matt didn't move, he just continued to stare at Jamison.

Her eyes narrowed in confusion. *Why isn't he calling an ambulance?* Frantic energy coiled in her. This wasn't a clean shot. Jamison needed to get to the hospital now. "He needs a doctor. I shot him," she said, stating the obvious. "You have to call an ambulance. His breathing is labored. He's bleeding a lot. He could bleed out."

Matt stared down at Jamison, stunned. He must be in shock. Of course he was, he worked in IT. He had never discharged his weapon. She took it for granted that every agent would know what to do in this situation, but most people that worked for the FBI, like Matt, had desk jobs. He would have never seen a gunshot wound.

Jess stood up. She tugged on his hand. "Come on, Matt. We need to call an ambulance."

Matt turned to face her. The expression on his face slowly changed, like a mask slipping. Anger and hatred replaced the carefree softness.

Jess took a step back. The hall table bit into her when she collided with its side. "He is going to bleed out! Where is your phone?" she demanded.

"This is a crime scene. You turned my house into a crime scene."

Jess's skin prickled at his reaction. "Come on, Matt. Look at me. It's okay. Everything is going to be fine I just need your phone. Give me your phone."

He still didn't move. He stared transfixed at the pool of blood around Jamison. His face drained of all color.

She tried to stay calm for him because any anxiety she had would be amplified in Matt and she needed him to not freak out on her. He was having an acute stress reaction but she didn't have time to deal with that now. Jamison was going to bleed to death if Matt didn't get his shit together. "Come on, Matt. You need to help me. Where is your phone? Come on. Stay with me. We need to get him to the hospital. Don't look at him. Look at me, Matt. Look at me." When Matt didn't immediately move, Jess dropped to her knees to search Jamison's pockets for a phone.

"You turned my house into a fucking crime scene. They will tear it apart." His voice rose in a potent mix of disbelief and anger.

Matt moved closer, stepping between her and Jamison so she could not reach him. A faint smell tickled her sinuses. The smallest bells of recognition rang somewhere deep in her subconscious. She stared at the small, wet patch beside his zipper. It was only the size of a dime but it was enough. With the next breath, the familiar odor was stronger. Slowly the bells rang louder, overwhelming her with a deafening cacophony she could not ignore. She knew that smell anywhere.

"Why do you have formaldehyde on your jeans, Matt?" Her voice broke.

For a moment time stopped. She couldn't breathe or think. Her synapses refused to fire. It was an act of self-preservation because every thought took her down an unimaginable path.

She had gotten it totally wrong.

A realization acute and painful stabbed into her consciousness. It was Matt. How did she not see it before? He had the skill set.

He had the opportunity. How did she miss it? She fucked up and now Jamison was paying the price.

Jess swallowed hard. She couldn't think about that right now. She just needed to get out of the house and get to a phone. Physically Matt had the upper hand. She couldn't fight her way out of this one. She needed to use her brain. That was all she had.

Jess took in a slow breath to calm her heart's violent assault against her ribs. She needed to sound calm, in control. Matt had been painted into a corner. Without options, he had nothing to lose. He needed an out. She needed to show him there was a way out of this for him. "It's okay, Matt. The EMTs won't even need to come inside. Help me drag Jamison to the street. You grab his feet. I'll take his arms. I'll call it in anonymously. I'll find a pay phone or flag down a taxi driver. I shot him, Matt. Me, I'm the one the police will be interested in. This has nothing to do with you. We just need to get him to the street and then it won't involve you at all."

Matt shook. His entire body vibrated with rage.

Jess glanced down at her gun. There was no talking him down. They both knew this was the end. She pounced, making a move, but Matt was too fast. He swiped the gun off the floor.

"You turned my house into a fucking crime scene!" he screamed again. "The police will do a search. You stupid cunt. I thought you were different." Matt turned and pointed the gun at Jamison. Jess threw herself on the gun just as Matt fired. The shot hit Jamison in the hip.

"Oh God, no!" Jess screeched. She dropped to the floor beside Jamison. She reached for him but she was catapulted backwards. Her head snapped back as Matt wrapped his hand around her hair and yanked. She kicked and thrashed as he dragged her through the hall and kitchen. When she screamed, he kicked her in the head.

Don't let him move you. She knew that the only reason men moved their victims to another location was to kill them. *You're going to have to kill me here, asshole.* She wasn't going anywhere without a fight. She clawed at his ankles, tearing chunks of skin. One of her nails broke, imbedding in his leg, but she kept fighting. If she died, she was going to leave enough DNA evidence to convict him. If she got close enough, she was going to bite him too. She would not die without a fight.

"Shut up!" Matt kicked her again, and the blow connected with the side of her head. Her ear rang from the impact.

Matt entered a code on the padlock of the cellar door. Why had she never noticed the lock on the door? Her head bounced off the stairs as he dragged her down to the basement. She closed her eyes because each bang of the stairs brought fresh terror. The impact hurt less when she didn't see it coming. Finally, they reached the bottom and Matt rewarded her with a swift kick to her ribs.

When she screamed out in pain his lip curled into a sadistic smile. Oh God, he got off on pain. Of course he did. She couldn't scream again. She would not give him that satisfaction. She closed her eyes again and pushed down her fear. It would not serve her now.

"Stand up!" he shouted. Matt pulled her hair until she was upright. She stumbled but he righted her by jerking her head to restore her balance. "It was supposed to be different with you. And now you've ruined it. Open your eyes, Jessica."

When she didn't immediately comply, he punched her in the face. She bit back her scream but opened her eyes.

"Oh God. Oh sweet Jesus, no," she rasped when she saw the contents of the basement. In the corner was a metal cage and shackles tethered to the floor. Along the concrete cinder-block wall were two metal shelves. On them were a total of twelve three-gallon glass jars; each one held a woman's head. There were more victims than they knew about. Immediately Jess recognized the broadly spaced eyes of Hannah Henderson. Beside her was Jennifer Thomson. Her long hair looped along the bottom of the jar like a disembodied mermaid. Some of them were staring at her with eyes wide open and others were closed, but each of the women's mouths were frozen in the perfect O shape. The last head on the shelf was a black woman with perfect tight curls and flawless caramel skin.

"Felicia." Jess's legs buckled under her and she stumbled, but Matt caught her.

"Look around. I wanted to share this with you. I have wanted to share this with you ever since I met you. I wanted to share my world with Jessica Randal. Yes, yes I know. Don't act so surprised, sweetheart." He smoothed down Jess's hair. "I knew who you were before we first met. I looked for you. When I found you, I applied for the FBI just to be near you. I watched you for a long time. And then I started my collection after the first night we met. You inspired me."

She winced when he ran a hand down the fresh bruise on her cheek. Bile burned in the back of her throat.

"You had formaldehyde on your jeans. You're taking them out of the jars, aren't you?" She had to get him talking. Buy herself some time. Someone would have heard the shots. Someone would call it in. *Someone please. Find Jamison.*

Matt continued to stroke her cheek.

"Answer me." She closed her eyes as she waited for the answer. She didn't want him to tell her what he was doing with the heads. She already knew. But she needed to keep him talking.

"Open your eyes. I want you to see them. They're beautiful, aren't they? My girls. I think they're even prettier now, sweeter, more compliant." Matt slapped her again directly on top of her already swollen cheek when she refused to open her eyes.

She whimpered like a puppy but did not cry out. The metallic zing of blood filled her mouth. He had split her lip when he hit her.

"Where do you think I got the idea?" he asked.

"I don't know."

"I thought you were more fun than this. Come on. Play along. Where do you think I got the idea from?"

She knew the answer but she refused to say it aloud.

"You disappoint me. Your dad. I got the idea from your dad. The heads were never discovered and I always wondered why. I thought about it all the time and then it came to me when I was coming, actually, ironically enough. He must have been keeping them to play with."

"No," she whispered. "That's not why he did it, you sick fucker." She had studied her dad's case in college. She sat in the back of the lecture hall with her head down as people around her pontificated about his MO. Was it ritualistic? Did it have religious significance? None of them guessed the true reason. It was simple counter-forensics from a bygone era when dental records not DNA confirmed identity, so he cut out the bite marks he inflicted on his victims and cut off their heads and incinerated them. "He did it so they were harder to identify. He was a child rapist and a killer, but you're the only freak defiling corpses."

"Now you're just trying to hurt my feelings." His lower lip protruded in an exaggerated pout. "Luckily I don't actually have any feelings, but how fucking brilliant am I at faking it? Go on, tell me. It was pretty great, right? My 'aw shucks, you're just so pretty' is as good as it gets. I know you liked that one. It took time to perfect. You have to walk the line between humble and bumbling, and if you overshoot it even a little, you end up pathetic. And no woman will fuck pathetic. Even the crazy ones with daddy issues."

Jess's gaze darted past Matt to the stairs. There wasn't a lock on this side of the door, so if she could make it past him she had a chance at getting out of here. She needed to keep him talking, distract him, and then make her move. She was fast. She could make it.

"Why? Why are you obsessed with my father?"

Matt shrugged. "Obsessed is overstating it a bit. But he has certainly inspired me. I remember the first time I read about him." His face split into a broad smile. "He was on the front page of the newspaper. I must have been ten maybe. The look on my mother's face when she saw the headline. That look..." His eyes glossed over and his smile deepened even further. "I had never seen anything like it. The fear and revulsion and curiosity. God, I love that look. I had to know what it was. She didn't even read the whole story. She shoved it in the trash under soggy cornflakes. I waited for everyone to leave and I pulled it out of the trash. It was amazing. People were terrified. That power he had: amazing. After that, I read everything I could find on him. I rode my bike to the library. Other kids were playing baseball at the park and I was looking through reels of microfiche. Every detail was more amazing than the last. And you got to live with him. See it firsthand." The awe in his voice made her shudder. "What was it like living with him? Did he ever let you play with them? Did your daddy hurt you too?"

Jess's stomach clenched in revulsion. Her mouth was almost too dry to answer. "No." The familiar question was a bolt of lightning to her heart. Ice, painful and destructive, tore through her veins, leaving everything in its path numb. Every mental health professional she'd ever seen had asked the same thing. He must have abused her too, that's what they thought. She was either a victim or a conspirator because there was no room for anything else.

"Oh." The corners of his mouth turned down. He looked genuinely surprised by her answer. "Well, that is rather selfish, keeping it all to himself. I'll share. I'll let you play."

The acidic burn of bile rose again in her throat. She was going to vomit. She knew she had to keep talking but she could not hear anything else about her father. "Why did you kill Felicia? Was it just to get back at Jamison?"

"It's not all about Jamison. I needed a little color on my shelf. She rounds out the dozen nicely. But yeah, jamming up your boyfriend was also a factor. Well, the biggest factor actually, but she has been quite fun so I'm not going to look a gift horse in the mouth."

"And the tattoo on the prostitute. Did you do that too?"

Matt laughed. "I knew you would see it too." He wagged his finger at her. "We think alike, me and you. I didn't do it, but when I saw it I knew I had to have her. The tattoo was some sort of tribal design, Maori or Aztec, I don't know, some culturally appropriated bullshit that she thought looked cool. She was a white chick from Canada. When I saw her pictures online I knew I needed her for my collection. She's not even my type but the tattoo sold it for me. I knew you would see the similarities to the delta branding. I wanted to make this fun for you too. You're welcome for that, by the way."

If he was expecting her to thank him, he would be waiting forever. While he was talking, she slowly slid her foot to the side, edging closer to the bottom stair. "How did you get access to Shoshone?"

Matt waved his hand dismissively. "That? That was easy. We were already investigating Shoshone for using illegal surveillance on their employees. Admittedly, taking that technology to the next level was a stroke of genius. I was out hunting for Isabella, I think it was, and I thought wouldn't it be easier if she just came to me? I was sick of waiting outside her gym. That woman never got off the damn StairMaster. She had a great ass. Shame I only got to use it the once." He pointed to the redhead on the bottom shelf. Her green eyes were wide open, fixed in a surprised stare.

Jess shifted her weight and tentatively slid her foot across the concrete floor. Slowly she would inch her way across until she was close enough to bolt.

"You know what is scary? How easy it was. I'm surprised someone hasn't done it before. There are a lot of sick people out there, Jessica." He shook his head.

"Yeah there are," she agreed, edging ever closer to the stair. Almost there. Matt was still partially blocking her path but this was as good as it was going to get for an opportunity. She closed her eyes and took a fortifying breath. She only had one chance at this. Jess lunged forward, throwing all her weight at Matt. He stumbled back and fell when he hit the bottom stair. Jess clambered over him. She used his chest to bolster her next step. Her nails scraped over a lacquered rung as she continued her frantic crawl to freedom. *Keep going.*

Jess swore as Matt's long fingers bit into her ankle. Frantically she kicked his face as she tried to free herself from his grip, but he was already dragging her back down. "No!" she screamed. "Help me!" she begged. But there was no one there to hear her.

Matt picked her up and slammed her against the wall. A splitting pain ripped through her skull as it connected with the concrete blocks. The impact robbed her of breath. It took a few seconds for her lungs to remember how to work.

To her left, within inches of her face, were the jars with his other victims, each young and beautiful in life and sentenced to an existence of morbid defilement in death. The display was mocking her, calling her, warning her. *You're next.*

She was not going to be one of them. If she died, she was going to die fighting and leave a face too ugly to add to his collection.

"No!" Jess screamed as she ran full force at the glass containers. She swung wildly at the jars, knocking the contents of the bottom shelf to the floor. Glass shattered and formaldehyde sloshed around, pooling at her feet beside the head of Liddy Steiner.

"You stupid bitch," Matt roared as he tackled her to the ground.

This time Jess saw the attack coming and she was able to shield her head from the concrete floor, but there was nothing to stop the fragments of shattered glass that pierced her naked flesh. Matt fell heavy on top of her. Embalming fluid and blood saturated the thin fabric of her shirt. It was wet on her thighs, seeping into the crack of her ass when she struggled under him. The smell assaulted her nasal cavity. There was no other stench like it.

He wrapped his hands around her neck and squeezed. She swung and thrashed but the blows didn't lesson his grip. She couldn't breathe. She gasped, desperately trying to get any air into her lungs, but her trachea was being crushed. Pressure built in her head with every stagnated beat of her heart. Her peripheral vision went black. The edges slowly crept in, pushing out the light. When the light was gone, so was she. She clung to consciousness, fighting with everything she had.

"We could have been great together, Jessica. I didn't even mind that you're a slut. I felt that connection as soon as I met you. I saw it. I see it in your eyes. You're like your dad. You and I are the same."

No! Her mind screamed. She was nothing like her dad and nothing like Matt. And she was not going to be one of his victims. She clenched a shard of glass in her hand. Blood made it slippery. She only had one chance. She could not drop it so she squeezed it until it tore into her palm and her own flesh kept it in place, wedged between skin and tendons.

She looked at Liddy Steiner's head, directly in the eye. Jess was doing this for her and for Hannah and Jennifer and Felicia and for the victims they hadn't named, the ones they hadn't even known about. And she was doing it for herself. She wasn't going to die this way.

Jess swung her arm at Matt's neck. She plunged the shard deep into his throat. His eyes bulged from the pain of the attack. Blood sprayed out of his jugular, spurting with every heartbeat. His hands went to his neck, desperately trying to quell the torrent, but Jess pushed deeper and then dragged the glass down across his neck towards his chest.

The harder Jess pushed the glass into Matt, the deeper the other end wedged into her hand. She screamed out from the pain of her flesh being torn from the bone.

Matt gurgled and blood dripped from his mouth as he tried to speak. His eyes widened, trying to communicate. And then they glossed over and he collapsed onto Jess, the glass still connecting their bodies.

For a long moment Jess lay with his dead body on top of hers, scared to move or even breathe, and then she screamed. It was a low, guttural sound that tore at her lungs and burned her throat. All the pain she hadn't let Matt see ambushed her. She rolled Matt's body off her and then began the torturous process of disengaging the fatal connection. Her hand looked and felt like she had stuck it in a meat grinder. There was no telling where her blood and tissue ended and his began. Her body trembled as adrenalin coursed through her. Jess held her breath and pulled up as quickly as her broken body would allow. The room spun as she raised her palm off the splintered glass that joined their bodies. Blood gushed from her hand but she was free.

Jess stumbled as she tried to stand up. The room would not stop spinning. She had been deprived of oxygen too long and lost too much blood. She slipped on the slick floor and fell. She was too weak to stand so she crawled to the stairs. Each step was torture as she put her weight on her hands to lift herself up.

When she made it to the top, she turned to look one last time at the women who had not made it out. The floor was a sea of blood, watery and diluted by embalming fluid. Four heads and shattered glass were scattered amongst the recent carnage. She didn't want to leave them behind with him again. If she could have, she would have gathered them all and taken them with her, but they were already gone. She had to tell herself again that she wasn't abandoning them because they were lost before she arrived.

She closed the door. Blood streaked the kitchen tiles as she dragged herself along. She held on to the wall for support. A crimson trail marked her path along the gray wall.

"Jamison," she called out when she reached the hall. Her voice was barely a whisper. "Jamison." She stumbled again and fell. She crawled to his lifeless body. His chest did not rise and fall. "Please, please be okay." With her good hand she reached out and found the place on his neck where his pulse should be. Her heart plummeted when she couldn't find a pulse. She moved her hand and pushed deeper. "Jamison," she cried when she felt the slow, faint beat of his heart. He was alive! She reached into the front pocket of his jeans, pulled out his phone, and dialed 911. She held his head in her lap as she waited for the ambulance to arrive.

CHAPTER THIRTY-TWO

Sirens screeched as the ambulance raced to the hospital. In addition to the firefighters and police, two ambulances had arrived for them, but Jess refused to leave Jamison. She was strapped to a backboard with a hard collar so she couldn't see anything past her oxygen mask, but she could feel the movements of the EMT and sensed their anxiety. Jamison wasn't doing well. Of course he wasn't doing well, she had shot him.

In the front, the driver radioed the ER to relay the extent of their injuries to the waiting medics. Jess could not make out most of the conversation but she picked up that he had requested a trauma surgeon and lots of blood. Jamison was going to need a transfusion. She also heard something about a hand surgeon, which would be for her.

Jess could no longer feel her hand. She didn't know if it was shock or if she had done permanent damage but it didn't feel like part of her body anymore. It felt like one of the limbs the killer, Matt, had disarticulated from his victims' bodies and thrown out into the bayou like swampland trash.

Oh God, Matt. How? How did she not see it? Were there signs and she missed them, or was she immune or so callous because it was normal to her? She had studied sociopaths, chased them for years. Jess knew the signs. And she had missed them. Her head swam in snapshots, flashes of memories from their time together. Nothing. She couldn't see any signs. But she had seen them in

Jamison where they didn't exist. She had assumed the absolute worst about the man she claimed to love.

She really was messed up.

She couldn't do it anymore, pretend that her dad's crimes hadn't impacted her. No more running from it because the past had caught up with her. Jamison's life was in jeopardy because of it. There was no more pretending that what she did was compartmentalizing; it was denial. She had to deal with it. As soon as she was out of the hospital she was going to ask Lindsay to recommend someone for her to speak to.

Jamison groaned. He was regaining consciousness. Jess pulled down her oxygen mask. "You're okay. Everything is okay. You're on your way to the hospital. They are taking care of you. I'm right here with you." Jess reached out her good hand to hold his.

She wrapped her hand around his long fingers. Relief rushed through her. He was okay. He was going to be okay. Jamison groaned something she could not make out behind his oxygen mask and then slowly he pulled his hand away.

Her chest ached. With the small movement, her hope shattered. Jamison was alive and that was more than she had the right to hope for. She had shot him. She had believed the worst and picked Matt over him. There was no coming back from that. They were never going to be the same again.

CHAPTER THIRTY-THREE

Someone was squeezing her arm. The pressure was so tight; it was going to cut off her blood supply. She moaned as she tried to pull away but the vice grip just got tighter.

"She's awake," a familiar female voice said. "Should we get a nurse?"

"Tina?" Jess croaked. She tried to open her eyes but they felt like they were glued shut. She was so tired. "Arm… my arm… squeezing… someone squeezing." Jess lifted her heavily bandaged hand to point out what she was talking about.

"That's the blood pressure monitor. It goes off every fifteen minutes. Don't worry about that. You're out of surgery. The surgeon said it went really well."

Lindsay? Lindsay was here too. Jess nodded because it took less energy than formulating words. The last thing she remembered was staring up at the bright lights of the operating room and counting backwards from ten. They hadn't been able to operate on her hand right away because there was no specialist available, so she'd spent thirty-six hours in a hospital room getting antibiotics and looking out the window at a flickering streetlight; the bulb was about to die so it flashed off and on at random intervals. Jess had counted the seconds between each flicker. It was the loneliest hours of her life. She had designed a life of isolation. She had done it to herself.

Every time a nurse came to check on her IV or top up her pain medication, Jess felt bereft when she left. Jess thought she loved being alone until she realized there was really no one there for her.

"Are you comfortable? It looks like she needs a pillow. Or maybe we should prop up the top of the bed. How does this work? I can never figure these things out. I don't want to send her flying. Tina, can you do it please? You're the technical one," Jeanie said. She sounded flustered. Jeanie was never flustered.

Jeanie was here too. Jess's lungs constricted. Jeanie had come to see Jess, and she was worried about her. Her eyes burned. She didn't realize until that moment how much she wanted someone to worry about her. She wanted someone to notice her and care.

"Jamison?" Jess croaked. She had given up asking for updates about him. She wasn't family so they couldn't tell her anything. In the end a shy Filipino orderly had told her he was alive so that she would stop asking every nurse, doctor, and cleaner that walked by.

"Jamison is fine. He was lucky. Both bullets missed vital organs. He'll be off work for a while but he is going to be just fine." Jeanie stroked Jess's hair and smiled, knowingly. Jess was glad she had told Jeanie about her feelings for Jamison. Her secrets had become a burden too heavy to carry alone.

"Did he… do you know what happened?" Jess asked.

"You and Agent Briggs were both injured in the line of duty. That is all that matters and that is the only things that will be reflected in the report."

Jess gave a small nod. Jeanie knew. "I'm sorry. I screwed up."

"I have no idea what you're talking about, Agent Bishop." Jeanie's tone was terse. The official story had been determined and no one was to question it. "You single-handedly defeated a dangerous predator in his home. Sadly, you and Agent Briggs received injuries but fortunately there were no other casualties other than the assailant." That was all Jeanie was ever going to say on the matter.

"And the women? Did you find them in the basement?"

"Yes. We are working on identifying them. Some have already been sent home for burial. You did a good job, Jess," Tina said.

"We were really close. Matt was on the list of people with access to passwords at Shoshone. He had been investigating them. You were right when you said to cross-reference people with the passwords with those who had bought embalming fluid. We were almost there. We would have found him. I'm sorry I didn't get there faster." Her bright eyes brimmed with tears.

"Don't apologize," Jess said. "You didn't do anything." She didn't shoot Jamison or force Jess to have an affair with a serial killer.

Tina swallowed hard. "He seemed so into you. I shouldn't have given him your number. That was wrong. I'm sorry."

"No, he would have found my number anyway or staged another meeting. He—" Jess looked away. It still scared her to talk about him. Every time she heard a bump or saw a shadow, she jumped. She wondered when that was going to go away. "He knew things about me. That's why he targeted me. It's nothing to do with you, Tina." Eventually Jess would have to explain everything. Tina deserved that.

"Because of who your dad is? What he did?" Tina asked tentatively.

The heart monitor beeped when Jess's pulse spiked. "You know about that? Is that part of the report? Will that be brought up by internal affairs?" Panic seized her.

Lindsay stepped forward. "Jess, we can't know what will come up but it doesn't matter. You—"

"It won't come up," Jeanie said with absolute certainty. "Children should never be punished for the crimes of their parents. The bureau knew your history coming in. This is not new information and there is absolutely no need for it to be brought up again."

Jess wasn't convinced. "But Tina knows now."

Tina shook her head. "No. No one else needs to find out. I've always known, Jess. I'm literally the background check queen. Like that is my official title." Her nose crinkled when she smiled.

Jess blinked. "You knew?"

Tina nodded. "I knew."

And she still wanted to be her friend. Jess didn't have words. A lead weight lifted from her chest. They all knew and they were all still here with her. She wasn't alone. She had people; she just needed to stop pushing them away.

"Ooh, I almost forgot." Tina reached into her handbag. "I brought you some books." She held up a cover with a shirtless cowboy looking off into the sunset. "This is Colt and Cheyenne's story. It's from the same series I was telling you about. She had a secret baby that she gave up for adoption when they were teenagers. Now she is a major country star. It's so good."

"Another unplanned pregnancy? Do the women in romance novels not know about birth control?" Jess smiled.

"I know, right? But this writer is so good you forget about that. Okay, now after you finish Colt's story you have to read his brother's story. Cane is a quarterback in the NFL."

"Of course he is."

Tina smiled. "I know. I know. Look at these abs though. You're going to love it. And no surprise baby. Ooh and there is a kiss in the lightning storm. Amazing." Tina lit up as she spoke.

"Thank you. I'm sure I will love it."

Lindsay stood up. "Now I wish I would have brought some bodice rippers. All I brought you was this." She placed a jar of jalapeños on the bedside table next to Jess's hospital notes. "I hear the food here is bland."

"Excellent. Thank you." Jess couldn't imagine facing a meal anytime soon, but when she did she had no doubt jalapeños would make it more palatable.

"I'm afraid I was rather staid with my offering. All I have is this stress ball. I spoke to a physical therapist and she said it will help rebuild the strength and mobility in your hand," Jeanie said as she produced a pink tennis-ball sized toy.

The gift was so sensible and so Jeanie. Jess smiled. Her throat tightened. Through all the darkness, Jess had managed to find these three beacons. She had spent so much time running from her past and from herself. But she didn't need to anymore because she had found what she was looking for. They were her people and she was loved.

A LETTER FROM KIERNEY

Thank you for reading *Forget Me Not*. I am truly grateful when readers choose to spend their time and money on something I have written, so thank you again. If you enjoyed the book, I would very much appreciate if you left a review. Reviews are the lifeblood of writing; they are how new readers find a book, so even a short review would be tremendously helpful.

If you did enjoy the book, and want to keep up-to-date with all my latest releases, just sign up at the following link. Your email address will never be shared and you can unsubscribe at any time.

www.bookouture.com/kierney-scott

I really enjoyed writing about Jess and learning about her world. If you have any questions or comments, please feel free to email me at KierneyScott@gmail.com. I love hearing from readers and I always write back. You can also find me on Facebook at www.facebook.com/kierney.scott and Twitter at twitter.com/Kierney_S. I hope to see you all again when Jess and the team are back for their next adventure.

ACKNOWLEDGEMENTS

It is a shame that only one name appears on a cover when it takes so many to create a book. Firstly, thank you to my husband Alistair who encouraged me to write a crime thriller. While I love writing romance, he knew I had other stories to tell and I needed a push. Thank you also to Gina Calanni and Lizbeth Crawford for being confident in my ability to switch genres even when I wasn't. I'm so grateful for your pep talks and plotting sessions, and most of all for not letting me give up. Thank you to Claire Ayres for being my friend and beta reader.

Thank you to Chris Mulsow for the fact-checking and providing me with an insider's perspective of law enforcement. Your insight and anecdotes are very much appreciated.

Thank you to Jo Hilton for discussing Jess with me at length like she was a real person and not even charging me for sessions. It was tremendously valuable to take Jess to a psychologist. I dare say she could use a few more sessions.

Last but not least, thank you to my wonderful publisher. I am honored to be part of such an amazing team. A few years ago I received my first contract thanks to a writing competition masterminded by Oliver Rhodes, so joining Bookouture felt like coming home. I am delighted to work with such dedicated, hardworking people. Thank you so much to Peta Nightingale and Helen Jenner for seeing potential in Jess's story. I am so grateful for all the time they put into this book to make it shine.

CPSIA information can be obtained
at www.ICGtesting.com
Printed in the USA
BVHW01s1643260218
509110BV00028B/1156/P